D1433911

York St John

3 8025 00561131 7

Virginia Woolf and Fascism

Virginia Woolf and Fascism

Resisting the Dictators' Seduction

Edited by

Merry M. Pawlowski
Professor of English
California State University, Bakersfield
California
USA

YORK ST. JOHN
COLLEGE LIBRARY

palgrave

Editorial matter, selection and Chapters 1 and 4
© Merry M. Pawlowski 2001
Chapters 2, 3, 5–13 © the contributors 2001

All rights reserved. No reproduction, copy or transmission of
this publication may be made without written permission.

No paragraph of this publication may be reproduced, copied or
transmitted save with written permission or in accordance with
the provisions of the Copyright, Designs and Patents Act 1988,
or under the terms of any licence permitting limited copying
issued by the Copyright Licensing Agency, 90 Tottenham Court
Road, London W1P 0LP.

Any person who does any unauthorised act in relation to this
publication may be liable to criminal prosecution and civil
claims for damages.

The authors have asserted their rights to be identified
as the authors of this work in accordance with the
Copyright, Designs and Patents Act 1988.

First published 2001 by
PALGRAVE
Houndmills, Basingstoke, Hampshire RG21 6XS and
175 Fifth Avenue, New York, N. Y. 10010
Companies and representatives throughout the world

PALGRAVE is the new global academic imprint of
St. Martin's Press LLC Scholarly and Reference Division and
Palgrave Publishers Ltd (formerly Macmillan Press Ltd).

ISBN 0–333–80115–6

This book is printed on paper suitable for recycling and
made from fully managed and sustained forest sources.

A catalogue record for this book is available
from the British Library.

Library of Congress Cataloging-in-Publication Data
Virginia Woolf and fascism : resisting the dictators' seduction /
edited by Merry M. Pawlowski.
        p. cm.
Includes bibliographical references and index.
ISBN 0–333–80115–6 (cloth)
    1. Woolf, Virginia, 1882–1941—Political and social views.
2. Politics and literature—Great Britain—History—20th century.
3. Fascism and literature—England—History—20th century.
4. Woolf, Virginia, 1882–1941—Views on fascism. 5. Fascism—
–England—History—20th century. 6. Dictatorship in literature.
7. Dictators in literature. 8. Fascism in literature. I. Pawlowski,
Merry M., 1945–

PR6045.O72 Z8922 2001
823'.912—dc21
                                              00–054528

10   9   8   7   6   5   4   3   2   1
10   09   08   07   06   05   04   03   02   01

Printed in Great Britain by Antony Rowe Ltd, Chippenham, Wiltshire

For Gordon, Neil, Allan, and Daniel

Contents

List of Abbreviations   ix

Acknowledgements   x

Notes on the Contributors   xii

1 Introduction: Virginia Woolf at the Crossroads of
Feminism, Fascism, and Art
Merry M. Pawlowski   1

Part I   Fascism, History, and the Construction of Gender   **11**

2 *A Room of One's Own* and *Three Guineas*
Quentin Bell   13
3 *Three Guineas*, Fascism, and the Construction of Gender
Marie-Luise Gättens   21
4 Toward a Feminist Theory of the State: Virginia Woolf and
Wyndham Lewis on Art, Gender, and Politics
Merry M. Pawlowski   39
5 Freudian Seduction and the Fallacies of Dictatorship
Vara S. Neverow   56

**Part II   Preludes to War: Politics in the Novels, Aesthetics
in the Nonfiction**   **73**

6 Acts of Vision, Acts of Aggression: Art and Abyssinia in
Virginia Woolf's Fascist Italy
Leigh Coral Harris   75
7 'Thou Canst Not Touch the Freedom of My Mind':
Fascism and Disruptive Female Consciousness in
Mrs. Dalloway
Lisa Low   92
8 Of Oceans and Opposition: *The Waves*, Oswald Mosley,
and the New Party
Jessica Berman   105
9 Monstrous Conjugations: Images of Dictatorship in the
Anti-Fascist Writings of Virginia and Leonard Woolf
Natania Rosenfeld   122

Part III   Voices against Tyranny: Woolf among Other Writers   137

10 'Finding New Words and Creating New Methods':
     Three Guineas and *The Handmaid's Tale*
     Maroula Joannou   139
11 Seduced by Fascism: Benedetta Cappa Marinetti, the
     Woman Who Did Not Write *Three Guineas*
     Lia Giachero   156
12 Eternal Fascism and its 'Home Haunts' in the Leavises'
     Attacks on Bloomsbury and Woolf
     Molly Abel Travis   165
13 Dystopian Modernism vs Utopian Feminism: Burdekin,
     Woolf, and West Respond to the Rise of Fascism
     Loretta Stec   178
Afterword
Jane Marcus   194

Notes   196
Select Bibliography   226
Index   230

List of Abbreviations

AWD	*A Writer's Diary.* Ed. Leonard Woolf. New York: Harcourt Brace Jovanovich, 1953.
BA	*Between the Acts.* New York: Harcourt Brace Jovanovich, 1941.
Diary	*The Diary of Virginia Woolf.* 5 vols. Ed. Anne Olivier Bell. New York: Harcourt Brace Jovanovich, 1977–84.
Essays	*The Essays of Virginia Woolf.* 6 vols. Ed. Andrew McNeillie. New York: Harcourt Brace Jovanovich, 1986–
Letters	*The Letters of Virginia Woolf.* 6 vols. Ed. Nigel Nicolson and Joanne Trautmann. New York: Harcourt Brace Jovanovich, 1975–80.
MB	*Moments of Being.* Ed. Jeanne Schulkind. 2nd edn. London: Hogarth Press, 1978.
MD	*Mrs. Dalloway.* 1925; rpt., New York: Harcourt Brace Jovanovich, 1953.
AROO	*A Room of One's Own.* 1929; rpt., New York: Harcourt Brace Jovanovich, 1957.
TGs	*Three Guineas.* 1938; rpt., New York: Harcourt Brace Jovanovich, 1966.
TTL	*To the Lighthouse.* 1927; rpt., New York: Harcourt Brace Jovanovich, 1955.
TY	*The Years.* 1937; rpt., New York: Harcourt Brace Jovanovich, 1965.
TW	*The Waves.* 1931; rpt., New York: Harcourt Brace Jovanovich, 1959.
VO	*The Voyage Out.* 1920; rpt., New York: Harcourt Brace Jovanovich, 1948.

Acknowledgements

My thanks to all the contributors of this volume; their valuable research adds new dimensions to our understanding of Woolf's responses to the rise and threat of fascism. Thanks are also tendered to panel participants and the audience at the panel I chaired on Woolf and Fascism at the Modern Language Association Convention in San Diego, CA, 1995; for it was there that the idea for this book was first conceived.

Permission to quote from the following sources is gratefully acknowledged:

From *Bloomsbury Recalled*, by Quentin Bell. Copyright © 1995 Columbia University Press. Reprinted with the permission of the publisher.

From *Elders and Betters*, by Quentin Bell. Copyright © John Murray (Publishers) Ltd. Reprinted with the permission of the publisher.

Excerpts from *Three Guineas*, copyright 1938 Harcourt, Inc. and renewed 1966 by Leonard Woolf, reprinted by permission of the publisher and The Society of Authors as the Literary Representative of the Estate of Virginia Woolf.

Excerpts from *A Room of One's Own* by Virginia Woolf, copyright © 1929 by Harcourt, Inc. and renewed 1957 by Leonard Woolf, reprinted with permission of the publisher and The Society of Authors as the Literary Representative of the Estate of Virginia Woolf.

Excerpt from *The Waves*, copyright 1931 by Harcourt, Inc. and renewed 1959 by Leonard Woolf, reprinted by permission of the publisher and The Society of Authors as the Literary Representative of the Estate of Virginia Woolf.

Excerpt from *Mrs. Dalloway*, copyright 1925 by Harcourt, Inc. and renewed 1953 by Leonard Woolf, reprinted with permission of Harcourt, Inc. and The Society of Authors as the Literary Representative of the Estate of Virginia Woolf.

Cover Illustrations

Photograph from *Virginia Woolf: a Biography*, copyright © 1972 by Quentin Bell, reproduced by permission of Harcourt, Inc. and The Society of Authors as the Literary Representative of the Estate of Virginia Woolf.

Still photograph from *Triumph of the Will*, copyright 1935 by Leni Riefenstahl, reproduced with the permission of Leni Riefenstahl and supplied by the Institute of Contemporary History and Wiener Library.

Notes on the Contributors

Quentin Bell, distinguished painter, sculptor, potter, writer, and art critic, was the nephew of Virginia Woolf. During his academic career, he was Professor of Art at the University of Leeds, Slade Professor of Fine Art at Oxford, and Professor of the History and Theory of Art at the University of Sussex. His classic study of his aunt, *Virginia Woolf: a Biography* (1972), authorized by the family, remains an invaluable resource for students of Woolf's life and work. Other books include *On Human Finery*, *Bloomsbury*, and the recently published *Bloomsbury Recalled* (1995).

Jessica Berman is an Assistant Professor of English and Women's Studies at the University of Maryland Baltimore County, where she teaches modernist fiction, literary criticism, and feminist theory. She has published on Henry James and Virginia Woolf and is completing a book entitled *Cosmopolitan Communities: the Politics of Connection in Modernist Fiction*.

Marie-Luise Gättens is Associate Professor of German at Southern Methodist University and author of a number of articles and chapters dealing with feminist theory, women's history, and German and contemporary women's literature. Her most recent book, *Women Writers and Fascism: Reconstructing History* (1996), discusses Virginia Woolf's *Three Guineas*, placing the work within a constellation of works by German women writers, including Ruth Rehman's *Der Mann auf der Kanzel*, Christa Wolf's *Patterns of Childhood*, Helga Schubert's *Judasfrauen*, and Monika Maron's *Silent Clove 6*.

Lia Giachero received her PhD in the history of art criticism from the University of Milan in 1995. She has published articles and essays, among which there are several on women in Italian futurism and on the Bloomsbury group. She recently edited a collection of writings by Vanessa Bell entitled *Sketches in Pen and Ink* (London: Chatto & Windus, 1997).

Leigh Coral Harris is currently on the faculty in the Writing Program and in the Women's Studies Program at the University of California, Santa Barbara. She received her PhD in English from Yale University in 1998, has published on the political aesthetics of Elizabeth Barrett

Browning's poetry, and is now writing a book on contemporary American feminism.

Maroula Joannou is Senior Lecturer in English Studies at Anglia Polytechnic University in Cambridge, England. She is author of '*Ladies, Please Don't Smash These Windows*': *Women's Writing, Feminist Consciousness and Social Change 1918–38* (1995) and co-editor with June Purvis of *The Women's Suffrage Movement: New Feminist Essays*, forthcoming.

Lisa Low is Professor of English at Pace University in New York City. She is co-editor with Anthony John Harding of *Milton, the Metaphysicals, and Romanticism* (1994) and author of a number of articles on Virginia Woolf and early modern literature. She is at work on a book-length study of Woolf's reception of Milton, *Unkind Masters: Woolf, Milton, and the Literary Tradition*.

Jane Marcus is Distinguished Professor of English at the Graduate Center, City University of New York. Her works on Virginia Woolf include *Virginia Woolf and the Languages of Patriarchy, Art and Anger: Reading Like a Woman*, and three volumes of collected essays, *Virginia Woolf Aslant, New Feminist Essays on Virginia Woolf*, and *Virginia Woolf and Bloomsbury*. *Britannia Rules the Waves* is soon to be published. She is a founding member of the Virginia Woolf Society and has been active in its work for many years. She is also preparing *A Key to A Room of One's Own*, with Angela Ingram, as well as the Shakespeare Head edition of *A Room of One's Own*.

Vara S. Neverow is Professor of English and Women's Studies at Southern Connecticut State University. She currently serves as the co-coordinator for the Women's Studies Program and as the director of graduate studies in English. Her publications include articles on Virginia Woolf, documentation of the bibliographic sources cited in *Three Guineas* (co-authored with Merry Pawlowski), and the first three volumes of the selected papers from the conferences on Virginia Woolf (co-edited with Mark Hussey). She has also published articles on utopian studies and composition theory.

Merry M. Pawlowski is Professor of English at California State University, Bakersfield, where she teaches British modernism, literary theory and criticism, and women's literature. She is the author of several articles examining Woolf within the context of 'male' modernism and English domestic fascism and is currently at work, with Vara Neverow, on an archival edition of Woolf's *Reading Notebooks for Three Guineas*.

Natania Rosenfeld teaches in the English Department of Knox College in Galesburg, Illinois. 'Monstrous Conjugations' is excerpted from her book *Outsiders Together: Virginia and Leonard Woolf* (2000). Her poetry has appeared in numerous journals.

Loretta Stec is an Associate Professor of English at San Francisco State University where she teaches Modern British and Postcolonial Literature. She has published articles on Virginia Woolf, Rebecca West, pacifist writers between the world wars, and the canon of African fiction. She is writing a critical study of Rebecca West's works.

Molly Abel Travis is Associate Professor of English at Tulane University where she teaches courses in modernist and postmodernist literature and literary theory. She is the author of *Reading Cultures: the Construction of Readers in the Twentieth Century* (1998) and a number of articles on women's writing, reader theory, and literary hypertext. She is at work on a study of feminist irony and intertextuality.

Introduction:
Virginia Woolf at the Crossroads of Feminism, Fascism and Art

Merry M. Pawlowski

> if those daughters . . . are going to be restricted to the education of the private house, they are going, once more, to exert all their influence both consciously and unconsciously in favour of war.
>
> (Virginia Woolf, *TGs*, p. 37)

A brief article in the Sunday London *Times* caught Virginia Woolf's eye on September 13, 1936. Its title, 'Praise for Women', captured the spirit of an address by Adolf Hitler to the Nazi Women's League celebrating the participation of German women in the triumph of Nazism. Since she was gathering materials to write an indictment of domestic fascism and patriarchy in *Three Guineas*, Woolf was especially interested in Hitler's assessment of women's willing collaboration in their own oppression, and quite aware of the insidious presence of a seductive ideology that played upon women's maternal and nurturing instincts in order to 'enslave' them. 'A woman lawyer', Woolf read from Hitler's speech, 'may be ever so efficient – but if there is a woman next door to her with five or six children all healthy and well brought up – then I say that from the standpoint of the nation's future the woman with children has accomplished more'. Woolf clipped the article to add it to a collection of news clippings and other documents which, by the time she was finished, would grow to fill three large scrapbooks, Woolf's personal contribution to the history of the 1930s and a 'triumph' as an example of one woman's resistance to tyranny.[1] The significance of Woolf's scrapbooks, and, indeed, of a voluminous collection of reading notebooks, has yet to be fully plumbed; but their very existence helps to establish Woolf as a serious student of the history of the oppression of women with special emphasis upon the role that European fascism has played in that oppression.[2]

1

After Woolf's death and following the horrible débâcle of the holocaust and the Second World War, scholars' examinations of the phenomenon of fascism described it as an umbrella ideology linking Germany and Italy (and in Woolf's view, Great Britain), which most closely represented itself as a Männerbund, a society of males that needed continuity in peacetime with the camaraderie of the trenches of wartime.[3] It was an easy step from this bond to an intense nationalism, perhaps the most powerful ideology of modern times; indeed, as Himmler worked upon the concept, the Männerbund transformed itself into the Männerstaat. Zeev Sternhell sees fascism as an extreme manifestation of a much broader phenomenon in modern times, not, Sternhell insists, a 'parenthesis' in contemporary history but an integral part of European culture.[4] Fascism is an utter rejection, Sternhell argues, of Enlightenment philosophy and the lessons learned from the English, French, and American Revolutions of the seventeenth and eighteenth centuries – a rejection of individualism, liberalism, and democracy and, in addition, a raising of nationalist consciousness among the masses.[5] On the other hand, George Mosse's most recent work explores the complex and contradictory self-perception of a people who believed they were governing themselves *democratically* in conjunction with a charismatic leader who was their living symbol.[6] Clearly, fascist ideology is contradictory, revealing what Richard Golsan has called its 'unstable ideological core', confusing the general public about its aims and its methods.[7] Despite its unstable core, fascism never seemed to be in doubt regarding its view of the feminine sphere in social relations; and it is this very aspect of its ideology that Woolf sought to interrogate.

The majority of studies written on the phenomenon of fascism have focused on the nature of totalitarian government, the management of the masses and Caesarist leadership, the philosophical vagueness of fascist theory, and the attraction fascism held for some intellectuals.[8] A few recent studies have centered their efforts on either Italian or German women in an effort to reconstruct the realities of women's involvement with fascism and Nazism.[9] But the voices many women writers raised against the intolerable nature of fascist ideology go, today, largely unheard. It is our intent to offer new perspectives on Woolf's voice against tyranny and her resistance to fascist seduction, so that the power and contemporaneity of her argument may be brought more fully to light.

Not until 1977, with the work of Klaus Theweleit, and 1979, with that of Maria-Antonietta Macciocchi, would there be specific scholarly attention to the production of a fascist ideology of gender. Theweleit, in his magisterial two-volume study *Male Fantasies*, produces a theory of fascism that searches for its origins in post-First World War Germany to argue, as Barbara Ehrenreich points out in her Foreword, that fascism is 'implicit in the daily relationships of men and women'. 'Theweleit refuses', Ehrenreich reminds us, 'to draw a line between the fantasies of the Freikorpsmen (the advance guard of the Nazis) and the psychic ramblings of the "normal" man'.[10] It would be a mistake, however, Ehrenreich warns, to conclude simplistically that all men are fascists and thereby court the danger of trivializing Nazi genocide by forgetting that real Jewish, Catholic, gypsy, and communist women and men were murdered. Woolf herself acknowledges that Jewish men were as much at risk from the tyranny of dictators as women had been for centuries:

> The whole iniquity of dictatorship, whether in Oxford or Cambridge, in Whitehall or Downing Street, against Jews or against women, in England or in Germany, in Italy or in Spain is now apparent to you.
>
> (*TGs*, p. 103)

It is, however, a masculine ideology, in Theweleit's terms 'male fantasies', in flight from women whose bodies are the 'holes, swamps, pits of muck that can engulf', that Woolf, who could not have been in full possession of the facts of Nazi genocide in 1938, would single out for feminist attack.[11]

Shortly after Theweleit, Maria-Antonietta Macciocchi advanced a similar argument about Italian fascism, suggesting the complex connections among sexuality, feminist theory, and fascist ideology and acknowledging Woolf as an important foremother to her argument. Faced, as Woolf was faced, with the troubling assumption that many women were complicit with fascism, Macciocchi reflects upon feminine silence regarding the expulsion of women as subjects from history. Fascism enlists women, Macciocchi suggests, by seducing and addressing them in the terminology of a familiar sexual ideology, a terminology already deeply inscribed in the unconscious and capable of constructing women's desires within fascism. Women are summoned, Macciocchi insists, like 'corrupt voyeurs' to enter the space which fascism has fashioned for them.[12]

Woolf, though, was not seduced by fascist ideology. The impression of Woolf as an apolitical, lyrical, modern novelist so carefully cultivated by generations of New Critics and fueled by Woolf's own nephew's assessment of her during the 1930s as a 'distressed gentlewoman caught in a tempest and making little effort either to fight against it or to sail before it'[13] is necessarily exploded by the weight of evidence to the contrary which the present collection of essays develops. From at least 1929, with the publication of *A Room of One's Own*, marked by the beacon of *Three Guineas* in 1938, and continuing to the end of her life and the composition of *Between the Acts* (1941), Woolf's work was explicitly infused with a sense of rage against injustice toward women. Just over a decade ago, the work of Jane Marcus, so foundational to this volume, introduced the Woolf of *A Room of One's Own* and *Three Guineas* as an engaged feminist, acting as a counterpoint to the view of her politics offered by her husband Leonard and her nephew, Quentin Bell.[14] Nor does Woolf's work before 1929 lack traces of feminist politics in the making, as several essays in this collection demonstrate.

It is the particular strength of this volume to build upon a vision of Woolf's political involvement shared by feminist readers to argue for the importance of her anticipatory vision of the inextricable links between power and gender and her awareness of the roles of fascism and patriarchy in the forging of those links.[15] The volume also foregrounds a debate between aesthetics and politics which has a natural connection to the study of a woman writer best known for her art rather than her political writing.[16] This is a debate which becomes especially significant in the context of Woolf as artist and political thinker, who reacts against fascist propaganda, but is complicated by Woolf's own apparent desire to rid her art of politics. In an October, 1932, diary entry, Woolf, in reaction to the letters of D. H. Lawrence, writes: 'Art is being rid of all preaching: things in themselves: the sentence in itself beautiful . . .' (*Diary 4*, p. 126). Our case, however, is that the evidence in and argument of *Three Guineas* undercuts that position; for that work at its very conception, as a novel-essay, was Woolf's effort to merge her art and her politics. The essays here present Woolf, therefore, as embedded in and actively engaged in making the history of her time, a view distinct from Marcus's argument that Woolf could propagate without preaching and from Pamela Caughie's emphasis upon a rhetoric 'uncommitted to any one position'.[17] To that end, the arguments of this volume fold back continuously into a reconsideration of *Three Guineas* as the strongest example in her oeuvre of Woolf working as a contemporary cultural critic and feminist historian.[18]

While our enemies assert that women are tyrannically oppressed in Germany, I may reveal that without the devoted and steady collaboration of German women the Nazi movement would never have triumphed.

(Adolf Hitler)[19]

The present volume divides into three sections, the first of which, 'Fascism, History, and the Construction of Gender', offers four essays which counterpoint each other in positioning Woolf's tract as a voice of feminist resistance to and revision of masculine constructions of femininity in the midst of a long history of misogynist patriarchy. The historical foundation for the essays in this section rests upon Virginia Woolf's prescience in recognizing the danger of fascism at a time when many men and women in her society blinded themselves to it. Winston Churchill, Neville Chamberlain, and Rudyard Kipling expressed their admiration for Mussolini in 1929; and in 1933, H. G. Wells wrote: 'Fascism indeed was not an altogether bad thing. It was a bad good thing; and Mussolini has left his mark on history.'[20] The work of fascists in the 1930s reveals an effective campaign and concerted effort against women's rights, equality, freedom, and access to education, jobs, and the professions which Woolf was quick to point out.

As the first essay, Quentin Bell's '*A Room of One's Own* and *Three Guineas*' suggests an ongoing view of his aunt's politics and feminism against which many feminist readers have reacted. Jane Marcus emblematized the tone of these responses when she wrote about the difficulty of 'explaining yet again to Quentin Bell how his Virginia Woolf is different from our Virginia Woolf'.[21] But the inescapable value in Bell's judgment of *Three Guineas* is that it has been a spur to scholars, goading us increasingly to look more closely at the text and serving as an important catalyst for an ongoing reassessment of the work. Bell tackles the interlocking issues of history, gender, and fascism, from quite a different perspective than those adopted in other essays in the volume, for he is especially concerned with what he believes was Woolf's misrepresentation and essentialization of masculine attitudes toward war at the time. He also takes a hard look at the problematic core of Woolf's solution to war – her 'Society of Outsiders', expressing gratitude that his aunt was spared by fate from the spectacle of a female Prime Minister 'joyfully leading her country into a short but bloody war fought over a "little patch of ground that hath in it no profit but the name" '.

Marie-Luise Gättens, in '*Three Guineas*, Fascism, and the Construction of Gender', is the first in the present volume to take a very different view of *Three Guineas* from that advanced by Bell. Gättens introduces an argument for the significance of Woolf's tract in establishing a theory linking gender to fascism and suggests that Woolf 'proposes a strategy of entry into the professions [for women] without identifying with its institutional structures and disassociation from the existing sex-gender system by an act of active remembrance of the history of female subjection'.

My essay, 'Toward a Feminist Theory of the State: Virginia Woolf and Wyndham Lewis on Art, Gender, and Politics', is next and resonates with Gättens by surmising that another impetus for Woolf's construction of gender in *Three Guineas* was her reaction to attacks on her artistry by 'male' modernists like Wyndham Lewis. Lewis's essays participate in a widespread cultivation of fascist ideology, but from within a modernist artistic enclave; while Woolf necessarily entwines aesthetics and politics in *Three Guineas* as she seeks to articulate a feminist theory of the state.

As the closing essay of the section, Vara Neverow's 'Freudian Seduction and the Fallacies of Dictatorship' adds to our growing understanding of Woolf's construction of gender through its relationship to Freud's psychoanalysis. Building upon the groundbreaking work of Elizabeth Abel, Neverow argues that Freudian psychology and fascism spring from the same ideological root; but Woolf ably exposes and mocks the pathology of the privileging of the phallus.

We must create a new art, an art of our times: a Fascist art.

(Benito Mussolini)[22]

The second section of the present volume, 'Preludes to War: Politics in the Novels, Aesthetics in the Nonfiction', offers four perspectives directly aimed at the debate over aesthetic value and political reality raised first by Bell. The essays, while continuing an overall concern with fascism and the construction of gender, select work rarely looked at in the context of fascism: two novels, *Mrs. Dalloway* and *The Waves*; prose by Leonard Woolf, and diary entries and letters written during Woolf's travels in Italy. The essays collectively argue that, given the historical moment of the 1930s, Woolf could no longer believe that 'art is being rid of all preaching'.

The danger of not eliminating preaching from art, however, as Woolf knew well, was in the potential for replicating propaganda which

Woolf as artist deplored. How, then, to express the passion of one's beliefs without slipping into propaganda? One manner indeed lay in Woolf's own and early recognition of fascist art as abortion: 'Poetry ought to have a mother as well as a father. The Fascist poem, one may fear, will be a horrid little abortion such as one sees in a glass jar in the museum of some country town' (*AROO*, p. 107). The appropriateness of Woolf's observation is borne out by the 1932 spectacular display of Mussolini's *Exhibition of the Fascist Revolution*; and, as Jeffrey Schnapp describes, the aesthetic overproduction found there among its surfeit of signs reveals the lack at the center, the shifting ideological vacuum of fascism.[23] Fulfilling Woolf's prediction, the exhibition reflects an outsized, overdetermined masculinity in the imagery surrounding all facets of the 'Duce', representing fascism's first sustained effort at a self-interpretation of its politics and its art in the mirror of twentieth-century history.

In 'Acts of Vision, Acts of Aggression: Art and Abyssinia in Virginia Woolf's Fascist Italy', the initial essay of the second section, Leigh Harris probes this dichotomy of art and politics, embedding it in a new context. Woolf, Harris argues, maintained two visions of Italy gathered from her travels there – one as a place of spiritual renewal and the other as the space of a fascist regime with a hypermasculine artistic identity – which together 'mutually construct one another in her work'.

Lisa Low's ' "Thou Canst Not Touch the Freedom of My Mind": Fascism and Disruptive Female Consciousness in *Mrs. Dalloway*' continues the argument that Woolf could not separate politics from aesthetics and suggests that while the aftereffects of the First World War in *Mrs. Dalloway* have been acknowledged, little attention has been given to the role this novel plays in the evolution of Woolf's resistance to fascism.

Jessica Berman's 'Of Oceans and Opposition: *The Waves*, Oswald Mosley, and the New Party' advances an innovative reading of the politics of Woolf's *The Waves*, suggesting the novel's linkage to the growth of the protofascist movement and Mosley's New Party as resistance to such a worldview. Berman tackles the very complex issue of fascism's relation to aesthetics, its desire to make life into art, its connections to modernism as a movement, and Woolf's differences from its vision.

In 'Monstrous Conjugations: Images of Dictatorship in the Anti-Fascist Writings of Virginia and Leonard Woolf', Natania Rosenfeld writes of the necessity both Woolfs felt to 'disrupt the litanies of the patriarchs, reactionaries, and dictators' and to find an alternative to fascist discourse. By examining *Three Guineas* and *Between the Acts* by Virginia and *Quack, Quack!* and *The War for Peace* by Leonard, Rosenfeld argues that the Woolfs release their use of satire as an effective discursive weapon against the dictators in favor of a new historical narrative, a reinvention of authorship.

> as a woman , I have no country. As a woman I want no country
> As a woman my country is the whole world.
> (Virginia Woolf, *TGs*, p. 109)

The third section, 'Voices against Tyranny: Woolf among Other Writers', concludes the volume with four essays which, incorporating the themes advanced by preceding essays, move to situate Woolf within the cultural geography of other women writers and their resistance to or complicity with tyranny. These essays respond, in large part, to the climate against women evolving in Germany and Italy from the 1920s onwards as women were blamed through the 'stab in the back' myth for losing the war on the homefront.[24] As a result of demobilization, unemployment, and competition for jobs, there was increasing tension between the sexes. Though the backlash mentality of the 1920s argued otherwise, women, who worked at the lowest end of the scale, rarely displaced men. In 1933, when Hitler came to power as Chancellor, the Nazis institutionalized a systematic campaign against women workers, whom they called 'double earners'. By 1934, the Nazis were actively disassembling women's organizations, using the severe economic crisis and high male unemployment to restrict women's access to jobs. Wherever possible and feasible, men were substituted for women workers. Women were dismissed if their husbands or fathers worked. In the professions, all married women teachers were dismissed, the Nazis had inaugurated a regulation to eliminate women doctors and women lawyers, and the quota for female university students was reduced to 10 per cent.[25] 'New women' represented degeneracy for Nazis, who initiated a discourse of racial hygiene, necessarily implicating women as responsible both for ensuring racial purity and for reproducing the species.

In the Italy of the 1920s, Mussolini was most responsible for crafting fascist ideology to support his view of the place of women in the state, taking them to himself as his 'brides' and encouraging them to bear children for Italy. While appearing to support women's rights on the one hand, Victoria de Grazia argues, the fascist state denied female emancipation.[26] But the state was caught by its need for cheap labor in the face of high male unemployment. On September 5, 1938, state and private offices were ordered to cut back their female workers to 10 per cent of their staff. Yet during the 1930s, women already represented one-fourth of the workforce despite a 15-year campaign of sexual discrimination coupled with state efforts to return women to the home and to persuade them to reproduce. The fact is that women were making efforts to resist the roles being forcibly crafted for them by Mussolini.

Nor was Woolf easily seduced by a dictator's charm. Her research to write *Three Guineas* provides an indelible record of one of the most extensive investigations of contemporary history conducted by a woman writer and offers a compelling collage of the atmosphere in which women in Europe and England lived and worked. The closing section of essays in this volume looks closely, as Woolf did in both research materials and published text, at feminist engagement with fascist, patriarchal oppression and enriches our reading of *Three Guineas* by contextualizing it within the work of other women writers who test, contest, and problematize the very nature of feminism.

Maroula Joannou, in ' "Finding New Words and Creating New Methods": *Three Guineas* and *The Handmaid's Tale*', moves forward in time from the 1930s to position Woolf within a context of modern 'feminism' and suggest the problematic associations of that term as well as the larger problematics of feminist resistance to domination.

Lia Giachero's 'Seduced by Fascism: Benedetta Cappa Marinetti, the Woman Who Did Not Write *Three Guineas*' puts Benedetta Cappa, wife of Futurist poet and manifesto writer Filippo Marinetti and a woman complicit with Italian fascism, in dialogue with Woolf for the sake of comparing two gifted women quite opposite in temperament and views on the point of fascist ideology.

Molly Travis, in the third essay of the section, 'Eternal Fascism and its "Home Haunts" in the Leavises' Attacks on Bloomsbury and Woolf', examines the motivations and assumptions of two of Woolf's contemporaries and most virulent opponents, F. R. and Queenie Leavis, to reverse the charge of fascism and elitism they make against Woolf and expose the 'ur-fascism' of their own ideas.

In 'Dystopian Modernism vs Utopian Feminism: Burdekin, Woolf, and West Respond to the Rise of Fascism', Loretta Stec argues that Katharine Burdekin, Virginia Woolf, and Rebecca West all participate in feminist utopian impulses as resistance to oppression but share a recognition of the complexity of a modernist dystopia for women. The work against fascism begun by Woolf, Burdekin, and West, Stec concludes, suggests that '[m]odernity has bequeathed us a state of deep scepticism as well as a desperate need to believe, nonetheless, in a utopian future'.

As contributors to this volume, we, too, need our utopian vision – that our work can add to an understanding of Woolf's feminist vision to reshape the world. It is our further hope that a number of irresistible echoes from our volume reverberate for the reader at its end. Among the most important are the inextricable linkages in Woolf's work between aesthetics and politics, art and life; Woolf's recognition of the indisputable history of masculine domination of women and its connections to all other forms of oppression; and the necessity and nature of Woolf's feminist resistance to fascist ideology in her writing. Her words, by way of concluding, provide a fitting correction to the misconceptions of the dictators about women's roles in society; indeed, Woolf here addresses all men, including the tyrants and dictators, as she instructs men and women both about resistance to oppression:

> A common interest unites us; it is one world, one life. How essential it is that we should realise that unity the dead bodies, the ruined houses prove. For such will be our ruin if you in the immensity of your public abstractions forget the private figure, or if we in the intensity of our private emotions forget the public world. Both houses will be ruined, the public and the private, the material and the spiritual, for they are inseparably connected.
>
> (*TGs*, pp. 142–43)

Part I

Fascism, History, and the Construction of Gender

2

A Room of One's Own and Three Guineas

Quentin Bell

Was Virginia, as Leonard suggested, 'the least political animal that has ever been since Aristotle invented the definition'? At times, rereading *Three Guineas*, I have agreed with him. But one does not feel this so strongly when one reads *A Room of One's Own*. Here Virginia is not concerned with politics in the ordinary sense of the word. Her subject is fiction, a subject which she addresses with the greatest authority and the work itself is presented to us as fiction so that one need not regard the various little taradiddles – as for instance those concerning university regulations – with any concern, for she has already told us that she will mix fact with fancy. But although this work keeps clear of party politics it is political.

Alex Zwerdling in his admirable *Virginia Woolf and the Real World* tells us that Virginia Woolf felt anger but suppressed it: 'In place of anger we have irony; in place of sarcasm, charm.' *A Room of One's Own* is indeed a condemnation of anger. 'Anger had snatched my pencil while I dreamt. But what was anger doing there?' What indeed? For she goes on to point out that if she, the female novelist, is angry 'she will never get her genius expressed whole and entire. Her books will be deformed and twisted. She will write in a rage where she should write calmly. She will write foolishly where she should write wisely.'

Talleyrand said that politics is 'the art of the possible'. If you want to get your brother to behave sensibly – and this roughly speaking is the essence of Virginia's kind of feminism – you may attempt to coerce him but you will probably find it easier to persuade him. This was at all events the policy of those whom one may call the 'suffragists'. But it was not the policy of the suffragettes. In America we still find a devoted band of feminist critics who believe that it is a fault in Virginia's work that she did not lose her temper. She smiles and mocks when she ought to be screaming and spitting. With enviable self-assurance they assume that they know better than Virginia how her books should be written; she should have understood that 'anger is a primary source of creative energy'. These critics seem unconcerned with policy, rather they are thinking in terms of aesthetic value and there I am not qualified to comment. But it is worth considering the political implications of a literature which aims at the cultivation of violent hatred. It cannot be denied that writing of this kind can have impressive results: the denunciation of nations, of minorities, of classes and perhaps above all of races, has had an undeniably important effect upon the world and perhaps the same kind of effects might be achieved by setting sex against sex. I do not think that Virginia had any such ambition.

For what it is worth, my opinion is that *A Room of One's Own* is a masterpiece and makes a convincing case which might have been weakened by yells of hatred. It is, however, difficult to measure its effect upon society. It was an immense success and it may be that it bore political fruit, but the chief aims had already been attained. Women had won the vote, subject to an age limit, in 1918 (it is worth noting that this was not the result of window breaking, although the memory of militancy may have helped; in principle the vote was given for patriotic work by women during the First World War). Virginia was not greatly interested, nor I think did she take much notice of the 1928 Act which gave women complete political equality with men. I think it is possible, even, that Virginia forgot that this important event had taken place. The years 1928 and 1929 were for her a happy time. Her fame was growing and Europe had some reason to hope that the enmities of the past might be forgotten and that those disputes which remained might be settled. But the years which followed were years of disaster. Everywhere reaction triumphed: in the Far East, in Abyssinia, in Germany and finally in Spain, everywhere it bred war or the threat of war. Meanwhile Virginia was engaged upon *The Years*, a work which, although it was a commercial success, did not quite satisfy her. It was also horribly difficult to write and nearly led her to a nervous breakdown. Finally, in 1937, public tragedy was merged with private tragedy: her nephew, Julian, was killed in Spain. By this time Virginia was at work on *Three Guineas*. I think it suffered from the deterioration of the political climate.

Three Guineas is a much less cheerful work than *A Room of One's Own* but I would not call it an angry book. There is a good deal of fun, witness the comic pictures of gentlemen disguised as historical monuments. There is also some fascinating and moving information concerning the achievements and tribulations of women. The book consists of three letters, the first of which is addressed to an imaginary man, a man who has been given a great many educational and other advantages and all at the expense of his sisters. This was undeniably true of a great many men, even though the division of wealth and power in 1938 was rather less extreme and less unfair than it had been. But to this she adds that men, unlike women, positively rejoice in war. 'Obviously' she writes, 'there is for you some glory, some necessity, some satisfaction in fighting which we have never felt or enjoyed.' This it seems to me is the main argument of *Three Guineas*, the assertion which gives the book its thrust and its character.

In order to explain her meaning Virginia gives examples of masculine militarism and, to be fair, one of masculine pacifism. She cites a young aristocrat who writes: 'Thank God, we are off in an hour. Such a magnificent regiment! Such men, such horses! Within ten days I hope Francis and I will be riding side by side straight at the Germans.' This surely is a period piece; it is clear that this imprudent young man knows very little about modern warfare – that is, war which was modern in 1914 – and one guesses that if his 'magnificent regiment' does ride 'straight at the Germans' it will not be magnificent for very long. It is no doubt typical of many young soldiers at that moment in history, the kind of thing one might expect from a young soldier, born in a nation which had only a very limited notion of what war was like. This romantic view of war had come to end long before 1918. If any young soldier had used such words in 1939 he would probably have been sent to a mental hospital.

The second example is of another young aristocrat who feared that 'if permanent peace were ever achieved . . . there would be no outlet for the manly qualities which fighting developed'. And yet a long period during which England had been engaged in no great war had not failed to produce those 'manly qualities' which were so evident in the courage, enthusiasm and ignorance of our first specimen.

These two rather slow-witted soldiers are hardly typical of mankind in general. The same may be said of Virginia's one non-conforming example, Wilfred Owen, who had indeed experienced war and objected to it on religious grounds. It is a remarkable fact that in the course of the past 1,500 years or so only a tiny proportion of Christians have opposed war; those who *have* done so were of both sexes. But the vast majority seem to have decided that, in preaching the Sermon on the Mount, our Saviour was talking through his halo. A rather odd example then and one that suggests that the male pacifist is a rarity. And yet, as Virginia should have remembered, there had in the last fifteen years or so been no lack of men willing, like General Sherman, to say: 'War is Hell'. Robert Graves, Richard Aldington, Edmund Blunden, Ernest Hemingway, Ford Madox Ford, Erich Maria Remarque and many others had all expressed their horror of war.

The literature of war in the period 1918–38 is very different from that of both the patriots and the pacifist quoted by Virginia; it describes the horrors, the beastliness and the boredom of the trenches. The only notable exception is T. E. Lawrence and he was not in the trenches; indeed his war seems almost to belong to another age. It reminds us that in former centuries, although the common soldiers may sometimes have been brutalized barbarians, their officers could be skilled professionals and these may indeed have enjoyed war. But they were a tiny minority of the nation; few gentlemen ever became soldiers, nor were they expected to do so. In the fearful struggle against Napoleon no one ever suggested that Frank Churchill should 'do his bit'; there were no white feathers for Mr Knightley nor, it should be added, was there an army of vociferous women baying for blood.

But if the nation under arms is a new idea in Europe and a very new idea in Great Britain, Virginia can still assert that in 1937 the great majority of men 'are today in favour of war. The Scarborough Conference of educated men, the Bournemouth Conference of working men are both agreed that to spend £300,000,000 annually upon arms is a necessity.[1] They are of the opinion that Wilfred Owen was wrong; that it is better to kill than be killed.' We may presume that 'educated' and 'working' are so to speak *noms de guerre* for Conservative and Labour and therefore the 'war makers' were representative of the great mass of the politically conscious population. But are there no politically conscious working women or conservative ladies? Obviously there are; Virginia herself had noticed the presence of women delegates at the Labour Party Conference in 1935. As for the Conservative ladies, no one who has taken part in a parliamentary election can have failed to notice them and I have yet to hear of a pacifist Conservative woman, indeed they seem sometimes more bellicose in their sentiments, more thirsty for the blood of foreigners and criminals than their menfolk; for them the gun, the rope and the birch offer a primrose path to eternal bliss.

Virginia tended to forget that she had a vote; not only did she have one, every adult woman in the country had one too. If women wanted peace and disarmament then, together with that not inconsiderable part of the male population which was of the same opinion, they could have thrown out any government which proposed to rearm the nation.

I do not think Virginia could admit that the great majority of women, if they have any political opinions, tend to share those of their brothers and husbands. She is more inclined to think that the bad treatment from which they have suffered for centuries has alienated women from the other half of society and made them, in a sense, stateless persons whose patriotism must be qualified: 'Our country still ceases to be mine if I marry a foreigner . . . in fact, as a woman, I have no country. As a woman I want no country. As a woman my country is the whole world.' But might it not be possible for a man to say the same thing? It is true that a man cannot marry his way out of his country but there are other means of escape. Virginia's friends T. S. Eliot and Henry James changed their country, while several million others have done likewise by crossing the Atlantic. I doubt whether these migrations had the effect of making the gentlemen less patriotic.

But Virginia clearly did think that in some way her sex excluded her from the full enjoyment of civil liberties. There had been woeful grievances in the past; some remained; the vote was useless, persuasion needed great wealth and clout to succeed. What then was to be done? How were women to prevent war? They were to found a society, a peculiarly unsocial society, without organization, officers or funds. If it had to have a name it could be called the 'Outsiders' Society', it was to be not only pacifist but passive. The members were not to incite their brothers to fight, but neither were they to dissuade them from fighting. They were to maintain an attitude of complete indifference. As Virginia says, the duty to which they would pledge themselves is one of 'considerable difficulty'. It is indeed. To bid a clever girl fall silent while her brothers talk nonsense is brutality worthy of a male tyrant. She is to be sure given a number of subjects upon which to meditate, she is to earn her own living and to agitate for maternity grants: for 'a wage to be paid by the State legally to the mothers of educated men'. A maternity grant to the rich alone would I think be a politically hazardous operation but to agitate for any kind of maternity grant would surely be difficult for a society with no organization.

Virginia believed that the 'Society of Outsiders' was already in being and supported her assertion with these examples: the Mayoress of Woolwich had declared that she 'would not even do as much as darn a sock to help in the war'. Miss E. R. Clarke of the Board of Education 'referred to the women's organizations for hockey, lacrosse, netball, and cricket, and pointed out that under the rules there could be no cup or award of any kind to a successful team'. Canon F. R. Barry, vicar of St Mary the Virgin (the University church) at Oxford observed that the daughters of educated men didn't go to church.

The fact that Virginia saw in these reports evidence of a silent feminist and pacifist revolt forces us to consider them with interest and respect. Nevertheless I cannot but think that if the mothers of Madrid, hunting in the debris of their bombed-out homes for the shattered limbs of their babies, had known of this passage in *Three Guineas* they would have said: 'What on earth is there here to save us from the fury of our fascist enemies?' I will return to those murdered children, but first it is necessary to say something about Virginia's kind of pacifism.

There are, I would suggest, two kinds of pacifism, limited pacifism and total pacifism. Limited pacifism condemns any kind of aggression, it also condemns military or imperial rule without the consent of the governed, but it would not condemn armed resistance to aggression, armed revolt against tyranny, the maintenance of armed forces for a purely defensive purpose, or the supply of arms to the victims of aggression.

Total pacifism simply forbids any use of military force for any purpose whatsoever. The total pacifist, it must be allowed, argues that all aggressors can find reasons for representing their aggressions as justifiable. Nevertheless I believe that there is a definable difference.

Now I can return to those murdered children: 'Here then on the table before us are photographs . . . They are not pleasant photographs to look upon. They are photographs of dead bodies for the most part. This morning's collection contains the photograph of what might be a man's body, or a woman's; it is so mutilated that it might, on the other hand, be the body of a pig. But those certainly are dead children . . .' 'War . . . is an abomination; a barbarity; war must be stopped' – such is Virginia's reaction; it is also the reaction of her correspondent. What then is one to do? One can agitate, write to the press and so on, sign a letter, join a society. But the emotion caused by the photographs, 'that emotion, that very positive emotion, demands something more positive than a name written on a sheet of paper; an hour spent listening to speeches; a cheque written for whatever sum we can afford – say one guinea . . . You, of course, could once more take up arms – in Spain, as before in France – in defence of peace. But that presumably is a method that having tried you have rejected.' But if the reply to this barbarity has to be something different from 'a name written on a sheet of paper' or the use of war in defence of peace, where is the alternative? Virginia's reply is not wholly clear, but I think that it may be not too unfairly summarized thus: being a woman and therefore politically powerless we can do nothing or practically nothing. It is necessary therefore that we should first change our condition and to do this we have to create the 'Outsiders' Society'.

But, as we have seen, the achievements of that society had not done much for the people of Madrid. In fact if we adopt the principles of the total pacifist there is practically nothing that can be done. But was Virginia a total pacifist? Reading *Three Guineas* one would certainly say that she was. I cannot believe, or believe that she could believe, that in the 1930s the British Government, or indeed the British nation, *wanted* to undertake an aggressive war. And yet, when considering the vote of £300 million for arms Virginia makes it clear that she considered this to be a vote in favour of war. This is quite in keeping with the views of the total pacifist; the total pacifist would tell even the Swiss to disarm. Nevertheless, although the authoress of *Three Guineas* seems to have been an absolutely uncompromising pacifist, Virginia Woolf in her diaries was not.

Let us suppose that she had allowed her fictitious correspondents to say: 'I do not think that we need to make war on behalf of the Spanish republic; we need do no more than is already being done by its enemies, that is to say, to give the people of Madrid the planes, the anti-aircraft guns and whatever else they may need for their defence? That might at least save some innocent lives.'

Now consider Virginia's diary for 1937 when she was writing *Three Guineas*. Julian Bell, her nephew, had been killed near Madrid in July of that year. On 13 October Philip Hart, a doctor who had been with Julian, came to see her and described the circumstances in which he died: 'A nice, sensitive thin man, an enthusiast. If we allowed arms through we should save thousands of lives. And then I go upstairs and find Leonard enraged with the Labour Party which sent a deputation to the Foreign Office and was diddled by Vansittart. So we shan't let arms through: we shall sit on the fence: and the fighting will go on – But I am not a politician: obviously, can only rethink politics very slowly into my own tongue.' No, she certainly was *not* a politician, and one has to allow for the horrible and heartbreaking circumstances of that dreadful time. One may sympathize with the apparent contradiction of one who regards the desire to fight as incomprehensible and at the same time calls for the supply of arms to the victim of aggression. These are the words of a 'limited pacifist'; perhaps if one could more perfectly understand what is meant by the 'rethinking of politics' one could arrive at a truer comprehension of those hard sayings in *Three Guineas* which I find so difficult to accept.

Here perhaps I should end this attempt to examine some of the arguments in *Three Guineas*. It is only fair to say that they are weaker than those in the magnificently successful *A Room of One's Own*. Both sexes deserve justice and I feel that it would be entirely unjust to suggest that, amongst the British, either sex actually *wanted* war in 1938.

Finally I would like to say a word of thanks to the fate that ordained that Virginia should not live to see a female Prime Minister joyfully leading her country into a short but bloody war fought over 'a little patch of ground that hath in it no profit but the name'.

3
Three Guineas, Fascism, and the Construction of Gender

Marie-Luise Gättens

War, the father of all things, is also our father. It has hammered us, chiseled us and hardened us into what we are. And always as long as the swirling wheel of life revolves within us, this war will be the axis around which it will swirl. It has reared us for battle and we shall remain fighters as long as we live.

(Ernst Jünger)[1]

Obviously there is for you some glory, some necessity, some satisfaction in fighting which we have never felt or enjoyed. Complete understanding could only be achieved by blood transfusion and memory transfusion – a miracle still beyond the reach of science.

(Virginia Woolf, *TGs*, pp. 6–7)

Virginia Woolf's essay *Three Guineas* is a comprehensive attempt to theorize the significance of gender for fascism. Woolf's analysis of fascism focuses on the patriarchal relationship between men and women, and she argues that the unequal distribution of power between the genders is a key element for producing fascism. In *Three Guineas* fascism is not treated as some kind of extreme aberration but as the consequence of the patriarchal sex-gender system. Instead of turning towards those countries that were experiencing fascist rule in the 1930s, Woolf examines England, a democratic country, and shows that women are systematically excluded from all public positions of prestige and power, excluded from all positions that would enable them to have real political agency, making that country far from democratic for women. Woolf traces women's lack of power and influence in the public affairs of England back to the nineteenth-century tradition of the separate spheres, which relegates women to the home and family. The relegation of women to the family, Woolf argues, not only causes women's lack of power in the public affairs, but also their lack of power within the family. Woolf's demystifying analysis of the middle-class family shows that far from being a haven from the power and strife of the public world, the family is an institution of vital importance for the reproduction of the conditions of the public world. For Woolf the production of gendered subjects in the family is of prime importance for the production of fascism. *Three Guineas* argues that for women anti-fascist politics has to first of all focus on gaining (relative) economic independence for women. Woolf, however, proposes no simple emancipation of middle-class women through their entry into the professions, for the professions, too, are part of the patriarchal structure that produces militarism and war. Instead, Woolf proposes a strategy of entry into the professions without identifying with its institutional structures and disassociation from the existing sex-gender system by an act of active remembrance of the history of female subjection.[2]

Three Guineas is written in the form of a fictitious letter in response to a gentleman who has requested the speaker's support in the struggle against fascism and war, 'to protect liberty and culture'. The request is used as an occasion to examine middle-class women's position within British society in the 1930s.[3] The essay is divided into three parts, each centered around a particular theme. At the end of each part the speaker gives a guinea in support of a certain organization. Part I focuses on women's lack and need of higher education and ends with the speaker's donation of a guinea to rebuild a women's college. Part II addresses women's position in the professions and ends with the donation of a guinea to an organization that helps women enter the professions. Part III concentrates on politics and culture and ends with the donation of a guinea to the gentleman's anti-fascist organization. The speaker, however, refuses to join this organization because she does not believe that it is aimed at transforming the existing gender relations. Instead, she proposes that women find their own form of political organization, the Outsiders' Society, and practice active non-involvement as a strategy for hollowing out the sex-gender system, pillar of family and fatherland.[4]

The First World War had changed the relations between the genders significantly. In Germany and in Great Britain, politicians expressed their gratitude for women's active support of the war by granting them the vote and by opening women's educational and professional opportunities. As the possibility of the independent woman emerged, a backlash formed, which was reinforced by the economic crisis. Many wanted women to return to home and hearth. The Nazis were outspoken proponents of a reactionary gender policy, claiming to save women from politics and to return them to their rightful place, the family – as mothers of the nation. Far from arousing widespread opposition, this gender policy gained the Nazis widespread support, from men as well as from women. Indeed, the Nazis' promise to implement gender-separate spheres appealed to many middle-class women, because they expected it to bring stability to their lives. For most analysts of fascism in the 1930s and in later years, gender, however, figures as an issue of secondary importance and Woolf's analysis has remained singular up to today.

In my ministry I directed departments of economics, education, colonial issues, consumer affairs and health, education and welfare. No man ever interfered with us; we did as we pleased . . . My women and I functioned as one big happy family. They knew they could always count on my support. In all my years in office, no one ever resigned, and I fired no one. Now that record shows how harmoniously we cooperated. No man ever represented us in the outside world. We spoke for ourselves.[5]

If it was not for the 'colonial issues' and the supremely patronizing 'my women and I', one might think of this as a description of government in 'Herland', or some other feminist utopia, rather than the description of the running of the Nazis' Women's Bureau. Yet this is how Gertrud Scholtz-Klink, the chief of the Women's Bureau, describes her work to the historian Claudia Koonz in 1981. Of course, Scholtz-Klink's characterization of this organization as 'one big happy family' where no one was 'fired' or 'resigned', not only suggests retrospective embellishment but indeed the desperate desire for a 'presentable past'. Gertrud Scholtz-Klink is obviously deeply concerned about her historical significance, a significance that she is determined to prove to this historian not only through her wide range of responsibilities but through her autonomy – in other words her power to act.

Gertrud Scholtz-Klink claims for herself as a historical figure agency – for agency is after all the vehicle for achieving historical significance in Western historiography. And while Scholtz-Klink's agency operates within the realm of a political organization, the organization and the women's field of action within it are firmly premised on the notion of separate spheres. The Nazis' belief in biologically determined gender roles clearly delimited the Women's Bureau's field of operation to the affairs of women, families, and children. Indeed, Gertrud Scholtz-Klink did not participate in any of the policy decisions. This preroga-tive remained with the male leadership of the party. Koonz compares the political power of this woman who held the highest office in the Nazi state with that of a district chief or deputy minister.[6] However, as Koonz observes, the very fact that the Nazis so firmly believed in gender segregated political institutions, offered women relative power and autonomy within their own organizations – which had to operate, of course, always within the Nazis' ideological frame-work. Indeed, I think one can argue that Gertrud Scholtz-Klink's political power under National Socialism was based fundamentally on her strict adherence to the Nazis' concept of femininity, which could be summarized as motherhood and work in the family reconceptual-ized as service to the nation. Koonz points to the irony that women such as Gertrud Scholtz-Klink, on the one hand, espoused the 'special nature' of women and ceaselessly preached their dedication to the traditional family, but themselves never thought of limiting their activities to the family, indeed, clearly enjoyed the opportunity of gaining the power that the Nazi state offered them.[7] These women, Koonz argues, engaged in a compensatory deal: 'Women who decided to support Nazism accepted their inferior status in exchange for rewards . . .'.[8]

Nazi women engaged in a 'compensatory deal' that while different in degree, is not fundamentally different from the one Virginia Woolf argues in *Three Guineas* middle-class (British) women have to engage in if they follow and accept traditional gender arrangements. As daugh-ters or wives, they are able to partake in the privileges of their class – Woolf's claim that their payment consists of 'board, lodging and a small annual allowance for pocket money and dress' shows the limits of even that participation – in return, they have to make themselves desirable to the men of their class. To be desirable equally means adherence to these men's notion of femininity as it means espousing their economic interests and political views:

> Because consciously, it is obvious, she was forced to use whatever influence she possessed to bolster up the system which provided her with maids; with carriages; with fine clothes; with fine parties – it was by these means that she achieved marriage . . . In short, all her conscious effort must be in favour of what Lady Lovelace called 'our splendid Empire'. . .
>
> (*TGs*, pp. 38–9)

Woolf uncovers a close connection between the gender arrangements on which the middle-class family is based, class interests, and nationalism, which in the case of Britain is tied to colonialism. Thus one of Woolf's central arguments in *Three Guineas* can be summarized in the following way. As the middle-class family produces gendered subjects, it not only continuously reproduces the division between the private and the public but also continuously reproduces militarism and war: 'Here, immediately, are three reasons which lead your sex to fight; war is a profession; a source of happiness and excitement; and it is also an outlet for manly qualities, without which men would deteriorate' (*TGs*, p. 8). The politics of the public sphere, specifically those of nationalism and colonialism, thus depend on the politics of the private sphere.

It is, however, a vital ingredient of the modern patriarchal order to regard the private as diametrically opposed to the public and thus as nonpolitical. Indeed, this opposition is necessary for maintaining the coherence of this order. In the third part of *Three Guineas*, in her discussion of the exclusion of women from the church (of England), Woolf shows that cultural authority as well as economic superiority depend on the gendered division of the private from the public in the western cultural order: 'But when the Church became a profession, required special knowledge of its prophets and paid them for imparting it, one sex remained inside; the other was excluded' (*TGs*, p. 124). Of course, the church would never admit that its exclusion of women, like that of other professions, not only serves men's vital economic interests but also their desire for domination. Instead, middle-class men utilize all instruments of their privilege to mask their desire for control: 'He has nature to protect him; law to protect him; and property to protect him' (*TGs*, p. 135). Woolf, furthermore, boldly argues that it is precisely this defense of their male interests which connects the institution of the church with that of fascism: 'The emphasis which both priests and dictators place upon the necessity for two worlds is enough to prove that it is essential to their domination' (*TGs*, p. 181n). As a consequence, Woolf argues, a break with the politics of the Empire for women has to begin with a refusal to assume their traditional role in the family. Anti-fascist politics for women, first of all means a job and her own income:

For to help women to earn their livings in the professions is to help them to possess that weapon of independent opinion which is still their most powerful weapon. It is to help them to have a mind of their own and a will of their own with which to help you to prevent war.

(*TGs*, p. 58)

The Nazis' policy towards women reveals even more starkly this connection between a notion of gender based on biology, militarism, and
nationalism. In a speech to the National Socialist women during the
1934 party congress in Nuremberg, Adolf Hitler defined the fundamental duties of men and women in the following way:

> The same heroic courage that man summons up on the battlefield,
> woman summons up in patient devotion, in patient suffering and
> endurance. Every child that she brings into the world is a battle that
> she undergoes for the Being or Non-Being of her people (*Volk*).[9]

While Hitler conceives of the essence of masculinity – and the Nazis
were irresistibly drawn to the notion of the essence – as military valor,
women are nothing but selfless devotion and quiet suffering, which
reminds me, by the way, of the title of the collection of essays about
nineteenth-century British women called *Suffer and Be Still*. As her most
'essential' feminine task of giving birth is coined by Hitler in military
language, 'a battle she undergoes for her people', he explicitly links
motherhood to the Nazis' national and racial project of the Nation and
openly acknowledges the power and control the state assumes over
women's reproductive capacities.[10] While Hitler reduces women to
their biology and thus leaves no doubt about their subordinate status
in the National Socialist state, he simultaneously flatters all those who
are allowed to think of themselves as 'German' women by conferring
superior status on them over all other non-German beings. The combination of requiring subordination and simultaneously granting eleva-
tion fundamentally characterizes Nazi ideology. Within Nazi ideology,
the fact that motherhood was always tied to the Nazis' national and
racial category of 'Germanness', made it very clear that women were
not existing within an autonomous or non-political sphere.

However, most women clearly preferred to think of their work
within the family as non-political, which, by the way, is an interesting
example of a collective (and in some ways self-serving) ideological
blindspot. Gertrud Scholtz-Klink's Women's Bureau thus emphasized
in their work with women, who were not party members, practical
advice and help. Ute Benz thinks that it was indeed this approach that
made the Women's Bureau's work so successful and which made it possible for the organization to integrate millions of German women and
girls into the Nazi state.[11] The Women's Bureau organized, for
example, training programs for mothers (Mütterschulung), which
taught basic infant and child care. These programs were extraordinarily

popular. However, as Ute Benz notes, the knowledge passed on here from one woman to the other was only seemingly 'neutral', but instead vitally informed by the Nazis' notions of race hygiene, hereditary value, and consequently military conquest.[12]

Indeed, Gertrud Scholtz-Klink's claim about the unity of 'her' women has to be seen within the context of the Nazis' policy that irreparably divided women. Although the Nazis continuously proclaimed the unity of all women and the end of all class divisions in their propaganda, Nazi rule produced the most radical differences between women. While the majority of women, namely those who were considered 'German', were designated as 'valuable', a minority of women was designated as 'inferior', or indeed, as in the case of Jewish, Gypsy, and mentally retarded women, as 'valueless' (*lebensunwertes Leben*). These women were first excluded and discriminated against and later persecuted and murdered. Ute Benz maintains that the majority of women accepted this difference in value:

> The majority of women did not protest against this fundamental differentiation and assignment in value. During National Socialism, the often summoned unity of women was not only a deceptive as well as self-deceptive phrase, but an aggressive and intolerant instrument, used by men as well as by women, in order to consolidate National Socialist rule.[13]

Benz adds to this, that women who were persecuted by the Nazis noted with great bitterness the general disinterest of the majority of women in their situation.[14] The Nazis thus successfully employed membership in the 'German' race as a compensation for women's otherwise inferior status. It is in light of this history that we have to see Woolf's rejection of a national status for women. For Woolf, the break with the patriarchal middle-class family has to be extended into a break with the nation or as she calls it 'the full stigma of nationality'.

The myth of the non-political status of women within their sphere of family and home was skillfully employed by the Nazis, in fact, in order to thoroughly politicize and control this sphere. Indeed, Gertrud Scholtz-Klink was chosen by the male party leadership to become the leader of all 'German' women because she projected precisely the kind of image of the German woman the Nazis wanted to promote. Koonz describes her in the 1930s as 'young, trim and blond . . . as the most "Aryan" of the clique of leaders surrounding Hitler'.[15] The mother of eleven children, she was the widow of a Nazi, who later remarried an SS man. Most importantly, however, while obviously highly ambitious and politically shrewd, Scholtz-Klink projected the image of the respectable, non-political mother. She accepted male leadership without questions and made no demands of political power outside of her sphere. Both Claudia Koonz and Renate Wiggershaus insist that the male leadership of the party chose her over the more radical Nazi women leaders from the early days precisely because she projected the image of a respectable middle-class woman rather than a Nazi leader and thus seemed better able to integrate millions of ordinary 'German' women and girls into the Nazi state.[16] By 1939 Scholtz-Klink and her organizations had absorbed 3 million girls within the Hitler Youth and 8 million women in other affiliated organizations. Over 1 million women subscribed to the journal that was directed at the most loyal Nazi women.[17] The women bureaucrats who worked under Scholtz-Klink, Koonz claims, had no illusions about their independence: 'They expected to wield power over women beneath them in exchange for rendering total obedience to the all-male chain of command above them.'[18]

After serving for more than eleven years, from 1934 until the end of the war, in the highest position a woman held in the Nazi state, Scholtz-Klink claims about herself in the interview with Koonz, who calls her a 'paragon of womanliness': 'Oh, I never cared much for politics.'[19] Scholtz-Klink's interested use of the myth of the separate spheres, on the one hand, gained her political power (however limited that might have been compared to men's power), and, on the other hand, allowed her to abjure herself of political responsibility for the Nazis' crimes. She had, of course, known of nothing and participated in nothing, a claim it seems that was largely shared by the Occupation officials as well as the post-war German government. In 1949, the Occupation officials certified her as de-Nazified and after retirement age she received a handsome civil servant's pension.[20]

Nazi women embraced the notion of the separate spheres, as they accepted their position of 'trapesing along at the tail end of the procession' of the Nazi party, which is, of course, a slightly contradictory position. But in this Nazi women are not so different from many other women, who align themselves with a male political movement. There are, of course, also important differences between the alignment of Nazi women with the Nazi party and, say, middle-class British women, who aligned themselves with the dominant political institutions of the 1930s. Nazi women participated in the massive repression and murder of the political enemies of the Nazis, and, even if indirectly, in the war and the Holocaust.

Keeping the important differences between Nazi women and conformist British women in mind, I would like to explore the systematic exclusion of women from the 'public sphere', which is as Woolf argues in *Three Guineas*, a vital ingredient for producing fascism. Woolf uses the figure of the 'procession' to express that the professions are based on exclusion and alignment. Membership in the procession is a sort of birthright, reserved for middle-class men, as the professions practice the systematic exclusion of women and other outsiders, such as working-class men. Those privileged enough to belong to the procession have to subject themselves, however, to its rigid alignment as it forces its members to fall into step:

> There they go, our brothers who have been educated at public schools and universities, mounting those steps, passing in and out of those doors, ascending those pulpits, preaching, teaching, administering justice, practising medicine, transacting business, making money. It is a solemn sight always – a procession, like a caravanserai crossing a desert.
>
> (*TGs*, pp. 60–1)

The procession is a massive production line of male subjects. It reserves to these subjects all the practices that are endowed with meaning and prestige, at the same time that it requires them to subject themselves to the discipline of its practices. 'According to its form, the procession is authoritarian, despotic', Gisela Wysocki maintains. 'It gathers its members under the principle of complicity. They have always been soldiers and fathers. The procession devours bodies, affects. It absorbs, it possesses. At the end, this big assimilation machine spits out deformed bodies.'[21] The procession's strictly hierarchical nature makes its meaning readable not only for those inside but also for those outside of it; even the daughter as outsider can read its significance. As the procession gives meaning and identity to its members through its ranks – 'some with ribbons across their breasts, others without' – it simultaneously rewards and punishes.[22] It is no surprise that those who are not able 'to keep in step' literally fall out of this system of meaning. They are no longer producing words themselves, but 'selling newspapers' are only selling the words of others and thus are economically at the very margins or, from the perspective of the center, are geographically at the very margins, 'in Tasmania', 'doing nothing'. However, the pull of the procession is so strong that most keep 'in step'.

Woolf's use of the figure of the procession, its requirement of keeping 'in step', immediately brings to mind the military and its habit of forming soldiers into formations. 'The rhetoric of war', as Wysocki puts it, 'refers back to the rhetoric of the procession. Conquered nature, the firing position, the assembling in the order of battle.'[23] Indeed, in her discussion of professional man's splendid clothing, Woolf stresses the centrality of the military:

> What connection is there between the sartorial splendours of the educated man and the photograph of ruined houses and dead bodies? Obviously the connection between dress and war is not far to seek; your finest clothes are those you wear as soldiers.
>
> (*TGs*, p. 21)

For the military is the professional institution that most clearly consolidates and expands the economic and political interests of the empire and that continuously produces a particularly prestigious brand of masculinity. The image of the soldier, just mentioned, furthermore, is clearly connected to the image of the uniformed fascist, which appears at the end of the text: 'It is the figure of a man; some say, others deny, that he is Man himself, the quintessence of virility, the perfect type of which all the others are imperfect adumbrations' (*TGs*, p. 142). In *Discipline and Punish*, Michel Foucault stresses the significance of the modern military for creating the modern individual:

> The human body was entering a machinery of power that explores it, breaks it down and rearranges it. A 'political anatomy', which was also a 'mechanics of power', was being born; it defined how one may have a hold over others' bodies, not only so that they may do what one wishes, but so that they may operate as one wishes, with the techniques, the speed and the efficiency that one determines. Thus discipline produces subjected and practised bodies, 'docile' bodies.[24]

The fascists, of course, elevated the soldiers to the quintessential embodiment of masculinity, as the earlier quote from Hitler shows. Nazis saw themselves as 'political soldiers' and the First World War as 'the father of their movement'.[25] And as Barbara Ehrenreich reminds us, 'it is not only that men make wars, but that wars make men'. Thus, the Freikorpsmen, the men who refused to disband after the First World War and who went on to fight working-class uprisings in the inter-war years and who later became the core of Hitler's SA, did not appear ready-made on the plain of history, but were shaped by the First World War.[26] Indeed, *Three Guineas* is a refutation of the fascists' adherence to a natural gender difference. As femininity is produced out of the various social practices and discourses so is masculinity – thus the significance of the procession, the giant machinery for producing middle-class men able to rule.

While the procession is clearly in sight, the family house, which is one of the rewards for those who belong to the procession, remains invisible, as do its female members remain unnamed. Only Arthur, whose education will enable him to join the procession, has a name as he has a meaning in terms of the procession. Here again, Woolf alludes to the power relation between the private and the public. Excluded from the public discourses, women remain invisible and powerless. In contrast to the private house, the procession is not only at the center stage but also engages in extravagant visual display:

> The first sensation of colossal size, of majestic masonry is broken up into a myriad points of amazement mixed with interrogation. Your clothes in the first place make us gape with astonishment. How many, how splendid, how extremely ornate they are – the clothes worn by the educated man in his public capacity!
>
> (*TGs*, p. 19)

Woolf's elaborate description of the procession draws attention not only to the fact that it is in possession of all the wealth and that it fetishizes power but also that it has a hold over the production of images.

However, Woolf refuses to invest this elaborate display of male power with a desiring gaze, instead she assumes a 'bird's-eye view of the outside of things', which not only refuses identification but also estranges. It allows her to reveal the power that structures the most commonplace. The refusal to invest with desire and to identify indeed is promoted as the central feminist strategy in the text. The aim of this strategy is to dismantle the sex-gender system that produces a masculinity based on militarism and a femininity of subjugation. In order to understand Woolf's feminist strategy, which, of course, in a way precisely refuses to be a strategy, it might help to summarize the political argument that leads up to Woolf's survey of the procession.

Woolf argues that the middle-class family is based on the radical inequality of the sexes. With nothing but marriage open to them, women are completely dependent on the men of their class and thus have to support these men's political and economic interests. The middle-class family, furthermore, continually reproduces gendered subjects, in other words, male subjects whose identity is shaped by a notion of virility that is closely allied to the military and female subjects whose femininity is vitally informed by subservience to men. In order to have a 'mind of their own', so that they can 'help prevent war', women need their own income, in other words they need to enter the professions and indeed, in the mid-1930s, when *Three Guineas* is written, women have joined the professions – a little bit: 'For there, trapesing along at the tail end of the procession, we go ourselves. And that makes a difference' (*TGs*, p. 61). If joining the professions means joining the procession, will women not become as aligned with this vast machinery that produces individuals able and ready to rule, with militarism as a vital ingredient of this rule? In this case they would end up supporting the same system they had to support within the family. Now Woolf proposes that women join the professions – to make their own money – but refuse to identify with them. The speaker locates her own position as on 'the threshold of the private house', as on 'the bridge which connects the private house with the world of public life' (*TGs*, p. 18). She is thus neither enclosed by the private house, nor has she joined the profession. The speaker inhabits this 'suspended' position, first of all for historical reasons: born in the late nineteenth century, her education was still vitally shaped by the tradition of the private house, which as a working woman she has left in the twentieth century. Secondly, her position is also determined by her profession: as a writer the speaker is not as bound by an institutional framework as the members of other professions. This 'indeterminate' position is precisely located in the text, because it determines the speaker's critical perspective of society. Just as the gentleman does not speak from a neutral position, neither does she.

Throughout *Three Guineas*, Woolf insists that middle-class women have different historical experiences from those of the men of their class. This difference is for Woolf the most important reason why there can be no identity between men and women. At the moment that women could become aligned with men's history by joining the procession, she urges women to use their own history to construct their own social identity. The four 'great teachers of the daughters of educated men', 'poverty, chastity, derision and freedom from unreal loyalties', are the memory of their own subjugation, which are used here precisely *not* to assume the status of the female victim, but in order to refuse identification and alignment with middle-class men's rule.[27]

In a similar way, the political program of the 'Outsiders' Society' consists primarily in a militant practice of 'indifference', a continual refusal to join in and to identify with the nation, its various institutions, and the men of her class. Rather than constructing a counter power, this feminist strategy aims at hollowing out the existing structures of power, by refusing not only practical support but more importantly by investing masculine activities with desire. In order for it to work, the patriarchal sex-gender system clearly not only requires women's participation in its social and cultural practices, but also needs women to invest men with their desire. If the patriarchal sex-gender potentially produces fascism, Woolf implicitly argues, one ingredient in this production is female desire. Reading *Three Guineas* it becomes quite clear that Woolf herself was quite immune against feeling desire for the masculinity of the fascist. Gisela Wysocki characterizes Woolf's texts as texts that 'maintain avidity': 'The texts live out of the rejection of patriarchal fetishes. They boycott the fantasies created by male culture. The belief in Gods, the language of heroes, the din of personality.'[28] And while Woolf sharply criticizes the systematic exclusion of women from almost all economic, political, and cultural enterprises, because it condemns women to dependency on the 'fathers', she uses women's history of exclusion as a critical tool of resistance against assimilation into the male order. For women's history has produced 'freedom from unreal loyalties'. Indeed, the speaker of *Three Guineas* uses the gentleman's request to help him figure out 'how to prevent war', precisely not to assimilate herself into his political speech, but to outline and insist on her difference. The difference she insists on, however, in contrast to the gender difference of the fascists, is not biological but historically produced. Indeed, as Nina Schwartz insists, Woolf rejects the notion of a 'natural' sex difference: 'Since she never defines the meaning of sexual difference except insofar as that difference has been interpreted culturally, the terms [*male* and *female* M.L.G.] can be taken to signify *difference* itself, in a far more complex sense than "polarity".'[29] The essay rejects the notion that middle-class men and women share in the face of fascism, the greater evil, a common interest. The three dots . . ., that appear throughout *Three Guineas*, indicate the gulf that separates men and women. Instead, the common interests between anti-fascist men and women are partial, because of this the speaker donates a guinea to the gentleman's anti-fascist society, but refuses to join his society and to subsume her own cause under the gentleman's.

Three Guineas offers an acute analysis of the power that structures the relationship between the genders, the connection between the private and the public, as well as convincing strategies for resistance, yet what Woolf perhaps underestimates is the desire that many women feel for the splendor of the procession and for that man in uniform, 'the quintessence of virility', the embodiment of power. Gertrud Scholtz-Klink as well as many ordinary middle-class German women, while insisting on their pure femininity were clearly eager to share in the power and superiority that the Nazis offered them. At one point in *Three Guineas* Woolf alludes to women's fascination for that most male of all enterprises: war. Woolf refers here to British women's enthusiastic support (they were, of course, not the only ones who felt this enthusiasm, German women did too) for the First World War. For women, Woolf insists, the war offered the opportunity to escape from the 'private house' and their support was an expression of their 'loathing' of it:

> So profound was her unconscious loathing for the education of the private house with its cruelty, its poverty, its hypocrisy, its immorality, its inanity that she would undertake any task however menial, exercise any fascination however fatal that enabled her to escape. Thus consciously she desired 'our splendid Empire'; unconsciously she desired our splendid war.
>
> (*TGs*, p. 39)

Women feel a desire for war, Woolf suggests, because war offers an escape from the narrowness of domestic life and from the dissatisfying relationships between men and women. Klaus Theweleit in his book *Male Fantasies* also observes the enthusiastic departure to war of the Freikorpsmen: 'Real men lack nothing when women are lacking.'[30] Indeed, military culture tends to celebrate its maleness and tends to equate all of civilian life with femininity. The reasons for men's desire to escape the domestic must be different from women's. After all men's activities are not even during peacetime restricted to the 'private house'. According to Theweleit it is, indeed, not so much the domestic that these men try to escape but more specifically women. The Freikorpsmen feel an unspeakable dread of women. They hate their bodies and their sexuality.[31] As women cannot function as love objects for these men, violence has become their supreme form of satisfaction.[32] While the Freikorpsmen were a relatively small group of men, who clearly identified with the fascist project, Theweleit, nevertheless, insists that their structure of desire is not fundamentally different from that of most men.[33] While the experience of violence remains for most women indirect, their fascination with the male figure that embodies violence can nevertheless be strong and direct. It seems to me, that Woolf describes the daughters' fascination much too simply as an opportunity to escape the narrowness of the domestic and not enough as a longing for fusion with the most dramatic of all national projects: war. Of course, Woolf is right that in reality the war experience divides men even more from women than any other experience but that nevertheless does not preclude that women feel desire for the men in uniform, as for the power they embody.

Only two years before Woolf began writing *Three Guineas* in 1936, Leni Riefenstahl staged the most grandiose massing of men in uniforms in her film *Triumph of the Will (Triumph des Willens)*. Indeed, this film of the National Socialist Party congress in Nuremberg in 1934 strings together a series of gigantic processions. These grandiose processions of uniformed men make it very clear that the Nazis understand themselves entirely in military terms. Thus the party congress is officially opened with a commemoration of Field Marshall Hindenburg, 'the first soldier of the Reich', and even the members of the Labor Service are lined up with their shovels as if they were guns, in a sense anticipating their own transformation into soldiers a few years later. In another sequence, Hitler, Himmler, and Lutze, three lonely figures in the vast Luitpold arena, walk on a wide aisle to a war memorial in order to lay down a wreath. This scene stages dramatically the relationship between leader(s) and followers. The vast mass of completely disciplined followers, although robbed of their individuality, nevertheless function through their participation in the vast formation as the embodiment of the German nation and its world-historic mission. '*Triumph of the Will*', Susan Sontag observes, 'uses overpopulated wide shots of massed figures alternating with close-ups that isolate a single passion, a single perfect submission: in a temperate zone clean-cut people in uniforms group and regroup, as if they were seeking the perfect choreography to express their fealty.'[34] The close-ups make it seem as if every follower pledges his allegiance personally and in return is recognized by his leader personally. We are presented with the indissoluble bond between men.

Sequence after sequence singles out the Führer and shows him from every angle always single-mindedly attending to the sublime task of leading. And while the followers proclaim their total devotion to their Führer, the Führer presents the total devotion of the ruler. The many

close-ups of Hitler in *Triumph of the Will* produce the spectator's sense
of intimacy and connectedness with the Führer that continues
throughout the film.[35] The contrast between the individual figure of
the Führer and the vastness of the masses produces a sense of the 'vastness' of his historical mission.

Riefenstahl in her film gives perfect expression to the National
Socialists' claim to be the embodiment of the German nation. The
scene of the Labor Service men literally enacts the unity of the people
(*Volkseinheit*): the leader asks a man where he is from and the man
answers from Friesenland, for example. In the course of this sequence,
every German region is named, making it clear that there are no more
geographical as there are no more class divisions, two important claims
of the Nazi state.[36] The lines Riefenstahl places at the beginning of the
film present National Socialist rule as a historic mission, one that will
bring salvation to the German people:

> 5. September 1934.
> Twenty years after the outbreak of the Great War.
> Fifteen years after the beginning of German suffering.
> Nineteen months after the beginning of German rebirth.[37]

National Socialist rule as the 'new beginning' is most impressively
enacted in the morning sequence that shows thousands of men in
their tent camp getting ready for the day, the German nation as a vast
boy-scout camp. The sequence radiates brightness, energy, and optimism.[38] This is a world far away from the dreariness of everyday life
that separates men. Here they all belong together, the ugly ones as well
as the good-looking ones, even the ones who are failures in their bourgeois existence, can here belong to the elite. It is this sense of belonging, as Theweleit argues, that makes these men feel whole as members
of the Nazi movement: 'The men in the film submit to orders and
connect into sites that promise to eliminate what they experience as
lack. The word they repeatedly scream at the party congress is "whole"
– heil, heil, heil, heil, heil – and this is precisely what the party makes
them. They are no longer broken; and they will remain whole into
infinity.'[39] Their sense of wholeness and belonging obviously requires
the absence of women.

There are hardly any women in this film. If they appear, they appear
only briefly as enthusiastic spectators who watch men make history. In
a brief sequence that is supposed to underline the devotion of the
people to their Führer, a woman brings her child to Hitler so that it can

give flowers to him. *Triumph of the Will* presents history as military history, as the history of the nation, whose people are passive sufferers, who wait to be delivered by men who are leaders, who bring about a quasi religious new beginning. In the two hours and 20 minutes of the film, Riefenstahl gives filmic expression to the idea that National Socialist men embody not only German history but World history. This is history as myth and Wysocki calls Riefenstahl appropriately 'ruler over men's myths'. 'Leni Riefenstahl elevates the lives of men into the world order. She stages masculinity as totality.'[40]

It seems ironic that the film that is generally regarded as the archetypal fascist film was made by a woman.[41] One explanation may be: recognizing that she would never be able to really join the procession, Riefenstahl decided to direct it. She directed a film crew that consisted of 170 people: 36 camera men, of which 9 were aerial camera men, and 17 light technicians.[42] For her work Riefenstahl received not only ample financial and technical support from the Nazis but her crew was carefully protected in their work. During the shooting of the film, the cameramen were dressed in SA uniforms and the SS supplied the film team with guards. Riefenstahl did, furthermore, not simply film the party congress, as it was taking place, but was involved in its planning, which was, as Sontag points out, 'from the start conceived as the set of a film spectacle'.[43] Moreover, the final product of the film also bears Riefenstahl's signature, as it was she herself who undertook the editing. Many critics have pointed out that it is through the skillful and innovative editing that the film gained its dramatic tension.[44] In other words, Riefenstahl was very much the author of this work which not only celebrates fascist masculinity but banishes women from history. Wysocki believes that it is the experience of humiliation, of being 'deceived' out of being subjects of history, that connects Riefenstahl with the fascists, who also believed themselves to be outsiders.[45] While Gertrud Scholtz-Klink and the other women of the Women's Bureau gained power within the Nazi state by embracing the Nazis' notion of femininity and their idea of the womanly sphere, Riefenstahl gained power by shamelessly celebrating fascist masculinity, or as Wysocki puts it: 'The film relentlessly illustrates the genealogy of phallic power. Every image presents the indispensability of male victory.'[46]

Woolf does indeed propose an antidote to the seductiveness of the figure of the uniformed man, the 'quintessence of virility', of power and action. It consists in placing next to his image, the images of destruction: 'And behind him lie ruined houses and dead bodies – men, women and children' (*TGs*, p. 142). Because the seductiveness of the images of the processions in *Triumph of the Will* works, of course, only by actively repressing the horrendous images from the First World War, for example those of trench warfare. And here I will conclude with Woolf's passionate plea to recognize our own investment in that figure in uniform, to recognize it as our own regressive desires for power and/or submission, which are after all two sides of the same coin:

> It suggests that the public and the private worlds are inseparably connected; that the tyrannies and servilities of the one are the tyrannies and servilities of the other. But the human figure even in a photograph suggests other and more complex emotions. It suggests that we cannot dissociate ourselves from that figure but are ourselves that figure. It suggests that we are not passive spectators doomed to unresisting obedience but by our thoughts and actions can ourselves change that figure.
>
> (*TGs*, p. 142)

4
Toward a Feminist Theory of the State: Virginia Woolf and Wyndham Lewis on Art, Gender, and Politics

Merry M. Pawlowski

> And the *feminization* of the white European and American is already far advanced, coming in the wake of the war.[1]
>
> (Wyndham Lewis)

> It is the figure of a man; some say, others deny, that he is *Man himself*, . . . He is called in German and Italian Führer or Duce.
>
> (*TGs*, p. 142, Virginia Woolf; emphasis added)

On October 11, 1934, Virginia Woolf learned that she was included in Wyndham Lewis's newly published *Men Without Art*; and she wrote in her diary:

> In todays Lit. Sup. [*sic*] they advertise Men without Art by Wyndham Lewis. Chapters on Eliot, Faulkner, Hemingway, Virginia Woolf . . . Now I know by reason and instinct that this is an attack . . . My instinct is, not to read it.
>
> (*Diary 4*, p. 250)

But she did read it, taking the 'arrow of W. L. to [her] heart' (*Diary 4*, p. 250), at exactly the right time for the evolution of her thinking about the fascist state. Woolf tried to console herself that, despite his mockery of 'Mr. Bennett and Mrs. Brown' and her fundamental prudery, Lewis considered her 'one of the 4 or 5 living (it seems) who is an artist'. Nowhere in Lewis's chapter on Woolf can one find that judgment. It is hard to imagine, for example, that Lewis meant to send Woolf accolades when he wrote: 'While I am ready to agree that the intrinsic literary importance of Mrs. Woolf may be exaggerated by her friends, I cannot agree that as a symbolic landmark – a sort of party-lighthouse – she has not a very real significance' (*VW*, pp. 159–60).

Far from finished with his attack on Woolf, however, Lewis metaphorically chooses her back to transport him across the territory of militant feminism. Indeed, Lewis's use of the 'party-lighthouse' to represent the emasculation or 'feminization' of a phallic image suggests the direction he will take in his attack on Woolf. It is this very feminine standpoint, and the shift in a power base it seemed to represent, that Lewis so feared.[2] Woolf could not have missed the maliciously gendered satire that Lewis saved for his chapter on her; indeed, it would prove yet more fuel to the fire of her rapidly evolving theories. Framing his remarks within a 'Woolf vs the realists' context, Lewis could barely contain himself as he surveyed an age where he felt the balance of power in favor of men had been disturbed by women like Woolf.

> It has been with considerable shaking in my shoes, and a feeling of treading upon a carpet of eggs, that I have taken the cow by the horns in this chapter, and broached the subject of the part that the feminine mind has played . . . in the erection of our present criteria.
>
> (*VW*, pp. 170–1)

Woolf's feminine assessment of modern literature ten years before in 'Mr. Bennett and Mrs. Brown', one which Lewis argued was based on a gendered dichotomy, is his target here. Lewis ventures no real assessment of Woolf's artistry; rather, because she is a woman who threatens masculine power, he makes her appear unworthy of true aesthetic judgment. Possibly Woolf's view of society that, 'on or about December, 1910, human character changed',[3] rankled Lewis, whose opinions were openly elitist. Woolf believed that she was witnessing a transformation in the twentieth century, that is to say, just the sort of leveling of power relations between 'masters and servants, husbands and wives, parents and children'[4] which Lewis deplored as the 'feminization' of human character.

Regardless of Lewis's motive, Woolf believed that she had resisted his attack; and, specifically referring to *The Pargiters*, the 'ur' version of *Three Guineas*, she reminded herself that it would be fatal to arrange it 'so as to meet his criticisms' (*Diary 4*, p. 252). At the end of several days' torment over Lewis's satire, Woolf even imagined herself strengthened by the attack, with her 'back against the wall', 'possessed of a remarkable sense of driving ey[e]less strength', 'rapid, excited, amused: intense', and ready to 'let fly, in life, on all sides' (*Diary 4*, p. 260). Yet, within just two and a half months, Woolf changed the working title of *Three Guineas* from 'A Tap on the Door' to 'On Being Despised', a significant moment in the process of her thinking about the early stages of this work.[5]

The conflict between Woolf and Lewis portrayed here reveals the interanimation of art and politics which infused the beliefs of both writers, resulting in irrevocably opposed positions on gender, power, society, and the state. A microcosm of any society, the state as its ruling body wields power, incorporating and reflecting its society's views on gender. For Lewis, we could say, as Catherine Mackinnon suggests in general, that formally the state is male and objectivity is its norm.[6] The state sees women as men do, Mackinnon argues, and the very form of the state recapitulates the male point of view. Is masculinity inherent, Mackinnon asks, in the state form as such, or is some other way of governing imaginable? I can imagine Woolf asking herself the same question, experiencing from the very attack Lewis had launched against her, the depths to which 'gender is a social system that divides power',[7] and recognizing how entirely women were (and continue to be) exploited and excluded from public life. And though it may be as Mackinnon suggests, that feminism has articulated no theory of the state, I believe that Lewis's overly emphatic defense of a masculine status quo coupled with the rise of fascism in Europe inspired Woolf to build the foundation necessary to formulate a feminist theory of the state.

Lewis's attack on Woolf reaches a new height of malignant satire for the very reason that he believes the arbiters of taste and the wielders of power collected in the form of the state should be one and the same – and that gendered masculine. Balanced against what he writes about Woolf and other 'feminized' minds, Lewis's chapter on himself in *Men Without Art* continues a practice of gendered aesthetics pervasive throughout the book and reinforces objectivity as the norm to which one should aspire. He poses himself as satirist and 'externalist' par excellence in sharp opposition to all those practitioners of interior monologue, '*the tellers-from-the-inside* . . . the masters of the "interior monologue", . . . those Columbuses who have set sail towards the El Dorados of the Unconscious, or of the Great Within' (*WL*, p. 128). Rejecting the 'jelly-fish that floats in the centre of the subterranean stream of the "dark"

Unconscious', Lewis chose for himself the 'shield of the tortoise, or the rigid stylistic articulations of the grasshopper' (*WL*, p. 120), the hard carapace of external appearance. Lewis's remarks offer insight into a gendered imagery which suggests compelling alignment to what Klaus Theweleit has called the imagery of a fascist, masculine unconscious.[8] Indeed, it is in his attack on Woolf that Lewis's 'fascist unconscious' explodes most overtly in print, crystallizing his efforts to link art to politics and power/domination to gender.

Theweleit's work in *Male Fantasies* suggests an important feminist analogue to the development of Wyndham Lewis's thought, as Theweleit, in his research into the writing of pre-Hitlerian German Freikorpsmen, suggestively uncovers a masculine 'unconscious' that is violently anti-feminine: 'Women's bodies are the holes, swamps, pits of muck that can engulf.'[9] Central to Theweleit's approach, and a factor which distinguishes his work from other socio-psychological investigations of fascism, is his insistence upon the primacy of violence which originates in a fear and loathing of females.[10]

Theweleit's work is also significant for assuming a continuum between ordinary 'male fantasies' and their violent counterparts in a fascist unconscious, suggesting the horrifying possibility that such fantasies and desires are 'the common psychic property of bourgeois males – and perhaps non-bourgeois males as well'.[11] Theweleit's views resonate compellingly with Woolf's conclusions about the antifeminism found at the heart of patriarchal societies and prepare a context from which to view Lewis's political and social statements in three key texts, 'The Code of a Herdsman' (1917), *The Art of Being Ruled* (1926), and *Hitler* (1931). In examining these texts, I plan to use Woolf's *Three Guineas* and *Between the Acts* as much needed corrective lenses through which to view Lewis's conception of the state, itself emblematic of the fascist paternalism of society at the time.

By 1934, when he wrote on Woolf, Lewis's gendered vision of aesthetics, politics, and power was firmly in place; but even early in his career, in 'The Code of a Herdsman', his ideas had begun to crystallize. Informed both by the protofascism of Charles Maurras and the misogyny of Nietzsche,[12] Lewis offered the following advice in 'Code': 'As to women: wherever you can, substitute the society of men . . . women, and the processes for which they exist, are the arch conjuring trick: and they have the cheap mystery and a good deal of the slipperiness, of the conjuror' (*Code*, p. 6). Lewis does, however, condescendingly suggest that a woman might be a kind of 'bastard herdsman', and that, perhaps, there is a 'female mountain', a mirage-mountain, somewhere where women might retreat from the herd. By this, Lewis would have meant that women might have their own domain of power, a pale reflection of and absolutely separate from, the domain of male power. Nowhere does Lewis allow women a space among (male) herdsmen.

Lewis ends on a note that seems, tragically, and in the spirit of *Joyful Wisdom*, to welcome violence: 'The terrible processions beneath are not of our making, and are without our pity. Our sacred hill is a volcanic heaven. But the result of its violence is peace' (*Code*, p. 7). Even in this early satire, Lewis displays himself as a rather sociopathic personality; but more importantly, he had begun to draft his own theory of the state, inextricably merging his belief in an elitist, aesthetic, and masculinist superiority with his view of the weak, 'feminine' need to be governed shared by a common human mass.

Oddly enough, Woolf, too, was thinking about herds in 1917, an early impulse which would deepen much later when she began to read Freud seriously. Woolf wrote of dining with Roger Fry and Clive Bell one night in November of 1917:

> Old Roger takes a gloomy view, not of our life, but of the world's future; but I think I detected the influence of Trotter & the herd, & so I distrusted him. Still, stepping out on Charlotte Street, where the Bloomsbury murder took place a week or two ago, & seeing a crowd swarming in the road & hearing women abuse each other & at the noise others come running with delight – all this sordidity made me think him rather likely to be right.
>
> (*Diary 1*, p. 80)

Woolf's class prejudice is surely evident here, but her reluctance to lump masses of humanity beneath her in class is clear as well. When she first read Wilfred Trotter's *Instincts of the Herd in Peace and War*, Woolf (despite her insistence that she didn't read Freud seriously until 1939) would have been exposed to Trotter's quarrel with Freud's 'psycho-analytic' psychology in favor of a biological psychology which emphasizes humanity as part of the evolutionary scale and subject to instincts which dominate all life.[13] She would have also read Trotter's exploration of herdlike behavior and instinctual gregarious behavior, yet she seems uneasy with a 'psychology' which predicates that human masses and animal herds are simply points along a continuum. Like Lewis, Woolf would become increasingly concerned with the nature of power and control, but these concerns with the leader, the group, and the place of the feminine within and/or outside the 'crowd' take an opposing path. In fact, years later, in 1939–40, Woolf would utter an ebullient and visionary pronouncement on the nature of humanity: 'From this I reach what I might call a philosophy . . . that the whole world is a work of art . . . we are the words; we are the music; we are the thing itself' (*MB*, p. 72). Where Lewis establishes a hierarchy which dichotomizes the world and art in terms of gender and spatial arrangement – elite and mass, high and low, superior and inferior, Woolf equalizes the genders into humanity and Lewis's mountains/plains into a vast, level playing field.

Lewis, however, posing increasingly as an 'enemy' to the human masses, refines, in a subsequent work, *The Art of Being Ruled* (1926), the notions he had begun to flesh out in 'Code'. This text is among four of Lewis's major works published between 1926 and 1930; and in it, he would embellish the core of his Manichaean vision in the 'Code'. *The Art of Being Ruled* contains Lewis's most visible cultural model, a simple, two-part construction which divides humanity into a small class of intellects who are capable of individual thought and unthinking masses who wish for nothing better than to be ruled.[14] Lewis has few qualms about predicting in this work the coming of an enlightened authoritarianism, announcing in an often quoted statement: 'I am not a communist; if anything, I favour some form of *fascism* rather than communism' (*ABR*, p. 27). Such a statement underscores Lewis's antipathy toward democratic liberalism and individual freedom which he believes has prevented the 'white' race from unifying the world's 'large mud-ball' (*ABR*, p. 67). Rather, it is authoritarianism, leninism so extreme it turns right, in a word, 'fascismo', that should emerge when European democracy is strangled offstage (*ABR*, p. 69).

> *Fascismo* is merely a spectacular marinettian flourish put on to the tail, or, if you like, the head, of marxism: that is, of course, fascism as interpreted by its founder, Mussolini. And that is the sort of socialism that this essay would indicate as the most suitable for anglo-saxon countries or colonies . . .
>
> (*ABR*, p. 369)

Lewis's prototypes of the future state of England are Russia and Italy, where the rulers know the human being well enough to realize:

that he finds his greatest happiness in a state of dependence and subservience when (an important condition) it is named 'freedom'. It matters very little, then, if you outrage often, as you must do to rule successfully, the most elementary principles of 'freedom'. He will be happier with you dependent, than with other people, *in*dependent.

(ABR, p. 91)

Shortly, as we shall see, Lewis's models for competent states would grow to include Germany and its leader, Hitler.

Charting a cultural profile which increasingly characterizes the leader and his masses as gender-specific, Lewis writes: 'This division into rulers and ruled partakes of a sexual division; or rather, the contrast between the one class and the other is more like that between the sexes than anything else. The ruled are the females and the rulers the males, in this arrangement' (*ABR*, p. 95). Indeed, Lewis jokingly suggests castration for the masses (the ruled) in his chapter on the problem of the white European 'Yahoo', yet closes on a more serious note when he writes: 'the feminization of the white European and American is already far advanced, coming in the wake of the war' (*ABR*, p. 51).

At a deeper level, Lewis suggests a view of the feminine uncannily reminiscent of Theweleit's insights:

> Finally, the bergsonian (jamesesque, psycho-analytic, wagnerian Venusberg) philosophy of the hot *vitals* – of the blood-stream, of vast cosmic emotion, gush and flow – is that of a blind organism.

(ABR, p. 403)

'Venusberg' is the space where 'feminized' (read also Woolfian) aesthetics may be found; but art must be concerned, Lewis argues, with 'the hard, cold, formal skull or carapace' of form (*ABR*, p. 403).

The Art of Being Ruled, as David Ayers points out, shows clear signs of influence from Weininger's *Sex and Character* (1904), a work which reeks of misogyny.[15] 'Women', Weininger wrote, 'have no existence and no essence; they are not, they are nothing . . . Woman has no share in ontological reality.'[16] In Weininger, Lewis would also find and echo the identification of the Jew with the feminine, a key element for Theweleit's notion of a fascist unconscious. Weininger had, in fact, a central role in the crafting of a fascist unconscious dependent upon misogyny and antisemitism, his work profoundly influencing Hitler and the course of modern racism.[17] Derived from his reading of Weininger, Lewis displays a tone of superiority in his flight from the feminine and an unmistakable desire to separate men from women throughout *The Art of Being Ruled*:

> Eventually, I believe, a considerable segregation of women and men must occur, just as segregation of those who decide for the active, the intelligent life, and those who decide (without any stigma attaching to the choice) for the 'lower' or animal life, is likely to happen, and is very much to be desired.
>
> (*ABR*, p. 199)

Lewis's argument that no stigma would attach to the choice of 'lower' life is, of course, a ridiculous gesture toward 'political correctness' as Lewis might have understood it in 1926. In addition to fleshing out his philosophy of elitist separatism of the masculine intellectual leader from the feminine 'herd', Lewis, in the 434 pages of *The Art of Being Ruled*, attacks and denounces liberalism, communism, democracy, feminism, individualism, and homosexuality. His vision of the present climate in *The Art of Being Ruled* would lead Lewis to a satiric and utterly naive conception of women having more than won their freedom. I offer the following as an example, which, though lengthy, bears repeating in its entirety: and note that the italicized words are a feature of Lewis's satiric style:

> When *feminism* first assumed the proportions of a universal movement it was popularly regarded as a movement directed to the righting of a little series of political wrongs. Woman had been unjustly treated, had been a chattel to be bought and sold and disposed of: men were *free*, women in chains – chained to the hearthstone in the home, which was also referred to as the *castle* of the male gaoler. A thousand chivalrous gentlemen leapt to arms and rushed to the assistance of this matron in distress. With great gestures of christian magnanimity they divested themselves of all traditional masculine authority or masculine advantage of any sort. Tearfully they laid them all at the feet of the dishonoured matron, who dried her burning tears, and with a dark glance of withering indignation picked them up and hurried away. The general herd of men smiled with indulgent superiority. So that was all settled; it was a bloodless revolution.
>
> (*ABR*, pp. 215–16)

What disturbs Lewis most deeply finally becomes clear; there can be no question of female equality, for the very suggestion of it threatens masculine power.

Concluding *The Art of Being Ruled*, Lewis reaffirms his belief in elitist authoritarianism over a mass of common humanity incapable of self-rule:

> Our minds are all still haunted by that Abstract Man, that enlightened abstraction of a common humanity, which had its greatest advertisement in the eighteenth century. That No Man in a No Man's Land, that phantom of democratic 'enlightenment', is what has to be disposed of for good in order to make way for higher human classifications, which, owing to scientific method, men can now attempt.
>
> (*ABR*, p. 434)

By 1939, when she acknowledged in her diary that she was reading Freud's *Group Psychology and the Analysis of the Ego*, Woolf had been thinking for some time about the nature of groups and their leaders, but in a manner quite different from Lewis. Perhaps at the very core of conceptualizing any theory of the state lies the leader and the 'herd'. Her reading of Trotter years before introduced her to an emphasis on the herd instinct; but Trotter, as Freud points out, takes no account in his theory of the group leader or herdsman, an oversight which, for Freud, weakens Trotter's exposition.[18] Lewis, in the work we have examined so far, indicates leader types – Mussolini is one example – and we suspect that Lewis's herdsman would have to be someone very much like himself: artistic, elitist, educated, and, of course, manly. The irony of the title, *The* Art *of Being Ruled*, suggests an inverse, intensely comic vision Woolf had of the *art* of the *ruler*, a vision she offers in *Between the Acts* (1941).

Woolf's posthumously published novel produces an alternative vision of both Lewis's authoritarian leader dominating common humanity as well as Freud's leader and his herd.[19] Through the lesbian playwright Miss La Trobe, the producer of an annual village pageant, Woolf *negatively* reproduces Freud's charismatic leader-hero and Lewis's self-image of the elitist artist and herdsman as a woman and a failed artist while associating the villagers, both the gentry and commoners who are her audience, with the herd. The possibility of ironic contrasts between Hitler and his horde as subtext is far from lost on Woolf as she describes Miss La Trobe's military airs. La Trobe has '. . . the look of a commander pacing his deck' (*BA*, p. 62). Furthermore, the villagers call Miss La Trobe 'Bossy', linking her by that common bovine 'nickname' to the real herd in the novel, the cows who are always in the meadows beyond the pageant taking place on the terrace of Pointz Hall, enriching the comedy implicit in the concept of humanity as a herd. In fact, the cows participate both as actors and audience in bringing La Trobe's vision to momentary fruition:

> Then suddenly, as the illusion petered out, the cows took up the burden. One had lost her calf. In the very nick of time she lifted her great moon-eyed head and bellowed. All the great moon-eyed heads laid themselves back. From cow after cow came the same yearning bellow. The whole world was filled with dumb yearning. It was the primeval voice sounding loud in the ear of the present moment . . . The cows annihilated the gap; bridged the distance; filled the emptiness and continued the emotion.
>
> Miss La Trobe waved her hand ecstatically at the cows.
> 'Thank Heaven!' she exclaimed.
>
> (*BA*, p. 141)

The 'ruler' here has become dependent on the herd for the production of art and humanity; and when Woolf records her desire for a vision of unity, bringing together audience, actors, and cows for one moment, she presents a feminine ideal which subverts Freud's masculinist theory of the leader of a horde as well as Lewis's arrogant notion of the herdsman. For Woolf, though, failure at achieving that unifying vision is still the most likely result.

The culmination of Lewis's notion of the leader in *The Art of Being Ruled*, in my view, occurs in *Hitler* (1931), a work which collected a series of articles serialized in *Time and Tide* and which displays Lewis's naive conjecture that Hitler could be a rational man. Lewis's own account of the composition of *Hitler* indicates that he hastily got up the articles in response to the 'unmistakeable accent of passion and of impressive conviction' he found in his travels to Germany (*Hitler*, p. 5). John Constable, however, insists that Lewis's work on this book was rather a premeditated study masked as a report developed on the spur of the moment.[20]

Lewis announced his intention in *Hitler* to 'lift' from the rather obscure *The Art of Being Ruled*, signaling the relationship of the latter work as a continuation of his conceptualization of a masculine intellectual leader of the (feminine) masses. Lewis's wrongminded appraisal of Hitler's imperialism and antisemitism is appalling, as the following reveals:

> I do not think that if Hitler had his way he would bring the fire and the sword across otherwise peaceful frontiers. He would, I am positive, remain peacefully at home, fully occupied with the internal problems of the *Dritte Reich*. And, as regards, again, the vexed question of the 'antisemitic' policy of his party, in that I believe Hitler himself – once he had obtained power – would show increasing moderation and tolerance.
>
> (*Hitler*, pp. 47–8)

Despite the opinion of some critics that many British would have held similar opinions of Hitler in 1931, it is important to note that the editor of *Time and Tide*, where the book was first serialized, wrote: 'We do not find ourselves in agreement with Mr. Wyndham Lewis's attitude towards the German National Socialist Party and the political situation generally.' Furthermore, the Berlin correspondent wrote to *Time and Tide* to insist that Lewis, in his ignorance, was conveying Nazi propaganda.[21] In fact, the contemporary reception of *Hitler* has been inaccurately recorded, for there were far more reviews than acknowledged by Lewis's biographer, many of which demolished Lewis as an elitist and artist whose book clearly demonstrates his utter ignorance of the contemporary political scene.[22] As Lewis's biographer cogently argues, Lewis participated in the failure of many writers to understand the most significant political issues of their time. Indeed, Constable adds the view that the composition of *Hitler* represents a conscious attempt on Lewis's part to revitalize his career based on a new readership and 'to involve himself in the social reform, or, more accurately, covert resistance to racial enemies, which he considered necessary'.[23]

Lewis's completely inadequate grasp of the facts is further borne out by the fact that he had not read *Mein Kampf* thoroughly and would not do so until 1938.[24] Hitler's desire for an alliance with an England he believed no longer had designs to annihilate Germany, his anti-Marxist stance, and his belief in the importance of an intellectual leader over the masses all would have appealed to Lewis. 'It lies in the nature of an *organization*', Hitler wrote, 'that it can only exist if a broad mass, with a more emotional attitude, serves a high intellectual leadership.'[25] Hitler would extend his examination of the leader and the masses to formulate an identification of leader as masculine and mass as feminine, much as Lewis was doing throughout his political and social writing:

> Like the woman, whose psychic state is determined less by the grounds of abstract reason than by an indefinable emotional longing for a force which will complement her nature, and who, consequently, would rather bow to a strong man than dominate a weakling, likewise the masses love a commander more than a petitioner and feel inwardly more satisfied by a doctrine, tolerating no other beside itself . . .[26]

We might further assume that what Lewis witnessed in his travels through Germany in 1928 and again in 1930, preparing to write *Hitler*, including his firsthand observations of Hitler and the fascist ideology being drafted by the Nazi party, would have made him optimistic about the future of male domination. For Lewis, Hitler was a 'herdsman' who could be depended upon to shape the unthinking masses into the form that they could never achieve alone. But in attempting to account for Hitler's 'Blutsgefühl', or blood relationship, Lewis has to squirm to deliver an analysis that skirts the issue of Hitler's intense German nationalism. Railing against the 'frenzy of exoticism', a fascination with what is different or strange that has held England in its grip, Lewis argues vigorously that white civilization is threatened by the non-white world (*Hitler*, pp. 111, 121). Lewis's constant refrain suggests that Europeans and Americans must band together as Anglo-saxons against non-whites, 'all the Blacks, Browns, and High Yallers' (*Hitler*, p. 119). But at the end of his section, Lewis must convince himself, and his reader, that Hitler means the 'Aryan World' to include Europe, not just Germany, as united in Hitler's mission to convert the world: *'All that is not Race is dross!* Herr Hitler cries. But "race" not being identical with "nation" – as no one better than Hitler knows, born as he was a few miles outside the frontiers of "Germany" ' (*Hitler*, p. 143).

At least two of Lewis's critics suggest that for Lewis, Hitler offered an alternative to that crisis of the masculine self which was the very crisis of literary Modernism.[27] Where the male self might be dissolved at the level of the individual, in Hitler's Männerstaat, it 'was to be recuperated and reintegrated at the level of the nation'.[28] This implies not only a validation of male bonding and domination of all others but also a conception of the nation which reveals the sexism and racism at its core. Furthermore, Lewis's notion of the leader and the herd first fleshed out in

'The Code of the Herdsman' evolves by the time of *Hitler* to allow for a collectivity of nation to be subsumed by the power of the leader's ego. It is important to note here, however, that Lewis's emphasis remains not on Hitler's genius but on his typicality, 'Adolf Hitler is just a very typical german "man of the people" – . . . the core of the teutonic character' (*Hitler*, p. 31). Hitler's doctrines, Lewis continues, are specially fitted to ensure the survival of the racial traditions which he embodies because Hitler allows the German nation to 'act *as one man*' (*Hitler*, p. 33). Even though the sexism of Lewis's language was most likely unintentional, it reveals the conceptualization of the true German state under Hitler as, consciously or unconsciously, masculine.

Throughout its 202 pages, though, *Hitler* gives very little substantive information because, as Constable argues, it 'is not an exposition, but a defense structured around possible objections to Hitlerism'.[29] Despite the fact that Lewis would recant his ignorant version of Hitler, realizing that he had been quite politically incorrect and publish *The Hitler Cult* in 1939, Fredric Jameson insists that even Lewis's second book on Hitler ' . . . is informed by *all* the ideological positions which will remain constant to the very end of Lewis' life . . . fascism remains for Lewis the great political expression of *revolutionary* opposition to the status quo'.[30] As Jameson points out, it is the 'European White Male Will' which must be preserved at all costs in Lewis's view of politics.[31] Appropriately, Lewis called for the support of White Western Europeans and Americans in *Hitler*: 'Why not all of us draw together and put our White Civilization in a state of defence?' (*Hitler*, p. 121).

By 1938, Woolf would have certainly agreed that Hitler was the epitome of Germanic manhood, an exemplar of the German Männerstaat; only, in her mind, this was no cause for admiration. Woolf's verbal icon of the dictator in *Three Guineas* provides a sharp contrast to the kind of ideology espoused by Lewis:

> It is the figure of a man; some say, others deny, that he is Man himself, the quintessence of virility, the perfect type of which all the others are imperfect adumbrations . . . His hand is upon a sword. He is called in German and Italian Führer or Duce.
>
> (*TGs*, p. 142)

First, Woolf accomplishes a stunning reversal of a centuries-old tradition of social representation of *Woman* as icon to fix the reader's gaze instead upon essential *Man*, as the leader, the image of Hitler or Mussolini, so eagerly applauded by Lewis as the type of his people. Woolf summons instead a Platonic masculine form for ironic description and predicts just that sort of masculine, fascist unconscious about which Theweleit would theorize decades later. The equation between *Man* and *War* as posed by Woolf in her portrait is absolute. With his uniform, sword, and mindless, belligerent stare, Man is no longer the leader but the mindless Mob itself, spoiling for the fight. Hence, Lewis's idealistic notion of an intellectually elite but typical 'man of the people' who wields power over the masses is stripped in Woolf's vision to reveal that, in reality, the leader and the mob are one and the same.

Once again, Woolf has drawn a negative image of Lewis's leader. For Woolf, of course, this form of dictatorship militates against individual freedom and democracy, and her analysis demonstrates a deeper understanding of the true nature of Hitlerism than posed by Lewis in his naive appraisal of Nazi Germany. Certainly the most effective way of shocking her English audience, especially the men in it like Lewis, was for Woolf to insist that there was no *essential* difference between those men about to go to war for England and their fascist and Nazi enemies.

Woolf's most compelling and passionate attack on domestic fascism would come just a few pages later in *Three Guineas*:

> And are we not all agreed that the dictator when we meet him abroad is a very dangerous as well as a very ugly animal? . . . And is not the woman who has to breathe that poison and fight that insect, secretly and without arms, in her office, fighting the Fascist or the Nazi as surely as those who fight him with arms in the limelight of publicity?
>
> (*TGs*, p. 53)

Women, especially women who *work*, as Woolf points out in her reference to a woman fighting the fascist 'in her office', these are the ultimate enemy of the masculine will to power. Rather than focusing on the antisemitism of Nazi Germany or the militarism of Fascist Italy, Woolf targets patriarchal states in any national form as the oppressors of women, and women, by extension, become the icons for all oppressed groups. As we have seen in the work of Lewis, Theweleit, Weininger, and Hitler, the feminine becomes the space in which to collect all outsiders, all marginalized individuals who are expelled from the 'European White Male' center of power.

Realizing the impact of a masculine psychology determined to dominate while in flight from the feminine, Woolf wrote in *Three Guineas*,

'Society it seems, was a father, and afflicted with the infantile fixation too' (*TGs*, p. 135). The memory of her own father's irrational rages, as the incarnation of the Victorian patriarch, reflected for Woolf the growling discourse of Hitler's ranting speeches. Woolf had written in her diary on Tuesday, September 13, 1938:

> Hitler boasted & boomed but shot no solid bolt. Mere violent rant, & then broke off. We listened in to the end. A savage howl like a person excruciated; then howls from the audience; then a more spaced & measured sentence. Then another bark. Cheering ruled by a stick. Frightening to think of the faces. & the voice was frightening.
>
> (*Diary 5*, p. 169)

Woolf's writing, as her life neared its end, was consumed with the political scene and with the desire to theorize a space for the feminine other than that given to it by fascist, patriarchal ideology. She vacillated, in my view, between a desire for an ideal where all humankind creates a vast, communal artistic pattern and her recognition of reality by assuming the position of 'outsider' to her own society, as she would do in *Three Guineas* and beyond. Lewis's work in *The Art of Being Ruled* and *Hitler* provides an important reverse echo, and exists in antipathetic relation to Woolf, suggesting the general framework of his version of a fascist ideology. With the passing of democracy and all its vulgarities, Lewis argues, the freeing of the greatest intelligences of the race to rise above the common (feminine) mass as leader can occur.

Woolf's desire for unity among the 'common mass', though, is problematic, and her works indicate a failure of vision as much as a vision achieved. The record Woolf left in her diaries reveals that while she was deep in the composition of *Pointz Hall (Between the Acts)*, she was 'gulping up' Freud, finding her reading on groups upsetting, a whirlpool. 'I tried to center by reading Freud', Woolf wrote in her diary on June 27, 1940, as she reflected on the coming war, 'We pour to the edge of a precipice . . . & then? I cant conceive that there will be a 27th June 1941' (*Diary 5*, p. 299). Woolf is, on this date, in the midst of composing *Pointz Hall*, the preliminary title for *Between the Acts*, and writing almost daily reports in her diary of news of the war. La Trobe, as Woolf's mask in *Between the Acts*, echoes Woolf's despair: 'It was failure, another damned failure! As usual. Her vision escaped her' (*BA*, p. 98). A sense of failure echoes again as La Trobe's pageant ends, 'This is death, death, death, she noted in the margin of her mind; when illusion fails' (*BA*, p. 180).

Her growing concern with war, nationalism, community, and subjectivity led Woolf to ponder in just what space the feminine consciousness (or unconscious) might abide. In *Three Guineas*, Woolf had determined that, rather than accept a place on the margins of life prepared for women by a patriarchal society, she would propose her own feminine 'dystopia', an 'Outsiders' Society', where women might engage in resistance to masculine social power:

> . . . the Society of Outsiders has the same ends as your society – freedom, equality, peace; but that it seeks to achieve them by the means that a different sex, a different tradition, a different education, and the different values which result from those differences have placed within our reach . . . – we, remaining outside, will experiment not with public means in public but with private means in private.
>
> (*TGs*, p. 113)

Woolf proposes a community, primarily of women, as a counterpoint to the masculine state, making a personal commitment to it.[32] Woolf's vision is even a magnificent substitute for Lewis's conception of humanity as a common herd already inscribed as feminine. The Society of Outsiders does not, in my view, parallel Lewis's thinly sketched 'female mountain', where the more elite among women can retreat from the herd, but is rather Woolf's way of placing the power of the *Männerstaat* under erasure, of suggesting power in its negative form. Without doubt, and as Woolf is well aware, this space 'outside' is where women have always already been. The difference now resides in choice. Choosing the figure of Antigone as her icon of choice, Woolf suggests the despair which must attend women's determination to resist masculine domination.

> And Creon said: 'I will take her where the path is loneliest, and hide her, living, in a rocky vault.' And he shut her not in Holloway or in a concentration camp, but in a tomb. And Creon we read brought ruin on his house, and scattered the land with the bodies of the dead . . . Things repeat themselves it seems. Pictures and voices are the same today as they were 2,000 years ago.
>
> (*TGs*, p. 141)

Woolf wrote defiantly in her diary to comfort herself after the appearance of *Three Guineas* to heavily mixed reviews: 'I am an outsider. I can take my way: experiment with my own imagination in my own way. The pack may howl, but it shall never catch me. And even if the pack – reviewers, friends, enemies – pays me no attention or sneers, still I'm free' (*Diary 5*, p. 141). Once having finished *Three Guineas* and observing its fate in the reviews, Woolf would return again to Lewis's attack on her and seek comfort in the cultural space outside male society that she had mapped for women in her book. Writing in November of 1938, four years after Lewis's *Men Without Art*, she reflected:

W[yndham].L[ewis]. attacked me. I am aware of an active opposition. Yes I used to be praised by the young & attacked by the elderly. 3 Gs. has queered the pitch . . . I'm fundamentally, I think, an outsider. I do my best work & feel most braced with my back to the wall.

(*Diary 5*, pp. 188–9)

Before closing the chapter on Wyndham Lewis and his attack on her work and her politics, Woolf had given her feminist manifesto in *Three Guineas* to the world and set her course of feminist resistance to masculine, fascist tyranny. It was no easy course she set for herself, to select the outside rather than the inside, to reject all honors and awards, to refuse participation in a society bent upon war and self-destruction even to the point of choosing suicide, 'It is essential to remain outside & realize my own beliefs: or rather not to accept theirs' (*Diary 5*, p. 34). But Woolf's despairing vision is the threshold beyond which lies hope in the faint outlines of a feminist theory of the state yet to be born.

5
Freudian Seduction and the Fallacies of Dictatorship

Vara S. Neverow

In *A Room of One's Own* and *Three Guineas*, Virginia Woolf interweaves her version of Freudian psychoanalytic theory and her interpretation of fascist dogma to explain the origins of patriarchal violence. With surgical precision, she reduces psychoanalysis and fascism to a homology in which the patriarchal father is the dictator and vice versa. As the narrator of *Three Guineas* notes, the Victorian feminists who fought for women's autonomy were 'the advance guard' in an ongoing war. They defied 'the tyranny of the patriarchal state' and thereby set the stage for the struggle against 'the tyranny of the fascist state' (*TGs*, p. 102). Woolf's analysis of the patriarchal system of domination depends on her belief that 'the public and the private worlds are inseparably connected; . . . the tyrannies and servilities of one are the tyrannies and servilities of the other' (*TGs*, p. 142). Woolf believes that these tyrannies and servilities gratify a male obsession with dominance and contends that the gender hierarchy endorsed by both Freud and the fascists in which anatomical distinctions are used to situate females as genetically defective and inherently inferior is derived from a deep-seated male sexual anxiety. According to Woolf, this anxiety, which manifests itself simultaneously in a fear of castration and a con-comitant overvaluation of the male sexual organ, translates into an obsessive need to subjugate women. Woolf traces these psychological and ideological configurations to a cultural disorder which in *A Room of One's Own* she identifies as an inferiority complex and in *Three Guineas* she terms an 'infantile fixation'. Both the inferiority complex and infantile fixation are Woolf's revisionary interpretations of Freud's castration complex and constitute an emphatic refutation of his theory of penis envy. She suggests that penis envy is a convenient fiction intended to justify an excessive male investment in the penis which can only be validated by enforced female inferiority. Thus, culturally, the male organ is fetishized and transformed from a biological appendage into what Jacques Lacan would later term the transcendental signifier, the phallus, endowed with the patriarchal authority of the Law of the Father. Woolf identifies this privileging of the phallus as pathological.

Both *A Room* and *Three Guineas* are satirical case studies of this patriarchal pathology which manifests itself not only in the subjugation of women but also in masculine aggression in the public sphere. This aggression is evidenced not only in military conflicts and colonization of other cultures but in hierarchical social stratification, the compulsive accumulation of wealth and the glorification of competition. The narrator of *A Room* suggests that, under the threat of castration, male dominance becomes almost an involuntary reflex. 'Great bodies of people' (one suspects she means the male 'half [of] the human race', *AROO*, p. 36) are 'driven by instincts which are not within their control' (*AROO*, p. 38). Men as a group are so deeply 'concerned about the health of their fame' that they cannot 'pass a tombstone or a signpost without feeling an irresistible desire to cut their names on it as Alf, Bert or Chas. must do in obedience to their instinct, which murmurs if it sees a fine woman go by, or even a dog, Ce chien est a moi' (*AROO*, p. 52). This instinctual urge for immediate gratification affects not just the individual male but the entire patriarchal culture: 'And, of course, it may not be a dog, I thought, remembering Parliament Square[.] . . . [I]t may be a piece of land or a man with curly black hair' (*AROO*, p. 52). The narrator of *A Room* reflects that 'the patriarchs, the professors' are victims of 'the instinct for possession, the rage for acquisition which drives them to desire other people's fields and goods perpetually; to make frontiers and flags; battleships and poison gas; to offer up their own lives and their children's lives' (*AROO*, pp. 38–9).

Confronting what she perceives as a profoundly diseased culture, Woolf advocates a compound of mockery and indifference as the best remedies for the affliction. Thus, the narrator in *A Room* suggests that women 'should . . . learn to laugh, without bitterness, at the vanities – say rather the peculiarities, for it is a less offensive word – of the other sex' (*AROO*, p. 94). In the larger context of *A Room* and *Three Guineas*, this passage is a representative instance of the narrator's wicked wit directed at the male anatomy, a tactic which intensifies in *Three Guineas*. The narrator demonstrates the technique of mockery by referring to the cherished male genitals first as 'vanities' and then,

more stingingly, as 'peculiarities'. Similarly, in *Three Guineas*, the narrator prescribes 'pelt[ing] the [patriarchal mulberry] tree with laughter'
(*TGs*, p. 80) as a remedy. As the narrator points out, 'great psychologists, like Sophocles', discern that dominators are 'peculiarly
susceptible . . . to ridicule or defiance on the part of the female sex'.
Thus, 'laughter as an antidote to dominance is perhaps indicated'
(*TGs*, pp. 181–2, n32).

Such laughter is invited by the five photographs included in the 1938
edition of *Three Guineas* published by Hogarth Press but omitted from
most subsequent editions. The photographs are captioned as A General,
Heralds, A University Procession, A Judge, and An Archibishop even
though, as Alice Stavely points out, these individuals were well known
public figures of the period.[1] All the photographs are of men in full
professional regalia. Not only are the men in these photographs decked
out in their most elaborate ceremonial garb; in each of the five
photographs one or more of the men is equipped with a ritual object that
represents male authority and resembles a phallic signifier. The General
sports an erect feather in his dress helmet; the Heralds raise elongated
trumpets to their lips; the University Procession is distinguished by
several dons bearing large ceremonial staffs; the garb of the Judge
includes a dangling cord at the waist; and the Archbishop holds a long
ornate rod of obvious religious significance. The calculated anonymity of
these photos illustrates the indifference Woolf advocates as an alternative
to ridicule. The photographs objectify these representatives of the patriarchy, denying them individuality. The necessary indifference fostered by
this suppression of identity not only creates disinvestment and distance;
it has a distinct political impact. Drawing on '[t]he psychology of private
life', the narrator of *Three Guineas* argues that such indifference can 'help
materially to prevent war': '[t]he small boy struts and trumpets outside
the window; implore him to stop; he goes on; say nothing; he stops'
(*TGs*, p. 109).

In *A Room* and *Three Guineas* Woolf wields Freud's ideas as a double-
edged sword, mocking his theories of sexuality but also applying
psychoanalytic concepts to support her diagnosis of the fascist disease
and its patriarchal etiology. Woolf's ready access to Freudian psychoanalytic theory is confirmed in several studies. Elizabeth Abel argues
that 'Woolf's aversion to writing about psychoanalysis is matched by
her resistance to reading about it [and s]he claims to have avoided
reading Freud until 1939',[2] but Abel acknowledges that Woolf refers
specifically to psychoanalysis at least once in *A Room* and frequently
in *Three Guineas*.[3] Although Shari Benstock asserts that Woolf 'was

powerfully influenced by Freud's writings, which she read from the early 1920s through the 1930s',[4] it is uncertain whether Woolf actually read Freud prior to writing *A Room* and *Three Guineas* or acquired knowledge of his theories through what she herself called 'superficial talk'.[5] What is unquestionable is that Woolf was familiar with the basic premises of psychoanalysis and had, at minimum, a secondhand (and perhaps somewhat distorted) understanding of Freud's work. Freudian thought saturated contemporary culture, especially the culture of Bloomsbury.[6]

The cultural obsession with all things Freudian would have been virtually inescapable for Woolf. Her brother, Adrian Stephen, was himself a psychoanalyst and was married to an analyst, Karin Stephen (née Costelloe). The Woolfs also had frequent professional and social contact with James and Alix Strachey since the Hogarth Press published all of Freud's work.[7] Despite the lucrative Hogarth Press connection to the psychoanalytic industry, Virginia Woolf herself rejected psychoanalytic thought emphatically. Meisel and Kendrick state unequivocally that, even though 'by the late twenties, the close connection between Bloomsbury and psychoanalysis had been confirmed[,] Virginia, alone among her circle, was entirely hostile to the idea of being analyzed'.[8] Woolf's continuing aversion to psychoanalysis is evidenced in a letter of May 14, 1925 from James Strachey to Alix Strachey in Berlin. Having dined with the Woolfs the night before, James recounts the conversation, noting that 'Virginia made a more than usually ferocious onslaught upon psychoanalysis and psychoanalysts, more particularly the latter';[9] interestingly, Woolf's own diary entry makes no reference to this topic of discussion.[10]

Alix Strachey, toward the end of her life, observed that 'James [Strachey] often wondered why Leonard did not persuade Virginia to see a psychoanalyst about her mental breakdowns'.[11] However, if Woolf definitively equated psychoanalysis with the abuses of patriarchy, then her sustained resistance to being analyzed would scarcely come as a surprise. Woolf's own experiences with the paternal histrionics of Leslie Stephen and the incestuous sexual assaults of her stepbrothers Gerald and George Duckworth are well documented in her memoirs 'A Sketch of the Past' and '22 Hyde Park Gate' (*MB*, pp. 64–159 and 164–77).[12] Given these factors, there can be no doubt that Woolf, despite her claim never to have read Freud until 1939, not only would have been exposed to Freud's theories of sexuality as they evolved over several decades but also – given her feminist convictions – would have been alert to the patriarchal assumptions in Freud's writings.

While Freud's inquiries into the subject of sexuality did not at first distinguish sharply between male and female developmental patterns,[13] as his Oedipal concept crystallized he envisioned a developmental disparity between male and female psychical processes which he traced back to an initial (and traumatic) recognition of genital difference. Of the four volumes of Freud's *Collected Papers* which were published by the Hogarth Press between 1924 and 1925, the second included Freud's landmark essays 'On the Sexual Theories of Children' and 'The Passing of the Oedipal Complex' in which he advances his theories of the castration complex and its relation to the 'mutilated' female genitals, states his view that the clitoris is an inferior penis which must be relinquished as a source of pleasure in adulthood, argues that anatomy is destiny[14] and makes his preliminary case for penis envy stating that 'when [girls] express the wish "I should love to be a boy", we know what lack the wish is to remedy'.[15]

In 'Some Psychical Consequences of the Anatomical Distinction Between the Sexes', translated by James Strachey and published by the Hogarth Press in 1927, two years prior to the publication of *A Room*, Freud again advances his theory of penis envy,[16] stating that when a little girl 'notice[s] the penis of a brother or playmate, strikingly visible and of large proportions, [she] at once recognize[s] it as the superior counterpart of [her] own small and inconspicuous organ [the clitoris] and from that time forward fall[s] victim to envy for the penis'.[17] As both Abel and Benstock argue, Woolf was familiar with this assertion and I hope to demonstrate that she deliberately ridicules these ideas in both *A Room* and *Three Guineas*, punning frequently on the absurdity of patriarchal fascination with the male genitalia.

From Woolf's perspective, Freud (and all patriarchs including the fascists), use the mere biological fact of an anatomical distinction between the sexes to legitimate male dominance. The textual evidence indicates that Woolf interpreted Freud's theoretical model to mean that the little girl is forced to accept her innate female inferiority, while the little boy realizes his male superiority even though that superiority is severely chastened by castration anxiety. Thus, misogyny is situated as a 'natural' and, indeed, inevitable function of female genital lack. In Freud's words, the male child, 'when some threat of castration has obtained a hold upon' him, immediately recalls the moment when he first 'ca[ught] sight of a girl's genital region'. This recollection 'permanently determines the boy's relations to women' generating two possible responses: 'horror of the mutilated creature or triumphant contempt for her'.[18]

Freud himself seems to demonstrate this precise combination of horror and contempt when, in the same essay, he makes an abrupt and illogical transition from the physiological to the mental and moral asserting that 'though [he] hesitate[s] to give it expression', he 'cannot escape the notion . . . that for women the level of what is ethically normal is different from what it is in men'. He explicitly identifies this difference as female deficiency and, fully realizing that such a claim is likely to provoke resistance, he makes a pre-emptive strike: 'We must not allow ourselves to be deflected from such conclusions by the denials of the feminists, who are anxious to force us to regard the two sexes as completely equal in position and worth.'[19] Freud's defensive allusion to 'the feminists' is evidently an index of his own sexual anxiety and of his desire to justify patriarchal privilege. His explicit references to the threat of feminism reveal that he and Woolf are positioned as ideological antagonists.[20]

Deliberately challenging Freud's brief for patriarchy, Woolf, in both *A Room* and *Three Guineas*, makes a laughingstock of his blatant overvaluation of the male organ, exposing the preposterous phallic delusion that size is a synonym for superiority. In *Three Guineas*, the more caustic of the two manifestos, the references to Freud's theory of anatomical distinctions, penis envy and female genital deficiency are particularly explicit. The narrator of *Three Guineas*, examining the reasoning behind the exclusion of women from 'the profession of the Church', cites a study by one 'Professor Grensted, D.D., the Nolloth Professor of the Philosophy of the Christian Religion in the University of Oxford' who was solicited by the Archbishop's Commission on the Ministry of Women to provide 'relevant psychological and physio-logical' reasons for the clerical ban on women in the priesthood. Grensted's findings indicate that the 'strong feeling . . . aroused by any suggestion that women should be admitted' to the ministry is a func-tion of an 'infantile fixation' which must be traced back to 'theories of the "Oedipal complex" and the "castration complex" '. Grensted further indicates that the very ideas of 'male dominance' and of 'female inferiority' are caused by a 'non-rational sex-taboo' based on 'infantile conceptions' and 'subconscious ideas of woman as "man manque" '. As the narrator observes, Grensted has 'dissected the human mind', and 'laid bare for all to see what cause, what root lies at the bottom of our fear. It is an *egg*. Its scientific name is "infantile fixation". We, being unscientific, have named it wrongly. An *egg* we called it; a germ' (*TGs*, pp. 126–7; emphasis in text). The 'non-rational sex-taboo' to which Professor Grensted refers is, of course, Freud's anatomical distinction between the sexes. The infantile fixation – which Woolf links to the castration complex – results in anxious efforts to establish and defend male dominance by whatever means necessary. For example, as the narrator dryly remarks, 'Science, . . . infected [with an infantile fixation], produced measurements to order: the [female] brain was too small to be examined' (*TGs*, p. 139).

In *A Room*, the narrator notes the curious inaccuracy of 'measuring rods' that 'rise and fall' as they gauge gender differences and remarks that 'delightful as the pastime of measuring may be, it is the most futile of all occupations, and to submit to the decrees of the measurers the most servile of attitudes' (*TGs*, p. 110; see also *TGs*, p. 40). However, she appropriates the discourse of the scientific method to refute the theory of female inferiority. Thus, she urges 'the psychologists of Newnham and Girton' to study the effect of deprivation on the female psyche just as 'a dairy company measure[s] the effect of ordinary milk and Grade A milk upon the body of the rat' (*AROO*, pp. 54–5). As the narrator implies, referring to her dismal dinner at the women's college, 'women as artists', when fed on 'prunes and custard' (*AROO*, p. 55), are significantly at a disadvantage. In *Three Guineas*, the narrator takes a far less whimsical approach to the same issue and measures the vast economic disparity between men and women of a certain social strata, a disparity so severe that it actually creates two distinct sub-classes; while the class of educated men 'possesses in its own right and not through marriage practically all the capital, all the land, all the valuables, and all the patronage in England', the class of daughters of educated men 'possesses in its own right and not through marriage practically none' of these resources. '[T]hat such [material] differences make for very considerable differences in mind and body, no psychologist or biologist would deny', the narrator remarks (*TGs*, p. 18).

Investigating the causes of this massive gender inequity, the narrator also examines the educational system, 'measur[ing with a foot-rule] the money available for scholarships at the men's colleges with the money available for their sisters at the women's colleges' (*TGs*, p. 30; see also p. 164 n20). As she points out, the list of scholarships for men's colleges 'measures roughly thirty-one inches'; the list for the two women's colleges 'measures roughly five inches' (*TGs*, p. 154 n27).[21] In an implicitly related passage, the narrator notes that, although the 'Right Honourable Sir Sampson Legend, O.M., K.C.B., LL.D., D.C.L., etc., etc.' (*TGs*, p. 83) can sport an astonishingly long list of honors and degrees, male undergraduates at the universities vehemently protested against giving this privilege to women, rioting and running amok, even though female graduates, who 'could not put B.A. after their names[,] were at a disadvantage in obtaining appointments'. As the narrator slyly suggests, in seeking the motive for such behavior one must 'look for it in psychology' (*TGs*, 29). She speculates that education 'makes [people] . . . anxious to keep their possessions . . . in their own hands' and observes that such impulses '[are very] closely connected with war' (*TGs*, pp. 29–30) for, 'if we help an educated man's daughter to go to Cambridge are we not forcing her to think not about education but about war? – not how she can learn but, how she can fight in order that she may win the same advantages as her brothers?' (*TGs*, p. 31).

Continuing the same theme of measurement, the narrator addresses the vexed issue of comparable worth in the workplace and wonders disingenuously 'why the pay of the professional woman is still so small' (*TGs*, p. 53). She discovers that, in the Civil Service, as in the distribution of scholarships, degrees and other honors, 'all the names to which the big salaries are attached are gentlemen's names' and it is '[o]nly by putting on a stronger pair of glasses . . . [and] read[ing] down the list, further and further down [, that we a]t last come to a name to which the prefix "Miss" is attached. So, then it is not the salaries that are lacking; it is the daughters of educated men' (*TGs*, p. 47). The word play on 'lacking' seems quite calculated. Simply stated, the narrator subtly suggests women are absent at the higher levels of the Civil Service because they lack the appropriate genitalia. As the narrator points out in a passage fraught with suggestive sexual references: 'those to whom the word "Miss" is attached do not seem to enter the four-figure zone' and 'the reason for this may lie not upon the surface but within': 'it may be that the daughters of educated men are in themselves deficient' and 'lacking in the necessary ability' (*TGs*, p. 48) for 'rising and falling' in the professions 'is . . . by no means . . . a cut-and-dried clear-cut rational process' (*TGs*, p. 49).

Woolf's quarrel with both Freud and the fascists pivots on this double standard and is consummately illustrated by her caricature in *A Room* of Professor Von X., whose monumental and definitive study of women, *The Mental, Moral, and Physical Inferiority of the Female Sex* (*AROO*, p. 31), echoes both Freudian and fascist doctrines on female subordination. The very title of Professor Von X.'s work suggests a parody of Freud's 'Some Psychical Consequences' for, like Freud, the professor is given to using 'measuring-rods to prove himself "superior" ' (*AROO*, p. 92). If, as the narrator muses, the professor 'had written dispassionately about women, had used indisputable proofs to establish his argument, and had shown no trace of wishing that the result should be one thing rather than another', she would have accepted his findings; however, she believes the professor's study was motivated by the deeply repressed 'black snake' of anger, 'anger that had gone underground and mixed itself with all kinds of other emotions. To judge from its odd effects, it was anger disguised and complex, not anger simple and open' (*AROO*, p. 34). The narrator, particularly enraged by just 'one phrase' (*AROO*, p. 34) in this misogynistic treatise, distracts herself therapeutically by 'drawing a face, a figure. It was the face and the figure of Professor Von X. . . . He was not in my picture a man attractive to women. He was heavily built; he had a great jowl; to balance that he had very small eyes; he was very red in the face' (*AROO*, p. 31). While the narrator's caricature of the professor does not correspond precisely to photographs of Freud from the period, the title of his study suggests that the professor may nevertheless be a parody of Freud himself. As the narrator scrutinizes her own psychological motives for making an angry sketch of the angry professor, she speculates that 'it is in our idleness, in our dreams, that the submerged truth sometimes comes to the top', but she terms this observation '[a]n elementary exercise in psychology, not to be dignified by the name of psychoanalysis' (*AROO*, pp. 31–2), subtly disparaging Freud's major study of the unconscious and its defense mechanisms as detailed in his *Interpretation of Dreams*.[22]

Woolf explicitly turns Freud's own arsenal against him by 'adopt[ing] . . . Freudian theory' (*AROO*, p. 31) and treating Professor Von X.'s profound hatred of women as a psychological disorder. Symptomatically, the professor suffers from a repetition compulsion driven by an obsessional neurosis,[23] for 'some emotion made him jab his pen on the paper as if he were killing some noxious insect, but even when he had killed it . . . he must go on killing it'. This pathological behavior is caused by adult sexual jealousy compounded by a childhood sexual trauma: the professor '[had] been laughed at . . . in his cradle by a pretty girl' (*AROO*, p. 31).[24] Here, as elsewhere in both *A Room* and *Three Guineas*, the laughter of a woman functions as a castrating gesture linked to the etiology of patriarchal phallic pathology and, simultaneously, as a potential remedy for the disorder.

For most readers, these Freudian references are only a faint trace memory by the time the narrator of *A Room* begins to pun on penis envy and castration anxiety, noting that '[r]ich people, for example, are often angry because they suspect that the poor want to seize their wealth' (*AROO*, p. 34). The narrator stresses that the motive for this hostility may not even be conscious:

Possibly when the professor insisted a little too emphatically upon the inferiority of women, he was concerned not with their inferiority but with his own superiority. That was what he was protecting rather hot-headedly and with too much emphasis, because it was a jewel to him of the rarest price.

(AROO, pp. 34–5)

The narrator's commentary on the professor's attempt to protect his superiority – 'a jewel to him of the rarest price' – is almost certainly a pun, part of the pattern of sexually disparaging commentary sustained throughout both *A Room* and *Three Guineas*. Eric Partridge, in his definitive dictionary of slang, defines 'family jewels' as '[a] man's sexual apparatus: both domestic and, between man and man . . . joc. and often bonhomously ironic'. As Partridge himself recollects that 'within my own memory, it goes back to the 1920s; what's more it smacks of educated Edwardian raffishness'.

The narrator of *A Room* implies that patriarchal subordination of women originates in the illusory opposition of male genital privilege and female genital deficiency: 'Hence the enormous importance to a patriarch, of feeling that great numbers of people, half the human race indeed, are by nature inferior to himself.' As the narrator indicates, for 'the patriarch, who has to conquer, who has to rule', the anatomical distinction between the sexes 'must indeed be one of the chief sources of his power', authorizing 'some innate superiority'. This sense of superiority is validated by the '[w]omen [who] have served all these centuries as looking-glasses possessing a magical and delicious power of reflecting the figure of a man at twice its natural size'. Without such enhancement, 'Supermen and Fingers of Destiny would never have existed' for 'mirrors are essential to all violent and heroic activities. That is why Napoleon and Mussolini both insist so emphatically upon the inferiority of women, for if they were not inferior, they would cease to enlarge' (*AROO*, p. 35). Female inferiority thus authorizes and affirms masculinity, 'explain[ing] in part the necessity that women so often are to men' (*AROO*, p. 35). Again invoking the antidote of ridicule, the narrator observes that men are 'restless . . . under [a woman's] criticism for when a woman begins to tell the truth the figure in the looking-glass shrinks[.] . . . How is he to go on giving judgement, civilising natives, making laws, writing books, dressing up and speechifying at banquets, unless he can see himself at breakfast and at dinner at least twice the size he really is?' (*AROO*, pp. 35–6). The passage puns satirically on male physiology, mocking male preoccupation with genital size, for the narrator implies that the 'figure of a man' reflected in the female 'looking-glass' 'at twice its natural size' is a kind of psychological prosthetic – an apparitional phallus.

To illustrate how a woman's honesty can make 'the figure in the looking-glass shrink', the narrator offers a humorous anecdote: 'Z, the most humane, the most modest of men, taking up some book by Rebecca West and reading a passage of it, exclaimed, "The arrant feminist! She says that men are snobs!" ' As the narrator observes, although Z's response seems excessive, it actually has an underlying psychological motive that seems to be a form of castration anxiety: 'This exclamation, to me so surprising . . . was not merely the cry of wounded vanity; it was a protest against some infringement of the power to believe in himself' (*AROO*, p. 35). The narrator's stress on castration anxiety is particularly evident in her meditation on the Manx cat who 'did look a little absurd, poor beast, without a tail' (*AROO*, p. 13). In the Fitzwilliam Manuscript of *Women and Fiction*, Woolf explicitly refers to 'some fluke of the . . . subconscious . . . which I leave to Freud to . . . explain'[25] and, as Abel documents, the phallic significance of the cat's missing tail as a 'parod[y of] the Freudian construction of sexual difference as a question of castration' was noted as early as 1931 in the psychoanalytic community.[26]

Using selected fiction authored by men as an index of typical male psychology, the narrator of *A Room* cites the sexually explicit novels of Mr. A. and the virile works of Galsworthy and Kipling in which, despite critical acclaim, she as a female reader, fails to find the 'fountain of perpetual life':

> It is not only that they celebrate male virtues, enforce male values and describe the world of men; it is that the emotion with which these books are permeated is to a woman incomprehensible. It is coming, it is gathering, it is about to burst on one's head.
>
> (*AROO*, p. 106)

When reading Kipling, who is seemingly obsessed with 'Sowers who sow the Seed' and 'Men who are alone with their Work', the narrator finds herself 'blush[ing] at all these capital letters as if one had been caught eavesdropping at some purely masculine orgy' (*AROO*, p. 106), a comment that seems calculated to remind the reader of the erect capital 'I' that dominates Mr. A.'s novel.[27]

The narrator contends that Mr. A. and his ilk suffer from arrested development and are engaging in a male pre-pubescent display of their sexual abilities for, while 'Shakespeare does it for pleasure[,] Mr. A., as the nurses say, does it on purpose. He does it in protest. He is protesting against the equality of the other sex by asserting his own superiority' (*AROO*, p. 105) because he fears the diminution of his phallic power. As the narrator observes, 'the suffrage campaign was to blame. It must have aroused in men an extraordinary desire for self-assertion' (*AROO*, p. 103). Analyzing the response apparently provoked by the suffrage movement, the narrator comments that 'one retaliates . . ., if one has never been challenged before, rather excessively' (*AROO*, p. 103). The narrator's pseudo-Freudian critique of masculine literature culminates in her speculation that the fascist poem, a literary form born of 'unmitigated masculinity', is the ultimate product of this anxiety. The offspring, described as 'a horrid little abortion', a 'monster' with '[t]wo heads on one body' (*AROO*, p. 107), is a hyper-masculine appropriation of the female reproductive function. This masculine totality is similarly invoked in *Three Guineas* through the image of venomous patriarchal caterpillars that lay eggs (*TGs*, p. 53; see *TGs*, p. 140 for another version of male egg production).

In *Three Guineas*, Woolf seems to counter directly the theories Freud presents in *Totem and Taboo*.[28] In this work, Freud traces the origins of civilization to a prehistoric Oedipal scenario which not only generates a prohibition against both patricide and incest but mandates exogamy. In *Three Guineas*, Woolf, however, insists that nineteenth-century European society, rather than enforcing this prohibition, fully authorized and systematically justified incestuous patriarchal appropriation of the women within the family. Freud's version in *Totem and Taboo* of the earliest social order is that the 'primal horde' of brothers defied the autocratic rule of 'a violent and jealous father who ke[pt] all the females for himself and dr[ove] away his sons as they gr[e]w up'. In rebellion, 'the brothers who had been driven out came together, killed and devoured their father';[29] 'based upon complicity in the common crime'[30] of cannibalistic patricide, the brothers not only were drawn into a fraternal bond of guilt but recognized that 'they were all one another's rivals in regard to the women. Each of them would have wished, like his father, to have all the women to himself.' Rather than 'collaps[ing] into a struggle of all against all', the brothers 'institute[d] the law against incest . . . and renounced the women whom they desired and who had been their chief motive for despatching their father'.[31] Freud argues that the collective guilt of the brothers generated both patriarchal religion and the 'socially based prohibition against fratricide'.[32]

Reversing Freud's scenario, the narrator of *Three Guineas* contends that '[Victorian s]ociety it seems was a father, and afflicted with the infantile fixation' (*TGs*, p. 135). While Freud's translators rarely use the term 'infantile fixation' (it is not even included in the index of the *Standard Edition* although there are references to 'fixation – infantile incestuous' and 'infantile – incestuous fixation'[33]) and Woolf probably acquired it from Professor Grensted, it is interesting that the term occurs in Freud's article 'Types of Neurotic Nosogenesis' in the second volume of the *Collected Papers*. In this article, Freud argues that one type of neurosis results from an '*inhibition of development*' in which 'libido has never forsaken its infantile fixation'.[34] In what may be a deliberate reference to Freud's vision of a fraternal social structure, the narrator of *Three Guineas* comments that it was 'the fathers in public, massed together in societies, in professions' who 'were even more subject to the fatal disease than fathers in private'. Because '[t]he disease . . . was connected with manhood itself' (*TGs*, p. 138), women, when they initiated their struggle for equal rights, aroused the rage associated with this infantile fixation: 'an emotion perhaps below the level of conscious thought but certainly of the utmost violence' (*TGs*, pp. 138–9). In advancing this theory, Woolf also counters Freud's argument that the little girl, as a direct result of her penis envy, immediately 'gives up her wish for a penis and puts in place of it a wish for a child and *with this purpose in view* . . . takes her father as a love-object'.[35] Instead, Woolf anticipates subsequent feminist critiques of Freud arguing that his assertion is a psychological projection that attributes to the little girl the father's pathological desire to dominate the daughter, forcing her into an incestuous dependency on him.

This dependency is central to patriarchal control of women. As the narrator of *A Room* argues, her own economic autonomy demolishes the phallic fiction of male superiority (an economic theory developed in much greater depth in *Three Guineas*). Because of her inheritance, the narrator 'need not hate any man' or 'flatter any man': 'my aunt's legacy . . . substituted for the large and imposing figure of a gentleman, which Milton recommended for my perpetual adoration, a view of the open sky' (*AROO*, p. 39). The narrator's economic autonomy guarantees her sexual and intellectual freedom as well, for she no longer is forced to see the world in the shadow of a vast ideological obstruction, the male organ which, in this instance, is personified as the patriarchal deity. The legacy permits her to elude that very interesting and obscure masculine complex which has had so much influence on the women's movement; that deep-seated desire, not so much that *she* shall be inferior as that *he* shall be superior, which plants him wherever one looks, not only in front of the arts, but barring the way to politics too.

(*AROO*, p. 57; emphasis in text)

In *Three Guineas*, the narrator, discussing what she designates as a representative 'case' (Sophia Jex-Blake's vexing relationship to her domineering father), argues that 'at the root of Victorian psychology' is the father's injunction that 'the daughter must not on any account be allowed to make money because if she makes money she will be independent of her father and free to marry any man she chooses' (*TGs*, pp. 132–3). The narrator's analysis of the dictatorial relations between father and daughter actually echoes Freud's original seduction theory.[36] As the narrator of *Three Guineas* argues, '[t]he infantile fixation was protected by society'. Thus, '[i]t was easy for [the fathers] to hide the real nature of their emotions from themselves' (*TGs*, p. 135).

The narrator compares the voices of the fathers and the dictators to 'an infant crying in the night, the black night that now covers Europe[.] . . . [I]t is a very old cry. Let us shut off the wireless and listen to the past. We are in Greece now' (*TGs*, p. 141). Using Sophocles' *Antigone* – not his *Oedipus* – as a proof text, the narrator argues that 'infantile fixation' originates in the ancient mandate that '[w]omen must not rule over men'.[37] It is 'the voice of Creon, the dictator' that insists '[w]e must . . . in no wise suffer a woman to worst us' asserting that '[t]hey must be women and not range at large'. Noting that '[t]hings repeat themselves it seems', another possible allusion to Freud's theory of the repetition compulsion, the narrator summarizes 2000 years of male violence for her male correspondent: 'Creon we read brought ruin on his house, and scattered the land with the bodies of the dead. It seems, Sir, as we listen to the voices of the past, as if we were looking at the [Spanish Civil War] photograph again' (*TGs*, p. 141).

The ancient creed 'women must not rule over men' reveals the intersection between Freud's psychoanalytic theory and fascist politics. Woolf argues that fascism, like Freudian psychoanalysis, endorses the view that anatomy is destiny and overvalues the masculine; Woolf is convinced that all fascist ideologies culminate in the same patriarchal subordination of women. As the narrator of *Three Guineas* indicates, quoting from one of Hitler's own speeches, '[t]here are two worlds in

the life of the nation, the world of men and the world of women . . .
The woman's world is her family, her husband, her children and her
home' (*TGs*, p. 53).

Woolf believes both Freudian psychoanalysis and fascism explicitly
limit women's proper sphere to 'the private world', discouraging
or even forbidding entry into the public forum, the world of self-
determination and action strictly reserved for men.[38] Christine Froula,
in a crucial footnote to her article 'St. Virginia's Epistle to an English
Gentleman' reveals that even linguistically the patriarchal ideology of
the public and the private are inseparably connected:

> *Public* and *pubic* derive from Latin *pubes*, which means both 'adult'
> and 'the adult male population'. . . . That, etymologically, the
> public is literally the privates highlights the arbitrary construction
> of the public sphere as an arena of male *pubes* that subordinates (or
> veils) female *pubes*.[39]

As Woolf sees it, patriarchy mandates female subordination not only as
a means of controlling female sexuality but as a means of generating
masculinity itself. However, she argues that female subordination can
only be fully achieved if women are systematically forced into economic dependency on men and this dependency can only be ensured
if women are excluded from the public arena. Thus, both *A Room* and
Three Guineas examine the male sexual anxieties aroused when women
enter the public sphere and become financially independent. In a controversial passage in *Three Guineas*, the narrator disingenuously indicates that the word 'feminist', which 'means "one who champions the
rights of women"', is 'now obsolete . . . since the only right, the right
to earn a living, has been won' and 'the word no longer has a meaning'
(*TGs*, p. 101). Of course, as *Three Guineas* documents, the word *feminist*
cannot yet be considered outmoded when a woman's very right to
earn her living is threatened and her financial situation is by no means
equitable, adequate or secure.

To define the fascist mentality, the narrator invites us to 'turn to the
public press' (*TGs*, p. 51). Comparing Hitler's speech quoted above to
three letters written by men to the editor of the *Daily Telegraph*,[40] the
narrator demonstrates that the identical sentiments are expressed:
that women as a group should, indeed *must be* economically restricted
and confined to the home. The narrator asks rhetorically 'are not
the[se] both the voices of Dictators?' Answering her own question, she

asserts that they are 'the egg of the very same worm that we know under other names in other countries. There we have in embryo the creature, Dictator we call him when he is Italian or German' (*TGs*, p. 53).

If the narrator is deliberately punning on the *dick* in *dictator* in the preceding passages, using the crude slang term to expose the exaggerated violence of dictatorship,[41] her double entendre powerfully illustrates how Freudian and fascist (ph)allacies and fantasies of power intersect. The slang term *dick* was definitely available in the lexicon of Woolf's own era. As a reference to the male genitals, *dick* was in military use in the 1880s in England.[42] Another possible derivation is the term *dirk*, 'a short dagger used by sneak thieves in Old England'.[43] Partridge defines the word *dirk* as 'the penis: orig. Scot.' Alan Richter offers the most complete definition of *dirk*: 'penis, especially an erect one. This 18th-century term derives from the standard sense of a type of Scottish dagger.'[44] The term *dick*, thus, is etymologically associated with various weapons from its very origin.

The narrator's description of the dictator is vivid: 'Are we not agreed that the dictator when we meet him abroad is a very dangerous as well as a very ugly animal? And he is here among us, raising his ugly head, spitting his poison, small still, curled up like a caterpillar on a leaf' (*TGs*, p. 53; see also p. 97). The phallic caterpillar is a precise synecdoche for the dictator, a part that signifies the whole. However, while the metaphor is anatomically correct, it is non-sequential[45] – the initial image is of a penis becoming erect and spurting vitriolic semen; the subsequent image is of a flaccid penis, 'small still', curled against the testicles represented by the leaf.[46] This non-sequential representation calls attention to the typographical toggle between the capitalized Dictator (recognized as a genuine threat) and the lower-case dictator (regarded as harmless by society). Woolf's deliberate masculinization of capital letters in *A Room* reinforces this reading. The narrator of *Three Guineas* insists that England must help women fight the lower-case dictators first:

> Should we not help her to crush him in our own country before we ask her to help us crush him abroad? What right have we, Sir, to trumpet our ideals of freedom and justice to other countries when we can shake from our most respectable newspapers any day of the week eggs like these?
>
> (*TGs*, p. 53)[47]

In both *A Room* and *Three Guineas*, Woolf links the private (Freudian psychoanalytic theories of sexuality) to the public (the fascist agenda), arguing that the false gender hierarchy in which men are 'superior' and women 'inferior' is the fundamental model for all acts of oppression and aggression. To invoke the words of the narrator of *Three Guineas* in a slightly different context, 'the causes are the same and inseparable' (*TGs*, p. 144).

Part II

Preludes to War: Politics in the Novels, Aesthetics in the Nonfiction

6
Acts of Vision, Acts of Aggression: Art and Abyssinia in Virginia Woolf's Fascist Italy

Leigh Coral Harris

At the end of a letter to Lady Ottoline Morrell on October 4, 1935, Woolf wrote: 'Now Leonard has turned on the wireless to listen to the news, and so I am flicked out of the world I like into the other. I wish one were allowed to live only in one world, but thats [*sic*] asking too much' (*Letters 5*, p. 429). As registered in her letter to Morrell, Woolf's response to the BBC's broadcast of Italy's invasion of Abyssinia that was launched that very day encapsulates her phenomenal and ideological relationship to the Italian nation. The two worlds Woolf imagines here are the world she 'likes' – defined in the letter as a private realm of reading, writing, friendship, and landscape contemplation – and the 'other' world of Mussolini's aggression in Africa. This dual vision mirrors the dichotomy in Woolf's thinking about Italy that remains a constant feature of her work. On the one hand, Woolf represents Italy as an intensely private, peaceful place of spiritual renewal that enables her to achieve a liberating sense of anonymity. On the other hand, she depicts Italy as fascism embodied, perceiving that its dictatorial regime assigns a debilitating hypermasculine identity to its art as well as to its nationalistic and impe-rialistic politics. But these opposing images of Italy in Woolf's thought are only apparently opposed in her writing; indeed, they exist for her as mutually constitutive states. Woolf's touristic and political accounts of Rome and its environs demonstrate the way in which Italy's two identi-ties – the place itself defined by life, art, and meaning; its fascist policies defined by death, propaganda, and annihilation – mutually construct one another in her work.

This analysis will chart the way in which Woolf's theory of anonymity or identitylessness (a conceptual companion to the theory of androgyny advanced in *A Room of One's Own*) evolves out of her experience of Italy over one crucial decade. In revealing Italy's unrecognized role in fashioning the familiar ideas of androgyny and anonymity in Woolf's writing, a new reading of Woolf's artistic vision in the late 1920s and of her reaction to fascism in the 1930s emerges. Understanding the origins of these ideas in Italy discloses a novel dimension of Woolf's aesthetic and political philosophy: Woolf transforms the sterile, culture-destroying properties inherent in Italian fascism into the rejuvenating, creative, and inspirational possibilities of the Italian experience. While Jan Morris comments that 'Virginia Woolf's responses to Italy were, especially in later life, hyperbolic',[1] Woolf conjoins her romantic understanding of Italy to a political critique. Indeed, *la bella Italia* reveals a fresh vision of artistic and ethical authority to Woolf that equips her with artistic, cultural, and political solutions to counter fascism's violence and domination. Paradoxically, it is Woolf's profound antifascist stance that enables her to invest even fascist Rome with a moral dimension. Woolf's multiple journeys through fascist Italy in the late 1920s and early and mid-1930s greatly influenced her feminist political thinking.[2] Her experience of Mussolini's Italy is registered in these terms in *A Room of One's Own* (1929) and *Three Guineas* (1938), as well as in her 1927 and 1935 travel writing on Italy.[3]

Woolf's interest in Italy stems in part from the historical British cultural obsession with Italy and things Italian. Indeed, her essays' and novels' references to Italy often reflect the Victorian and Edwardian passion for Italy as picturesque cultural exotica. *The Voyage Out* (1915) mines the notion of Italy's primitivism when old Mrs. Paley claims that using Seltzer water is 'all the precaution I've ever taken, and I've been in every part of the world, I may say – Italy a dozen times over . . .' (*VO*, p. 362). In *Mrs. Dalloway* (1925) Septimus Smith finds temporary security in Milan when news of peace comes – he was 'billeted in the house of an innkeeper with a courtyard, flowers in tubs, little tables in the open, daughters making hats' – and makes an Italian war bride of the younger daughter, Lucrezia (*MD*, p. 131). Rome is one of the 'shapes of a world not realised but turning in their darkness, catching here and there a spark of light' (*TTL*, p. 281) that forms in Cam's mind as she sails with James and Mr. Ramsay in *To the Lighthouse* (1927). In 1928 Woolf composed the introduction to a new edition of Laurence Sterne's *A Sentimental Journey through France and Italy*; in it she describes Sterne's pursuit of happiness on the continent as a 'pirouette about the world, peeping and peering, enjoying a flirtation here, bestowing a few coppers there, and sitting in whatever little patch of sunshine one can find'.[4] In an attempt to shed ' "one of [his] life- skins" ' (*TW*, p. 188), the melancholy Bernard travels to Rome for rejuvenation in *The Waves* (1931). *Flush* (1933) explores the nine-teenth-century British experience of Italy through the perspective of Elizabeth Barrett Browning's cocker spaniel, Flush, who often 'fol-lowed the swooning sweetness of incense into the violet intricacies of dark cathedrals' in Florence.[5] And in her introductory letter to the essay collection, *Life As We Have Known It* (1931), Woolf uses images of the Mediterranean to mark class difference. The impossibility of a middle-class woman's adopting the perspective of a miner's wife becomes evident when Woolf realizes their different worlds: 'One saw landscapes or seascapes, in Greece or perhaps in Italy, where Mrs. Giles or Mrs. Edwards must have seen slag heaps and row upon row of slate roofs in a mining village.'[6]

Despite these traditional views, Woolf certainly recognized Italy's complex political and historical identity. From helping her husband Leonard compile statistics for his book, *Empire and Commerce in Africa: a Study in Economic Imperialism* (1920), as well as reading it at least twice, Woolf would have been thoroughly acquainted with Italy's imperialistic history that precedes and folds into its fascist regime.[7] Leonard claimed his book plunged the reader 'into a maze of facts and details';[8] Virginia thought it 'superb' (*Letters 2*, p. 413) and delighted 'in the closeness, passion, & logic of it' (*Diary 2*, p. 5). His study delin-eates Italy's economic and colonial involvement in Africa, devoting space to circumstances surrounding Italian hopes for 'an Empire of Ethiopia'.[9] But beyond this textbook familiarity with Italy's political and imperial history, Woolf's many trips to Italy between 1904 and 1935 enabled her to witness directly Italy's increasingly militaristic and imperialistic policies.

In the midst of a busy London spring in 1933, Woolf confides in her diary that she wants 'that escape which Italy & the sun & the lounging & the indifference of all that to all this brings about. I rise, like a bubble out of a bottle' (*Diary 4*, p. 151). Woolf escaped to the intoxica-tion of Italy on at least ten different occasions. The first time she trav-eled to Italy was in 1904 with Violet Dickinson and the Stephen children after the death of their father; the last time was in 1935 with Leonard on a motoring holiday through Europe. Woolf toured the major Italian cities, the Italian Riviera, as well as the countryside of Umbria and Tuscany (where she and Leonard contemplated buying a farm to settle in 'for ever and ever' [*Letters 5*, p. 185]). She adored Rome, describing it as 'a revelation' (*Letters 3*, p. 394) and the 'place I love the best in the whole world' (*Letters 6*, p. 321).

Woolf's letters from her spring stay in Italy in 1927, particularly those to her sister, the artist Vanessa Bell, suggest a preoccupation with ideas about artistic vision. Indeed, the letters themselves were in exchange for a painting Vanessa had promised to make for her sister (*Letters 3*, p. 360). Woolf's comments to Vanessa emphasize the architectural relation of color, form, and space; she notes Italy's 'very light, gay and spacious' buildings boasting '[p]illars of pale green and pink marble like avenues of birch trees disappearing one behind another: immense distance; vast spaces'. She calls Rome's surrounding countryside, the Campagna, 'perfection' in its texture, palette, and composition – 'smooth, suave, flowing, classical, with the sea on one side, hills on the other, a flock of sheep here, and an olive grove' (*Letters 3*, p. 361).

The images of Rome and the Campagna function importantly in Woolf's letters to Vanessa. In her powerful descriptions of them, Woolf links her concern with artistic creation and perspective to the idea of identitylessness, a concept she describes in her first diary entry after returning to London from Italy that year. While Woolf apparently kept no journal during this trip to Italy in 1927, she summarized her travels in her diary after arriving home to Tavistock Square. She describes a different mode of visually and conceptually relating to natural and cultural phenomena, a new perspective made possible by the experience of Italy. 'We came back on Thursday night from Rome', Woolf writes, 'from that other private life which I mean to have for ever now. There is a complete existence in Italy: apart from this. One is nobody in Italy: one has no name, no calling, no background. And, then, not only is there the beauty, but a different relationship' (*Diary 3*, p. 133). Not simply a picturesque country, the peninsula constitutes for Woolf a distinctive conceptual space. Italy is 'that other private life' she considers 'apart' from her more public life in Britain, with telephones ringing and guests arriving for tea. Paradoxically, Woolf defines the 'complete existence' she captures in Italy as an existence in the mode of anonymity: 'One is nobody in Italy.' Reversing the element of despair in Bernard's existential recollection at the reunion dinner in *The Waves*, during which he thinks, ' "we felt enlarge itself round us the huge blackness of what is outside us, of what we are not" ' (*TW*, p. 277), the possibility of *not being* while in Italy represents renewal and strength. Writing in the third person in her own diary, Woolf emphasizes the idea of namelessness, speculating that in Rome 'one has no name' – that is, no present identity; 'no calling' – that is, no future direction; and 'no background' – that is, no past. According to

Woolf's theory, an individual achieves a sort of triumph over the strictures of cultural identity when one's personal history, and history yet to be, gives way to a condition of wholeness through which a different understanding of the world is made possible. For Woolf, being 'nobody' in Italy represents an alternative state of being that offers a new view of spiritual and concrete 'beauty'. She notes that the mode of non-identity heightens her 'faculty of enjoyment' of Italian culture, its language, 'art', and 'literature' (*Diary 3*, p. 133).

Woolf's epistolary descriptions of the city of Rome and the Campagna in 1927 communicate a peaceful, almost hypnotically picturesque, beauty. From a lush and blooming Rome she writes to Vanessa about a 'perfect day' in which 'all the flowers are just out, there are great bushes of azalea set in the paths; Judas trees, cypresses, lawns, statues, among which go wandering the Italian nurses in their primrose and pink silks with their veils and laces . . .' (*Letters 3*, p. 365). Natural and cultural elements blend seamlessly in the language composing this scene: 'primrose' represents the pale yellow color of the nurses' pastel silk, and 'statues' is listed as if it were a variety of tree. Instead of reading Proust, as she had intended, she finds herself 'undulating like a fish in and out of leaves and flowers and swimming round a vast earthenware jar which changes from orange red to leaf green'. Thus Woolf's literate, touristic identity metaphorically dissolves into an impressionistic and instinctive fish, who experiences Rome as its private earthenware universe. Woolf's imaginative transformation into a fish dramatically portrays her sense of being 'nobody'. The sense of identitylessness Woolf projects onto the image of the fish changes her relationship to the city's wondrous sights, as a walk in a Roman piazza becomes a colorful, smooth wavelike glide through an immense aquarium.

Wave thematics also inform Woolf's depictions of the Roman Campagna. In its structure as well as in its content, the following passage about the Roman countryside evokes the fluid images in Woolf's account of the city. The flow of the descriptive point of view suggests Woolf's rambling over the Campagna with Leonard. In a letter, she directs Vanessa's imagination using language of the plastic arts:

> Figure us sitting in hot sunshine on the doorstep of a Roman ruin in a field with hawk coloured archways against a clear green grape coloured sky, silvery with mountains in the back ground. Then on the other side nothing but the Campagna, blue and green, with an

almond coloured farm, with oxen and sheep, and more ruined arches, and blocks of marble fallen on the grass, and immense sword like aloes, and lovers curled up among the broken pots ... We lunched at a restaurant hung above the lake, which is almost round, very deep, with Roman ships sunk in it, and of the colour first of olive trees and then of emeralds. It was rather cloudy so the colour was always changing very slowly, and round the lake was a little path with horses and goats. We went down after lunch and found wild cyclamen and marble lapped by the water.

(*Letters 3*, p. 367)

The undulating focus circles to one side of the Campagna and then over to the other, creating linguistic folds of space throughout. The passage's rising and falling point of view anticipates the end of Bernard's soliloquy in *The Waves* when he describes 'the eternal renewal' as 'the incessant rise and fall and fall and rise again' (*TW*, p. 297). In this epistolary excerpt, as in *The Waves*, Woolf embeds signs of destruction in the modulating perspective that ultimately becomes a rejuvenating force.

Woolf's description of the Campagna both subtly and graphically juxtaposes markers of past violence with signs of survival and growth. She understands the ancient ruins as more than simply picturesque decay: they are signs of creative endurance. The doorsteps and archways that are remnants of interiors and exteriors function differently in the open air, aesthetically enriching the surrounding landscape as well as serving as reminders of past conflict. The archways' 'hawk' coloring adjectivally evokes the idea of Roman aggression, but their placement against a surreal 'green grape coloured sky' mutes the association. And Woolf inverts earthy and airy qualities (hawk-like arches, a grape-like sky), further devitalizing images of violence by descriptively remaking them. The 'lovers curled up' together on the ground redeem destructive images of 'broken pots' and 'sword like aloes', which also combine opposing associations of wounding and healing. Like the tidal pool in which Nancy sees the world and experiences her moment of being in *To The Lighthouse*, this lake, with ancient ships sunk deep within, constantly reflects the changing heavens. The image of wild cyclamen thriving next to 'marble lapped by the water' is a visual echo of 'the lovers curled up among the broken pots'. The Roman landscape illustrates for Woolf the idea of the past surviving into the present in a way that positively changes the contours of the here and now. In the essay she wrote at the end of her life, 'Anon', Woolf affirms that 'only when we put two and two together – two pencil strokes, two written words, two bricks . . . do we overcome dissolution and set up some stake against oblivion'.[10] Since Woolf's scene presents men and women harmoniously paired beneath archways and coupled among the ruins, it would seem that the couples' rambling and loving, 'two and two together' among the fragmented artifacts of an ancient culture, set a 'stake against oblivion' by becoming part of a restorative landscape in which peace absorbs violence in the end.

During the period when Woolf was rambling over the Campagna and wandering through Rome, the obliterating potential of Mussolini's fascist regime was focused on the domain of culture and art. Prompted by Mussolini's 1926 call for the creation of a uniquely fascist culture, a cultural and artistic debate was raging in Italy during Woolf's trip there in 1927. Mussolini's call for a fascist art was more than exhortation; it was an order. But 'whether or not the new art would be forthcoming, it made discussion of the problem a duty'.[11] The regime's most unrestricted ideological forum, the journal *Critica Fascista*, hosted this discussion most openly.[12] Over several months in 1926 and 1927, the editor, Giuseppe Bottai, gathered politically charged *'opinioni sull'arte fascista'* from various fascist cultural figures. Although Woolf did not speak or read Italian as proficiently in 1927 as she did in the 1930s, there is the possibility that with her 'dog Italian' (*Letters 3*, p. 362) Woolf might have read *Critica Fascista*, most likely while in Rome. In *A Room of One's Own*, published just two years after her 1927 sojourn in Italy, Woolf works out more fully the themes of culture and artistic vision that saturate her travel writing from Rome that year. The brief but critical passage in *A Room of One's Own* commenting on Italian fascist art implicitly explores the question Alessandro Pavolini asks in his contribution to *Critica Fascista*, about whether it makes sense to expect an artistic rebirth from a political one: '*Ha un senso qualsiasi attendersi da un rinascimento politico un rinascimento artistico?*'[13] But whether Woolf actually read *Critica Fascista* (there is no direct indication that she had) is less important than the fact that she indirectly participates in its debate by offering her own *opinione* of the creation of fascist art.

In the following vignette from *A Room of One's Own*, Woolf examines Italian fascism's doomed endeavor to infuse cultural formulations with its hypermasculine political, military identity. She critiques the tenet of fascist thought that considers fascist creative power unlimited and fascist politics, according to Bottai, 'the art of impossible, the marvelous, the miraculous'.[14] Addressing the paradoxes of a cultural discourse that positions the birth of literature in the virile domain of self-conscious *maschilità*, Woolf informs her readers about a meeting of high-profile Italian men, famous ' "by birth, or in finance, industry or the Fascist corporations" ' (*AROOO*, p. 113), who want to create fascist literature:

> We may all join in that pious hope, but it is doubtful whether poetry can come out of an incubator. Poetry ought to have a mother as well as a father. The Fascist poem, one may fear, will be a horrid little abortion such as one sees in a glass jar in the museum of some country town.
>
> (*AROO*, p. 113)

The scene Woolf visualizes is a members-only, and therefore male-only, gathering of the fascist party.[15] Women's exclusion from this scene of cultural production bears out the earlier pronouncement in *A Room of One's Own* regarding Mussolini's emphatic insistence 'upon the inferiority of women' (*AROO*, p. 38). But the tenuousness of such a mandate of gender hierarchies is also revealed. Woolf turns fascist intention on its head through parodying the hypertrophic product of fascist poetic labor. The passage exposes as illusory and ironic the claim that fascist art, in words from Mario Puccini's article, has expelled the '*intonazione femminea*'.[16]

Indeed, despite the absence of actual women, fascist cultural work nevertheless appropriates the properties of women's bodies. It imagines producing the poet 'worthy of the fascist era' in terms of human reproduction. While using the gendered metaphor of birth to describe artistic labor may be conventional in Western literary tradition, Woolf points to the troubling implications of such gendered imagery. Moreover, Woolf's analysis of the way in which fascism links power with masculinity addresses the preoccupation of *Critica Fascista* with the idea of virility. She argues that the fascistization of culture, writ small as the inculcation of 'unmitigated masculinity' on 'the art of poetry' (*AROO*, pp. 112, 113), results not in a masculinized culture but only in a perversely feminized creative effort, for the Italian novel is conceived and incubated solely by the fascist-father acting doubly as the mother. Fascist (male) cultural work thus produces a deformed progeny without viability because it emphatically rejects the 'natural fusion' (*AROO*, p. 107) of male and female elements in what Woolf considers in *A Room of One's Own* a 'fertilised' (*AROO*, p. 114), and therefore successful, poetic creation.

The specter of fascist art helps Woolf formulate the creative condition that opposes it: the state of androgyny. The concept of androgyny that Woolf features in *A Room of One's Own* surrounds her discussion of the fascist poem, and it is linked closely in her mind to the idea of anonymity, that sense of identitylessness she experiences in Italy ('one has no name, no calling, no background'). Both modes of subjectivity, androgyny and anonymity, enhance acts of vision and creation. The discussion in the final chapter of *A Room of One's Own* explores the relation of the body to thought in the creation of artistic works; Woolf resolves this problem in the pacific image of the androgynous mind. In that section of her text, Woolf defines what Coleridge meant by an androgynous mind as one 'resonant and porous', transmitting emotion 'without impediment', and 'naturally creative, incandescent and undivided' (*AROO*, p. 108). It is a dual-sexed consciousness: 'If one is a man, still the woman part of the brain must have effect; and a woman also must have intercourse with the man in her' (*AROO*, pp. 107–8). A 'purely masculine' mind cannot create 'any more than a mind that is purely feminine', for a creative mind must be androgynous.

Woolf tacitly contrasts the forced and rigid nature of fascistic creation to the porousness of the androgynous intellect. Fascist art is the extreme example of a collective 'purely masculine' mind barrenly engaged in literary production; *A Room of One's Own* warns that 'whatever the value of unmitigated masculinity upon the state, one may question the effect of it upon the art of poetry' (*AROO*, pp. 112–13). Indeed, fascism's self-conscious masculinization botches the conception and execution of its art, rendering it grotesque. The coerced 'Fascist poem' represents a creation antithetical to that born of the serenity of the androgynous mind. Woolf provides images such as plucking 'petals from a rose' or watching 'swans float calmly down the river' (*AROO*, p. 115), to highlight the contrasting peacefulness of androgynous creation authored by Shakespeare, and '[i]n our time', Proust (*AROO*, p. 113). The figure of Proust in *A Room of One's Own* evokes themes both of androgyny and anonymity since it is his work that Woolf is in the midst of reading when she relaxes into Rome in 1927 and imagines herself as a fish gliding through silky surroundings.[17]

The urgency surrounding ideas about artistic vision and creative freedom that infuses her letters from Rome in 1927, as well as her passage on fascist art in *A Room of One's Own* in 1929, becomes in 1935 a political urgency, an anxiety over the endangerment of life, peace, and culture in Europe.[18] While Woolf originally applies the mantra, '[t]here must be freedom and there must be peace', to the conditions for androgynous 'woman-manly or man-womanly' writing in the late 1920s in *A Room of One's Own* (*AROO*, p. 114), she forcefully repeats the spirit of its meaning when she faces the threat of death and war in the 1930s. While Mussolini's fascist state had been building its power base since its establishment in the years 1925–27, it made clear to the world its aggressive, imperialist intentions when it invaded Abyssinia in October 1935 (Woolf listened to the BBC's coverage of the event). In the spring prior to Mussolini's aggression against Abyssinia, Woolf made her final trip to Italy, meeting Vanessa, Vanessa's daughter, Angelica, and son, Quentin, for more than a week of holiday in Rome. The diary entry Woolf writes on the eve of this journey abroad reflects the increased intensity of the political situation. 'In the public world', she notes, 'there are emphatic scares' and 'incessant conversations – Mussolini, Hitler, Macdonald ... incessantly arriving at Croydon, arriving at Berlin, Moscow, Rome; & flying off again ...' (*Diary 4*, p. 303). The entry's closing thought, that 'Stephen [Spender] & I think how to improve the world', identifies the diary's other theme concerning Woolf's role, as woman and writer, in the political world. She wants to 'investigate certain questions' of herself, among these, 'why do I always fight shy of my contemporaries? What is really the woman's angle?' (*Diary 4*, p. 303). Thus Woolf leaves Britain to travel through fascist Italy and Nazi Germany preoccupied by questions surrounding her own ethical, gendered positioning in relation to the ominous political volatility of Europe. Woolf responds to Italian fascism and Nazism's threat to civilization by turning, in Brenda Silver's words, 'a critical eye on the discourses and the impact of a patriarchal culture dedicated to hierarchy, dominance, capitalism, imperialism, and war'.[19]

The intense militarism displayed during Woolf's 1935 stay in Rome forecasts the impending conflict. In a *New Statesman* article that details his impressions of Mussolini's Italy, Leonard observes during this tour with his wife that even 'to the casual traveller Italy externally gives one the impression of a country already at war. There are soldiers everywhere, marching, marching, marching.'[20] The preponderance of military displays in the Roman streets as well as the ubiquitousness of Mussolini's image combine to create an intensified version of what Woolf had described in *A Room of One's Own* as an atmosphere of 'unmitigated masculinity' (*AROO*, p. 112).

In Woolf's spring visit to Rome, less than six months prior to Mussolini's invasion of Abyssinia, another image of virile nationalist hubris supplemented the spectacle of soldiers marching and *Duce* icons in bookstore windows: maps of Northeast Africa.[21] Reporting on Mussolini's propagandizing cartographic campaign in April 1935, the *New Statesman* reports that these maps of Northeast Africa showed 'green Italian land bearing down on the pale, colourless Abyssinia, so that the hand fidgeted to paint out what looked an irritating intrusion, a sterile island holding apart two waves of fertile civilization'.[22] The fascist maps emblazoned across bookstore windows in Rome represent fascism's appropriation of culture by its masculine military politics. As if imperialism were for sale, or were selling itself, maps filling windowfront space depict fascism's attempt to substitute itself for culture. Exactly one month after the *New Statesman* published this account, Woolf herself was in Rome encountering firsthand the propagandistic imagery of Rome's imperial hopes.

In contrast with the more methodical way she writes in her diary about other European cities she visits on this 1935 trip, Woolf's entries about Italian cities consist of 'notes' recorded in a 'pencil book' kept in her purse to write in 'when taking in petrol, waiting for something or other' (*Diary 4*, p. 312). The relatively brief, spontaneously composed entries are a montage of first impressions. They are verbal snapshots, fragmented thoughts forming sensual images. Although Woolf questions the usefulness of 'such notes', thinking that '[p]erhaps when the editing of the mind has gone further one can see & select better' (*Diary 4*, p. 312), the unedited nature of the two entries dealing with Rome is telling in terms of how Woolf experiences Rome – synecdoche for Italian fascism itself – differently from the rest of Italy. First, her jottings from Rome are more fragmentary and choppy than those she writes in a similar 'note' format when visiting other Italian locales. Second, unlike the other passages, those on Rome bring fascism and ethics into relief. In full, the notes on Rome read:

Rome. tea. Tea in cafe. Ladies in bright coats & white hats. Music. Look out & see people like movies. Abyssinia. Children begging. Café haunters. Ices. Old man who haunts the Greco.

Sunday cafe. N. & A. drawing. Very cold. Rome a mitigated but perceptible Sunday. Fierce large jowled old ladies. Q. talking about Monaco. Talleyrand. Some very poor black wispy women. The effect of dowdiness produced by wispy hair. The Prime Ministers [*sic*] letter offering to recommend me for the Companion of honour. No.

(*Diary 4*, pp. 313–14)

These two short passages make manifest the ideas Woolf expresses in the only letter she writes from Rome in 1935 (to Smyth), that 'all is splintered' and full of 'unlinked melodies' (*Letters 5*, p. 394). The poetic snippets reveal in structure and theme a city transformed from the sensuously intense, artistically stimulating one that Woolf enjoys in 1927. The experiential intensity of a day in Rome has faded: 'Rome a mitigated but perceptible Sunday'. The shimmering atmosphere through which Woolf walks in 1927 has become cracked and dry; the halting rhythm and staccato composition of the notes is aurally and visually disturbing. Much of the Roman scenery is similarly raw: 'Children begging' suggests urban misery exacerbated by escalating military spending. The frothiness of Rome's 1927 display of 'the loveliest women in Europe, with proud little heads' (*Letters 3*, p. 365), gives way to a more sober scene that highlights women on the economic periphery as loveliness has been replaced by 'dowdiness'. The more concrete version of Roman women Woolf notices in 1935 takes into account racial and class difference: there are 'Ladies in bright coats & white hats', as well as harsh 'large jowled' and 'very poor black wispy' women. Woolf also registers sensory experience differently in 1935 than during her prior visit. In contrast to the phenomenal immersion in the Roman element she indicated by imaging herself as a fish during her 1927 visit to Rome, Woolf adopts a more fixed stance this time. Terse words and phrases such as 'tea', 'Music. Look out & see people like movies', 'Very cold', record in a detached fashion simply the externality of phenomena. Fascism's cacophonous presence violates the 'different relationship' to Rome in which she used to revel. By 1935 Mussolini's reign seems to have corrupted her aesthetic vision, as she is fixed in place, as if she were watching a muted cinematic image of Rome from a seat in a movie theater.

Woolf's concern with artistic vision recedes dramatically from its epistolary prominence in 1927, while thoughts about personal and nationalistic identity become more prominent. For example, the fragment 'N. & A. drawing' reduces the names of Vanessa ('Nessa') and Angelica in the act of artistic production to minimal pencil strokes, illustrating the way in which oppressive fascist atmosphere compromises the function of Rome as a place where artistic vision and creation flourish. But however dark the scene fascist Rome presents, whether through military spectacles or advertisements of imperial expansion into Northeast Africa, the act of making art in the face of fascism nevertheless survives in her writing through the statement itself of 'N. & A. drawing'.

The casual placement and abrupt formal qualities of the word 'Abyssinia' suggest at once Woolf's resistance to fascism's extreme nationalism and the dangerous banality of fascism.[23] Woolf places the one-word symbol for Mussolini's territorial greed apparently at random among the words and phrases of the notes, as if fascist politics had been incorporated into the culture of the everyday. 'Abyssinia' could be an endeavor as quotidian as that which 'Café haunters' undertake. Woolf's naming Abyssinia directly, however, endows the Ethiopian country with a subjectivity that opposes fascism's imperialist egocentrism and denies its appeal to the commonplace, figuratively extricating it from its impending Italian colonization that is garishly staged in those maps of Northeast Africa. By calling attention to the as-yet free nation of Abyssinia itself, Woolf disrupts fascist propaganda's message that Mussolini's plan to conquer Abyssinia is a natural stage in the evolution of the Italian nation.[24]

The single word sentence which brings these notes on Rome to an end, 'No', represents the ethical counterpoint to another single word in the notes, 'Abyssinia'. With this pair of words, Woolf both links and repudiates national and individual egomania. Having proclaimed in 1927 that 'one has no name' in Italy, Woolf now refuses egotism in Rome by not accepting the Prime Minister's offer to be named as a member of the Order of Companions of Honour as part of the King's birthday honors. By not having her name presented to the King and nationally publicized, she rejects participating in what she calls later in *Three Guineas*, 'the great modern sins of vanity, egotism, and megalomania' (*TGs*, p. 82), through the individuating and ultimately disunifying markers of 'personality'. As a moral gesture against the 'egotism' of the 1930s, Woolf symbolically erases ego by remaining royally uncommemorated.

Where hypermasculine fascist art makes clear the value of androgyny, fascist nationalism, staged all around Woolf in 1935, illuminates the value of anonymity. Her emphatic 'No' to the birthday honors marks a stage in her theory of anonymity that began with feeling that '[o]ne is nobody'. Woolf succinctly presents the ethical implications of anonymity in a memoir of Julian Bell she writes two years later in 1937. Recalling how 'immensely generous' Julian's regard for her as a writer was, and how 'touchingly proud'[25] he sometimes was of her writings, Woolf reflects:

> But then I came to the stage 2 years ago of hating 'personality'; desiring anonymity; a complex state which I would one day have

discussed with him. Then, I could not sympathise with wishing to be published. I thought it wrong from my new standpoint – a piece of the egomaniac, egocentric mania of the time.[26]

This 'new standpoint' Woolf came to '2 years ago' would have been in 1935, a suggestive date coinciding with her last trip to Rome. Julian's memoir in part solidifies Woolf's thinking, evidenced in her diary notes from Rome, about political and personal egocentrism. The new perspective she explains in the piece on Julian is the ethical position taken by renouncing identity as a cultural imperative.

Woolf explores further the 'complex' nature of anonymity for women a year after writing her memoir of Julian. In *Three Guineas* Woolf suggests that anonymity is not the endpoint of a moral stance; in her view, anonymity is not a passive state and not without responsibility to the world. Rather, anonymity is an active state that enables women, in particular, to practice their freedom from a constructed social-sexual identity by asserting freedom for others. *Three Guineas* faces the issue of social responsibility when it historicizes Woolf's production as an educated man's daughter and explores the moral possibilities of what Woolf calls the outsider position.[27] In the 'Outsiders' Society' proposed in the book, the daughters of educated men would work 'in their own class' and 'by their own methods for liberty, equality, and peace' (*TGs*, p. 106). But in order to secure these noble abstractions in the concrete, women outsiders must first free themselves from ' "unreal loyalties," ' especially, ' "pride of nationality" ' (*TGs*, p. 80). Fortunately, the law of England enjoins antipatriotism in women, *Three Guineas* argues, since ' "[t]he law of England sees to it that we do not inherit great possessions; the law of England denies us, and let us hope will long continue to deny us, the full stigma of nationality" ' (*TGs*, p. 82). In fact, a British woman contemplating nationalistic idealism can argue that ' "our country" ' has ' "throughout the greater part of its history has treated me as a slave" ' and ' "it has denied me education or any share in its possessions" ' (*TGs*, p. 108).

A crucial aspect of the argument advanced by *Three Guineas* is here. While it seems that the woman-outsider would repudiate the idea of 'country', fraught with its associations of inequality, injustice, and servitude, Woolf's logic in *Three Guineas*, shaped by her experience of fascist Italy, demands precisely the reverse of disavowal. Instead of claiming non-responsibility for the society, country, and world in which an outsider has no historical or present stake, a woman is required to engage her freedom. Liberated from oppressive identifying traits, including the burden of national identity, she is able to work for change – ' "to assert 'the rights of all – all men and women – to the respect in their persons of the great principles of Justice and Equality and Liberty" ' (*TGs*, pp. 143–4) by 'finding new words and creating new methods' (*TGs*, p. 143). The outsider will say: ' "as a woman, I have no country. As a woman I want no country. As a woman my country is the whole world" ' (*TGs*, p. 109). These three sentences encapsulate the case on patriotism in *Three Guineas*. The first part speaks to the fact that as a woman, her country has exploited and excluded her; the second recognizes that as a woman-outsider, she wants no part in exploitation or exclusivity. In the final sentence – ' "As a woman my country is the whole world" ' – Woolf enlarges the sphere a woman is responsible for by conceptualizing 'world' as a greater vision than mere 'country'. Paradoxically, Woolf's antinationalist philosophy represents her great love for Britain and for Italy.

Three Guineas thus endorses a fierce antipatriotism that counterintuitively makes possible an active love of country in the interest, not to the exclusion, of the rest of the world. Fascist Italy, then, enables Woolf to discern a more subtle fascism at home. While the figurative adversary of *Three Guineas* is fascism, it is a fascism understood in the double sense ascribed to it by Foucault – 'not [only] a historical fascism, the fascism of Hitler and Mussolini . . . but also the fascism in us all, in our heads and in our everyday behaviour, the fascism that causes us to love power, to desire the very thing that dominates and exploits us'.[28] But even before Foucault, Woolf recognized that the 'egocentric mania of the time' has as much to do with an individual's local desire for power as it does with fascism's global drive. At the end of *Three Guineas*, therefore, Woolf asks that we recognize in the fascist figure not exclusively the *Führer* or the *Duce*, but also, and perhaps especially, individual and institutional patriarchy at home. According to Woolf, the fascist figure suggests 'that the public and the private worlds are inseparably connected; that the tyrannies and servilities of the one are the tyrannies and servilities of the other'. She continues: 'we cannot dissociate ourselves from that figure but are ourselves that figure', and 'we are not passive spectators doomed to unresisting obedience but by our thoughts and actions can ourselves change that figure' (*TGs*, p. 142). Woolf's repudiation of the King's birthday honors in 1935 – 'No' – at once acknowledges complicity with fascism in the Foucauldian twofold understanding of fascism as both within and without and alters that association by refusing inscription by fascist politics.

Woolf's 1940 essay, 'Thoughts on Peace in an Air Raid', shows how the gendered activity of 'private thinking, tea-table thinking' is capable of, and even responsible for, countering the sterility of 'fear and hate' that fascist war-making universally imposes.[29] Her dramatization of thinking through the process of peace in the midst of a German air attack reveals the way in which Italy dually functions in her writing as both building and destroying a peaceable world.

'Thoughts on Peace in an Air Raid' explores the dark side of women's outsider position. The essay argues that women's historical and present exclusion as power brokers from the national and international scene can serve as an excuse that 'damps thinking, and encourages irresponsibility' (*Essays*, p. 173). But it must not. Woolf articulates her belief here that fascist consciousness finds its counterpart in the subconsciousness of common individuals as 'the desire for aggression; the desire to dominate and enslave' (*Essays*, p. 174). Women must work to free themselves from psychological and political fascism, as well as work to free the men more obviously engaged in fighting for or against it. Woolf's listening to the bombers overhead, waiting for the bomb that does not drop, suspends all thinking and all feeling 'save one dull dread':

> Directly that fear passes, the mind reaches out and instinctively revives itself by trying to create. Since the room is dark it can create only from memory. It reaches out to the memory of other Augusts – in Bayreuth, listening to Wagner; in Rome, walking over the Campagna; in London. Friends' voices come back. Scraps of poetry return. Each of those thoughts, even in memory, was far more positive, reviving, healing and creative than the dull dread made of fear and hate.
>
> (*Essays*, p. 176)

'Thoughts on Peace in an Air Raid' features Rome as one of the spiritually rejuvenating place experiences from which Woolf draws the moral and creative strength to oppose fascism. Recalling the moment in *Three Guineas* when 'the sound of guns' prompts the question of 'how to prevent war' (*TGs*, p. 143), the sound of deadly aircraft here tacitly asks, and offers a response to, the same dire question. Roaming the Roman Campagna; listening to opera in Germany; life in London: these memories energize the mind's shell once the fear has subsided. While the 'young Italian' and the 'young German' (*Essays*, p. 176) may be slave to tyrannical dictatorship when terrorizing Britain, Woolf's recollected encounters with Italy, and indeed even with Germany, counteract fascism's paralyzing effect. More than an arbitrary choice, Woolf's remembrance of other seasons spent 'walking over the Campagna' speaks eloquently to her touristic experience of Italy as a revitalizing, 'healing and creative' place. Rome and the Campagna function for Woolf as art to reinvigorate what she calls in *Three Guineas* 'the recurring dream that has haunted the human mind since the beginning of time; the dream of peace, the dream of freedom' (*TGs*, p. 143). Although Woolf's Italy produces Mussolini's sterile fascist regime, it also offers fertile conditions for the moral courage to resist it.

7

'Thou Canst Not Touch the Freedom of My Mind': Fascism and Disruptive Female Consciousness in *Mrs. Dalloway*

Lisa Low

The Leavisite reading of Virginia Woolf as an effete snob who wrote politically irrelevant upper class novels of manners has altered radically in the last two decades. Particularly among American Woolf scholars, Woolf has emerged not only as a major voice, but as a political revolutionary whose essays, letters, and diaries; whose novels; and whose two great polemical works *A Room of One's Own* and *Three Guineas* provide a radical philosophical critique of a variety of social ills, among them nationalism, colonialism, imperialism, misogyny, and war. *Three Guineas* in particular – that radical feminist polemic which Woolf wrote to condemn not only Italian, German, and Russian, but also English fascism – has enjoyed a reprise in recent years. For the most part poorly received in her own time, even by her supposedly liberal male peers; largely ignored for decades even by Woolf scholars, *Three Guineas* has emerged in the past two decades as a document of major consequence that offers not only powerful proof of a political Woolf, but material for utopian and most significantly, feminist reconstructions of culture.

Although much attention has been paid to *Mrs. Dalloway* as a political novel, and particularly to its critique, through Septimus Smith, of the First World War, little attention has been given to the role it plays in the evolution of Woolf's resistance to fascism.[1] In fact, however, Woolf began *Mrs. Dalloway* at the exact time of the emergence of Mussolini and, although she does not record the event in her letters or diaries, it is likely that Mussolini's rise to power in October of 1922, the same month in which she began seriously to 'think out Mrs. Dalloway',[2] provided Woolf with a particularly sobering historical context for the novel. *Mrs. Dalloway* foreshadows many of *Three Guineas'* principal themes: its hatred of war, violence, and dictatorship; its definition of fascism as the 'quintessence of masculinity'; its indictment of the professions generally, and of psychiatry and the medical profession in particular. Perhaps most importantly, *Mrs. Dalloway* develops – in ways impossible to the more rhetorical *Three Guineas* – the theme of female consciousness as resistance to fascist seduction.

For a variety of reasons, Italy's transition to a fascist state was accomplished with remarkable speed. According to Thompson, widespread economic depression and spiritual torpor made the masses in Italy especially susceptible to Mussolini's nation-building rhetoric about the fatherland. Modern technology brought Mussolini into private homes where fascist propaganda could be spread more easily and where a sense of a personal relationship with the dictator could be readily established.[3] Workers responded with enthusiasm to promises of a new and stronger Italy. Through a variety of methods – sporadic violence, control of the press, dissolution of parliament, banning of secret meetings, re-education in the schools, and establishment of the death penalty and the Special Tribunal to enforce it[4] – Mussolini, who came to power in 1922, established fascism with terrifying swiftness. Indeed, 'by 1929', four years after the publication of *Mrs. Dalloway*, 'Fascist Italy had been transformed into an authoritarian police State in which the ordinary citizen, once in the hands of the police, had few legal rights and very little hope of redress'.[5]

If the climate was less obviously meet for totalitarian takeovers, in *Downhill All the Way*, Leonard Woolf nevertheless describes the post-First World War atmosphere in England as one similarly rife with despair: in 1914 in the 'background of one's life and one's mind there were light and hope', but 'by 1918 one had unconsciously accepted a perpetual public menace . . .'.[6] The seeds of a 'cruel, mechanized, barbarous age' when people had become 'robots, puppets jerked through life by history, governments, and computers'[7] had been sown, and in the 1920s and the 1930s 'one impotently watched a series of events leading step by step' to the 'barbarism' of Nazism and fascism.[8] By 1918, one year after Leonard and Virginia had founded the Hogarth Press (in large part to circumvent censorship), public events had so invaded consciousness that private life ceased to exist: 'ever since 1914', Leonard writes, 'in the background of our lives and thoughts has loomed the menace of politics, the canker of public events'; in the end 'one has ceased to believe that a public event can be anything other than a horror or disaster'.[9]

Mussolini's takeover was widely reported in *The Times*, and to the Woolf who felt, even from childhood, hemmed in by enemies, that paper's relatively positive response to the *fascisti* must have seemed particularly appalling. Though one English reporter analyzed Mussolini's takeover in terms with which Woolf may have been in sympathy,[10] *The Times* was otherwise remarkably sympathetic to the crushing of the Facta Government in October of 1922. In a typical report, one *Times* journalist writes that there is 'some reason to hope for internal peace' now that the fascists have seized power.[11] Another reporter describes fascism as good in its aggressive attacks on the Bolsheviks and Socialists; bad only if, now that it has 'become the state', it continues its terrorist tactics.[12] *The Times'* response to fascism could only have redoubled Woolf's resolve 'to criticise the [English] social system, & to show it at work, at its most intense'.[13] Unlike George Orwell who in the 1940s could still argue that England could never become fascist since its culture did not predispose it to totalitarian rule ('England, Your England'),[14] the Woolf who always considered herself an outsider to even the most liberal of boys' clubs, had begun at least as early as *Mrs. Dalloway* to conceive of England as itself already fascist.

Woolf describes the fascistic character of English society throughout *Mrs. Dalloway*. From the novel's first page, when Clarissa Dalloway remembers the pleasure of childhood in the context of 'something awful [that] was about to happen', Woolf establishes a connection between private beauty and public horror, between the delicate Mrs. Dalloway and the invasive male-dominated state which would control her. In the war-scarred consciousness of Septimus Smith, in the airplanes that drone overhead, in the backfiring motor cars and dangerously careering omnibuses that are the peacetime equivalent of weapons of war, in the love of science that promises Holmes and Bradshaw their power and Smith his demise, and most pointedly, in the military parade that marches through the novel twice, Woolf emphasizes the 'excess of masculinity' that dominates 1920s England.

In 1932 in the *Enciclopedia Italiana*, under the heading 'fascismo', Mussolini describes the ideal fascist male as willing to give up 'the daily round of pleasure' in favor of a sacrificial identification – even unto death – with the state:

[Fascism aims at] the individual who is nation and fatherland, which is a moral law, binding together individuals and the generations into a tradition and mission, suppressing the instinct for a life enclosed within the brief round of pleasure in order to restore within duty a higher life free from the limits of time and space; a life in which the individual, through the denial of himself, through the sacrifice of his own private interests, through death itself, realizes that completely spiritual existence in which his value as a man lies.[15]

In her description of an English military parade, Woolf offers a vision of post-First World War England remarkably true to Mussolini's idealized conception of the suppression of the individual to the state. As he walks up the Strand Peter Walsh hears:

> A patter like the patter of leaves in a wood . . . and with it a rustling, regular thudding sound, which as it overtook him drummed his thoughts, strict in step, up Whitehall, without his doing. Boys in uniform, carrying guns, marched with their eyes ahead of them, marched, their arms stiff, and on their faces an expression like the letters of a legend written round the base of a statue praising duty, gratitude, fidelity, love of England . . . now they wore on them unmixed with sensual pleasure or daily preoccupations the solemnity of the wreath which they had fetched from Finsbury Pavement to the empty tomb . . . on they marched, past him, past every one, in their steady way, as if one will worked legs and arms uniformly, and life, with its varieties, its irreticences, had been laid under a pavement of monuments and wreaths and drugged into a stiff yet staring corpse by discipline. One had to respect it; one might laugh; but one had to respect it, he thought . . . all the exalted statues, Nelson, Gordon, Havelock, the black, the spectacular images of great soldiers stood looking ahead of them, as if they too had made the same renunciation . . . trampled under the same temptations, and achieved at length a marble stare.
>
> (*MD*, pp. 76–7)

In images of pleasure-less boys marching with 'eyes ahead of them', and 'as if one will worked legs and arms uniformly', Woolf portrays England as a fascist state in the making. The soldiers are not themselves, but the nation (England) for which they will die; indeed, they are already corpses, their souls sacrificed to the 'regular thudding sound' of the death they will deal and receive. In her description of Peter's desire to laugh at, and then ultimately to respect the English military, Woolf satirizes the professionally educated Englishman's respect for war. In the military parade itself, Woolf pulls aside the veil of English hypocrisy to show the serpent lying beneath English gentility: behind the pretense of good-heartedness, behind the Bradshavian smile and polite shake of the hand, is the boot without ruth in the face, the 'marble stare[d]' readiness to crush the individual for the greater glory of the state.[16]

In *Mrs. Dalloway* the violence of the masculine state is represented not only by abstractions such as Big Ben, Whitehall, and the military parade, but by members of the middle and upper classes, professionals who collaborate with war and oppression. If the military parade forms an underlying refrain, a drumbeat of masculine invasiveness thrumming at the back of the novel's mind, and if the backfiring of the Prime Minister's motor car represents the omnipresent threat of war imposing itself even in a supposed time of peace, Woolf's Hugh Whitbread, Dr. Holmes, and Peter Walsh are the novel's polite civil servants and respectable professionals who wear 'for God and empire' (*TGs*, p. 70) around their necks and who, though they pretend to gentleness and compassion, in fact wish to control.

Both Thompson and Wiskemann point out that fascism was supported by the middle and upper classes who benefited economically from the making of war. Wiskemann writes, for example, that 'inevitably some of the entrepreneurs in Italy's new heavy industry were interested in the fabrication of weapons',[17] and Thompson writes that while 'the disciplining and regimenting of primarily the lower classes . . . was the real meaning and function of the corporate State',[18] fascism was endorsed by 'the majority of large landowners, industrialists, businessmen, bankers and other financiers, intellectuals, professional classes, police, armed forces, shopkeepers and white-collar workers' who were 'offered a central role in planning the future of the State and its economy'.[19]

In *Three Guineas*, Woolf offers a similar analysis of the economics of fascism. Far from alleviating suffering, the professions encourage war by causing hostility with its competitive and hierarchizing 'barriers of wealth and ceremony' (*TGs*, p. 34). Education teaches not cooperation but 'the arts of dominating other people . . . of ruling, of killing, of acquiring land and capital' (*TGs*, p. 34). The professions do not provide a check and balance to, but rather collaborate with, the corporate state. 'If you succeed' professionally, Woolf writes, you sell your soul degradingly to the state, for 'the words "for God and the Empire" will very likely be written, like the address on a dog-collar, round your neck' (*TGs*, p. 70).

If successful professionals like Whitbread, Holmes, and Walsh have become pillars of a system that protects and benefits them, even as it exploits the masses of disenfranchised women, workers, soldiers, and the poor, the demonic egotism of the dictator himself is most clearly exemplified by the 'obscurely evil' (*MD*, p. 281) and privacy-invading Sir William Bradshaw, the state-protected psychiatrist who makes Clarissa shudder and who drives Septimus Smith to his suicide. Punishing, violent, egomaniacal, Bradshaw symbolizes not only the collaboration of the professional classes, but the censorship, propaganda, and sporadic violence of dictatorship itself. Where Clarissa has no wish to pry into what she calls 'the privacy of the soul' (*MD*, p. 192) ('Let her', she says of the old woman outsider across the street, 'climb the stairs if she wanted to' [*MD*, p. 191]), Bradshaw 'believes that he has the right . . . to dictate to other human beings how they shall live; what they shall do' (*TGs*, p. 53).

Pretending to be kind[20] – looking like the flower but being the serpent under it – Sir William demands obeisance. Idealizing the 'twin goddesses' Proportion and Conversion, Sir William imposes himself upon all who come within his compass, but particularly on the weak and defenseless.[21] Not only does his wife, whom Clarissa admits 'one didn't dislike' (*MD*, p. 279), succumb to 'the slow sinking, water-logged, of her will into his' (*MD*, p. 152) until she 'minister[s] to the craving which lit her husband's eye so oilily for dominion, for power' (*MD*, p. 152), but before him his patients often 'weakly broke down; sobbed, submitted' (*MD*, p. 153) until 'naked, defenceless, the exhausted, the friendless received the impress of Sir William's will' (*MD*, p. 154).

Sir William's evil comes in part from his occupation. Among the professions criticized in *Three Guineas* Woolf singles out medicine as particularly malevolent. Medical men blocked female entry into the College of Surgeons in the nineteenth century, and medical science itself is tainted – as totalitarianism was to show gallingly in the death camps – with a particularly ugly and for women dangerous form of masculine egotism. Citing Bertrand Russell, and with him anticipating the arguments of Barbara Ehrenreich, Deirdre English, and especially Mary Daly,[22] Woolf writes that 'the views of medical men on pregnancy, childbirth, and lactation were until fairly recently . . . impregnated with sadism' (*TGs*, p. 140). In Woolf's estimate psychiatry is more heinous than medicine, for it rapes the mind, which, 'people say, is nobler than the body' (*TGs*, p. 82). More dictatorial than Holmes, Bradshaw is, Mrs. Dalloway thinks in the climactic moment of her encounter with him, 'obscurely evil . . . capable of some indescribable outrage – forcing your soul' (*MD*, p. 281).[23]

Mussolini claimed just prior to taking over Italy that fascism must 'become the state'.[24] If Whitbread and Holmes have, in a sense, sold themselves to the state, Bradshaw is more horrifying than either for he has become it. Sir William is the exemplary man of the future, the quintessential fascist. At the very top of his profession, his power confirmed by his discussion of a bill regarding the rights of war veterans, surpassing the Prime Minister in power, especially as a menace to the individual conscience, it will be Sir William's and not the Prime Minister's voice to which the people will listen. Through his position at the head of a sadistic medical profession; through his state-urged and state-protected invasion of that final refuge – the mind – Sir William can practice more effectively than anyone else the usurpation of 'human and civil rights' that make up what Thompson calls 'the supreme act of violence by the Fascist State'.[25]

Given this 'supreme act of violence by the Fascist State', what is one to do? In 'Thoughts on Peace in an Air Raid' Woolf alludes to Blake's 'mental fight' to argue that 'there is [a] way of fighting for freedom without arms; we can fight with the mind'.[26] In Clarissa Dalloway – the first Woolf character whose mental life is completely revealed to us[27] – Woolf describes the female mind (hitherto almost totally suppressed by the patriarchy) as plural and evasive; as both inaccessible to patriarchal control and destructive of the patriarchal social order. As she thinks – meanderingly – Clarissa unravels the left-right-left grammar; the bootprint of fascism.

In *Three Guineas*, Woolf argues that the fascist state is characterized chiefly by the suppression of the female. This argument anticipates more recent feminist theories of fascism by at least five decades. According to Thompson, fascist theorists believed that females were physical and spiritual inferiors to males and that they must be rooted out of the society which their softening influence might corrupt. The family, which gave 'well nigh unimpeachable authority to the male head of each unit',[28] was at the core of fascist policies. 'Not only were women to be removed from the labour market', Thompson writes, 'but their mitigating and moderating influence throughout Italian society was to be severely curtailed'.[29] Mussolini argued that 'women were made to obey and could carry no weight in political life. [Instead] their role . . . was that of "wife and mother" '.[30] Rooting woman out of public life, even from the schools where women had traditionally worked, but that were now the front-line of fascist re-education, was imperative. Thompson writes, for example, that

> As early as May 1926, the Fascist deputy Vittorio Cian had expressed concern about the possibly grave consequences the 'female invasion' of the educational system would have on the ethics and subsequent military fibre of the nation, with their non-combative instincts, their patience, their willingness for compromise rather than self-assertive conflict. He deplored the notion 'which, until yesterday, was accepted more or less universally' of the equality of the sexes.[31]

In *Three Guineas*, Woolf urges women to capitalize on their outsider status and on the feminine culture of difference which fascist theorists like Cian scoffed at, but feared would bring 'grave consequences' to their program of masculinist nation-building. If fascism 'glorified war and colonial expansion, and demanded the just rewards of victory'; if it 'penalized open disagreement in every way' and 'based itself upon a system of propaganda involving large-scale deception',[32] Woolf argues that women should instead pursue difference: they should teach peace, self-containment, and tolerance; allow others to do as they please; expect neither reward nor victory; welcome open disagreement; and remain indifferent to propaganda. They should refuse to support war; become members of an 'outsiders' society'; dispense with 'the dictated, regimented, official pageantry, in which only one sex takes an active part'; increase private beauty (*TGs*, p. 114); nurture the development of the simple and peaceable arts in colleges that focus not on economics and military history, but on cooking, sewing, crafts; and they should practice vows of poverty, humility, chastity, and freedom from unreal loyalties. In *Mrs. Dalloway*, the most important of these may be mental chastity.

Commentary on Mrs. Dalloway's mental chastity is not uncommon. For T. E. Apter, 'the most real part of [Clarissa] is hidden, and wants to keep itself hidden'.[33] 'Images of cloistral isolation and virginal inviolability attach to [Clarissa]', writes Avrom Fleishman,[34] and for Suzette Henke, Clarissa 'jealously guards [a chastity of spirit] in the privacy of her attic room'.[35] Indeed, Jane Marcus writes that 'perhaps the most interesting case [of chastity used to resist patriarchal invasion] is that of Clarissa Dalloway'.[36]

In a sense Mrs. Dalloway – though hardly morally perfect (indeed, her economic position of undeniable privilege is often read as contemptible)[37] – is the perfect vehicle for Woolf's delineation of mental chastity. Empathetic, kind, and spiritually fertile; emotionally isolated from even as she is vulnerable to and in some ways chooses male domination, Mrs. Dalloway is the ideal artist, sensualist, and nun-lesbian who lives a submerged and secret life behind the face she presents to the world. In her thoughts as she walks to and stands within the flower shop; in her return to the cool vault that is her home and in her subsequent ascent to the attic room where she sleeps alone; in her meditation on Sally Seton's kiss; in her thoughts as she sews quietly in the parlor; and climactically in her withdrawal into a private room to contemplate the meaning of Septimus Smith's suicide, Woolf reveals not only the specificity, but the evasiveness and impermeability of female consciousness; the 'that's not it' and 'that's still not it' of a negative 'feminist practice'.[38]

The novel begins with Clarissa's walk toward Bond Street where she will buy flowers for her party. Clarissa enjoys the morning, describing it as 'fresh as if issued to children on a beach' (*MD*, p. 3), and comparing it to mornings remembered from her childhood at Bourton. In the flower shop where the 'button-faced Miss Pym' greets her with 'bright red' hands (*MD*, p. 17), Clarissa is amazed by the beauty of the flowers, and pressing her nose up against the petals and 'snuffing' in the palatable odors, she takes in the colors, shapes, and 'delicious scents' as if her mind were becoming stained glass, dyed by them. Her head turns from 'side to side' with 'her eyes half closed' (*MD*, p. 18), and she experiences wave after wave of the very thing Mussolini would deny her: pleasure (*MD*, p. 19). This pleasure is short-lived, however, for Clarissa is suddenly interrupted by what she thinks is a gun shot. The gun shot turns out to be a backfiring motor car, inside of which a 'male hand' draws the blind (*MD*, p. 19). The never-identified 'male hand' is curiously detached, even robotic. Even so, Woolf suggests, fascism startles the sealed-off female mind from its revery, 'violent explosion[s]' (*MD*, p. 19) reminding the female dreamer of the regime in which she lives and by which she is, in some ways, ruled.

After visiting the flower shop, Clarissa returns home, where she 'misinterprets' the airplane as beautiful and pleasurable: Lucy, the maid, opens the door, and Clarissa imagines the airplane as flying up, 'straight up, like something mounting in ecstasy'. When Clarissa enters the hall of her private house (*MD*, p. 42), it is 'cool as a vault' and she suddenly feels sealed away from the 'heat of the sun'.

At home, isolated in the privacy of her attic room, Clarissa meditates on Sally Seton, the novel's most outspoken revolter against domination and conformity. Unable to find a sponge, Sally 'ran along the passage naked' (*MD*, p. 50). Harassed by Hugh Whitbread, Sally nevertheless 'bicycled round the parapet on the terrace' and 'smoked cigars' (*MD*, p. 50). When they were young, Sally and Clarissa 'sat, hour after hour . . . talking about life, how they were to reform the world' (*MD*, p. 49). Sally's unexpected kiss is the most exquisite moment of Clarissa's life: 'Then came the most exquisite moment of her whole life passing a stone urn with flowers in it. Sally stopped; picked a flower; kissed her on the lips. The whole world might have turned upside down!' (*MD*, p. 52). Undisciplined and self-inspired, Sally is Clarissa's once-rejected but daily remembered ideal lover. Like Clarissa, Sally evades instinctively the fascist ideology that would contain and suppress her.

Clarissa's meditation on Sally lies at the core of the novel, where, alone in her attic room, Clarissa drifts in the indecipherable waters of the female soul, a sea where past and present, and self and other, are mixed unresolveably. Fascism requires uniformity and conformity: in order to dominate, the human soul must be rigidified into an wholly artificial self-presence. For this, the syntax of self must be strident, its grammar unviolated. Clarissa's soul is comprised instead of an infinitely complex, grammatically obtuse mixture of thoughts, words, sensations, images, and memories. Her thoughts move about freely and aimlessly, wandering indefatigably in alinear and self-reflexive multi-plicity, confirming Irigaray's claim that the female mind is amorphous and without boundary; that it is whatever 'eludes the "Thou art that" . . . That is, any definite identification'.[39] While random motion is suited for the experience of pleasure, it is fatal to the fanatical purposes of fascism, for in her distracted, bemused, diffused, grammatically attenuated state – the state in which Clarissa nearly constantly floats – she would make a very poor soldier.

Irigaray writes that 'Woman never speaks the same way. What she emits is flowing, fluctuating'.[40] Zwerdling writes that Clarissa is the first character in Woolf's novels whose 'inner life' is revealed completely.[41] Clarissa is Woolf's experimental female self. (Woolf herself puts the word in question to indicate her inability to say what a female is.) She is multi-ple, fluid, and anarchic; refracting and dreamlike; in some sense, given over entirely to pleasure. Indifferent to the fascist ideal of puritanical/stoical self-abstinence, Clarissa plunges instead into the moment, where she prefers what is always already falling/fulfilling – a 'drop' – a life confessed as evanescent and pleasurable. Clarissa's relaxed, even dazed, dreaminess displays a state of mind that cannot easily be convinced of anything. Where the soldiers Walsh admires march to a regular thud which 'drum[s]' thoughts into the strict measure of rational discourse, Clarissa in her saving island solitude 'leans and loafs' at her ease, swimming in a wide sea of self-reflecting un-selfconsciousness. It is only when Clarissa looks in the mirror and remembers her forgotten public self that her face comes into a 'point' (*MD*, p. 55), and only when Clarissa pauses on the landing before her party to assemble 'that diamond shape, that single person' (*MD*, p. 56), that the syntax of a once again permeable, violable self is restored and the 'mere sensibility' that refuses bodily incarnation hardens.

'*The transformation of fluid to solid' seals 'the triumph of rationality*' for Irigaray.[42] So in the mirror Mrs. Dalloway's shape, diamond hard and glittering, is temporarily restored. She becomes again the helpful 'hostess of the patriarchy',[43] that protective, incorruptible, glittering surface which administers kindness, and which, ironically, restores 'a precarious balance'[44] in a patriarchal world which normalizes only rationality.

At the party the state, and most especially Bradshaw, is brought into Clarissa's home and Clarissa's challenge is to defend herself against it (and him). Typically trivialized by masculinist culture, the party, like female consciousness, is in many ways benign and sociable, a 'privileged',[45] symbolic, communal space for Woolf, and, at least theoretically, the exact opposite of war. Mrs. Dalloway's party forms both the structural climax of the novel (the coming together of the various characters and plots which memory has revealed) and the thematic climax as well, especially because it plays host to the encounter between Clarissa and Bradshaw. As she lies 'on the sofa, cloistered, exempt' (*MD*, p. 184), instinctively preferring the sensuous pleasures of social life to the soul-destroying abstractions of soldiers who march stiffly in uniform, bearing 'on their faces . . . duty, gratitude, fidelity, love of England' (*MD*, p. 76); as she wards off the disparagers of her parties, 'the self-important men in white waistcoats who look down from the windows of their clubs on the world they control',[46] Clarissa glitters with the pleasure of bringing people new life by bringing them together at a party (*MD*, p. 185).

In midst of 'kindl[ing] and illuminat[ing]' (*MD*, p. 6), however, Clarissa is interrupted with news of a young man's death. In her nun-like meditation on that death, and through an empathy impossible for Holmes or Bradshaw, Mrs. Dalloway experiences Septimus's death as if it had been her own: she imagines the earth coming toward her as she falls, the rusty spikes piercing her flesh, and then death itself, the darkness. This empathy enables Clarissa not to die with Septimus, but to rise phoenix-like from his ashes into an affirmation of happiness in her own life: 'No pleasure could equal, she thought . . . this having done with the triumphs of youth . . . [only] to find [them], with a shock of delight, as the sun rose, as the day sank' (*MD*, p. 282). Where Holmes and Bradshaw enjoy the 'dubious [and soul/body killing] pleasures of power and dominion' (*TGs*, p. 105), the empathetic Clarissa, having experienced the horror of Septimus's death, finds satisfaction instead in the shocking, pleasant, brief delights of natural beauty, especially as that natural beauty, caught in exquisite, unexpected, and always fleeting moments, flowers in the imagination. Walking to the window to see the sky and finding that 'It held, foolish as the idea was, something of her own in it, this country sky, this sky above Westminster' (*MD*, p. 282), she sees to her surprise the solitary old woman opposite staring 'straight at her!' (*MD*, p. 283). In parting the curtains, Clarissa is met with another self exactly like herself, a fellow participant in what turns out to be a *community* of female outsiders (*TGs*, p. 106).

Woolf's lifelong concern was with the cultural construction of the sexes and their unequal valorization. According to Woolf, to the overall detriment of the human community, women and 'female values' have historically and globally been forced into the margins and silenced, while men and 'male values' have flourished. In Woolf's analysis, this gendrification of culture, this repression of the feminine, has taken us as far from Eden as we can get; we are, in fact, on the brink of global annihilation. Ironically, it is only in capitalizing on female difference (whether constituted genetically or culturally) that Woolf sees hope. Not only in *Three Guineas*, but in *Mrs. Dalloway* as well, Woolf suggests that female mental life is more than a finger in the dyke against global annihilation.

If *Three Guineas* represents the culminating philosophization of Woolf's revolutionary proposal for the reconstruction of gender, *Mrs. Dalloway* represents a significant forerunner to it, especially in its preoccupation with the female consciousness through which individuals can resist the cultural and material death-threat of fascism. Indeed, in some senses, *Mrs. Dalloway* is more effective than *Three Guineas*, for it uses stream of consciousness and a 'tunneling process' to show us the grammar-disturbing narrative codes of a, by definition, feminist underground. Labyrinthine and wandering; fundamentally impermeable to the phallus, the female imagination diffuses, multiplies, and complicates the subject; separates the 'I' from direct action or its object;[47] and, in the end, subverts the violent convincings of fascism, unnerving and unravelling completely the maniacal left-right-left logic and bootprint of fascist domination.

The spiritual torpor and economic depression that made a masculin-ized Italy vulnerable to fascism does not apply to Clarissa or to the female outsiders' society she represents. Although much might be said by the Marxist to criticize the *aristocratic* Mrs. Dalloway, Clarissa nevertheless symbolizes woman herself. Always and inevitably, Clarissa is an outsider whose inner life reveals a fascism-resisting feminist underground. Clarissa's 'mental life' is characterized by a mechanics of fluids rather than of authority and order; she prefers love to war; the concrete to the nationalist abstraction; beauty and pleasure to self-sacrificial renunciation. Unseduced by domination – the fascism that threatened to destroy England after the First World War – loving nature and the flowers which symbolize it, as well as 'whatever one loves' for the fleeting moment one loves it; empathetic, kind, and spiritually fecund, Clarissa Dalloway is in the female outsider's position of powerful resistance to fascism. Indeed, according to Woolf, neither the patriarchy, nor its most extreme and bullying form – fascism – can deflower Clarissa where she swims – unapproachably – in the still waters running deep of a diffused and ultimately *untraceable* female consciousness.

8
Of Oceans and Opposition: *The Waves*, Oswald Mosley, and the New Party

Jessica Berman

> Symbiosis and oceanic feeling are produced in fascism's 'gathering' stages – produced in its rhythms, the intonations . . . What was liberating in aesthetic terms can look dangerous as soon as it is socially conceived.
>
> Alice Kaplan[1]

It is no surprise that Alice Kaplan should speak of fascism's gathering stages in aesthetic terms, for she and others following Walter Benjamin have persuasively elaborated on his claim that 'fascism is the introduction of aesthetics into political life'.[2] Indeed, the fascist desire to re-create society often emerges most powerfully in its utopian fantasies and in the mass spectacles organized to enact them. But as Kaplan's analyses make clear, the fascist effort to make life into art was not confined to dramatic forms, nor did its nostalgia for pre-modern plenitude always imply a rejection of stylistic modernism.[3] In fact, as Russell Berman has claimed, 'modernism articulated alternative models in which . . . life and art were to be merged . . . for modernism in any case the social character of the various aesthetic endeavors was constantly underscored, and among those socially motivated literary projects a fascist version arose . . .'[4] We can draw no clear formal boundaries around the fascist aesthetic, especially in those gathering stages, just as we cannot easily judge, in its earliest days, the fascist potential of a political movement.

This difficulty becomes more salient when we consider that Kaplan describes the early fascist aesthetic as encapsulating 'symbiosis and oceanic feeling', terms that will be familiar to readers of Virginia Woolf's *The Waves*. The ocean in darkness as the novel opens is an ocean without limits or boundaries, indistinguishable from the sky. As the sun rises on the children at Elvedon their monologues run together, with images spilling from one child to the next. The children are 'edged with mist', in Bernard's celebrated phrase, they 'melt into each other' (*TW*, p. 16), and create the edenic Elvedon as a realm of symbiotic plenitude.

And yet, as the birds which first sang in chorus fly off, leaving only one singing 'by the bedroom alone' (*TW*, p. 11), so the characters constantly come together and separate, quickly discovering the limits of the connection even as they continue to desire it. *The Waves* begins and ends as a novel about the potential for plenitude in a group, about the forces, whether personal or political, that undermine it, and about the dangers, to both individuals and the group, of insisting upon it. Percival's imperial adventures, Louis's status-hungry strivings, even Rhoda's doomed quests for wholeness, all underscore the social forces which make the kind of unfettered communion that Bernard craves impossible. Still, the waves of the interludes fall 'in one long concussion' even as the sun sinks (*TW*, p. 207) and Bernard still wonders 'Am I all of them? Am I one and distinct?' (*TW*, p. 288).

But all of this is not new. What has not been adequately discussed is the extent to which in *The Waves* Woolf's aesthetic is bound up with the emergence of British fascism in the period of crisis from 1929 to 1932. For this is fascism's gathering stage in Britain, the period in which the populist appeal of the proto-fascist movement is often indistinguishable from that of left-leaning political groups and in which fascism can be 'especially appealing to the intellectual who dreams of gaining "community" . . . without losing "self" '.[5] In fact, in this period of rising unemployment, economic crisis, and dearth of leadership on both the right and the left, there were many British intellectuals whose quest for community brought them to the brink of fascism.[6] Yet, even as *The Waves* expresses an oceanic feeling, desire for wholeness, and pressure for international community like that which pervades the proto-fascist rhetoric of Mosley's New Party, and as well as much twentieth-century neo-conservative and fascist literature,[7] *The Waves* specifically confronts the limitations of this political and literary discourse.

As the sun rises further and further, the waves thunder on the beach, stamping and crashing[8] but never dispelling the desire to be caught up in their flow (*TW*, 192). Klaus Theweleit has abundantly argued that oceanic images and particularly images of undammed, feminine waters which flow indiscriminately and transgress boundaries, ultimately *threaten* the fascist desire to 'stand with both feet and every root firmly anchored in the soil'.[9] The threat here seems to lie in a dynamic feminine aesthetic opposite to the masculine symbiosis Kaplan discusses in French fascism.[10] In other words, though the power of Woolf's waves massed together may stamp with the might of a beast, ultimately in their ebb and flow they undermine any effort to stand firm. Within this context then *The Waves* may be seen as acting through its central imagery, creating a feminist narrative that swirls water against fascist boots. This chapter will examine the power of that narrative swirl as a countercurrent within the crisis of 1930–31, both marking and resisting the gathering of political force.

It's not always easy to see the close proximity of Mosley's fascism and the left-leaning cosmopolitanism of Woolf's Bloomsbury cohorts. To begin with, fascism in Britain is often either written off as unsuccessful, or written up as a phenomenon that does not get under way until the mid-1930s.[11] In fact Mosley's version of fascism, which was to grow into the British Union of Fascists (BUF), came into being in 1931 within a transitional organization called the New Party, a party that, at least at its outset, drew a startling number of adherents from the ranks of Labour, and held appeal to a wide range of dissatisfied citizens. If Zeev Sternhell is correct in claiming that 'fascist ideology in all its essentials is best perceived in its origins'[12] then it is to this party that we must turn to understand British fascism.

But the distinction between right and left within the oppositional movements of the late 1920s, and even within the New Party itself, was very rarely clear.[13] Mosley was a member of the Labour Party's inner circle and a minister in its government until he resigned in 1930, and he began the New Party as a means to solving the unemployment crisis.[14] His ideas were therefore seen by many as an extension of Labour Party policies. In fact, 'The Mosley Memorandum' that was rejected by the Labour cabinet in 1930, and which precipitated his resignation, was predominantly a Keynesian approach to solving unemployment through public works, the regulation of the market, and the creation of new industries via expanded government credit.[15] And since the Labour Party had all but abdicated its agenda in the face of the international economic crisis of 1929, to many Mosley's New Party seemed like a viable form of political opposition.[16]

The common bond among those attracted to Mosley seems to have been desire for organized and decisive action that would wrest Britain's economic policy from the hands of the international banking community, action that would unite Great Britain even as it connected it to people's movements in other nations. For, as Mosley was to claim over and over again, fascism was 'a worldwide creed. Each of the great political faiths in its turn has been a universal movement: Conservatism, Liberalism, and Socialism are common to nearly every country . . . In this respect fascism occupies precisely the same position.'[17] Like socialism, Mosley's fascism was conceived as a people's revolutionary movement, but one which relied upon the corporate state as its vehicle. Thus its connection to a universal movement could not lie in the dissolution of national boundaries and international solidarity (as in communist internationalism). Rather, it would ultimately be in shoring up British trade barriers, granting almost unlimited power to the central authority, and drawing the people together as a 'team' that Mosley's 'Greater Britain' would become an example of the universal appeal of fascist principles.[18] 'The human race is not prepared for internationalism', Nicolson writes, 'for its fulfillment we require a similar attitude of sanity on the part of other nations. That sanity does not, at present, exist. Our sanity therefore must begin at home.'[19]

But in 1930, when Woolf was writing *The Waves*, Mosley's politics were not yet openly fascist, and the claims of his followers were that they were continuing the work that the Labour Party had given up. The country needs action, wrote Oswald Mosley in the New Party journal which Nicolson edited, and 'a movement of order, of discipline, of loyalty but also of dynamic progress; a movement of iron decision, resolution and reality; a movement which cuts like a sword through the knot of the past to the winning of the modern state'.[20] And if we find Harold Nicolson giving up all else to edit this journal (entitled simply: *Action*), Vita Sackville-West writing a gardening column for it, and John Strachey and others intimately involved in its creation, then why, we might ask, didn't Virginia Woolf contribute as well? The answer is not, as so often used to be claimed, that she was not concerned with organized politics. While she was never so deeply involved as was Leonard Woolf, Virginia Woolf concerned herself with 'the pedestrian operations of the Labour Party and the Co-operative Movement . . . the grass roots of Labour politics . . .'.[21] She felt a long-term[22] solidarity with the Fabians and shared their preferences for gradual amelioration rather than revolutionary change; metropolitan forms of solidarity rather than nostalgia for the bygone rural community; and the ideal of a classless society rather than class antagonism.[23]

But in 1931 the Labour Party itself evoked no strong emotions from Woolf. To begin with, because of the variety of positions subsumed within the heading Labour, those in power did not necessarily represent the Fabian perspective that had drawn her to the movement.

Ramsay MacDonald was not a Fabian leader – in fact, the period of the 1920s when he was twice leader of a Labour government was also the period of the Fabians' least influence in Labour politics. Second, Labour was clearly closely aligned with the Trade Union Congress and the trade union movement in general, especially since it derived its main income from fees paid by trade unionists. But this was a movement from which Woolf often felt quite distant, in part because the trade unions were seen to be a male-dominated movement, of which the female counterpart was a cause much closer to Woolf's heart and politics, the Women's Co-operative Guild.[24]

The main failings of both the Labour Party and the Fabians, from Woolf's perspective, however, were that they were not wholly committed either to anti-imperialist pacifism or to the emancipation of women. While along with many others, MacDonald had protested Britain's entrance into the First World War, favoring a negotiated peace,[25] this did not mark a generalized opposition to war within the various sections of Labour. On this issue, the difference between Labour in general and the Co-operative Movement in particular stands clearly drawn. While the reaction of Labour to war might be best described as ad hoc, the Women's Co-operative Guild (WCG) adopted a consistent and persistent pacifism that was based on the principles of internationalism. 'Their condemnation of militarism extended even to the Boy Scouts, the Girl Guides, and the Church Lads' Brigades, as well as to Armistice Day celebrations and The League of Nations Sanctions policy.'[26] Thus, when she writes in a 1931 letter, 'I admit fighting to the death for votes, wages, peace' (*Letters 4*, p. 333), she is then writing specifically of her commitment to the WCG agenda of international pacifism and to the Fabian socialist approach to economic equality.[27] Clearly, this agenda diverges radically both from the Labour Party of 1930 and from the proto-fascist proposals of the New Party.

But Woolf's absence from the pages of *Action* was not a result of her unwillingness to conform to New Party political codes or to particular modes of writing. As the pages of *Action* attest, in its short run of one year Nicolson managed to assemble an exceptionally eclectic group of contributors. The editorial pages insist from the beginning that the paper was to be open to a variety of political perspectives and that all manner of contributions would be welcome. Thus along with Sackville-West's 'Your Garden' columns there were weekly columns from Francis Birrell, and contributions from Osbert Sitwell, Christopher Isherwood, and Keynesian economist Rupert Trouton. After the opening invective by Mosley, and Nicolson's corresponding editorial, there were reports on science, advice columns on housekeeping, and many reviews of general interest books. One might have imagined Nicolson soliciting a review or two from Woolf – that he didn't, or at least that if he did she didn't deem it important enough to record in her diary, seems clear.

On the contrary, the only time Woolf appears in *Action* is as the subject of an article – Nicolson reviews *The Waves* on the day of its publication in the premier issue of his journal. He calls our attention to 'the flux and reflux' in the novel, to the way that 'this symbol [of the waves] cuts across her vision, intruding into her images its battering restlessness, its unplumbed mobility, its incessant renewals of shape and energy'. According to Nicolson 'Her whole intention is to depict the fluidity of human experience . . . She succeeds triumphantly.'[28] This review is worthy of mention for two reasons: not only does it attest to the openness of Nicolson's publication, but it also highlights the paradoxes inherent in New Party politics at the time, and in the proto-fascist sensibility in general. Just as Kaplan's French writers are swept away in the restless energy of fascist feeling[29] so Nicolson admired Woolf's 'battering restlessness', and the 'incessant renewals of shape and energy' in her novel. Action in and of itself is a value for New Party members, from the metaphor of dynamic progress used from the first issue of *Action* to the later institution of a sports-oriented Youth Movement. In particular, Mosley's vision of 'regeneration' through the corporate state is specifically one of symbiosis through co-ordinated activity.

But clearly this is not flux and reflux of the kind inscribed on every page of Woolf's novel. There is no room for the sort of fluidity that the interludes in *The Waves* present or for a moment where 'all . . . wavered and bent in uncertainty and ambiguity, as if a great moth sailing through the room had shadowed the immense solidity of chairs and tables with floating wings' (*TW*, p. 183). Rather, the kind of boundless energy that *Action* endorsed is directed, unwavering, 'co-ordinated, co-operative and controlled',[30] action much more akin to the Hitler youth than to the young community at Elvedon. The watch-word for the New Party is 'VOLT': Vigor, Order, Loyalty, Triumph;[31] its body is the corporate state.

Nothing could be farther from Woolf's politics, and particularly here, nothing could be farther from the version of it she expresses in *The Waves*. It is in this way that her novel may be seen as marking the limitations and the dangers of proto-fascism within her circle and in British political life in general, and especially its inability to admit any version of dynamic feminine force within its emphasis on action.

Much has been recently written about the anti-imperialism of Virginia Woolf's writings.[32] My intent is not to negate the power of that aspect of Woolf's work. However, the vagaries of nationalism at home and the rising spectre of fascism in 1930 (and afterwards) are also direct targets of Woolf's fiction and her political writings. If as Jane Marcus has argued, *The Waves* critiques the imperial image of Britannia as ruler of the sea, then on the home shores it also presents the sea as pitted against the rigid and increasingly masculinized edifice of British nationalism.[33] *The Waves* presents an alternative feminine force of action that directs itself against the proto-fascist responses to national crisis.

Thus, the pages of *The Waves* not only critique empire through the fall of Percival but also contend with the domestic effects of international crisis. Although there are no legions of the unemployed in *The Waves*, material wealth often appears tenuous, especially in the bankruptcy of Louis's father 'a banker at Brisbane', which forces 'Louis the best scholar in the school' to work in an office instead of attending university with Bernard and Neville (*TW*, p. 92). We also see occasional glimpses of London squalor, as for example seen from Louis's window: 'I see the broken windows in poor people's houses; the lean cats; some slattern squinting in a cracked looking-glass as she arranges her face on the street corner . . .' (*TW*, p. 170).

But we also see the sexual politics which for Woolf mark all aspects of British social life. Despite Woolf's intentions not to have any characters in the novel at all (*Diary 4*, p. 47), Rhoda emerges as a compelling portrait of the kind of woman who is maimed by patriarchal values, and most especially, by the restriction of women to a certain sphere of manners. As the party scene makes clear, when Rhoda is deprived of a sphere of influence, importance, or comfort she is deprived of strength and integrity of both body and spirit. Jinny finds ease in the social world by discovering the bodily communication among those at the party (*TW*, p. 101). Susan has discovered that 'hard thing' (*TW*, p. 98) within herself away at school in Switzerland and brings it with her to her rural life. When she finds she 'cannot float gently, mixing with other people' (*TW*, p. 98), Susan can turn to the natural world where she establishes not only connection, but also escape from the confines of her gender identity. 'I am not a woman, but the light that falls on this gate, on this ground. I am the seasons, I think sometimes, January, May, November; the mud, the mist, the dawn' (*TW*, p. 98). But Rhoda has no alternative to being a woman, no other sphere where she can solidify her being, and so, while Susan and Jinny consolidate themselves in this episode, Rhoda disintegrates under the pressure of impending (and imposed) womanhood.

> Here, twisting the tassels of this brocaded curtain in my hostess's window, I am broken into separate pieces; I am no longer one . . . I am to be broken. I am to be derided all my life. I am to be cast up and down among these men and women, with their twitching faces, with their lying tongues, like a cork on a rough sea.
>
> (*TW*, pp. 106–7)

In these closely connected episodes Woolf's feminist critique makes clear that the political maiming of women is one which has corporeal consequences; without a means of enabling body and mind to flourish within the female sphere, both break up.

As Gillian Beer has pointed out,[34] each character in *The Waves* has a different relationship between body and world, and that relationship also governs the ephemeral give and take of the group's communal corpus. But the implications for the female outsider are more dire than for the male – than they are, for example, for Louis, who finds himself restricted by social codes of conduct but can nevertheless succeed within the masculine domain of business. This is partly because while Rhoda is made marginal through the immutable fact of her sex, for Louis the expression of exclusion arises in his Australian accent, which he attempts to hide or transform over the course of the book. While language and body are strongly connected in this novel of natural, visceral, and often sexual images, it is the male figures Neville, Louis, and especially Bernard, who reach toward a sort of idealized connection of the two realms. The possible uses of language hold out an ideal, potential wholeness of body and completenesss of interconnection that is not so available to the female characters. If Susan is at first content with the 'natural happiness'[35] of motherhood, by the end of the book she wearies of it. On the other hand, as Beer points out, Bernard experiences a kind of physical well-being when his animal nature asserts itself in his final monologue, establishing a kind of ' "gutteral, visceral" inner voice . . . [as] the unreachable ideal language which Bernard always seeks'.[36]

In the context of 1930–31, however, gendered images of the body also necessarily refer to the question of the body of the nation. The essence of British government as defined for many political writers was perceived as a question of establishing the cohesion of a group (nation, party, house of Parliament, national government, etc.) which would preserve the unity and strength of the nation. Organic metaphors and reference to the body abound in these writings[37] making clear that the proto-fascist call for a corporate state was only one of many ways of conceiving of the nation as a wounded body in need of assistance.

The New Party writings highlight the interrelationship between organic conceptions of statehood, war-mongering, and patriarchy that were also common within more mainstream movements. 'What therefore, is the alternative between the flag-waving jingo and the pimpled pacifist?' Nicolson asks. 'It is the belief that every man or woman is born into this world to fulfill a certain function. It is the belief in the Organic State.'[38] Compared to those in both Italy and Germany, Mosley's New Party seemed better able to admit that women might serve a public function, (as did for example, Mosley's wife Cynthia, who was a Member of Parliament). Still, the rhetoric of physical 'efficiency', 'athleticism', and youth becomes increasingly masculinized.[39] And that ruling bodies in general appeared both male-dominated and patriarchal to Virginia Woolf is made abundantly clear in her writings from the short story 'The Society' to *Three Guineas*. The call to save the nation by shoring up the state, or consolidating party ranks, or changing leadership, all were calls to restore a wholeness and unity to the seemingly 'natural' realm of masculine values, and to reinforce the system by which Louis triumphs while Rhoda disintegrates.

At the same time it is clear that the fascist fascination with the body, and particularly with gender distinctions as expressed by the body, is also bound up with desire to destroy these bodies. Within the Italian context with which Mosley was aligned, for example, there is a tension between physical liberation and bodily discipline ever tied to the image of the body politic.[40] As Andrew Hewitt puts it, writing of futurism, 'just as the politics of nationalism is split on the fault line of plenitude and transgression, so Marinetti's politics of the body strains between an ideal of discipline and an ideal of liberation. Bodily liberation . . . is not simply (or not even) a liberation *of* the body but also a liberation *from* it'.[41] And if for the Italian futurists this aesthetic often implied a sense of *self*-destruction as well as the effort to overcome the demands of one's own body, for many German fascists the body to be destroyed belonged to another and was very often female. Klaus Theweleit's exhaustive compendium of male fantasies has made clear the extent to which the reduction of disobedient or potentially threatening female bodies to 'bloody masses' was part and parcel of the fascist cult of the ideal body.[42] And even when not destroyed absolutely, the German woman within the Freikorps writings that

Theweleit presents is deprived of her bodily sensuality, emerging as an amalgam of sister/mother/nurse, dressed in uniform white, or else got up in the images of the united nation, Germania or Luisa of Prussia, safely de-sexualized and distanced by her symbolic role.[43]

From this perspective Rhoda's disintegration begins to take on more specific significance as an indicator of the potential corporeal destruction of the non-conforming female body within the proto-fascist situation. If Susan and Jinny can accommodate themselves to the available roles of mother and lover, at least enough to be able to preserve themselves intact, Rhoda becomes the equivalent of that bloody mass, dashed not by Freikorps blows or even the sword of Percival, raised in the imperial adventure, but by the false promise of a charismatic leader and the violence that emanates from his centralized authority. If the promise of plenitude held out by the proto-fascist, nationalist impulse is dual edged, verging on both liberation and destruction at once, then Rhoda's is the body that succumbs.

But the destructive aspect of the collectivist enterprise is not only limited to the female figures in the novel. While the cult of Percival is crucial to the development of the first half of *The Waves*, it is undermined as often as it is supported. If, as Melba Cuddy-Keane remarks, *Between the Acts* is a novel about the subversion of prevailing assumptions about leaders,[44] *The Waves* is its direct antecedent. Percival is not only laughable as a representative of empire, as Marcus has pointed out, but also very limited in his ability to act within the domestic arena. Woolf gives him no voice, so that we can only sense his presence in the effect he has on the others. But that effect is either illusory, or, as in the case of Rhoda, negative, created more by the function he fulfills than by the quality of his actions. This negative effect is especially clear after his death, as, for example, in Rhoda's comments: 'now I will walk down Oxford Street envisaging a world rent by lightening: I will look at oaks cracked asunder and red where the flowering branch has fallen . . . Look now at what Percival has given me. Look at the street now that Percival is dead' (*TW*, p. 159).

This is not simply the result of the loss of Percival. In fact, he is missing before the fact, so that his charismatic appeal may be seen as a certain sort of communal misapprehension. Not only is he voiceless but he is always viewed from afar, leading the 'smaller fry' or looking on with indifference. 'His blue, and oddly inexpressive eyes, are fixed with pagan indifference upon the pillar opposite . . . He sees nothing; he hears nothing. He is remote from us all in a pagan universe' (*TW*, p. 36). He inspires devotion simply by laughing (*TW*, p. 38), love by 'flick[ing] his hand to the back of his neck' (*TW*, p. 36), and poetry by 'blunder[ing] off, crushing the grasses, with the small fry after him' (*TW*, p. 40). Even when face to face with him, Percival inspires Louis with resentment (*TW*, p. 39) and need (*TW*, p. 40). His lack is felt before he ever leaves; the desire for him is for what is missing, in both self and other.

In this sense *The Waves* comments upon the limitations of both charismatic leaders and their followers. And it is also in this light that we must read the sections of the novel following the death of Percival. For, since he leaves the scene after the first third of the novel and dies by its mid-point, the group of characters that make up *The Waves* ultimately construct their community without him. Nor can either Louis or Bernard take over as the focus of desire or obedience, despite Louis's short-term appeal for Rhoda. As they come to adulthood the characters of *The Waves* form a group that has no static, organic identity and which no longer proffers itself to a single leader. Theirs is a community that exists in fragmentation, that constantly is in the process of becoming, without ever resolving itself into a common being. And while the group no longer has a single identity, neither do any of the characters alone. In Jean-Luc Nancy's terms the characters 'compear', existing together, yet not merging identities.[45] As Bernard puts it, 'We are divided; we are not here. Yet I cannot find any obstacle separating us. There is no division between me and them' (*TW*, p. 288).

From a political perspective, *The Waves* may be seen as a novel about the possibility of community not only without charismatic leaders but also without any totalizing structure like that of state or nation. Woolf's social vision here moves beyond simply critiquing either the notion of empire or the problem of leadership. Rather, in the positive interconnection of her community of characters she constructs an alternative model of social organization, that, I would argue, is directly targeted at those in search of political answers to the British crisis.

Thus in *The Waves* it is not as a bloody mass that Rhoda ends up but rather as fragments tossed into a current, pieces flung into the water that ebbs and flows throughout this narrative. If Percival's heroism is diminished both in the manner of his death and in the way it is announced in the novel 'Percival has died; (he died in Egypt; he died in Greece; all deaths are one death)' (*TW*, p. 170), then Rhoda's is enhanced, but not because she is a martyr. Rather, the power of the river into which she flings flowers to the dead Percival (*TW*, p. 164) or of the waves into which she falls as if in a dream (*TW*, p. 206) is the power of a symbiotic connection that dissolves and disassembles, at the same time as it creates a network of connection that flows to all corners of this narrative. From the struggle of her isolation ('I have sunk alone on the turf and fingered some old bone and thought: When the wind stoops to brush this height, may there be nothing found but a pinch of dust') to the satisfaction of a fleeting communion ('Who then comes with me? . . .') (*TW*, p. 206), there is only a gap of a few sentences. The sense of the 'we' is created the instant the dreamer leaves land and allows herself to fall into the sea.

> We launch out now over the precipice. Beneath us lie the lights of the herring fleet. The cliffs vanish. Rippling small, rippling grey, innumerable waves spread beneath us. I touch nothing. I see nothing. We may sink and settle on the waves. The sea will drum in my ears . . . Rolling me over the waves will shoulder me under. Everything falls in a tremendous shower, dissolving me.
>
> (*TW*, p. 206)

Just as the flowers flung as an offering to Percival travel with the waves to 'the uttermost corners of the earth' (*TW*, p. 164), connecting Rhoda to her dead friend as well as to the woman and man she sees pacing the embankment, so Rhoda's body itself here reaches its utmost connection to other people and places as it dissolves under the waves.

This is not to say that Rhoda's disintegration is a positive event in the novel – far from it. Yet, her role seems to be to highlight the dispersal within the natural flux of human experience that pervades the entire community of characters. And just as her difficulties throughout are tied to the limitations of her feminine role, so are her strengths. It is Bernard, Louis, and of course Percival who, throughout this narrative, struggle to organize and command the flux of interconnections. Despite his desire to 'feel close over [him] the protective waves of the ordinary' (*TW*, p. 94) Louis is 'conscious of flux, of disorder' as linked to 'annihilation and despair' and therefore worthless, something that must be overcome by directed activity (*TW*, p. 93). And if Louis wants in this way to be like Percival, Bernard wants to contain him by setting Percival down on paper, neatly summarized and categorized.

But the female characters, even in their enormous differences, seem less insistent about the teleology of their lives, and therefore more susceptible to natural, cyclical rhythms. In addition, the images connected to these female characters refer far more frequently to ebb and flow, their metaphorical life within the novel touches far more often upon the presiding figure of the waves. For example, Susan who is perhaps the most conventional of the female characters and who claims to 'have reached the summit of [her] desires' growing trees, fruit and children on a rural farm, regrets ending up 'fenced in, planted here like one of [her] own trees' (*TW*, p. 190). At night, however, remembering her childhood, she 'can feel the waves of [her] life, tossed, broken, round [her]' and though rooted, still harbors the value of lives spent 'eddying like straws round the piers of a bridge' (*TW*, p. 192). And Jinny, who finds her strength in the social whirl of London, experiences it not as the conquest of a realm or the launching of a career, but rather as the sense of almost limitless and directionless capacity.

> I am arch, gay, languid, melancholy by turns. I am rooted but I flow. All gold, flowing that way, I say to that one 'come' . . . This is the most exciting moment I have ever known. I flutter, I ripple. I stream like a plant in the river flowing this way, flowing that way, but rooted . . .
>
> (*TW*, p. 102)

So too in the interludes the figure of the waves promulgates an oceanic sensibility intrinsically linked to the rising of the sun and the cyclical progress of the lives of the characters. While the waves may 'thud like a great beast stamping' (*TW*, p. 150) they are not simply symbols of imperialist violence as Jane Marcus would have it, but part of the dissolving power of the natural world which sets to blazing an island 'on which no foot could rest' (*TW*, p. 165) and lets nothing stand immobile, untouched. In fact, much of what is so striking in the interludes of *The Waves* is the very subtlety with which Woolf weaves together images of power and movement, sun and water. The sun, figured as a girl who rises from a watery bed to disperse her light, wears 'water-globed jewels that sen[d] lances of opal-tinted light falling and flashing in the uncertain air like the flanks of a dolphin leaping, or the flash of a falling blade' (*TW*, p. 148). Her light strikes, 'pierces', and 'beats' even as it descends 'in floods dissolv[ing] the separate foliage' of a tree into an indistinguishable mass (*TW*, p. 149). At times, the waves pound like drums (*TW*, pp. 75, 109), the birds dart like warriors (*TW*, pp. 74–5), and the sunlight shoots like darts (*TW*, p. 165), yet by end of day 'sea and sky [are] indistinguishable' fanning out over the shore and rolling back in a sigh (*TW*, p. 236). Warlike imagery is clearly not restricted to the waves: the mid-day sun shoots arrows into the water (*TW*, p. 165), even the clouds fling nets across the sea (*TW*, p. 183).

There is no doubting the power of this natural world – yet it is a power that cannot be categorized or compartmentalized. It changes with the cycle of the day and with corresponding events in the characters' lives.[46] Its metaphors mix modes, and dissolve boundaries between earth, sea, and sky, so that petals may be described as 'shell-shaped', leaves might run, and 'wave[s] of light' can pass through flowers 'as if a fin cut the green glass of a lake' (*TW*, p. 182). As this last example makes clear, there is constant movement here from sea to sky and back again and it is this movement, sometimes thundering violently, sometimes rolling peacefully, that is the figurative thrust of *The Waves*.

This forceful current also moves through the structure of the sentences in the novel, which often slip from one word to the next, either clipping an intervening sound or smoothing it into an alliterative stream. As Garrett Stewart has pointed out, 'a certain conjunction of words across the border or blank of their normal scriptive segmentation proliferates with unusual frequency in *The Waves*'.[47] In phrases like Susan's: 'the silver-grey flickering moth-wing quiver of words' (*TW*, p. 215), we can hear little distinction between the *g* at the end of 'wing' and the *q* at the beginning of 'quiver' which tend to run together as we pronounce them. Even the *g* in 'grey' and the *ck* in 'flickering' participate in a stream of sounds whose distinctions have been elided. What Stewart calls 'phonemic clotting or "thickening," ', accomplishes the same goal.[48] When Woolf writes in an interlude 'all the blades of the grass were run together in one fluent green blaze' (*TW*, p. 149) she creates linguistic echoes (blades/blaze; run/one) that help accomplish the meaning of the phrase, running sound fluently past the borders of the individual words, dissolving distinctions.

This is what I mean by the untrammeled, oceanic impulse of this novel – not a kind sweep of flowing waters which one might figure as stereotypically feminine – but an unceasing current of powerful change. This current respects no boundaries, whether between natural realms or between individual characters. Nor does it respect life, often stranding fish (*TW*, p. 166) or washing the substance from the earth (*TW*, p. 236). And though the narrative moves with the image of the girl rising from her bed, it is not a stereotypically feminine force we see in the interludes but what I would call an alternative version of action, a feminist combination of 'muscularity' (*TW*, p. 108) and flow. The boundaries that are muddied by its waters include the gendered roles that the lives of its characters also critique. Finally, the interludes carry a power that neither can be directed nor has its own direction, and so despite its warrior drums (*TW*, p. 75) cannot be approximated to the dynamic progress of the fascist call to arms.

We can hear the challenge of Woolf's narrative more clearly when we turn back to the pages of *Action* and the Mosley-Nicolson call for the corporate state. For example, while Nicolson might claim that the modern crisis might be traced back to the policies of 'our shabby grandfathers' who 'robbed this country of their sense of corporate purpose' by insisting on laissez-faire economics,[49] Mosley blames the current crisis on what he calls 'the rule of the old woman' which extends beyond economics and politics into the social life of the country.[50] The nation, according to Mosley, is 'hag-ridden', which means that there can be no forward movement, no efficiency, no discipline.

> Liberty of life in this country is thwarted at every turn by the omnipresent grandmother. Strength, efficiency, modernism in Government are excluded, however menacing the economic situation. But the nagging whining voice of the universal grandmother is ever at our elbow to thwart and to impede every natural impulse of man.[51]

The only solution is to hone the body and mind of the individual (man) into 'disciplined moderation or athleticism of life' placed in service to the state.[52] And while many New Party documents seem to accord a role to women members, by the end of 1931, and the end of *Action's* short-lived run, this disciplined athleticism, promoted in the New Party youth groups and in Mosley's thuggish entourage, was only a step away from the hyper-masculinity of the black shirts.

Mosley's embrace of para-military youth organizations after his defeat at the polls seems to have marked the turning point for many in their understanding of Mosley's fascist aspirations. John Strachey and several others among the founding members defected quickly in the fall of 1931. Nicolson ultimately followed suit, if only after accompanying Mosley on a trip to consult Mussolini. According to Nicolson's notebooks, Mussolini seems to have counseled Mosley not to try to import Italian militarism into Britain but to evolve his own home-grown fascism,[53] advice that would have stood Mosley in good stead had he heeded it. For it seems that the use of thugs at rallies and the para-military training urged on the young was to a great extent what disaffected his Labourite followers. At least to Nicolson, it didn't quite seem 'suited to England',[54] though he did his best to make it more so by suggesting to Mosley that the youth groups adopt grey flannels and white shirts as their uniforms.[55] The heightened emphasis on masculine power as directed towards accomplishing political action ultimately soured Nicolson on the entire concept of the corporate state, and he returned to the Labour Party, eventually becoming one of its most influential members.

Yet this all happens quite late in the game. In October Nicolson is still trying to mask the already severe disintegration of New Party consensus by shoring up its collective voice and empowering its proposals. 'We believe that the intelligence of man is capable of creating a modern State as organic as the human body. . . . A State in which energy and efficiency are always rewarded, and in which the bungler and the sluggard must go to the wall.'[56] What is most intriguing here is Nicolson's evocation of a firing squad as a mode for dealing with those incapable of the right sort of 'energy and efficiency'. Energy and efficiency are of course code words for masculinized, directed power that is harnessed to the goals of the state. As we remember, they are forces meant to combat the 'universal grandmother', who keeps the nation from moving forward as an organic, unified whole, forces, in other words, meant to prevent the dispersal or free flow of social energy associated with the feminine.

While Nicolson and Mosley never overtly express the violent, masculinist bent of their model of the corporate state, both of their wives react negatively to the New Party. Though Vita Sackville-West contributes a gardening column to *Action*, not once does it make any allusion to politics or Mosley's campaign. In fact, one must surmise that she produced it as an attempt to shore up the publication, not as an affirmation of its politics, for, as Nicolson's biographer notes, she mistrusted Mosley's motives and disliked him as a man.[57]

Cynthia Mosley's reaction is even more telling. As a self-described 'ardent Socialist'[58] and member of the House of Commons, Cynthia Mosley traveled to Russia in 1930, in order to meet with Trotsky. Nonetheless, she supported Oswald Mosley's resignation from the Labour Party and was one of the staunchest campaigners in the elections of 1930.[59] She ran as a New Party candidate and garnered a larger margin than did her husband. Yet after these efforts to launch the New Party she seems simply to have ceased all political activity. One of her last public speeches was at a Women's Peace Conference where she is reported to have said 'There is only one way that people could stop war – by refusing to fight', to which Nicolson responded: 'Poor C[ynthia] . . . She was not made for politics. She was made for society and the home.'[60] When she makes specific objection to the New Party's tendency toward fascism, reportedly telling Nicolson and Oswald Mosley that she wants 'to put a notice in the *Times* to the effect that she dissociates herself from [Oswald's] fascist tendencies', the two men assume it is a joke.[61]

A joke? Or sincere opposition to the increasingly ominous fascist rhetoric of the Mosley-Nicolson venture? That these men do not even engage with Cynthia Mosley's criticism, that they place it outside of sincere political or social commentary, despite her position as a twice-elected MP, demonstrates not only the misogynist dimensions of the New Party, but also its increasingly closed rhetorical world. While the opening issues of *Action* were open to all political perspectives, the final ones are not. Nicolson begins by claiming the paper not to be fascist; by its demise it openly proclaims its allegiance. And this allegiance is to the masculinist principle of VOLT: Vigor, Order, Loyalty, Triumph, on the way to the corporate state.

So if Nicolson admires the flux and flow of Woolf's 'masterpiece', he cannot yet heed its call. For, in its insistence on fragmentation-in-coherence, on free flow and cyclical progress, and especially on the forceful border crossings of feminist oceanic movement, *The Waves* undermines all that. Woolf's work runs determinedly counter to the onward rush of fascism, presenting an oppositional politics that resists the lure of the corporate state and that is prescient in its understanding of the danger of the fascist aesthetic. The gathering stages of fascism may produce rhythms, intonations, and oceanic feelings that hide its hard-booted political identity – but the waves of Woolf's novel, by moving according to another logic, uncover its masculinist, violent danger. The tone of *The Waves* has long been seen as highly aesthetic – its implications, however, are highly political.

9
Monstrous Conjugations: Images of Dictatorship in the Anti-Fascist Writings of Virginia and Leonard Woolf

Natania Rosenfeld

Old words

In her description of a masculinist novel in *A Room of One's Own*, Virginia Woolf complains of the shadow cast over its pages by the recurrent pronoun 'I'. The ego of the writer looms so large that all interest and all variety are obscured. There are no perspectives except those of the author and his male protagonist. The book is finally dull and unreadable.

In the 1930s, a similar shadow loomed over the lives of Virginia and Leonard Woolf, as it loomed over all Europe. It was the shadow of the authoritarian proclaiming his will. He had taken over and was dictating the narrative of European history. Other voices and other perspectives were squelched by his insistent 'I', which could only evoke an echo: the cry of misery Woolf transcribes in *Three Guineas* as 'Ay, ay, ay, ay' (*TGs*, p. 141). 'It is not a new cry', she writes, 'it is a very old cry.'

History was repeating itself, and repetition in history and language became a theme in both Woolfs' writings in the late 1930s. To disrupt the litanies of the patriarchs, reactionaries, and dictators became their necessary aim as writers. One tactic was derisive mimicry: Virginia Woolf describes the status quo of male dominion and capitalist greed as:

> the old tune which human nature, like a gramophone whose needle has stuck, is now grinding out with such disastrous unanimity[.] 'Here we go round the mulberry tree, the mulberry tree, the

mulberry tree. Give it all to me, all to me, all to me. Three hundred millions spent upon war.'

(TGs, p. 59)

Elsewhere in the same book, Woolf describes the female response to the word 'society', which 'sets tolling in memory the dismal bells of a harsh music: shall not, shall not, shall not' (*TGs*, p. 105). Leonard Woolf gives his 1935 analysis of fascist rhetoric, *Quack, Quack!*, a title which encompasses both repetition and nonsense, and uses repetitive nonsense words throughout the book to debunk Hitlerian incantation.

On the heels of this satirical mimicry, however, both Woolfs' writings of the late 1930s indicate their concern with finding an alternative to fascist discourse. As Hitler's territorial ambitions grew and his persecutions became more monstrous, satire must have seemed less efficacious. It was, after all, still an echo. Some new narrative, some entirely different voice, must be inserted between the Dictator's 'I' and the resultant universal wail of 'Ay, ay, ay, ay'; the authoritarian's solipsism had to be disrupted. Authorship needed to be reinvented along democratic lines, a new, more egalitarian relationship between author and audience had to be discovered. Virginia Woolf's last long work, the generically hybrid *Between the Acts*, represents such an attempt, as does Leonard Woolf's anti-realist political tract, *The War for Peace*, published in 1940. This essay will briefly examine the two satirical works, *Three Guineas* and *Quack, Quack!* before focusing on both Woolfs' attempts to recover language from the dictator's grasp and posit a new historical plot in *Between the Acts* and *The War for Peace*.

Words without meaning

In the 1930s, Virginia Woolf's letters and diaries are dotted with the complaint that the public life has permeated the private. Her reluctance to engage in discussions and activities which seemed to her not only peripheral to her real vocation but often futile as well is evident in her many complaints about committees on which she refuses to sit and organizations she would rather not join.[1] She pities the refugees she meets but has little to offer them; after meeting Sigmund Freud in January, 1939, she described the encounter thus:

> Difficult talk. . . . When we left he took up the stand What are you going to do? The English – war.

> . . . Freud said It would have been worse if you had not won the war. I said we often felt guilty – if we had failed, perhaps Hitler would not have been. No, he said, with great emphasis; he would have been infinitely worse. . . . A certain strain: all refugees are like gulls with their beaks out for possible crumbs. . . . The strain on us too of being benefactors.
>
> (*Diary 4*, p. 202)

Virginia clearly felt her sympathies being enlisted in a way she was inclined to resist. She uses the word 'strain' twice to describe the aura of the visit, as if to indicate a conflict of wills; and her use of pronouns is telling. By emphasizing the word 'you' in Freud's question she stresses the responsibility he places on the shoulders of his adoptive country, and, by implication, the power relations between Freuds and Woolfs: the latter voting citizens of a nation which can go to war, the former a family in flight, deprived of the rights of citizenship. Thus Virginia is drawn into a declaration of national allegiance she would probably have denied in another situation: 'we often felt guilty'. But what had she to do with the previous war when, as she so vehemently stated in her 1938 polemic *Three Guineas*, women neither make nor fight wars, nor do they possess nationality? It is Freud's own interpellation – 'What are you going to do?' – that forces the pronoun 'we' into her response before she has time to think about it.

Virginia Woolf's eschewal of the pronoun 'I' in favor of solidarity with the homeless and the disenfranchised – ' "I" rejected: "We" substituted. . . . "We" . . . all waifs & strays' (*Diary 5*, p. 135) – is often cited as the stance that dominates her work of the 1930s. In *Three Guineas*, she easily identifies herself as an outsider, excluded from the society men have constructed; yet she uneasily confronts her other identity, that of potential benefactress, witholding her guineas while the beaks clamor. The photographs her male correspondent has sent her face her with her responsibility, implying the complicitousness of inaction. In October, 1935, she wrote in her diary, 'Happily, uneducated & voteless, I am not responsible for the state of society' (*Diary 4*, p. 346), and this observation became the premise of her famous distinction in *Three Guineas* between patriarchal society, which excludes, and the Society of Outsiders, to consist of the excluded. The excluded are not responsible for the actions of the patriarchs. Yet the recognition that they are complicit if they remain silent compelled Virginia Woolf in the end to 'fight . . . for freedom without arms; [to] fight with the mind'.[2]

Fighting with the mind meant, of course, using words. The 'strain' between Woolf's continuing reluctance to engage and her sense of responsibility to 'fight . . . on the side of the English'[3] is linked to her misgivings about the use of words as weapons, and permeates her writing of the 1930s. She begins *Three Guineas* by admitting that she has dragged her feet for more than three years, and ends by stating that 'this letter would never have been written had you not asked for an answer to your own' (*TGs*, pp. 3, 144). The fictional letter from a gentleman thus plays the same role as Freud's interpellation: it demands an answer to the question, 'What are you going to do?' While doing, for Virginia Woolf, could only mean writing, she had moral hesitations about using words for political ends. Rhetoric and propaganda were the method of the enemy, of Hitler and Mussolini, and this awareness continually complicates her writing of the 1930s.

The primary question for both Woolfs was how to clear the slate of history, to begin again. In *Between the Acts*, Virginia posits a rewriting of Genesis which might redeem the world from bloodshed. Isa and Giles, at the end of the novel, become the new Adam and Eve whose first words constitute the start of Miss La Trobe's next composition. Leonard, too, uses a textual analogy with biblical resonances in his discussion of how to effect political change. In *The War for Peace* he writes,

> In history and all human affairs it is never possible to turn over a page and begin writing on an absolutely clean sheet of paper. Every page is blotted with the sins and stupidities of the fathers which are visited upon the children for generation after generation.[4]

In pursuing the recovery of an innocent, connective language, both Woolfs knew the odds were immense. They had to combat not only the ur-texts of oppression, all the major and minor propagandists for patriarchy and fascism, but also the nature of words themselves. Words define and differentiate; the moment of access to language is the moment when self is distinguished and other distanced with a label. It is this very distancing that tyrants and warmongers employ so effectively in their rhetorical constructions of the enemy.

Three Guineas becomes a proving-ground in the battle against such rhetoric. Woolf debunks old phrases and creates neologisms. She exposes the contradictions and intellectual weaknesses in the texts of men. At times she appears to become entangled by contradictory devices and even to employ the methods of the enemy. In Germany, too, books were being burned, neologisms created, old words eradicated. In a text that uses so many rhetorical devices to refute rhetoric, certain pitfalls are inevitable. While polemics differ in their method, and *Three Guineas* is distinguished by its irony and dexterity, the form could not ultimately satisfy a writer who was constantly searching for a wholly new genre. She returned to fiction in the late 1930s in the desire to find a way of communicating without symbols, which had become profoundly suspect; *Between the Acts* performs her quest for a language beyond representation – for words that might free instead of ensnaring.

In *Quack, Quack!*, Leonard Woolf links susceptibility to symbols to the fears that make primitive people turn to medicine men, and gave rise to the notion of divine kingship. In England today, he says, this manifests itself in 'the emotional attitude which the ordinary man is encouraged and expected to adopt towards the king and royal family, the ruling classes and "the flag" '.[5] In Germany, he perceives it in the hysteria with which the masses acclaim the Führer. The very word 'Führer' is invested with symbolic significance by Nazi rhetoric; literally translated, it merely means leader, a vague enough title, but for Hitler's followers, it had transcendent meaning. If he was their leader, then they were naturally followers, and the fixed categories were not to be questioned. Virginia Woolf, it is worth noting, unfixes them through a deliberate mistranslation at the culmination of her description of the dictator:

> [S]ome say, others deny, that [the dictator] is Man himself, the quintessence of virility, the perfect type of which all the others are imperfect adumbrations. . . . He is called in German and Italian Führer or Duce; in our own language Tyrant or Dictator.
>
> (*TGs*, p. 142)

Woolf's description is a portrait of a portrait, its gist that Hitler is no more than his own effigy. In *Quack, Quack!*, Leonard also focuses on the tyrant's physical self-representation in order to emphasize the artificiality and emptiness of his charisma. Leonard's aim is to shatter the mirror between the tyrant and his audience by questioning his use of symbols, the delusion he fosters that his stare, his medals, his raised hand, and his uniform possess magical powers. He begins with the tyrant's visual rhetoric in order finally to debunk his verbal rhetoric. Like Virginia, he purposely mistranslates: power, he explains, is nothing but exploited fear, just as the 'Führer' is not, in fact, a benevolent leader but a 'Tyrant', one who dictates.

The link between political dictatorship and verbal dictation characterizes fascism for both Woolfs. The dictator deprives his audience of the ability to respond, except through echo. Words' meanings are decided over their heads; there is no communication, there is only a sort of infernal catechism. 'The clamour,' Woolf writes in *Three Guineas*, 'the uproar . . . is such that we can hardly hear ourselves speak; it takes the words out of our mouths; it makes us say what we have not said' (*TGs*, p. 141). The dictator uses language not only to silence dissent, but also to mystify and obfuscate. What seems clear is in fact sheer nonsense: this is Leonard's thesis in *Quack, Quack!*

Yet the crowd also hears what it wants to believe, and it is the crowd's gullibility that the dictator cunningly exploits, by appealing to his audience's desire for certainty rather than their ability to comprehend subtleties. He is, Virginia Woolf might say, the consummate craftsman. Without referring explicitly to politics, Woolf debunked fascist discourse in a BBC lecture on April 20, 1937, entitled 'Craftsmanship'. The writer as craftsman, she maintains, is doubly a contradiction in terms:

> The English dictionary, to which we always turn in moments of dilemma, confirms us in our doubts. It says that the word 'craft' has two meanings; it means in the first place making useful objects out of solid matter. . . . In the second place, the word 'craft' means cajolery, cunning, deceit. Now we know little that is certain about words, but this we do know – words never make anything that is useful; and words are the only things that tell the truth and nothing but the truth. Therefore, to talk of craft in connection with words is to bring together two incongruous ideas, which if they can mate can only give birth to some monster fit for a glass case in a museum.[6]

From a woman who continually revised her own works, an argument against craftsmanship seems disingenuous. But the essay argues against the use of language as a means to an end. Woolf's aim is to unfix words, to insist on limits to the writer's or the speaker's control over them. Thus she even demotes the dictionary from its position of absolute authority to that of a text which 'confirms . . . doubts'. Words, Woolf goes on to say, cannot be used purposefully: first, because they are suggestive and protean instead of solid and fixed, then because they speak for themselves. To deny their autonomy is to produce a monster. It is a specific monster, too, very like the one that Woolf had described ten years before in *A Room of One's Own* when she wrote: 'Poetry ought to have a mother as well as a father. The Fascist poem, one may fear, will be a horrid little abortion' (*AROO*, p. 107).

Indicting the leftist poets of the Auden generation in 'The Leaning Tower', Woolf insists that they write too self-consciously. Their work, she maintains, is 'oratory, not poetry'.[7] No matter that Day Lewis, Spender, Auden and friends are all anti-fascists: their method is to preach instead of to engage their audience. The writer is making a point of himself, making a point of his point – he is attempting to convert. His product, too, is an abortion, though Woolf does not use the metaphor in this essay. But like the other literary abortions she discusses, it is the result of a travestied relationship: in this case, between writer and audience.

What all literary travesties have in common is the writer's denial of a vital element in the creative process: the autonomy of words themselves. Like the fascist, who denies the feminine and gives birth parthenogenetically,[8] the leaning tower poets ignore the needs and presence of the other. Invoking the sexual metaphor once again, one might say that they commit a rape rather than engaging in intercourse.[9]

What solution, then, does Woolf propose to writers whose social conscience prevents them from ignoring politics, at a time when politics have become unavoidable? The leaning tower poets' one virtue is the frankness they have learned 'with help from Dr. Freud', what she calls their 'unconsciousness'. The distinction she makes is implicitly one between private and public voices; thus, her own decision was to turn away from the more public form of the essay and back to fiction, for her the only intimate, and therefore the most honest, form of writing. While she knew and acknowledged that this was an escape from what was happening around her, she felt also that 'reality' had itself become fantastical. Fiction was a way to rectify the obscenity of 'the ravings, the strangled hysterical sobbing swearing ranting of Hitler', to counteract the radio's din of lies. 'Theres no getting at truth now all the loud speakers are contradicting each other', she wrote in November 1939. '[I]ts all bombast, this war', she wrote the following May. 'One old lady pinning on her cap has more reality' (*Diary 5*, p. 245, p. 285).

Thus Woolf returned to the old lady, whom she had invoked so many times before as an antidote to stultifying notions of literary realism. Mrs. Brown of the famous essay becomes Mrs. Swithin in *Between the Acts*. But the latter has a weakness that suggests a change in Woolf's attitude toward her own project. Maria DiBattista describes Mrs. Swithin as 'the incorrigible, perhaps anachronistic monist indigenous to Woolf's fictional world, a reminder of the effortless epiphanies – and certitudes – of the past'.[10] A potentially redemptive figure who falls short, Mrs. Swithin suggests the insufficiency of Woolf's traditional literary goal – a goal she still espoused in 1932 when she recommended to John Lehmann as his 'task . . . to find the relation between things that seem incompatible yet have a mysterious affinity, to absorb every experience that comes your way fearlessly and saturate it completely so that your poem is a whole, not a fragment'.[11] *Between the Acts* is a work that insists on its own fragmentedness, its disruptions and disjunctions, as inseparable from its moments of harmony. Thus Mrs. Swithin's 'one-making' is her limitation.

What makes Swithin ultimately questionable is her inability to resist authority in the form of patriarchal symbols. She wears a cross around her neck in a novel that invokes yokes, rings, and nooses as images of enslavement by convention, and whose subtext is biblical revision. 'How could she weight herself down by that sleek symbol?' William Dodge wonders. 'How stamp herself, so volatile, so vagrant, with that image?' (*BA*, p. 73). In rejecting the fiction of harmony Swithin represents, compromised as it is by her adherence to old gospels, Woolf paradoxically embraces an even purer fiction. It is Isa Oliver who articulates Woolf's desire for a restorative writing when she wishes for 'a new plot', even as Miss La Trobe begins to conceive her next work in 'words without meaning – wonderful words'. The language Woolf imagines and La Trobe engenders lacks verisimilitude: there are no objects behind its words. It is language used entirely without craft, and in it lies the only hope of a new plot for the world.

This idea of language is a consummately political conception, much as Woolf may have thought she was insulating herself from politics by returning to fiction. In casting La Trobe as the rewriter of Genesis, she was reconceiving international relations. Her project is echoed in more explicitly political terms in Leonard Woolf's tract, *The War for Peace*, published in 1940. The book is an argument against the Realpolitik which conceives of relations between people and states in terms of power rather than cooperation. Over and over Leonard attacks the terms used by the promoters of power politics, insisting that such words as 'realistic' and 'utopian' have no fixed meanings. Like Virginia, he sees history as a narrative shaped by the rhetoric of politicians. To undermine the power of such rhetoric, he employs a number of rhetorical devices of his own. One is to cast certain central terms in quotation marks, to question their accepted meanings:

> 'Realists' deride the view that there can be a harmony of interest among all nations in peace. But the whole history of Europe since 1815 makes it probable that the view is correct. It is true that at any particular moment, if the international system is based upon conflict

and the psychology of the majority of Europeans is nationalist, it may be to the immediate interest of a particular nation not to keep the peace. But for the realist to say that would be to beg the question. For by changing the system and psychology the interest of that nation might have been served far better by peace than war. That people, looking round Europe to-day, can refuse to change the word 'might' in the last sentence into 'would' reduces one to amazed despair.[12]

Leonard's emphasis, like Virginia's, is on diction as the molder of plot. Although Leonard does not go so far as to imagine a language without meaning, he echoes Virginia's insistence in 'Craftsmanship' on the protean character of words. A 'realist' means one thing to one person, another to the next. A change of tense could change the world order. And such change, Leonard insists, can and must be made by ordinary people: individuals must reclaim the historical narrative from the irresponsible leaders who impose upon the public a false notion of their 'interests'. Both Leonard's argument and his method are fundamentally anti-dictatorial. He attempts to engage his audience through a fiction, a fantasy about the future which, he claims, only they can make fact. Like the invisible author at the end of *Between the Acts*, who recedes into blank space just as the 'new plot' begins, he leaves the writing of that story to his readers.

The three emotions

Sigmund Freud, whose theories underlie much of both Woolfs' thinking about war and fascism in the 1930s, finds aggressive and erotic instincts battling beneath the consciousnesses of all human beings. *Between the Acts* dreams of a space between the two instincts, a lull in the fight. The deadlock of love and hate, and the impossibility of finding a solution that doesn't merely reverse the terms and re-start the cycle, are dramatized in *Between the Acts* by an episode critics fix upon. No single interpretation ever seems sufficient to comprehend the disturbing scene Giles Oliver stumbles on in the pageant's first intermission:

There, couched in the grass, curled in an olive-green ring, was a snake. Dead? No, choked with a toad in its mouth. The snake was unable to swallow; the toad was unable to die. A spasm made the ribs contract; blood oozed. It was birth the wrong way round – a monstrous inversion. So, raising his foot, he stamped on them. The mass crushed and slithered. The white canvas on his tennis shoes was bloodstained and sticky. But it was action. Action relieved him. He strode to the Barn, with blood on his shoes.

(BA, p. 99)

This strange image seems vastly overdetermined. In her diary entry of September 4, 1935, Woolf describes its original, and, without explanation, the profound, seemingly disproportionate psychological impact the sight had upon her:

> Oh how it pours! I used my umbrella . . . to cross the garden. Cant write today. I suppose after yesterday. Nessa in London. We saw a snake eating a toad: it had half the toad in, half out; gave a suck now & then. The toad slowly disappearing. L. poked its tail; the snake was sick of the crushed toad, & I dreamt of men committing suicide & cd. see the body shooting through the water.

(Diary 4, p. 338)

Virginia was often elliptical in her diary, and is especially so in this passage. The links between events are unclear: what happened 'yesterday' to keep her from writing 'today'? When and where did she see the snake and the toad? If yesterday, then her dream must have occurred that night. Or, by 'dream', did she mean 'fantasize'? Evidently, her vision of drowning men is connected both to the snake regurgitating the crushed toad and to the pouring rain in the garden. But there is a political backdrop, too, which surely plays into the psychological impression made by the snake and the toad. The diary entry begins with a brief description of the political atmosphere of the last two days:

> The most critical day since Aug 4th 1914. So the papers say. In London yesterday. Writings chalked up all over the walls. 'Dont fight for foreigners. Briton should mind her own business.' Then a circle with a symbol in it. Fascist propaganda, L. said.

(Diary 4, p. 337)

The day was critical because the Council at Geneva was trying to find means to stop Mussolini using force in Abyssinia. The question of isolationism or intervention was acute; Virginia at this time still favored isolation, along with such friends as Clive Bell, who insisted as late as 1938, in his pamphlet entitled *Warmongers*, that even a German invasion would be preferable to another world war. The dilemma was terrible, and images of a small entity being devoured by a larger might be applied to both possible solutions. On the one hand, there was Mussolini attempting to swallow up Abyssinia, and the necessity of going to war to stop such acts of engulfment. On the other, there was the threat that England itself might be sucked into another maelstrom, in which thousands of civilians as well as young men of military age might lose their lives. Hence, perhaps, the image of young men drowning.

The tension of watching 'helplessly and hopelessly' the rise of fascism and the approach of war resulted for Woolf in doubts about the efficacy of her own words. In her diary, she often describes her sense of the tininess of her enterprise in animal images which echo that of the toad and the snake. '[I]ts odd,' she writes on March 13, 1936, 'how near the guns have got to our private life again. I can quite distinctly see them & hear a roar, even though I go on, like a doomed mouse, nibbling at my daily page' (*Diary* 5, p. 17).[13] On May 24, 1938, she speculates that *Three Guineas* 'may be like a moth dancing over a bonfire – consumed in less than one second' (*Diary* 5, p. 142). And on August 19 she describes the experience of looking up at a German war plane, 'like a minnow at a roaring shark' (*Diary* 5, p. 312).

The question of how to rescue the toad occupied Virginia Woolf on two levels. There was her own position as a writer. Words themselves were being devoured and disgorged by the fascist serpent; how did one restore their innocence? How did one find a language to appeal not to love, not to hatred, but to the simple desire for peace? Words could do nothing, because words were part of what was being destroyed. In the end, England had to abandon her isolationist stance, and even Virginia Woolf had to concede, as she does in 'Thoughts on Peace in an Air Raid', that peace must be fought for – a paradoxical notion, tormenting to all those who despise war.

The complexity of the scene in which Giles destroys the snake and toad derives in part from its being an illustration of this very paradox. Giles is confronted by the quandary which occupied all England: to intervene, or to stand aside and watch. Either way, lives are lost. If the snake-toad scene can be seen as an articulation of Woolf's ambivalent feelings toward a national and personal dilemma in the late 1930s, it can also be read as a response to her husband's less ambivalent stance. In *The War for Peace*, Leonard expresses his 'sympathy with the pacifist view'. 'If you are on the side of civilization', he writes,

> you must be against the use of force. But that unfortunately does not settle the matter. In human affairs the choice is rarely between what is good and what is bad; it is usually between what is bad and what is worse.[14]

He goes on to cite an incident which proves the inefficacy of pacifism in certain situations:

> When I hear the pacifist arguing . . ., I am often reminded of something which I once saw in a Ceylon jungle. It was a pitilessly hot day. . . . I was traveling on foot in thick jungle. . . . Suddenly I saw upon a tree rather higher than the rest a group of monkeys. . . . They jumped up and down, up and down, up and down, always in the same place, raising their thin arms to heaven. And then . . . I heard a strange noise – click, click, click. The tracker behind me whispered: 'leopard'. . . . When a leopard sees monkeys on a tall tree, he lies down under it and clicks his teeth together. The monkeys, fascinated or hypnotized by the sound, begin to leap up and down with their arms raised to heaven above him until sooner or later one of them misses his footing and falls to the ground. He is eaten by the leopard. All my sympathies were, and are, with my collateral ancestor, the grey monkey, the pacifist, silhouetted against the sky with his thin arms raised, as it seemed to me, imploringly to heaven and protesting by non-resistance against the violence of jungle life. I crept round . . . and fired with a .303 British army rifle at the aggressor. It was a bad shot; there was a flash of yellow fur and the leopard had disappeared into the shadow. But it was force used against force and power against power, and the pacifists on the branch above my head scuttled away in safety. If they had been left to themselves . . . one at least of them would have died a violent death.[15]

The moral of this story, Leonard concludes, is that

> in so far as [the monkey's] near relation man has escaped from the life of the jungle, it has been by resisting force, not by the anarchic individualism of the lion or the tiger, but by establishing a communal law which forbids the use of force and controls the use of the individual's power and then places communal force behind the law.[16]

Well aware of the tragic absurdity of a war for peace, Leonard was also conscious that in certain situations, only violence can bring a new beginning. To this extent, he is himself a political realist. He argues for the use of force at the present moment so that the ideal of international cooperation, whose supposed 'utopianism' he ardently denies, can be realized when the enemy has been defeated.

As a Jew and a Socialist, Leonard could hardly concur with Clive Bell that even a Nazi invasion would be preferable to war.[17] As a political thinker, he advocated a reinstatement of the League of Nations along more efficacious lines, making a distinction between 'confederations' and 'federations'. The League of the future is to be a confederation consisting, presumably, of smaller federations of nations. Federations, he writes, would be much tighter alliances, and would be unnatural among nations run along entirely different principles. He uses a sexual metaphor to describe the impossibility of certain types of federation:

> It is . . . inconceivable that a dictatorship could be married successfully with a democracy in a federation; the marriage service might be read over them in a conference and treaty, just as you might read the marriage service over a dog and a cat, but in neither case would the union be real, permanent, or fertile. . . . It is a delusion to think that you could produce such political monstrosities as a federation of the Persia of Xerxes with the Athens of Themistocles or of the Spain of General Franco with the democracy of Switzerland and make them live. They would merely remain specimens in the museum of history.[18]

Here, again, is Virginia's image of the monster in a glass case. Leonard's monster, however, is not the fascist's spawn but the sexual alliance itself, in which two become one. His fascist-democratic marriage bears a striking resemblance to the 'olive green ring' of snake and toad in *Between the Acts*. Inevitably, the dictatorship would incorporate the democracy by force, like the tiger clicking its teeth until the monkey falls into its maw. Such obscene conjugations, Leonard suggests, must themselves be prevented. Failing prevention – and it is the fact that Hitler's gluttony might have been foreseen and prevented that Leonard continually bemoans – they need to be destroyed.

For Virginia, the question remained morally problematic, and *Between the Acts* dramatizes her incertitude. While readings casting Giles as a villain oversimplify, it is impossible to read him as a hero, either. He is, in a sense, one of the drowning young men in Virginia's dream: unable to stop the maelstrom, he flings himself in. But he seems aware, however dimly, that the old methods are no longer good. There is a spark of potential in Giles; he represents the young man Virginia Woolf pities and wants to nurture in 'Thoughts on Peace in an Air Raid', when she writes:

> We must help the young Englishmen to root out from themselves the love of medals and decorations. We must create more hon-

ourable activities for those who try to conquer in themselves their fighting instinct, their subconscious Hitlerism. We must compensate the man for the loss of his gun.[19]

To rescue her audience from their subconscious Hitlerism is Miss La Trobe's quest in *Between the Acts*. Like Woolf in and after *Three Guineas*, La Trobe is confronted with the difficulty of persuading without dictating. In her effort to unite her audience in a common vision, she fears mimicking the dictator's methods. The continual collapse of unity into dispersal among the audience, which to La Trobe feels like failure, is in fact a hopeful movement. Too much unity, as Woolf has already demonstrated in her image of the snake-toad, is dangerous.

Both Virginia and Leonard Woolf were ardent individualists. Only by maintaining the distinction between 'I' and 'you' could human beings, in their view, truly communicate. Empathy, so easily lost when self is distinguished from other, paradoxically also depends upon that boundary. Only respect for the other's differences leads one to prevent the other's suffering. Amorphous groups scapegoat the unassimilable. Virginia Woolf's last novel is dominated by a vision of solidarity founded upon individualism. Her stated intention to 'reject "I", substitute "we" ' does not mean an erasure of individuality. Instead, it denotes an authorial stance intended to be anti-authoritarian and communicative. This stance is embodied by Reverend Streatfield, who falters in his speech at the end of the pageant and refuses to proffer a definitive interpretation. La Trobe, while more talented than Streatfield, is also more ambivalent: at times she wishes to dictate, at others to withdraw. This very ambivalence, however, defines her achievement – an achievement dependent not solely on herself, but also on the cooperation of the audience and even of nature, as in this moment at the pageant's center:

> The view repeated in its own way what the tune was saying. The sun was sinking; the colours were merging; and the view was saying how after toil men rest from their labours; how coolness comes; reason prevails; and having unharnessed the team from the plow, neighbors dig in cottage gardens and lean over cottage gates.
>
> (*BA*, p. 134)

The synaesthesia which this description of peace and harmony initially suggests is belied by its emphasis on difference and boundaries. The view says what the tune says, but in its own language. Colors merge, but neighbors do not: their communication is defined by the gate. Unlike the national boundaries being so fiercely drawn and threatened as Woolf was writing, the gate can be opened or closed, according to the neighbors' need for privacy. Open or closed, it admits dialogue.

The first words[20]

Virginia Woolf's last novel ends with the possibility of renewed recognition between an 'I' and a 'you' which may, in turn, renew the world. Marriage is posited as a microcosm whose repair can renew the world. Miss La Trobe, indeed, becomes a kind of Creatrix in the final pages of *Between the Acts*. Sitting in her pub after the pageant, she fashions a new man and a new woman out of primeval mud: 'The mud became fertile. Words rose. . . . Words without meaning – wonderful words' (*BA*, p. 212). These words of La Trobe's become, in the book's last sentence, the deferred words of reconciliation between the protagonists. If Giles and Isa can begin again, their story will displace Genesis and even Darwin. But not until the war has been fought will the slate be wiped clean:

> Before they slept, they must fight; after they had fought, they would embrace. From that embrace another life might be born. But first they must fight, as the dog fox fights with the vixen, in the heart of darkness, in the fields of night.

> (*BA*, p. 219)

This is Woolf's concession that the war had to be, that only force could destroy force. It is also a statement of hope in the face of horror. Men and women, she says, have the ability to speak like neighbors across the garden gate, to engage in an intercourse defined by respect for difference. Marriage need not be an olive-green coil in which one ego incorporates the other, choking in the process. And if marriages between individuals are capable of redefinition, so are marriages – or, to use Leonard's term, confederations – between nations. But the first words must still be spoken.

Part III

Voices against Tyranny: Woolf among Other Writers

10

'Finding New Words and Creating New Methods': *Three Guineas* and *The Handmaid's Tale*

Maroula Joannou

In 1935 Virginia Woolf wrote to the organizers of an anti-fascist exhibition in London seeking assurances that this would include a section about the position of women under the Nazi regime in Germany. But feminist ideas had fallen out of favor with many anti-fascist intellectuals in Britain during the 1930s. Naomi Mitchison observed in *Left Review* that the very women who had started before the war as good little bourgeois feminists, determined to beat, or at least equal, men at their own game, had 'ceased to be militant feminists, ceased to regard men as enemies' after the vote had been won and had sometimes come to think of 'the economics of feminism as part of the general economics of possessor and possessed'.[1] As Johanna Alberti has put it,

> the very real threat to the lives of European opponents of Fascism and their children meant that the specific threat of Fascism to women assumed secondary importance for many feminists. Those feminists who worked with refugees, or called attention to the victims of Nazism, were unequivocally opposing Fascism but could also be distracted from Fascism's specific attack on women.[2]

By the mid-1930s there was little support in Britain for the proposition that resistance to fascism might take a gendered form. The reply that Woolf received from Elizabeth, Countess Bibesco was distinctly unhelpful, for Bibesco refused to see sexism as a part of the fascist programme, writing '. . . it had not occurred to me that in matters of ultimate importance even feminists could wish to segregate and label the sexes'.[3]

But Virginia Woolf, who had visited both Hitler's Germany and Mussolini's Italy, had become convinced of the necessity to establish an independent feminist opposition to fascism. Her classic anti-fascist treatise *Three Guineas* (1938),[4] is the product of much reflection on how men and why women are situated differently in relation to violence: 'scarcely a human being in the course of history has fallen to a woman's rifle' (*TGs*, p. 13). Although she never joined any anti-fascist organization, *Three Guineas* is also a meditation on how best women might collectively express their opposition to tyranny in all its manifestations, domestic, public, national and international, and irrespective of whether the 'iniquity of dictatorship' was to be found in 'Oxford or Cambridge, in Whitehall or Downing Street, against Jews or against women, in England, or in Germany, in Italy or in Spain' (*TGs*, p. 187).

I wish to analyse Virginia Woolf's importance as the inheritor and perpetuator of a cultural tradition that assumes the existence of a specific and highly polarized relationship between women as peace-makers and men as warmakers. According to the political theorist, Jean Bethke Elshtain, this cultural legacy is made up of socially fabricated and perpetuated myths and memories whereby men are deemed to 'fight as avatars of a nation's sanctioned violence' and and women 'to work and weep and sometimes protest within the frame of discursive practices that turn one out, militant mother and pacifist protestor alike, as the collective "other" to the male warrior'.[5] Elshtain has analysed how 'in time of war, real men and women – locked in a dense symbiosis, perceived as beings who have complementary needs and exemplify gender-specific virtues – take on, in cultural memory and narrative, the personas of Just Warriors and Beautiful Souls'.[6]

She contends that man is 'construed as violent, whether eagerly and inevitably or reluctantly and tragically; woman as nonviolent, offering succor and compassion'. Moreover, 'these tropes on the social identities of men and women, past and present, do not denote what men and women really are in time of war, but function instead to re-create and secure women's location as noncombatants and men as warriors'.[7]

In *Three Guineas* Virginia Woolf berates man, whether in uniform or not, for his bellicose attitudes, resolutely maintaining, in the face of much evidence to the contrary, including the disclaimers of prominent feminists with whom she corresponded after the publication of *Three Guineas*, that woman was by her nature non-combative in disposition

('But in my heart I find, it seems to me, such echoes of all the pride, vanity, and combativeness I ever see in men that I don't need to have it explained – I know.' Margaret, Lady Rhondda)[8]

For Virginia Woolf the differences between male and female behavior were not innate but socially constructed and she held the twin evils of fascism and war responsible for the extreme behavioral traits of both sexes which she detested ('manliness breeds womanlinesss – both so hateful').[9]

In *Three Guineas* she noted that:

> the nature of manhood and the nature of womanhood is frequently defined by both Italian and German Dictators. Both repeatedly insist that it is the nature of man and indeed the essence of manhood to fight. Hitler, for example, draws a distinction between a 'nation of pacifists and a nation of men'. Both repeatedly insist that it is the nature of womanhood to heal the wounds of the fighter.
>
> (*TGs*, pp. 326–7)

In a paper written for an American symposium on women, and published after her death as 'Thoughts on Peace in an Air Raid', Virginia Woolf argued that women were charged with a special responsibility to temper male aggression and belligerence: 'We must create more honourable activities for those who try to conquer in themselves their fighting instincts, their subconscious Hitlerism. We must compensate the man for the loss of his gun.'[10]

The intellectual tradition to which Virgina Woolf's impassioned defense of women's moral judgment would appear to belong is the tradition of 'feminine' moral reasoning which has been analyzed by the feminist philosopher Carol Gilligan. Gilligan has contended that women often approach moral issues differently from men because relationships, and particularly issues of dependency, are experienced differently by each of the sexes.

> For boys and men, separation and individuation are critically tied to gender identity since separation from the mother is essential to the development of masculinity. ... Since masculinity is defined through separation, while femininity is defined through attachment, male gender identity is threatened by intimacy while female gender identity is threatened by separation.[11]

Whereas men often see ethical questions in terms of abstractions or fixed principles, women 'not only define themselves in a context of human relationships but also judge themselves in terms of their ability to care',[12] valuing interdependence, relationships, and commonality: 'Thus it becomes clear why a morality of rights and noninterference may appear frightening to women in its potential justification of indifference and unconcern.'[13]

Although virtue in Virginia Woolf's scheme of things is generally equated with women, the female and feminine and that which is violent and/or vicious usually with men, the male and the masculine, she was aware that the positions of both men and women are much more complicated than such a schematization would suggest, and, on occasion, provides male characters who are not associated with militarism and aggression, for example, William Dodge in *Between the Acts*. She also intimates in her fiction that women may sometimes be complicit in imperialistic, militaristic, antisemitic, or pro-fascist behavior. Lady Bruton in *Mrs. Dalloway* is an enthusiastic supporter of the British imperial presence in India and some of the Pargiter women in *The Years* appear to be no less implicated in the history of empire than Abel Pargiter and his clubmen. Sara Pargiter also makes dismissive comments about the behavior of her Jewish neighbors in the same novel.

As a number of critics from Toril Moi onwards have argued,[14] there is in Woolf's writing an awareness of the metaphysical nature of gender identities and an attempt to deconstruct the binary oppositions of masculinity and femininity. This is in tension with the need for women to oppose war and the 'demands it made to be fought at least partially within the terms of the patriarchal discourse which created it'.[15] The historical responsibility for war is placed unhesitantly at the door of men: 'scarcely a human being in the course of history has fallen to a woman's rifle' (*TGs*, p. 11). But there is in Woolf's work a movement towards a redefinition of the terms 'masculine' and 'feminine' which takes place, as Gill Plain has observed,

> not along the traditional lines of gender, but along the boundary between power and the exclusion from power – in the terms of *Three Guineas*: the division between the patriarchy and the outsider, between those whose whole being promotes war and those whose whole being rejects it.[16]

Moreover, as Plain has put it, 'there is a sense in which *Three Guineas* strives towards a more flexible form, longing to pursue its ideas further, but sacrificing these desires to the overriding need to engage with the political issues of the threat of war'.[17]

Woolf's attitudes to sexual difference and to male and female behavior traits in *Three Guineas* may be usefully compared and contrasted to those in a much later work about women's relationship to totalitarian regimes, Margaret Atwood's *The Handmaid's Tale* (1986), a novel in which such fixities and oppositions are systematically contested and dissolved.

Atwood has argued that women both as characters in fiction and as human beings must be allowed to exhibit their imperfections:

> If I create a female character, I would like to be able to show her having the emotions all human beings have – hate, envy, spite, lust, anger and fear, as well as love, compassion, tolerance and joy – without having her pronounced a monster, a slur, or a bad example.[18]

Moreover, Atwood has objected strenuously to literary representations in which men 'have been seen as individuals, women merely as examples of a gender' arguing that 'perhaps it is time to take the capital "W" off woman'.[19]

As Susan Faludi has pointed out in *Backlash*,[20] there was an orchestrated backlash against women in the 1980s following the achievements of the women's liberation movement in the 1960s and 1970s. This was analogous to the anti-feminist backlash of the 1930s in many European countries, including France, Germany, Italy, Spain and Britain, where feminist ideas had been influential in the first two decades of the century but later appeared to be irrelevant to the organized struggle against fascism. While fascism strengthened the resolve of some feminists, it also deflected the energies of others away from specifically feminist work. The restitution of traditional gender demarcations was an important aspect of fascist ideology as it is in *The Handmaid's Tale* in which the women in Atwood's post-revolutionary dystopia suddenly find themselves forbidden to own bank accounts or to have paid employment. In Spain, Germany, and Italy the triumph of fascist ideas militated towards the removal of women from positions in the public sphere and their restoration to traditional domestic roles. The displacement of women from public life was one area in which fascism was generally acknowledged to present an obvious threat to the hard-won rights of women and in which protest was vocal and organized. This was widespread throughout Europe and was particularly marked in Hitler's Germany where, as Winifred Holtby observed, 'it was precisely because the women's movement had advanced so far under the Weimar Republic that its retrogression under Hitler struck observers as peculiarly significant'.[21]

Although the analogies between the anti-feminist political climate of the 1980s and the anti-feminist political climate of the 1930s should not be extended too far, *Three Guineas* and *The Handmaid's Tale* are both important feminist and anti-totalitarian interventions in the cultural politics of their respective day and each text will be analysed in the specific historical context out of which it emerged.

Any discussion of Margaret Atwood as the inheritor of Virginia Woolf's anti-totalitarian mantle must begin with the historical moment that *The Handmaid's Tale* mediates and interrogates; the ascendancy of economic, religious, and political fundamentalism in Britain and America represented by the election of Thatcher and Reagan and the revival of Islamic politics throughout the world after the Iranian revolution of 1979. As Edward Said has put it in *Culture and Imperialism*, 'this has been the age of Ayatollahs, in which a phalanx of guardians (Khomenei, the Pope, Margaret Thatcher) simplify and protect one or another creed, essence, primordial faith'. Said describes how 'one fundamentalism invidiously attacks the others in the name of sanity, freedom, and goodness'. He notes the appearance of 'an avalanche of images, writings and postures in the "West" underscoring the value of "our" Judeo-Christian (Western, liberal, democratic) heritage and the nefariousness, evil, cruelty, and immaturity of theirs (Islamic, Third World, etc)'.[22]

Although Atwood's opposition to totalitarian systems began in her adolescence ('I used to read Second World War stuff in the cellar when I was twelve or thirteen'),[23] it was given a new impetus by the international developments of the 1980s. In *The Handmaid's Tale* Atwood used the mode of speculative fiction in order to satirize the latent fundamentalism of American society, and the authoritarian direction in which much of the rest of the world appeared to be proceeding. The dangers and trends that *The Handmaid's Tale* dramatizes include the possibility of global destruction, the political triumph of totalitarian ideas, and the extermination of women's rights. In common with Virginia Woolf, who foresaw in *Three Guineas* the ultimate dangers of fascism and militarism, which she perceived as the logical consequences of the anti-feminist policies of her own day, Atwood feared imminent catastrophe if the trends she identified were not reversed. Addressing Amnesty International she argued that the author's responsibility to her public extended beyond her art, observing that 'placing politics and poetics in two watertight compartments is a luxury, and is possible only where luxuries abound'.[24] Like Woolf, who assiduously gathered information in her *Reading Notebooks* in the period between 1931 and 1937 as a basis for the anti-fascist arguments that she was later to make in *Three Guineas*, Atwood kept a file of press cuttings while she was writing *The Handmaid's Tale* 'to prove that there was nothing in Gilead that wasn't happening or hadn't happened, somewhere in the world'.[25]

Although much of Atwood's writing had hitherto been concerned with questions of Canadian identity, the setting of Gilead in *The Handmaid's Tale* is Massachusetts in the United States. The customs and observances of the theocracy are those associated with the American New Right, with Jerry Falwell's Moral Majority, and the charismatic American evangelists:

> I set it in the States because I couldn't fly it in Canada. . . . Because it is not a Canadian sort of thing to do. Canadians might do it after the States did it, in some sort of watered-down version. Our television evangelists are more paltry than yours. The States are more extreme in everything.[26]

Atwood's male-supremacist society is not merely a metaphorical equivalent for the society in which she lived but also a metonymic extension of it. Metonymic continuity and metaphoric distanciation separate the policies of the Commanders in *The Handmaid's Tale* from the policies advocated by the spokesmen of the American New Right.

The state of Gilead has come into being after a period of ecological disaster that has vindicated the worst fears expressed in the latter part of the twentieth century about the probable consequences of man's misuse of the earth's resources: 'The air got too full, once, of chemicals, rays, radiation, the water swarmed with toxic molecules' (*HT*, p. 122). Rivers have become contaminated, atomic power plants have exploded, mutant strains of syphilis have become rampant. But most disturbing of all is the widespread sterility that must ultimately threaten the survival of the human species. The sole function of the few surviving fertile women, the handmaids who are given the patronymic of their Commanders, is to give birth to children as surrogate mothers in place of the infertile wives of high-ranking men. However, the statistical probability of any of the handmaids giving birth to a baby without deformities is a mere one in four.

In their different ways both Woolf and Atwood are preoccupied with the pronatal policies of totalitarian states. The rewards conferred on women who bore large families and the reduction of women to their sexual and reproductive functions were important aspects of the fascist programme in Nazi Germany. In *Three Guineas* and her essay, 'Thoughts on Peace in an Air Raid', Virginia Woolf poses a feminist challenge to fascist ideology by reversing the usual equation between women and childbearing and contemplating women's refusal to become mothers: 'But if it were necessary, for the sake of humanity, for the peace of the world, that childbearing should be restricted, the maternal instinct subdued, women would attempt it.'[27] In Atwood's dystopia as in Nazi Germany, the handmaids are expected to produce as many children as possible to secure the victory of the state against its enemies. The Marxist slogan, 'from each according to his ability; to each according to his needs', has been expediently altered into 'from each according to her ability; to each according to his needs' (*HT*, p. 127). Like much else in Gilead the practice of surrogacy is authorized by literal quotation from the Old Testament and is based on the example of Rachel in the book of Genesis who used her maid, Bilah, to bear children for her husband, Jacob.

One of the most disturbing facets of Atwood's dystopia is the apparent ease with which the demands of feminists appear to have been incorporated into a male supremacist, anti-feminist agenda. Crimes of violence against women are treated with the utmost severity: rape is punishable by execution, pornography has been officially abolished – the Commanders have stockpiled it for their own use – and prostitution does not exist outside the state-controlled brothels frequented by men in high office. Women's bodies are not exploited and they need no longer submit to starvation diets or feel under any compulsion to wear revealing clothes or undergo plastic surgery in order to attract men. However, the state forbids women to read and denies women all rights as citizens. Moreover, as 'natural' childbirth is the only state-approved form of reproduction they are required to give birth without the benefits of technology. Atwood means to warn her readers against the dangers of allowing themselves to be lulled into a false sense of security merely because some of their demands appear to have been achieved. In an imaginary dialogue with her lost mother, who had been an active feminist in the 1970s, the hand-maid declaims, 'you wanted a women's culture. Well, now there is one. It isn't what you meant, but it exists' (*HT*, p. 137).

As there was an irony inherent in Hitler's Germany in the Nazis' successful mobilization of many conservative women to appear on public platforms to persuade other women that their proper place was in the home so, as the 'The Historical Notes' explain, in Gilead 'there were many women willing to serve as Aunts, either because of a genuine belief in what they called "traditional values", or for the benefits they might thereby acquire. When power is scarce, a little of it is tempting' (*HT*, p. 320). It is the Aunts who organize the Rachel and Leah Reeducation Centre and superintend the reinstatement of traditional gender precepts: 'For this there were many historical precedents; in fact no empire imposed by force or otherwise has ever been without this feature; control of the indigenous by members of their own group' (*HT*, p. 320).

One difficulty that must be addressed in relation to Atwood's feminism is her protagonist's apparent consent to, and dialogic interaction with, oppressive patriarchal systems. This is despite the celebrated declaration of the unnamed protagonist at the end of *Surfacing*, 'this above all, to refuse to be a victim'.[28] In *Feminist Dialogics: a Theory of Failed Community*, Dale Bauer has made use of Mikhail Bakhtin's idea of heteroglossia to show how the interplay of different voices within a novel produces that novel's linguistic community and has advocated a model for reading based on a feminist dialogics which attempts to 'read the woman's voice back into the dialogue in order to reconstruct the processes by which she was read out in the first place'.[29] The use of Bauer's model allows us to see how language in Atwood's dystopia becomes a site of contestation between those for whom it is a means of imposing conformity upon others and those for whom it is a means of resisting, subverting, and destabilizing authority.

Although the handmaids' voices have been officially stilled they have learned to whisper among themselves 'almost without sound' (*HT*, p. 14). Whispering becomes a potent mode of resistance: 'There is something powerful in the whispering of obscenities about those in power. There is something delightful about it, something naughty, secretive, forbidden, thrilling. It's like a spell, of sorts' (*HT*, p. 234). Whispering about the Aunts reduces them to size, deprives them of their pretensions and their dignity: 'Serena Joy, what a stupid name. It's like something you'd put on your hair, in the other time, the time before, to straighten it' (*HT*, p. 55). While the handmaid/narrator's inner commentary punctuates the text with many instances of dialogic resistance, ironic observations, and subversive humor, Moira is the more outspoken and outrageous in her use of spoken language: 'There is a hymn: There is a Balm in Gilead. "There is a bomb in Gilead", was what Moira used to call it' (*HT*, p. 230). ' "It doesn't do any good to talk like that" ', says the narrator when Moira suggests that the Aunts engage in forbidden sexual practices, 'feeling nevertheless the impulse to giggle' (*HT*, p. 234).

   Arguably, an example of what Atwood has identified as the figure of 'the solitary weeper' in literature ('that passive female victim to whom everything gets done and whose only activity is running away'),[30] the narrator appears to value her own physical survival above all else. Indeed, her greatest desire is 'to keep on living in any form' (*HT*, p. 298), to avoid the prospect of becoming a 'wingless angel', 'a doll hung up on the Wall' (*HT*, p. 298). 'Thinking', she explains, 'can hurt your chances, and I intend to last' (*HT*, p. 17). The fate that has befallen those dissidents close to her is the strongest deterrent against foolhardy action. She knows 'why the window only opens partly and why the glass in it is shatterproof' (*HT*, p. 17).

   The fate that has befallen other dissidents is the strongest deterrent against foolhardy action. The narrator's mother has been shipped off to the colonies to sweep up deadly toxins and Moira sentenced to a life of state-controlled prostitution. Another handmaid, Ofglen, decided that suicide was preferable when she saw the authorities coming to arrest her (*HT*, p. 297). The woman who had inscribed the motto 'don't let the bastards grind you down' had also taken her own life hanging herself from the hook on the closet door. 'Nole te bastardes carborundorum', reflects the handmaid/narrator. 'Fat lot of good it did her. Why fight?' (*HT*, p. 237). The only risks that she is prepared to take are in a sexual relationship: 'The fact is that I no longer want to escape, cross the border to freedom. I want to be here, with Nick, where I can get at him' (*HT*, p. 283). Even the fantasy of freedom evoked by Moira's dramatic escape and brazen defiance of the Aunts is vertiginous: 'Moira was like an elevator with open sides. She made us dizzy. Already we were losing the taste for freedom, already we were finding these walls secure' (*HT*, p. 143).

   The narrator of *The Handmaid's Tale* appears quiescent, inwardly mutinous but outwardly conforming, an example of Atwood's woman with the 'capital W removed'. She admits that her passivity had effectively amounted to collusion with totalitarianism: 'Ignoring isn't the same as ignorance, you have to work at it' (*HT*, p. 66). Although the warning signs had been plentiful she had taken no notice: 'There were stories in the newpapers, of course, corpses in ditches or the woods, bludgeoned to death or mutilated, interfered with as they used to say, but they were about other women, and the men who did such things were other men. None of them were the men we knew' (*HT*, p. 66). In contrast to her friend, Moira, the narrator confesses to having been fundamentally apolitical: 'There were marches, of course, a lot of women and some men. But they were smaller than you might have thought . . . I didn't go on any of the marches. Luke said it would be futile.' Her first concern was to protect her family, 'I had to think about them, my family, him and her' (*HT*, p. 189).

But as Barbara Rigney has observed, Atwood's concern for the survival of women is seen not merely in terms of the individual but also in terms of sisterhood. Furthermore, she points out that there is usually a sister-figure in Atwood's fiction, a secondary character, sometimes a confidante, who often aids the protagonist.[31] In *The Handmaid's Tale* this is the lesbian Moira. The handmaids are not officially permitted to form friendships but despite their differences in temperament the relationship between Moira and the narrator is very strong: 'We could fight and wrangle and name-call, but it didn't change anything underneath. She was still my oldest friend' (*HT*, p. 181). An avenging angel, who engineers the most brazen of escapes, Moira is all of the things that the narrator is not: 'I don't want her to be like me. Give in, go along, save her skin. That is what it comes down to. I want gallantry from her, swashbuckling, heroism, single-handed combat. Something I lack' (*HT*, p. 261).

Like Margaret Atwood, who observed that 'the place where all the little Nazis come out of the woodwork is more likely to be personal relationships',[32] Virginia Woolf insists on the interconnectedness of the public and the private worlds, 'the tyrannies and servilities of the one are the tyrannies and servilities of the other' (*TGs*, p. 258). Moreover, she finds beneath the overt script of male warmongering and bravado in the image of fascist man a submerged text of masculine anxiety based upon fear of disempowerment. The fascist soldier, whose erect posture and stiff, medallion-encased body she ridicules in *Three Guineas*, 'is called in German and Italian Führer or Duce; in our own language Tyrant or Dictator' (*TGs*, pp. 257–8). But his more familiar counterpart is the paterfamilias who refuses to have his authority challenged demanding total obedience in the domestic sphere.

The relationship between the rise of fascism in Germany during the inter-war period and the decline of the patriarchal family in European countries at this time was controversial. The research on the subject published by Horkheimer, Marcuse and others as *Studies on Authority and the Family* in 1936 was largely inconclusive. But Woolf confidently attributed the origins of fascist behavior to the power structures within the nuclear family, provocatively arguing that 'every family is essentially authoritarian because it is patriarchal, and every known society is also patriarchal, authoritarian, and ultimately war-like'.[33] According to this logic, the woman resisting tyrannical behavior in her home was 'fighting the Fascist or the Nazi as surely as those who fight him with arms in the limelight of publicity' (*TGs*, p. 98). *Three Guineas* extends the hand of sisterhood to the woman struggling to defeat the tyrant in her own home: 'Should we not help her to crush him in our own country before we ask her to help us to crush him abroad?' (*TGs*, p. 98).

In both *The Handmaid's Tale* and *Three Guineas* the importance attached to love distinguishes those who are in sympathy with autocratic regimes and those to whom such regimes are anathema. Margaret Atwood's Gilead is a society which permits no 'toeholds for love' (*HT*, p. 146), no opportunities for intimacy: ' "Love", said Aunt Lydia with distaste. "Don't let me catch you at it. No mooning and Juneing around here, girls." Wagging her finger at us. "Love is not the point" ' (*HT*, p. 232). But love is precisely the point for the narrator: 'Nobody ever dies from lack of sex. It's lack of love we die from' (*HT*, p. 113). In the *Antigone* of Sophocles, Antigone is prohibited from burying the brother she loves in the fashion decreed by the gods by the tyrant Creon, who speaks in the full authority of the patriarchal state. As Maria diBattista has noted, 'the state of war, civil or global, preempts or abrogates those rights in the name of that martial law whose basis necessarily resides in hating'.[34] But in opposition to the military ethos, Virginia Woolf cites with approval the words Antigone utters to Creon, 'tis not my nature to join in hating, but in loving' (*TGs*, p. 303). Moreover, Woolf presents Antigone as a feminist icon whose defiance of the tyrant removes her from the jurisdiction of her family thus transforming her so that she is seen to have the potential to become a full citizen.

Virginia Woolf argues that Antigone's example constitutes 'a far more profound statement of the duties of the individual to society than any of our sociologists can offer us' (*TGs*, p. 148). And in so doing she prefigures the appropriation of Antigone by contemporary feminist theorists such as Patricia Jagentowicz Mills, who has recently taken issue with Hegel's well-known interpretation of Antigone's behavior as paradigmic of ethical behavior within the family unit.[35] In the final analysis, the punishment which women defying patriarchal rule must be prepared to face is death. For Creon's words of warning to Antigone are unambiguous: 'Pass, then, to the world of the dead, and, if thou must needs love, love them. While I live, no woman shall rule me' (*TGs*, p. 303).

Despite what would appear objectively to be their white, middle-class, and socially privileged status, both Virginia Woolf and Margaret Atwood have insisted in designating themselves as 'outsiders' within their respective societies. Their self-descriptions may be understood in the context of what Susan Stanford Friedman has termed 'cultural narratives of relational positionality'.[36] These are narratives whereby situational identities and entities shift with a changing context dependent always on a point of reference so that 'power and power-lessness, privilege and oppression, move fluidly through the axes of race, ethnicity, gender, class and national origin'.[37] Such narratives can be understood differently according to the vantage point of their formation and function.

In Atwood's case the claim to 'outsider' status would appear to rest on her apprehension of her dual status as a Canadian citizen and as a woman: 'Women as well as Canadians have been colonized or have been the victims of cultural imperialism.'[38] Atwood contrasts herself to American feminists who are situated 'on the inside looking at each other, while I am on the outside . . . someone who understands my position would more likely be from a peripheral culture such as my own, someone from Scotland or the West Indies or a black feminist in the States'.[39] The figure of the outsider in *The Handmaid's Tale* is Moira, a radical feminist who had previously attempted 'to create Utopia by shutting herself up in a women-only enclave' (*HT*, p. 181). The equivalent of Virginia Woolf's 'Society of Outsiders' in Atwood's novel is the Underground Femaleroad to which Moira and her lesbian friends belong; and the importance of Moira in the narrative would seem to contradict Patricia Duncker's observation that 'this is white, middle-class fiction. No one is black, disabled, homosexual or unemployed.'[40]

Attempting to escape from Gilead Moira is conducted from one safe house to another belonging to people of all beliefs and none (*HT*, p. 259). It may be assumed that the courage of Moira, and of those who risked their lives to shelter those whom the regime has ostracized, is instrumental in bringing about the destruction of the theocracy. The 'Historical Notes' section of the novel makes it clear that Gilead no longer exists except as a historical phenomenon which is of academic curiosity to seekers of truth in the twenty-first century.

In *Three Guineas* Virginia Woolf argues that the courage of both the ordinary woman, Frau Pommer, arrested for protesting against anti-semitism (*TGs*, pp. 301–2), and the extraordinary woman, Antigone, is necessary to defeat fascism. Moreover, women must detach themselves from all patriarchal institutions and actively work to promote peace and freedom for the whole of humankind. To this end, Virginia Woolf proposed to inaugurate a 'Society of Outsiders'. In a departure from her practice of thinking back through the mother, membership of this society is restricted to 'the daughters of educated men working in their own class – how indeed can they work in any other?' (*TGs*, p. 193). The duties of the outsider are, in the first instance, couched largely in negatives; to refuse to fight, to refuse to make munitions or tend the wounded in wartime – tasks that Woolf admitted devolve largely on to working-class women – and to neither persuade nor dissuade her brothers from taking up arms but to maintain instead an attitude of complete indifference. The attitude of non-cooperation is to be based on the outsider's sense of the past exclusions suffered by members of her sex and class. 'Our country', she will say, 'throughout the greater part of its history has treated me as a slave; it has denied me education or any share of its possessions' (*TGs*, p. 197). But positive actions must follow: the outsider would bind herself to earn her own living, to seek entry into the professions, to question their patriarchal ethos, and to insist on their adoption of ethical behavior. Although many of the ideas that Woolf proposes in relation to the Society of Outsiders appeared revolutionary at the time – 'By nature, both Vita and I were explorers, revolutionists, reformers'[41] – they prefigured ideas which were to be widely disseminated during the Second Wave of Feminism in the 1960s and 1970s. Such ideas included opposition to hierarchies, the quest for new ways of working (including job-sharing and wages for housework), the commitment to ethical investments and to fostering non-exclusive and non-discriminatory corporate practices. But perhaps the most important legacy to feminists of a later generation in *Three Guineas* is the idea that for women international responsibilities must override all national allegiances, 'as a woman, I have no country. As a woman I want no country. As a woman my country is the whole world' (*TGs*, p. 197).

It is a condition of membership that the outsider must vow to 'make no part of any claque or audience that encourages war; to absent herself from . . . all such ceremonies as encourage the desire to impose "our" civilization or "our" dominion upon other people' (*TGs*, p. 198). *The Handmaid's Tale* provides many pointed examples of the orchestration of public occasions for the purposes of state indoctrination beginning with ritualistic insemination of the handmaid by her Commander. These include the prayavaganza with its semantic linkage of prayer and extravaganza, the salvaging when political dissidents are publicly put to death, the atavistic collective rope ceremony suggested by an English village custom of the seventeenth century.

At one level, Atwood's attitude to feminism appears relatively straightforward: 'No one who observes society can fail to make observations which are feminist. That is just based on real-life commonsense.'[42] But at another her success in 'evading the pigeonholers', her strenuous resistance to any attempt to place her in any feminist straitjacket, has left some feminists dissatisfied. Asked 'Are you a feminist or aren't you a feminist?' Atwood chose to say the same thing as she 'would say about any political movement, namely, something that has immeasurably improved the lives of a great number of people has to be a good thing'.[43] But, as Jill Bihan has pointed out, 'in refusing to overtly align herself with the women's movement, Atwood has been seen as a reactionary artist, separating her art from her politics and undermining solidarity'.[44]

Virginia Woolf too exhibited some of the ambivalence to organized feminism which accounts for her troubled relationship to the women's movement of her day. *Three Guineas*, for all its inspirational qualities as a treatise on the unique role that women have to play in the defeat of fascism, is also, somewhat surprisingly, the book in which Virginia Woolf engages in a symbolic act of arson. As feminism is consigned to the flames the restrictive definition of feminism (as that which is synonymous with the rights for women) is also destroyed. The 'only right', Woolf wrote, deliberately inviting controversy, 'the right to earn a living, has been won' (*TGs*, p. 184). But Woolf is not severing her links with the past but publicly acknowedging intellectual debts and recognizing important continuities. Thus she draws attention to the courage of her feminist foremothers involved in the nineteenth-century battles to secure higher education for women and to safeguard the civic rights of prostitutes in Victorian England. These women were 'fighting the tyranny of the patriarchal state as you are fighting the tyranny of the Fascist state', and 'we are merely carrying on the same fight that our mothers and grandmothers fought' (*TGs*, p. 186).

Just as Virginia Woolf's description of Victorian feminists, 'those queer dead women in their poke bonnet and shawls' (*TGs*, p. 185), made their foremothers appear strangely antiquated to the first readers of *Three Guineas*, so the 'wiry, spunky' (*HT*, p. 130) feminist militancy of her mother's generation comes to seem curiously outdated to the handmaid/narrator of *The Handmaid's Tale*. But the narrator is identified as part of an anti-feminist backlash by her mother who reminds her how hard women had had to fight in the 1960s and 1970s to achieve the very freedoms that their daughters were to take for granted: ' "As for you", she'd say to me, "you're just a backlash. Flash in the pan. History will absolve me. . . . You young people don't appreciate things", she'd say. "You don't know what we had to go through, just to get you where you are." ' (*HT*, p. 131).

Like Virginia Woolf, Margaret Atwood is a reluctant feminist who argues that feminism cannot encompass all her aims and aspirations many of which she prefers to identify as humanist rather than feminist.

> 'Feminist' is to me an adjective that does not enclose one. It's not enough merely to say that someone is a feminist . . . I would not deny the adjective, but I don't consider it inclusive. There are many other interests of mine that I wouldn't want the adjective to exclude.[45]

Woolf appears to make no distinction between feminism and humanism:

> 'Our claim was no claim of women's rights only': – it is Josephine Butler who speaks – 'it was larger and deeper: it was a claim for the rights of all – all men and women – to the respect in their persons of the great principles of Justice and Equality and Liberty.'
>
> (*TGs*, p. 185)

As Sybil Oldfield noted, for Woolf, 'Fascist anti-feminism was simply Fascist anti-humanism, only applied to women.'[46]

Indeed, one might say of Atwood, whose imaginative writing is at once indebted to, and deliberately distanced from, the women's liberation movement of the 1960s and 1970s, what Alexander Zwerdling has said of Woolf, that her 'contribution to the woman's movement was to restore a sense of the complexity of the issues after the radical simplification that had seemed necessary for political action'.[47] Virginia Woolf's own words describe how women can best contribute to the struggle against militarism and the seductive power of fascist ideology, 'we can best help you to prevent war not by repeating your words and following your methods but by finding new words and creating new methods' (*TGs*, p. 260). As Gill Plain has put it, 'the textual practice of *Three Guineas* sat uncomfortably on Woolf's politics – or perhaps her politics settled uncomfortably on her textual practice'.[48] The irony is that the 'new words' and 'new methods' that Woolf so eloquently advocated in *Three Guineas* are less evident in the anti-war polemic itself than in the formal and stylistic innovation of the novels which preceded it.

11

Seduced by Fascism: Benedetta Cappa Marinetti, the Woman Who Did Not Write *Three Guineas*

Lia Giachero

For someone like me, a foreigner, English neither of mother tongue nor of education, to study Virginia Woolf (above all her essays) must be considered something of a challenge. She was really so English. It therefore follows that to study her biographical and artistic progress means to bear in mind all the things that, for those born in England, form an integral part of the everyday fabric of life, but which we foreigners have to look up in books. Typical things spring to mind: the Victorian age, Oxford and Cambridge, the conscientious objectors during the First World War, the Fabian Society, gossip over the tea-cups, Shakespeare and the Brontës, the feeling of London as it was then. In fact taking up the challenge of putting yourself in other people's shoes is an extremely salutary exercise in terms of getting to know yourself. In my efforts to understand the nature of the country where Virginia Woolf lived, I learned to understand my own country, Italy, better.

Seen from this point of view, *A Room of One's Own* and *Three Guineas* are obviously of particular interest. It would have been inconceivable to imagine two such works being written in Italy in the third and fourth decades of this century, not because it was impossible to talk about pacifism in 1938 (although in fact it was) or to talk about women's rights in 1929 (a few people were managing to do so[1]), but because there was no Virginia Woolf to write them. There were women political thinkers, both fascist and non-fascist (the latter reduced more or less to silence), and there were also women writers and journalists. However, there was no great and revered novelist, skilled in expressing her opinions, in the political and social fields too, sometimes stirring up wasps' nests, but nevertheless opinions which are still quoted and discussed today. There were some writers later, there are some today, but then there was no one.[2]

To understand why this was so is a task for historical, literary, and sociological research and is certainly too long to tackle in this chapter. What I would like to say here is how maddening I always found it not to be capable of enabling Virginia Woolf to talk to an Italian fellow writer. This feeling gave me the sensation that there was an unbridgeable gap between her country and mine for which fascism was only partly to blame. But my frustration was transformed into excitement after reading the 'Editorial Comment on Woolf and Fascism' on the *Virgina Woolf Miscellany* (Fall, 1994) in which Merry Pawlowski quotes Maria-Antonietta Macciocchi when she speaks about the necessity to understand why there were women fascists.[3] Why then shouldn't we allow Virginia Woolf to talk to an Italian woman contemporary, militant in the opposite camp to hers as far as feminism and pacifism were concerned? Why not read what this person wrote and compare it with *A Room of One's Own* and *Three Guineas*?

It seems to me that the most suitable candidate for this dialogue is Benedetta Cappa, wife of Filippo Tommaso Marinetti, founder of futurism, futurist herself, not particularly famous, but without doubt of extreme interest. If Virginia Woolf had met her – beautiful, elegant and confident as Benedetta[4] was – she would, I believe, have detested her. This makes the comparison even more interesting.

According to Vanessa Bell 'comparisons are the easiest form of criticism',[5] but we have to bear in mind that, just because it is so easy, it risks being used even when it is inappropriate. It is not so in this case. In fact, even though Woolf and Benedetta were different in nationality, character, and ideals, they were both women of the same generation,[6] they both lived a conventional life with a tendency towards eccentricity, they were both married to men with strong personalities, but, above all, they both wrote and not only fiction.

The literary production of Benedetta, who was also a painter,[7] is very limited. She could not in fact be considered a professional writer: she did not earn her living by her writing and she left us only three novels and a handful of articles and brief essays. The three novels[8] are extremely experimental. The writer seeks new ways of expression different from those of traditional narrative (and, by the way, different to those used by Virginia Woolf). They range from theatrical dialogues, the recounting of dreams, the use of illustration as a graphic transcription of the essence of the feelings of the characters. Then there are the aesthetic essays where Benedetta justifies her work both as a painter and as a writer. There are also political articles which are authentic propaganda for the fascist regime.

Total dichotomy therefore: the soul of an avant-garde artist and the everyday life of a woman of the New Order – a situation not all that rare in that kingdom of contradiction which was fascist Italy. Benedetta is therefore ideal for playing the game of opposites with Virginia Woolf. One is a professional writer for whom her writing has priority over everything else, the other a hostess, wife, mother of three daughters and part-time artist; carelessly beautiful Virginia, elegant and well-groomed Benedetta; the Englishwoman always at odds with whatever remained of the patriarchal system in the society of her times, the Italian supporter of a regime and way of life dedicated to the most extreme form of male chauvinism. 'Progetto futurista di reclutamento per la prossima guerra' (1932)[9] and *Donne della Patria in guerra* (1942)[10] are the two works by Benedetta which I found most suitable for comparative reading.

As I have already mentioned, Benedetta was a futurist by her own choice, not just because she was married to Marinetti. All the futurists shared in full the passion for experimentation, the taste for provocation, and a love of categorical statements. It is in this light that the 'Progetto futurista di reclutamento per la prossima guerra' should be read. It is a brief but significant article which came out on October 2, 1932, in issue n.4 of the weekly *Futurismo*. Since it is so short it can be quoted almost in full.

> Bisogna rovesciare il sistema della leva militare facendola partire dalle classi sessantenni o cinquantenni. Seguiranno le quarantenni e le trentenni. Questa leva futurista ha per vantaggi principali:
>
> 1. Conservare per il dopo guerra della patria vittoriosa il maggior numero di giovani e conseguentemente annullare la crisi dei giovani combattenti spostati. Supponendo . . . che la guerra futura distrugga tutti i combattenti delle prime classi mobilitate resteranno alla Patria tutti i giovani.
>
> 2. Valorizzare patriotticamente i vecchi offrendo loro una morte utile e gloriosa sul campo di battaglia . . . Tanto più che la guerra futura . . . non esigerà . . . sforzi muscolari . . ., mentre esigerà il coragio cosciente dell'uomo vissuto.
>
> 3. Riservare le classi giovani per l'urto finale . . . quando gli eserciti sono esauriti . . .
>
> 4. Eliminare il problema della gelosia dei giovani al fronte e delle loro donne insidiate dai quarantenni e cinquantenni rimasti nelle città. Nasceranno molti più figli alla Patria e in fatto di donne sole non rimarranno che le non più giovani.[11]

Benedetta's proposal must have struck the readers of *Futurismo* who hastened to send their opinions which were duly published. As a result, two months after the publication of 'Progetto', Benedetta wrote a reply to her readers,[12] responding to their objections 'd'indole militare e morale'.[13] She also tackled, albeit briefly, the question of a women's army saying, 'sono lieta di credere che tutte le donne saranno fiere di collaborare in guerra come collaborano in pace (nella famiglia e nella società) alla grandezza della patria',[14] and declaring her hope that, in time of war, and once she had finished bringing up her children, she herself would be part of the first contingent to be called up. This was certainly a long way from the thoughtful, disenchanted, and disconsolate reflections of Woolf writing about the risk of conflict in *Three Guineas*. Benedetta speaks through paradoxes; her message is hidden between the lines. She has no wish to make us reflect, but to provoke our reaction, maybe of indignation or even scandal. It was thus, in fact, that futurism behaved during its political phase[15] with the aim of shaking up the Italian bourgeois and provincial society, still held in thrall by the nineteenth century. The form and style of writing are, therefore, not comparable to those used by Virginia Woolf. But Benedetta too is a woman who talks about war and it is on this that it is interesting to reflect here. There is no trace in 'Progetto' of the lack of familiarity with weapons and death that for Woolf is typically feminine and about which she wrote: 'Scarcely a human being in the course of history has fallen to a woman's rifle; the vast majority of birds and beasts have been killed by you, not by us.'[16]

On the other hand Benedetta speaks calmly about the 'prossima guerra'[17] as if it were a fact. She reasons like a man, or rather like a woman used to considering it a virtue to feel like a man. This was certainly one of the great limitations of the futurist women. They had a genuine desire to revolutionize the way of living (and not only from a cultural point of view) of a country that, in many ways, was still provincial, but, at the same time, they lacked a social and political conscience strong enough to promote constructive action. The decision to be active in the Marinetti movement was usually personal and not political and sprang from their feeling ill at ease within the traditional feminine roles. This was because of their courage, defiance, and creativity, which were gifts considered typically virile. They probably never asked themselves to what extent other women were different. For many, certainly, their involvement was fleeting and not a way of life. Many futurist women worked under a pseudonym and then there were others who, like Benedetta, managed to reconcile belonging to an anti-conformist avant-garde movement with marriage[18] and the bringing up of children.[19] Therefore, while we may well expect unconventionality, creativity, and intelligence from the futurist women, it does not necessarily follow that we shall also find feminist awareness or class consciousness. If futurist women have barely made any impact on Italian culture, it is no coincidence that the effect they had on customs of the day was virtually non-existent. Nothing to be compared to Mary Quant, not to mention Emmeline Pankhurst.

It is therefore not to be wondered at that the consideration that Benedetta demonstrates that she has of the idea of her Motherland, the same Motherland which, according to Woolf, woman has never had, since it has treated her 'as a slave', by denying her 'education or any share in its possessions'.[20] For the benefit of this Motherland – this is the conclusion reached in 'Progetto' – Benedetta hopes to see the birth of many more sons, a desire shared by Mussolini, even if perhaps she has some reservations regarding his famous motto 'La guerra sta all'uomo come la maternità sta alla donna',[21] given that she seems to have no particular objection to the idea of a female army.[22]

It is worth noting that, if Benedetta does not speak about war as a woman, that is with the awareness of the terrible price paid not only by people in the trenches but by everybody concerned, neither does her final mention of maternity seem written by a woman, expressed as it is with the brisk detachment associated chiefly with the writing of a man. But this is not the only time that she has tackled this subject. On other occasions she expressed herself in these terms:

> La donna italiana non è, non sarà mai una concorrente dell'uomo. Ella è troppo essenzialmente madre. Quando si dice madre bisogna dare alla parola il suo grande significato di generatrice; generatrice di uomini, di sentimenti, di passioni, di idee.
> ('Spiritualità della donna italiana', 1935)[23]

> Poiché dal fascismo abbiamo avuto il dono di essere state poste spiritualmente al vertice della vita, poiché venne potenziata la famiglia unita e indissolubile, poiché facendoci fiorire dall'istinto della razza fummo benedette madri e la maternità è favorita e protetta . . .
> ('Spiritualità della donna italiana', second version, 1941)[24]

> Nel nostro cuore di mamma quando si materializzava la vita nuova del nostro figlio ed egli era per noi la primavera del mondo, gli donammo il nostro pensiero, il nostro sogno, il nostro volere,

perché fosse ricco di bontà umana . . . perché in lui fosse chiara l'intelligenza luce alla fatica quotidiana; perché possedesse la forza che difende e crea . . . serenamente accettammo che la nostra carne si lacerasse purché fossero risparmiate al figlio nostro ferite alla sua carne, ma anche e forse di più perché il suo corpo sapesse contenere l'offerta del sacrificio per ubbidire alla legge d'amore della vita.

(*Volontà italiana*, 1944)[25]

The change of style between a provocatory article such as the 'Progetto' and the three examples of propaganda just quoted is evident. The person who wrote 'Spiritualità della donna italiana' and *Volontà italiana* is obviously a woman and, moreover, a woman who wishes to be recognized as such, not only because she speaks firsthand about maternity, but because of the emotional intensity with which she approaches the argument. It is a way of writing bent on capturing the sympathy of men who cannot help but approve of a woman who speaks of her *natural destiny* with such passion.

Quite another thing is the reflection of Virginia Woolf that we read in *Three Guineas*. The intimate link between the oppression of women and oppression tout-court did not escape her, aware as she was of how the government's policy towards women, including the laws on motherhood, were an excellent bench-mark for evaluating its degree of democracy. It is a pity that Woolf, having taken the difficult and painful decision to deny herself motherhood, never had the chance to write anything about it firsthand.

As everybody knows, Mussolini gave prime importance to the increase of the Italian population, apparently without being aware of some fundamental practical problems. The 'prolific mothers' that he admired so much were forced by necessity to spend their time looking after their children, but money was needed to bring these children up and often one salary was not enough.[26] The mothers were therefore obliged to work outside the home, thus, according to the regime, depriving their children of their time and men of jobs. These men, however, had more difficulties than their wives in finding jobs because factory owners preferred to take lower paid[27] women workers. To remedy this, women were systematically discouraged from working – and not only through the reduction of pay – without, however, raising the salaries of the men to meet the cost of living. Result: the demographic policy never gave the results hoped for by Mussolini.

There is no trace of any of this in the writings of Benedetta because the question did not interest her. The fact of living in a regime which had suppressed the freedom of the press and of expression had relatively little importance because there were women social reformers who tried as best they could to make their voices heard even during the 20 years in question.[28] On the other hand the question of women's professions, key point of the feminist thinking of Woolf, did not interest her either. It is impossible to understand from the political works of Benedetta that they were written by a person who had formed part of an avant-garde movement such as futurism. In fact there are almost no references to her artistic works, which she, however, did not disown and which she defended vigorously when, as on at least one occasion, they were accused of immorality.[29]

With the exception of Gararà, who is an allegorical figure, the characters in her novels could, in effect, be accused of being decidedly out of step with the times. Luciana (*Le forze umane*) is a girl who wonders about the sense of existence and discovers it not within the family, not at work, not in love, but in art. Astra (*Astra e il sottomarino*) reveals, in a soliloquy on the last pages of the book, that her flesh 'sa tradire ma non attendere'[30] and proclaims in verse:

> Voglio la voce che sveglia echi nelle valli
> folte del piacere
> del calore per correggere il freddo degli spazi,
> del sangue per colorare gli orizzonti
> della passione per popolare la vita.[31]

They are two strong women, different from the female stereotype beloved by the regime, by the church and by a certain type of light literature, but also a long way from the everyday life of Benedetta or the models that she proposes in her political writings.

The collection of women-symbols that she presents in *Donne della Patria in guerra*, will suffice as an example. For this lecture, with which she toured Italy in 1942, Benedetta does not create a sister of Dante, to complete the diptych with the Woolfian Judith Shakespeare in Chapter III of *A Room of One's Own*, neither does she tell the story of the lives of women compelled to sacrifice their creativity because the times did not allow them to express themselves. Instead, she shows us a gallery of women amongst those who, 'quando gli eventi lo esigono',[32] can extract: 'dalla fragile persona una forza di passione e di eroismo che centuplica il vigore fisico, irradia un'influenza decisiva, rende l'intelligenza visione, gli atti d'amore prodigio'.[33]

Not surprisingly the first two which are presented to our attention are two saints, Chiara d'Assisi and Caterina da Siena. Naturally, given the fact that in 1942, Italy was in the middle of the Second World War, she chose to highlight the combative spirit of the latter rather than the mysticism of the former. She continues with Anita Garibaldi, the only well-known figure among the three wives of the *Eroe dei Due Mondi*, she who, a foreigner (she was South American), was prepared to die for the unity of Italy. Then comes Ines Donati, a sort of Joan of Arc of the first fascist period, who died of tuberculosis in 1924 and was buried, in 1933, in the fascist martyr chapel in the Cemetery of Verano. When writing about Ines, Benedetta forgets to mention the initial hostility of the regime, which was, as always, suspicious of a young woman who seemed to be too uninhibited.

'La vita è se non perché si possa offrirla alla Patria':[34] if this is true for Ines, it is equally so for the anonymous mother of the fighter, who is the final figure of this parade of women-symbols. She is a figure drawn intentionally without features, who can belong to whatever social class and ready to 'salire attraverso la solitudine di un dolore implacabile a sostare nella fierezza più grande'.[35]

The second part of the lecture is a call to Italian women, who one presumes galvanized by the innumeration of so many examples, to keep faith and to contribute their share to the battles raging at the front through their sacrifice in their daily life.

Fortunately, wars are not won through rhetoric, otherwise, perhaps, the Nazi-fascists might have succeeded. Instead, between 1943 and 1945, Benedetta sees the collapse of the regime, the death of her husband and the dramatic worsening of her economic situation. Her life after the war was lived in silence. She decided not to write and not to paint any more because she considered that the futurist period had come to an end. Years would pass before Italian culture realized that closing the doors on the fascist past did not necessarily mean denigrating the interesting results obtained by futurism in the artistic fields. Before dying in 1977 Benedetta would, however, be in time to see herself reinstated as an artist.

Studying her today is a challenge, because it means understanding how an intelligent woman like her failed to understand what a contradiction there was between her artistic and political choices. And yet, one would say that she, through exalting motherhood, but specifying, at the same time, that one could be mother both of men and of ideas, deluded herself that she could reconcile the two extremes.

In Chapter VI of *A Room of One's Own* Virginia Woolf writes of 'abortion' as the image of art in fascist Italy: 'The Fascist poem, one may fear, will be a horrid little abortion such as one sees in a glass jar in the musem of some county town. Such monsters never live long . . . Two heads on one body do not make for length of life.'[36]

If we may borrow this image for a moment it comes naturally to ask ourselves whether Benedetta should be considered a monster with two heads. Certainly all her works have a certain dichotomy that is in terms of the conflict spirit/matter. From *Le forze umane*, her first novel, in which the young main character seeks to reconcile daily life with the thirst for the absolute, to the last paintings, such as *Il monte Tabor*,[37] in which the artistic inspiration borders on mysticism, there is always a dialectic relationship between two components. These may be the violence of the water and the solidity of the rocks, as in *Ritmi di rocce e mare*,[38] or else the desolation of the desert and the animation of a modern city, such as in *Il grande X*,[39] or inertia and creativity, as in the novel *Viaggio di Gararà*, or love and the absolute, as in her last book *Astra e il sottomarino*. In these works it is the spirit that triumphs, but in day-to-day life, where the regime must be revered, conventions must be respected and the role of the wife of an academician[40] is played to the utmost, no: Benedetta is condemned to a double life.

On the other hand, Woolf, too, had two heads, one healthy, which she used to write her novels, and one flawed, which spoke to her with the voice of madness. Sometimes you have the sensation that there has always been an abyss ready to engulf women who stray from the path of convention, as soon as they put a foot wrong.

Benedetta embraced the fascist creed with the same defiance and impetuosity which served her to enter the futurist movement; the same passion for men larger than life led her to fall in love with Marinetti and believe in Mussolini. In the same way the ultra-sensitivity of Virginia Woolf enabled her to write her unforgettable works and led her to her appointment with the river Ouse.

The madness of Woolf was directed only against herself and the fascist Benedetta has no deaths on her conscience because, for better or for worse, 'Scarcely a human being in the course of history has fallen to a woman's rifle.'

12

Eternal Fascism and its 'Home Haunts' in the Leavises' Attacks on Bloomsbury and Woolf

Molly Abel Travis

The game is 'Familiar Fascism', and the category is England – 1920s and 1930s. For ten points apiece, identify the speakers of the following quotations.

1. 'If I had my way, I would build a lethal chamber as big as the Crystal Palace, with a military band playing softly, and a Cinematograph working brightly; then I'd go out in the back streets and main streets and bring them in, all the sick, the halt, and the maimed; I would lead them gently, and they would smile me a weary thanks; and the band would softly bubble out the "Hallelujah Chorus" .'

2. 'The new ethics will hold life to be a privilege and a responsibility, not a sort of night refuge for base spirits out of the void; and the alternative in right conduct between living fully, beautifully and efficiently will be to die. For a multitude of contemptible and silly creatures, fear-driven and helpless and useless, unhappy or hatefully happy in the midst of squalid dishonour, feeble, ugly, inefficient, born of unrestrained lusts, and increasing and multiplying through sheer incontinence and stupidity, the men of the New Republic will have little pity and less benevolence.'

3. '[T]he slow, soft days are behind us, perhaps for ever. Hard days and dark nights ahead, no relaxing of the muscle of mind and will. It is at once our privilege and our ordeal to live in a dynamic period in the history of man. The tents of ease are struck and the soul of man is on the march.'

4. 'There is no doubt that in our headlong rush to educate everybody, we are lowering our standards . . . destroying our ancient edifices to

make ready the ground upon which the barbarian nomads of the future will encamp in the mechanized caravans.'
5. 'The artist has no longer any belief or suspicion that the mass, the half-educated simpering general . . . can in any way share his delights. . . . Modern civilization has bred a race with brains like those of rabbits, and we who are the heirs of the witch-doctor and the voodoo, we artists who have been so long the despised are about to take over control.'
6. 'A stupid, or slow-witted, not very ambitious, conventional, slothful person has necessarily a great many feminine characteristics.'

Their responses to *Three Guineas* indicate that most of Virginia Woolf's closest companions would have done poorly on a 'Familiar Fascism' quiz; more likely they would have refused to answer the questions. They were not persuaded by Woolf's arguments connecting British patriarchalism – with all of its institutionalized machismo and pomp, 'the crest and spur of the fighting cock' (*Letters VI*, p. 380) – to continental fascisms. At first glance, their negative response seemed to derive from a well-worn argument for timeliness, which had served as an effective deterrent in the women's movement of the nineteenth century; in its various forms, this argument had claimed that, yes, women's rights, and in particular suffrage, were necessary and important but that at the moment there were more pressing political and social problems to solve. The critics of *Three Guineas* did complain about Woolf's incredibly bad timing in mounting such an argument in 1938, but the real thrust of their angry response was that her conclusions were non sequiturs – out of time, out of joint – the product of a paranoid vision that perceived all events as temporally and causally related in a grand malevolent design. Quentin Bell, though seemingly describing his own response, speaks for the Bloomsbury circle as well:

Maynard Keynes was both angry and contemptuous, it was, he declared, a silly argument and not very well written. What really seemed wrong with the book . . . was the attempt to involve a discussion of women's rights with the far more agonising and immediate question of what we were to do in order to meet the ever-growing menace of Fascism and war. The connection between the two questions seemed tenuous and the positive suggestions wholly inadequate.[1]

In his 1941 Rede Lecture, dedicated to Leonard Woolf, E. M. Forster delivered what was ostensibly a eulogy to Virginia, but the result was a decidedly mixed message. Forster's assessment of Woolf as an 'aesthete . . . [with] no great cause at heart' set the tone for the devaluation of her literary achievement that occurred in the decade after her death. He described Woolf's outlook as 'peculiar', with the peculiarity stemming from an outmoded extremist feminism. 'Spots' of this feminism marred all of her work and completely ruined some of her texts, such as the 'cantankerous' *Three Guineas*. Forster claimed that by the 1930s there was not much reason for complaint in terms of women's rights. He saw no great cause in *Three Guineas*, merely the habitual grumbling of a paranoid and passé feminism.

For Bell and Forster as well as for Leonard Woolf, fascism had to be the Other, a threat from the outside to the force of civilization and reason represented by England. They could not admit of a fascism within. Alex Zwerdling explains this response in terms of Bloomsbury's worship of reason:

> The power of reason to make the world a better place was an unquestioned assumption in the Cambridge circle that nurtured the young men of the group. They were convinced that most human problems could eventually be solved by patient and scrupulous intellectual investigation.[2]

Of the Apostles, Keynes alone came to see the bankruptcy in their belief in meliorative rationalism; he observed that not only were the Cambridge rationalists 'pre-Freudian' in terms of their conception of human nature, but bereft of an earlier religious notion of original sin that had dealt with the human propensity for depravity.[3] Virginia Woolf thought Keynes's 1938 critique of Bloomsbury rationalism brilliant.[4] Indeed, she and Keynes were both influenced by Freudian theory in the late 1930s. But the significant difference between their positions is that Keynes's critique stopped short of analyzing Freud's notion of human nature in terms of gender, which is why he failed to see the connection Woolf made between patriarchy and fascism. His ideas maintained fascism as the Other to reason – the instantiation of the dark side of human nature, the irrational and bestial. But Woolf's critique implied that in late modernity Enlightenment rationalism had evolved into numerous types of reason, some of them distinctly pernicious in their institutionalization of oppression.[5]

Thus, fascism was neither alien nor aberrant; rather it lay 'curled up like a caterpillar on a leaf . . . in the heart of England' (*TGs*, p. 53). The threat of fascism extended well beyond the totalitarian regimes of Spain, Germany, and Italy, and it could not be contained in Britain by simply defeating Oswald Mosley and the British Union of Fascists. Woolf felt that one must seek Hitler out in his 'home haunts', which in the case of domestic fascism meant the heart of British institutions and the hearth of the patriarchal family.

In an essay titled 'Ur-Fascism', Umberto Eco engages in a structural analysis of eternal fascism. Although fascism can take many different local and historically specific shapes, Eco argues that it is always 'firmly fastened to some archetypal foundations'.[6] He discusses 14 features, any one of which can give rise to a version of fascism. In this discussion, I use Eco's structural features to analyze the British domestic fascism that Woolf describes in *Three Guineas*. Although figures such as Wyndham Lewis, Ezra Pound, and Filippo Marinetti come readily to mind in respect of the fascist tendencies within modernism, I want to focus on F. R. and Queenie Leavis, who made careers of being outsiders within the walls of Cambridge and established an outpost at the periphery of modernism. When read symptomatically, the Leavises' virulent opposition to Bloomsbury and Woolf reflects the ideology of familiar fascism that Woolf perceived at the heart of British institutions. In their unbending gender norms, their adoration of virility and authority figures, their glorification of the robust body, their fixation on Englishness, their cult of tradition and the concomitant rejection of the modern world and evocation of the myth of an organic society, the Leavises built their critical project at *Scrutiny* on characteristics of ur-fascism.

Although they were anti-machine, F. R. and Queenie forged a 'muscular' criticism that insisted on rigor, masculine strength, and the erasure of emotion, sensuousness, and sentimentality. As such, it recalls Lewis's, Pound's, and T. E. Hulme's projects to construct a new classicism – hard, spare, dry, phallic – which, in turn, share characteristics with the proto-fascist, mechanized machismo Freikorps ideology that Klaus Theweleit details in *Male Fantasies*. The machoism of the Freikorps members posited an organless body, steeled against penetration from the outside or from base urges within, displaying an aversion to the red tide represented by women and the lower classes which threatened to submerge rationality. One is reminded of Andreas Huyssen's description of the principal impulse of high modernism as 'warding off', a defensive response by vigilant modernists to avert the danger of an insipid and devouring mass culture consistently gendered as female.[7] In *Men Without Art* (1934), Lewis complains of subsisting in the 'suffocating atmosphere' of the 'feminizing' of culture for the past 15 years, with Woolf and the other 'tittering old maids' of Bloomsbury being among the worst offenders.[8] In an increasingly feminine world, Lewis felt that 'the natural feminine hostility to intellect' was leading to cultural decay.[9]

Denied the possibility of permanent war and displays of heroism, 'the Ur-Fascist', Eco says, 'transfers his will to power to sexual matters. This is the origin of machismo (which implies both disdain for women and intolerance and condemnation of nonstandard sexual habits, from chastity to homosexuality).'[10] Ur-fascism is marked by a fear of difference,[11] and the policing of gender is one of the effects of that fear. Under the Nazi regime, celibate females were ostracized and illegitimate mothers celebrated. Which is not to say that female sexuality was liberated under National Socialism – quite the contrary. Sex was a strictly instrumental and procreative act. Thus, the state deemed it intolerable for a girl or a woman to refuse to give herself sexually to a uniformed soldier.[12] Extreme gender anxiety determined the sexual economy of fascism, with every attempt made to force sex back to its 'original' and 'organic' function. Such anxiety is rendered succinctly in one of Mosley's signature statements: '[W]e want men who are men and women who are women.'[13] When fascist eugenics promised to create a race of virile men and feminine women, it actually meant that such men would aspire to heroism, leadership, and struggle, while women would engage in their natural and sacred role as mothers, perpetuating the race.

In addition to a profound fear of difference, ur-fascism reveals contempt for the weak and an insistence on nationalism as the source of identity.[14] The Leavises conflated these elements in their near pathological fixation on gender 'normalcy' and English robustness,[15] valorizing literature that appeared masculine, vigorous, and English.[16] Certainly one of the unspoken reasons for the Leavises' antipathy toward Bloomsbury stemmed from their homophobia and their prudish response to 'open' sexuality, with their disapproval coded in terms such as *immaturity* and *irresponsibility*.[17] In homophobic discourse the homosexual male is dissolute, weak, effeminate, and diseased; similarly, in racist or jingoist discourse the foreigner is pathological. F. R.'s highest praise was written in such phrases as 'native good sense', 'sinewy toughness', and 'strength of spoken English'.[18] Thus, his criticism was inf(l)ected by eugenics. In virtually every memoir of Leavis, much is made of his fixation on and pride in

his athletic prowess;[19] this aspect of Leavis's personality is not inci-
dental to his critical work. As David Carroll has observed in his study
of French literary fascists, we should not view the fascist cult of the
body – with its discourse on sports and hiking – as a mere curious
eccentricity, for it was a foundational principle of fascist politics and
aesthetics in that the individual body metonymically represented the
body politic.[20] From this perspective, if the individual body is weak,
dysfunctional, or diseased so is the body politic of the nation.

In ur-fascism, life gains meaning through struggle; struggle must be
maintained as a constant against the threats posed by pacifism and
peace.[21] The Leavises perceived themselves as outsiders and members of a
serious intellectual minority in a struggle against the immense forces of
cultural massification and commodification. In her 1932 study *Fiction and
the Reading Public*, Queenie hearkened back to the 'lusty' traditional
culture of early seventeenth-century England, which had been ideally
homogeneous and had derived its vitality from peasant life, before the
damaging effects of industrialization, urbanization, and the degeneration
of literary taste. She believed that along with the stultification of the
masses a degeneration of the ruling and professional classes had occurred
so that the people in power no longer possessed cultural and intellectual
authority.[22] The only hope for the representatives of cultural values lay in
their becoming soldiers of culture, with their struggle taking 'the form of
resistance by an armed and conscious minority'[23] Of course, this minority
constitutes an intellectual elite, and elitism characterizes any reactionary
ideology.

Paranoia, which is central to the fascist worldview, maintains the
necessary condition for struggle. If F. R. was paranoid, Queenie was
even more so; together they constantly reminded each other that life
was a conspiracy, with the worst conspiracy of all situated in the
corrupt and influential Bloomsbury coterie. The Leavises perceived this
clique as completely controlling the public media in London. The Arts
Council, they felt, snubbed their own minority perspective while gen-
erously subsidizing Bloomsbury.[24] How, they wondered, had an exemplary Cambridge intellectual such as Leslie Stephen come to be
displaced by a Lytton Strachey, who was mere surface, sneer, elitism,
and effeteness? The Leavises' paranoid vision resulted from the cult of
tradition, which is the primary feature of ur-fascism.[25] They began with
the premise that once upon a time there had been a vital and natural
rural existence in which life was felt deeply and morality was clear and
uncomplicated. What had destroyed this English pastoral paradise was
a combination of technology, suburban shallowness, and upper-class

glitter. The native vitality had been drained by cosmopolitan Bloomsbury vampires, and the robustness of natural speech gelded by the effects of advertising. High culture, no longer serious and responsible, had become 'coterie culture'; Bloomsbury ignored real values for social and personal values.[26] In place of the former ideal of cultivated leisure, which had emphasized refined taste and sensibility, the Leavises substituted petit bourgeois strenuousness and a rigorous professionalism. The marginal anti-salon run by the Leavises in weekly sessions at their home served as an alternative to Bloomsbury, establishing intellectual but no social links.[27]

It was mainly through criticism of Woolf that the *Scrutiny* writers attacked what they perceived as the insular community of Bloomsbury, which substituted social loyalty and affinity for responsible, principled criticism and collaboration, and which inflated the importance of someone like Strachey and led to the sharp decline of Woolf's aesthetic achievements after *To the Lighthouse*. The Leavises/Leavisites saw Woolf's prose and her later fiction as insular, overly aesthetic, and lacking in intellectual rigor. *Effete* is the word that they used most frequently to express their censure, so frequently that it became a kind of bludgeon. In the Leavises' homophobic glossary, effeteness is a synonym for homosexuality and gender perversion, and signifies what lies at the heart of their criticism of Strachey, of Woolf, and of Bloomsbury in general.

As was his custom, F. R. devalued Woolf by comparing her unfavorably to those writers he valued. Of course for Leavis, the valuation was often followed by revaluation, sometimes with the valued and the devalued changing positions; for example, early on James won out over Dickens, while later Dickens was on top. But Woolf's position never changed. F. R. used her fiction as a constant negative measure to point to the positive qualities of James, Conrad, and Lawrence. In *The Great Tradition*, Leavis's critical assessments suggest the ur-fascist adoration of masculine authority, fixation on nationalist identity, and cult of tradition. He praises James as a 'poet-novelist':

> The qualities of his art that derive from the profound seriousness of his interest in life – it is these in general that one stresses in calling him a poet. . . . When these qualities are duly recognized it becomes ridiculous to save the word 'poet' for the author of *The Waves* and *The Years* . . . [28]

When Woolf is contrasted with Conrad,

The contrast brings out how little of human experience – how little of life – comes within Mrs. Woolf's scope. The envelope enclosing her dramatized sensibilities may be 'semi-transparent'; but it seems to shut out all the ranges of the experience accompanying those kinds of preoccupation, volitional and moral, with an external world which are not felt primarily as preoccupation with one's consciousness of it. The preoccupation with intimating 'significance' in fine shades of consciousness, together with the unremitting play of visual imagery, the 'beautiful' writing, and the lack of moral interest in action, gives the effect of something clearly akin to a sophisticated aestheticism.[29]

Leavis criticizes Woolf for removing the individual from society, and praises Lawrence for his keen awareness of the individual in society and for his creation of an historical record:

The wealth of [The Rainbow] in this respect is such as must make it plain to any reader that, as social historian, Lawrence among novelists, is unsurpassable. . . . The Rainbow shows us the transmission of the spiritual heritage in an actual society, and shows it in relation to the general development of civilization.[30]

In his protracted campaign to convince the world of D. H. Lawrence's greatness, Leavis went to tortuous extremes. Arguing the merits of *The Rainbow* on the basis of its veracity as historical record was tricky enough, but the most glaring instance of Leavis's overdetermined investment in Lawrence was his controversial assessment of *St. Mawr*. Most critics consider this novella to be one of Lawrence's least successful works, yet Leavis claimed for it 'a creative and technical originality more remarkable than that of *The Waste Land*'.[31] R. P. Bilan points out that Leavis's attraction to *St. Mawr* and the exalted place it occupies in his writings on Lawrence cannot be separated from his antagonism toward Bloomsbury, for in the novella, through the negative characterization of Rico, Lawrence reveals the sterility of the Bloomsbury world.[32] This was the first Lawrence text that Leavis discussed at length in *Scrutiny*, and his review (in 1949) came almost immediately after a review of Keynes's *Two Memoirs*. In his review of Keynes, Leavis uses Lawrence's negative assessment of Bloomsbury to bolster his own antipathy. Although Keynes tried to rationalize Lawrence's rejection of Bloomsbury's version of civilization, Leavis finds the explanation unconvincing: 'That Lawrence, judging out of his experience of something incomparably more worthy to be called a "civilization", loathed and despised what was in front of him merely because he saw just what it was, is inconceivable to Keynes.'[33] Lawrence perceived in Bloomsbury what Keynes was unable to see: a world of self-absorbed, petty egos with no reverence for life. Lawrence's message in *St. Mawr* is that this kind of triviality breeds evil, a vision with which Leavis heartily agrees.[34] For all of Leavis's talk about the precision of a rigorous literary criticism, there was nothing precise or literary in his consecration of Lawrence.

As a representative of petit bourgeois femininity (and combining the ur-fascist anxiety about gender correctness and condemnation of the upper classes), Queenie attacked Woolf in terms of class and gender, labeling her effete, sterile, and unnatural. Commenting on *A Room of One's Own*, Queenie pronounced it 'crude' and Woolf's feminism dated.[35] In her scathing, mean-spirited review of *Three Guineas* in *Scrutiny* entitled 'Caterpillars of the Commonwealth Unite!' Queenie castigates Woolf for being out of touch with her public, including the educated daughters of the petty bourgeoisie (such as Q. D. herself). Queenie sees Woolf as insulated within her class and within Bloomsbury and, thus, offering dangerously simplistic suggestions for reform. She claims that Woolf could only know of 'domineering and hostile man . . . second-hand',[36] implying that none of the educated men in Woolf's life could possibly have been domineering or hostile – a dangerously simplistic assumption if ever there was one. Of course, this observation comes from someone who revered Leslie Stephen and the ethos he represented. In perhaps the nastiest of moments, Q. D. declares that Woolf – childless and surrounded by domestic help – cannot speak for working mothers (i.e. 'real women') at all. And she twice accuses Woolf of exhibiting tendencies of Nazism. She says that the overall effect of *Three Guineas* is 'like Nazi dialectic, without Nazi conviction' in that its only unity is emotional unity.[37] Furthermore, Woolf's 'most cherished project of all is to uproot criticism root and branch in the Nazi manner. With access to some practical control Mrs. Woolf would evidently develop into a high-powered persecutor.'[38] Woolf is 'a social parasite. . . . And she wants to penalize specialists in the interests of amateurs, and so her university could only be a breeding-ground for boudoir scholarship (a term I once heard applied to the learning of one of Mrs. Woolf's group) and belletrism.'[39] Then again, Woolf has no authority to speak on the subject of university education at all, 'voicing an opinion on a subject of which [she] can have no first-hand knowledge'.[40] Thus, Queenie does the bidding of F. R., laying the eggs of domestic fascism.

Although proud of being a working intellectual woman, Queenie was no feminist. And although her dissertation '*Fiction and the Reading*

Public' was meant to emulate the sociological studies that had begun to appear in scholarship in the USA, she was no social analyst. Her review of *Three Guineas* repeatedly points to the poor showing female students at Cambridge have made, even claiming that they have proven a nuisance to serious male students.[41] Instead of complaining about discrimination, females need to be about the business of 'living down their sex's reputation for having in general . . . ill-regulated [minds]'.[42] In her cataloguing of the failures of female undergraduates, Queenie never asks why. She faults Woolf for blaming patriarchal institutions and for failing to convey a 'masculine sense of responsibility and that capacity for self criticism which impresses us as the mark of the best kind of masculine mind'.[43] Queenie was a 'man's woman' and an ideal woman in the fascist mythology – strong, loyal to her man and children, an accomplished cook and housekeeper, and a good breeder. And an ideal woman in her mission against feminism: 'with regard to further female emancipation . . . the onus is on women to prove that they are going to be able to justify it and that it will not vitally dislocate (what it has already seriously disturbed – and no responsible person can regard that without uneasiness) the framework of our culture'.[44] Like a host of gender police before and after her, Queenie proclaims that feminist calls for emancipation are self-indulgent and warns that this emancipation threatens to destroy the 'natural' gender order upon which the culture survives. Unless women remain self-effacing, self-sacrificing, and nurturing, the world as we know it will cease to exist. Just as F. R.'s boasting about his athletic prowess was closely related to his critical perspective, so Queenie's pride in her domestic skills figured significantly in her critical assessments. As the queen of scones, she found Woolf defective and myopic.

The nastiness of Queenie's invective hinted at a tension in her earnestness. In Denys Thompson's collection of recollections and impressions of F. R. and Queenie, one discerns a distinct sense of the 'theatricality' of the Leavises' commitment to gender maturity and normalcy and the absolute centrality of family. Normative gender and familial roles had to be performed and re-performed. As Judith Butler has convincingly argued, 'gender trouble' does not derive so much from the fact that gender can be performed as that gender must be performed. The Leavises' celebrated intellectual 'collaboration' was not a transaction between equals; rather, it was determined by strict gender propriety as well as a domestic division of labor. Francis Mulhern perceives that in her efforts to be the perfect wife and mother along with being a working intellectual, Queenie suffered 'conflicts of identity and interest from which her husband was largely exempt, and she knew it'.[45] *Three Guineas* spoke the resentment that Queenie dared not express.

What Bloomsbury males could not see and Queenie Leavis would not see was painfully apparent to most female modernists. Shari Benstock has observed that every female writer in the decade preceding the Second World War acknowledged the impending danger of a masculinist ethic of authoritarianism and domination.[46] Louise Bernikow, in discussing Woolf's response to the rise of fascism, asks us to

> Imagine the effect of an ideology that insisted that a woman's world was husband and children on women who had rejected both. It is not an ideology that arose in the 1930s – since it describes most of world history – but it did, then, thunder as it had not for some twenty years. It did cut off the routes of escape from that ideology that women had relied on those twenty years or more. It weakened the walls around a women's community within which women might be heretics against this particular ancient religion.[47]

Thus, this period of two decades of relative emancipation for women began to seem like a mere interlude between acts in an age-old drama of injustice and violence. Coupled with the fear of encroaching fascism was the perception that communism, which appeared to be the only other option available to Europeans, was no option at all. Rather than being an antidote to fascism, communism presented a similarly restrictive and authoritarian scenario. For feminists, both ideologies were patriarchal to the core.

Although Woolf's feminism seemed outdated to both Bloomsbury and the Leavises, Maria-Antoinetta Macciocchi, in her important 1979 essay 'Female Sexuality in Fascist Ideology', claims that Woolf's ideas put her in the vanguard of a small number of thinkers beginning to formulate theories on the connection between gender/sex and authoritarianism. She links Woolf's observations about sexual exploitation and fascism to Antonio Gramsci's ideas about ideological internalization and the irrationality of fascism and Wilhelm Reich's connection between institutionalized sexual repression and dictatorial domination.[48] Despite the promising theoretical beginnings in the 1930s and 1940s, Macciocchi claims that 'the connection between fascism and female sexuality [has] been passed over in silence'.[49] In analyzing women's complicity in fascism, her concerns coincide with Woolf's in *Three Guineas*, but even more so with the ideas Woolf expressed in

'Thoughts on Peace in an Air Raid'. Macciocchi writes, 'Fascism has shown in a dramatic way that women could be made to serve, in the sense of both regression and repression'.[50] The fascist angel in the house represented both Mother and Death. In the Marquess Casagrande's welcome to Mussolini in Venice in 1923, one discerns the perverse erotic of the cult of mystical motherhood:

> Women have brought children into the world, but you [Mussolini] have inspired and conceived them. It is true that it is in the depths of the woman that an aroma is found which stimulates the male vigour of the combatant and which we now feel you ready to spread in large handfuls, while we likewise have given our sons to the fatherland in large handfuls.[51]

In fascist familialism, the masochistic mother is the duce's/führer's whore. Woolf entreats women,

> Let us try to drag up into consciousness the subconscious Hitlerism that holds us down. . . . We can see shop windows blazing; and women gazing; painted women; dressed-up women; women with crimson lips and crimson fingernails. They are slaves who are trying to enslave. If we could free ourselves from slavery we should free men from tyranny. Hitlers are bred by slaves.[52]

Macciocchi insists that revolutionary feminists must strangle the angel in the house.[53] Without understanding the past relationship between women and fascist ideology, revolutionary progress is doomed.

In her wary introduction to Macciocchi's article, Jane Caplan points out that although fascism itself is a 'ragbag' of randomly assembled concepts, one should not arbitrarily isolate any of those concepts and label them as fascist. Caplan argues that this is the problem with Macciocchi's argument – 'the eclectic fallacy'.[54] Caplan's points are well taken, deriving from her concern that Macciocchi has overstated and oversimplified women's collusion with fascism by attributing it to an all-powerful ideological internalization of authoritarianism, while overlooking the effects of economic and political incentives which made it seem that fascism allowed women significant agency. But there is something about Caplan's criticism of Macciocchi's argument that reminds me of Queenie Leavis's of Woolf's, much carping about bad examples and faulty evidence and losing sight of, or refusing to see, the justness of the macro argument.

In this chapter, I have risked the eclectic fallacy. As Eco warns,

> It would be so much easier, for us, if there appeared on the world scene somebody saying, 'I want to reopen Auschwitz, I want the Black Shirts to parade again in the Italian squares.' Life is not that simple. Ur-Fascism can come back under the most innocent of disguises.[55]

Fascism can be fuzzy, familiar, and feminine. It can be seductive.[56] Of course, F. R. and Queenie (Roth) Leavis were not the gestapo or the death camp administrators, any more than were D. H. Lawrence (quotation no. 1), H. G. Wells (no. 2), Oswald Mosley (no. 3), T. S. Eliot (no. 4), Ezra Pound (no. 5), and Wyndham Lewis (no. 6).[57] But together they all contributed to a way of thinking and feeling, a collection of cultural habits that provided fertile ground for fascist tendencies to take root. Woolf perceived this habitus and tried to warn her readers in 1938 that fascism was not the alien or pathological Other; rather, fascism inhabited the home haunts. But the exhortatory tone and form of *Three Guineas* indicate that although Woolf perceived fascism to be familiar, she did not see it as inevitable (unlike the critical theory of Max Horkheimer and others at the Frankfurt Institute in the 1930s, which concluded that fascism was the last phase of capitalism). Her argument was impelled by the conviction that fascism could be resisted, a conviction shared by this writer and the other writers in this volume.

13
Dystopian Modernism vs Utopian Feminism: Burdekin, Woolf, and West Respond to the Rise of Fascism

Loretta Stec

> We were among the last of the Utopians . . . who believe in a continuing moral progress by virtue of which the human race already consists of reliable, rational, decent people, influenced by truth and objective standards . . . We were not aware that civilisation was a thin and precarious crust . . .
>
> (John Maynard Keynes)[1]

Utopian visions have come increasingly under attack during this century of world wars, nuclear threats, capitalist and technological domination, poverty, genocide, and other horrors; dystopian visions have tended to replace them.[2] Speaking from our postmodern moment, Seyla Benhabib clearly articulates the conflict between these modes of thought that I would like to explore in the works of three writers in England in the 1930s, a key decade for the shattering of utopianism. Benhabib asserts that, on the one hand, Enlightenment-inspired utopias of 'the wholesale restructuring of our social and political universe according to some rationally worked-out plan' to lead toward 'human emancipation' have 'ceased to convince'.[3] While numerous reasons exist for this shift in belief, I agree with those who see the impossibility of utopianism as due in part to the congruence of utopian and fascist-totalitarian thought most abominably displayed in the Nazi deathcamps. As a feminist, on the other hand, Benhabib is reluctant to give up wholly on utopian impulses, for feminist thought usually includes both a critical and a visionary project, and imagines a world transformed for the better; she declares: 'utopian thinking is a practical-moral imperative. Without such a regulative principle of hope, not only morality, but also radical transformation is unthinkable.'[4] Women writing at the end of the 1930s about the state of European civilization found themselves trying to negotiate the extremes Benhabib describes, among other polarizations of this decade, including fascism vs communism, nationalism vs internationalism, Christianity vs secularism, and pacifism vs militarism. Three such writers were Katharine Burdekin, Virginia Woolf, and Rebecca West, each of whom wrote works in which a dystopian depiction of modernity and utopian impulses of feminism were often complexly entangled, and most often at odds.[5] Burdekin, Woolf, and West employed utopian and dystopian discourses in complex ways to defamiliarize the fascist, patriarchal, and militarist realities of the 1930s;[6] each had a different threshold of hope for human emancipation.

Towards the end of Auden's 'low dishonest decade', these three writers each wrote works that can be seen as participating in broadly defined utopian and dystopian genres.[7] Katharine Burdekin's novel of a horrifying Hitlerian future, *Swastika Night*, was published under the pseudonym Murray Constantine in 1937, and fits squarely in the tradition of dystopian fiction. Burdekin shows how a rationalized and hierarchical society can be extremely repressive, while she maintains a small hope for positive change through Christian faith and the power of historical memory. Virginia Woolf's stunning expository and epistolary work, *Three Guineas*, published in 1938, indexes certain dystopian conditions of modernity, particularly for women, while attempting to counter them – not at all decisively – with pacifist and ambivalently feminist utopian moments. Woolf's text undermines the belief in 'objective standards' that Keynes alludes to in the epigraph, and is highly sceptical of the 'facts' and rationalizations men have used to shore up their domination. Rebecca West's philosophical travelogue of Yugoslavia, *Black Lamb and Grey Falcon*, written primarily in the late 1930s and published in 1941, imaginatively creates another country as a community that is utopian in its ability to defend itself and its creative culture but nevertheless figures as a dystopia for women; West's text becomes anti-utopian in her inability to imagine a possibility of change in gender relations, and ultimately provides a conservative vision of irrational male violence holding sway at the expense of women. The mix of pessimistic scepticism and modified feminist hope in these works anticipates later critiques of utopian thought and positions them in a moment when nightmare possibilities of utopian societies were becoming apparent, primarily in Nazi Germany, but feminist hopes allied with Enlightenment beliefs in human emancipation still smoldered. As these ideological dilemmas remain with us under current circumstances, we can begin with these writers to chart the range of possible responses to utopian impulses in a dystopian age.

Many historians and other thinkers, such as Adorno and Horkheimer,[8] posit a connection between an Enlightenment-inspired faith in human rationality and a logic of control and domination whose endpoint was Auschwitz.[9] Fascist ideology of the 1930s, however, joined the rational with the mythic, in fairy tales, in model agrarian communities, and in the works of Nazi ideologues such as Alfred Rosenberg, to create a visionary project[10] that 'displayed some of the characteristics of utopianism, most notably [a] conception of history leading to a future golden age'.[11] A vision of a total state rooted in a racially pure German *Volk* led to a 'utopian vision of demonic proportions – a vision that inspired an apocalyptic revolutionary program of genocide'.[12] What seems a utopian project from one angle, turns into the most hideous dystopian nightmare from another; this refocusing of perspective calls into question fundamental assumptions of Enlightenment thought, particularly the ideology of progress, and can make feminist visions of a restructured world suspiciously allied with the utopianism/dystopianism of fascist thought. The works of the three women writers under consideration in this chapter, particularly Woolf, grappled with the multiple perspectives of modernity, and considered how to salvage a hopeful vision for women in an era dominated by fascism.

As part of their utopian imaginings of the ideal fascist society, those in power in Germany and Italy had very circumscribed visions of the place of women. From its inception in 1922, 'Mussolini's regime stood for returning women to home and hearth, restoring patriarchal authority, and confining female destiny to bearing babies.'[13] In *Mein Kampf*, Hitler designated the role of women as that of guaranteeing 'the increase and preservation of the species and the race', and continued, 'This alone is its meaning and task.'[14] Burdekin, Woolf, and West were very aware of fascist attitudes toward women, and *Swastika Night, Three Guineas*, and *Black Lamb and Grey Falcon* (to a lesser degree) all explore the 'continuity between the ordinary practices of patriarchy and the exacerbations found in . . . nazism'.[15] Woolf, for example, collected clippings from newspapers and other periodicals, letters, and quotations from books, for the better part of a decade in preparation for writing *Three Guineas*. Among her papers is a series of articles on the Nazi movement, including one from *The Times* which quoted the following from Dr. E. Woermann, Counsellor of the German embassy: ' "To believe that a woman's principal work was family life and bringing up the young generation was simply to return to natural and eternal law." [16] This recourse to essentialist gendered identities – the 'natural' or 'total' woman – undergirds the strict separation of spheres in the ideological program of Germany and Italy. [17] Like Woolf, Burdekin and West were well acquainted with fascist social organization, and responded to such claims about women throughout their works.

While a remarkable number of women in Germany did pay homage to National Socialism and worked for its success – women were not simply victims of fascist regimes – Burdekin shows with the greatest specificity the potential results of this ideology by imagining a wholesale transformation of society in line with these masculinist principles. *Swastika Night* is a fine example of a dystopian novel; it is set seven centuries after Nazi forces have won control of Europe. The novel has little action and much dialogue, and is clearly a vehicle for Burdekin to explore the ideological logic or illogic of fascism, and contemplate the kind of resistance necessary to reverse fascist trends. In her Hitlerian world, Christians are outcasts and Jews are extinct. Unlike other dystopian fiction of this era, Burdekin incorporates a devastating critique of gender relations in the Hitlerian future, and in an only slightly veiled fashion, of both Germany and England during the time she was writing. [18]

Burdekin confronts the fascist-patriarchal conception of women's position by depicting the 'Reduction of Women' that has taken place during the centuries of Hitlerian rule. Women have been reduced to animals used for breeding, and are described in grotesque terms, as having 'small shaven ugly heads and ugly soft bulgy bodies' (*SN*, p. 9). They are kept in a mile-square cage, given barely enough rations to survive, and are assumed to have no souls or ability for affection. They must submit to any man's desire to rape them. If a child results, the woman keeps and cares for it if it is a girl; if it is a precious boy, it is taken from her at 18 months old, and raised by men to be a man. This text presents a dystopia, a 'bad place', perhaps most poignantly for women readers, not only in the allusions to the plight of women in this society, but in the fact that the entire book is focused on male characters. As Patai points out, none of these characters is a 'simple hero' who signals a definitively better future for women, not even the ostensible English hero Alfred who comes closest to understanding the need to liberate women for a transformation of society. [19]

Burdekin explicitly links the excesses of this era with the European society out of which they grew. In Burdekin's novel, the characters learn that a Nazi 'historian' wrote a book one hundred years after

Hitler's death supposedly proving that 'Hitler was God . . . [and] that women were not part of the human race at all but a kind of ape' (*SN*, p. 79). It becomes clear, however, that this Nazi 'history' book did not initiate the disastrous gender relations that the dystopian novel presents; rather, before Nazi 'history' was written, 'the Reduction of Women . . . had begun already. Rapes were extraordinarily common . . . and the sentences for rape were getting lighter and lighter' (*SN*, p. 81). These moments in a dystopian critique of the future carry with them a critique of the patriarchal society of England and Germany in which Burdekin lived.[20] In another very disturbing scene, the ancestor of one of the characters finds the dead body of a girl mutilated by other women because she refused to accept the Nazi vision of her role (*SN*, p. 84); he then decides to write 'a Book, a real book, the only one in the world' to record pre-Hitlerian history and thereby challenge the Nazi version of events and ideology (*SN*, p. 74). The gruesome murder calls attention to the violence against women in European society before the 'Reduction of Women', particularly against those who refused their appropriately 'feminine' roles.

The fact that the murder has been committed by other women illustrates that Burdekin criticizes women for 'complicity in their own subjugation'.[21] Her character explains: 'Once [women] were convinced that men really wanted them to be animals and ugly and completely submissive . . . they threw themselves into the new pattern with a conscious enthusiasm that knew no bounds' (*SN*, p. 82). While this passage and others seem close to the logic of 'blaming the victim', the narrative complicates that view. Since this male character, and all other characters in the novel, are unable to see past their gender myopia, the criticism of women is shown to be part of their masculinist ideology; the emphatic nature of those criticisms, however, is not challenged, and thus they have significant weight, and suggest that Burdekin is warning her female readers not to submit to patriarchal or fascist tyranny. This admonition is an important counterpoint to Rebecca West's reaction to male domination and militarism as we will see below.

What the women consent to in this version of the future is not only their own subjugation, but a society built on the values of militarism, as evidenced in the 'Creed' that men in the Holy Hitler chapel recite: 'I believe in pride, in courage, in violence, in brutality, in bloodshed, in ruthlessness, and all other soldierly and heroic virtues' (*SN*, p. 6). This hyperbolic presentation of beliefs functions to defamiliarize the masculinist values of a Europe that had just suffered through the First

World War and was gearing up for a second and even more devastating war. Burdekin's narrative discounts military resistance to Hitlerism in favor of slow, steady ideological change: 'if people no longer believe Hitler is God, you have nothing left' (*SN*, p. 26). The salvation of Europe, the novel suggests, will occur through the spread of knowlege gained from the Book that has preserved pre-Hitlerian history.

The creation of this dystopian society is in large part due to the nihilistic book burnings that the Hitler regime has carried out to 'destroy all records of truth', all evidence of a prior, alternative society (*SN*, p. 83), an echo of the Nazi book burnings that took place in May 1933 at German universities.[22] The Hitlerians are only able to achieve their vision of a utopian society by destroying all record of what has gone before, and replacing it with myths about a blond, seven-foot Hitler. By showing this legend of Hitler to be false, through a single photograph that survived of the 'small dark soft-looking Lord Hitler' (*SN*, p. 67), Burdekin comments on the power of literature and legend to shape new realities that then become difficult to escape once institutionalized: utopian visions can become dystopian traps. As one character exclaims, once that happens, creativity is impossible: 'We can create nothing, we can invent nothing . . . We are Germans. We are holy. We are perfect, and we are dead' (*SN*, p. 121). A common criticism of visions of utopian societies is that they include a 'monologic demand for conformity'[23] that will not tolerate difference, which Burdekin exposes and narrates. The form of the novel reinforces that static quality attributed to utopias through its minimum of action and dramatic incident, and premium on didactic conversation.[24] The Book that describes pre-Hitlerian history has as its function demonstrating that the world was at one point structured *differently*, not always as a static, hierarchical, mass society. The possibility of change lies in scepticism of the present order, and Burdekin's novel *Swastika Night* is of course one artifact profoundly skeptical of fascist ideology; the novel in some sense *is* 'the Book' that urges readers to see alternatives and create a better future.

While the novel presents a pessimistic vision of the future joined with a hint that the society can awaken from this Hitlerian nightmare, its potential solution is paradoxical, particularly with regard to Christianity. At the end of the novel, the outcast Christians in England are in charge of 'the Book' on which a better future rests. Throughout the novel the Christian community plays the hopeful role of the degraded alternative society within the dystopia; at the same time the Christian community is nearly as repressive of women as the Nazis, and the Nazi hierarchy models itself partly on institutional Christianity. The text indexes St Paul, whose teachings suggest woman is 'nothing', and 'nothing she must become' (*SN*, p. 175), beliefs indistinguishable from Nazi ideology. The novel seems able to present only alternative ideologies implicated in the fascist values it critiques. Another example is democracy: when Burdekin's characters discuss democracy, they see it as the antidote to authoritarianism, and yet one argues 'the end of democracy . . . is always the same: it breaks up into chaos, and out of chaos comes some kind of authoritarian government, a Fuehrer, an oligarchy' (*SN*, pp. 146–7). The dystopian form of the novel cannot present a positive future, a fleshed out utopian vision, and has suggested the danger of that form of myth-making. Dystopian fiction tends not to advocate a radical transformation from the current world, even as it critiques it. Hence, Jean Pfaelzer declares about the American fiction she analyzes: 'Dystopian fiction, formally and historically, structurally and contextually, is a conservative genre.'[25] What the novel does offer is a kind of ongoing resistance through skepticism that will destroy the Hitler Empire, but that leaves 'nothing left' (*SN*, p. 26), no alternative system, just a continual struggle. This is an anti-utopian position, akin to Foucault's 'fundamental suspicion of any and all idealized visions of society'.[26] In this way, Burdekin participates in the modernist suspicion of grand narratives and belief in Enlightenment emancipation even while her text proposes spiritual belief associated with Christianity and a strong commitment to pacifism as potential antidotes to the Hitlerian nightmare of the novel.

Unlike Foucault, Burdekin fuses the skepticism of this anti-utopian position with feminist hope: the birth of Alfred's daughter Edith. The 'Reduction of Women' in Germany had so oppressed women that, in a feat of strangely passive, biological resistance they stopped having female babies, and the race was in danger of extinction. This had not happened among the English yet. Alfred's 'woman' Ethel gives birth to Edith, and he glimpses the fact that she is very significant to the future, potentially a 'new kind of human being' (*SN*, p. 160). Early in the novel a character states: 'If a woman could rejoice publicly in the birth of a girl, Hitlerdom would start to crumble' (*SN*, p. 14). The utopian impulse of this novel rests with feminism, then, even though Alfred dies, and his son cannot imagine what to do with Edith that will make her plight different from that of other women. This novel presents a dystopian vision of what might occur in Europe if the fascists of the 1930s are not stopped; in that sense it participates in the pessimistic dystopian strain of modernist literature and is a powerful indictment of rationally planned societies that result in hierarchy and conformity. At the same time it presents a hopeful, feminist revision of one of the master narratives of the West, Christianity, and suggests that when women are more respected a better world will result.

Although Burdekin's skeletal realist novel set in the future is not modernist in form, its dystopian vision places it in a distinctly modernist category that includes Eliot's *The Waste Land*, Fitzgerald's ash heaps in *The Great Gatsby*, the grotesque worlds of Beckett's fiction, and Picasso's representation of 'Guernica', site of the first demonstration of saturation bombing. These blasted landscapes constitute a profoundly modernist dystopia of total war. In *Three Guineas* Virginia Woolf responded to the fact that another world war was looming by incorporating elements of both the modernist dystopia and the feminist utopia into her vision. Like Eliot in *The Waste Land*, Woolf in this work splices together numerous quotations, voices, addresses, and perspectives to create a powerfully modernist, satirical work. Although her case is closely argued and carefully documented, Woolf's use of the epistolary form, with multiple letters within letters, undermines a unitary perspective, complicating both dystopian and utopian modes. Like Keynes's, Woolf's utopian expectations had been shaken, and *Three Guineas* ultimately provides less room for optimism than *Swastika Night*.

Like Picasso's painting, Woolf's descriptions of photographs from the Spanish civil war are indexes to a contemporary dystopia in which violence tears apart democratic principles as well as individual lives. She describes these photographs as 'a crude statement of fact' that both men and women can react to with 'horror and disgust' despite the different perspectives that she posits are due to the differently gendered histories of men and women. The photographs are not properly dystopian in any generic sense; Woolf does not create an imaginary 'bad world' for her readers. Rather, she describes the war in Spain through these images, and by presenting them with 'horror and disgust' she defamiliarizes violence that had become too routine, in a traditional rhetorical strategy of utopian and dystopian fiction.[27] The rest of the book draws links between these photographs of violence and the seemingly genteel world of 'the daughters of educated men', placing the blame for the 'ruin' on a social system that privileges traditional masculine values of heroism, competition, and domination.

Woolf continues to use defamiliarization to criticize these masculine values. For example, her female narrator pretends to stand on a 'bridge which connects the private house with the world of public life' (*TGs*,

p. 18). Several pages describe with great scorn the 'splendid' and 'ornate' clothes men wear to display their professional and military honors, making strange what must seem routine to at least some of her readers. This defamiliarizing works to show how the common rituals and dress of educated English men are on a continuum with the grandiose mass rituals and fetishizing of uniforms of Nazis and Italian fascists. Women are to reject these distinctions.

In addition, like Burdekin in *Swastika Night*, *Three Guineas* presents patriarchal Europe as a 'bad place' for women. She highlights the often ignored connections between the gendered public and private worlds, claiming that 'The emphasis which both priests and dictators place upon the necessity for two worlds is enough to prove that it is essential to their domination' (*TGs*, p. 181). The doctrine of separate spheres has created in England a separate realm for middle-class women, which is not exactly a dystopia, but is a repressive place, as confining in its way as the cages Burdekin's 'reduced' women inhabit. The astonishing details from biographies, histories, newspapers, letters, and other sources with which Woolf documents the oppression and exclusion of women (while simultaneously satirizing academic conventions of research) cohere to present a well-documented world of subjugation that shares much with fascist tyranny. Woolf's sense that separate spheres are 'essential' to men's domination signals that a large part of her anti-fascism requires that separate spheres be abolished and this had begun to happen by the 1930s.

While one can read this analysis of fascism as dystopian, the rhetorical context of this book challenges Woolf to imagine a utopian world; she responds to a man's letter asking her how to prevent war, which demands imagining an ideally pacific world without war. A number of utopian moments appear in this work that attempt to counter the force of the dystopian photos from Spain. For example, Woolf presents a vision of a college that would not teach the old way, a new college 'in which learning is sought for itself' (*TGs*, p. 35). The 'aim of the college' she imagines will be to foster what have become known as Bloomsbury values: 'the arts of human intercourse; . . . the ways in which mind and body can be made to co-operate' (*TGs*, p. 34). This holistic vision of human interaction and learning was part of the Bloomsbury faith in the 'power of reason to make the world a better place', the conviction that 'most human problems could eventually be solved by patient and scrupulous intellectual investigation' that we saw above in the epigraph from Keynes.[28] *Three Guineas'* utopian moments, however, are continually challenged, for example, by the imagined interlocutor –

the treasurer of a women's college seeking funds – in this section of the book who chastises her: 'Dream your dreams . . . fire off your rhetoric, but we have to face realities' (*TGs*, p. 35). These include that students must be taught skills to enter the workforce. The college is implicated in capitalism, and capitalism thrives on producing weapons for war, and war perpetuates the fascistic gender division. Woolf's narrator admits that this chain of logic leads to a 'lame and depressing answer' to whether education can be used to prevent war (*TGs*, p. 36). The women at the college risk becoming part of the system Woolf is critiquing; *Three Guineas* does not present liberal or equality feminism as the answer to the problems she explores.[29] Yet Woolf does not completely negate her utopian vision, although she tempers it radically; the daughters of educated men must have access to a college education, 'which, imperfect as it may be, is the only alternative to the education of the private house' (*TGs*, p. 39). The utopian impulse here is countered by 'reality', and *Three Guineas* continually moves between these zones.

The deconstructive strategies of Woolf's rhetoric extend to her presentation of feminism, despite our expectations that her utopian vision would be most strongly located there. Rather, Woolf presents a utopian moment most disturbing to feminist critics: the burning of the word 'feminist'. As part of her mockery of male rituals Woolf invents a 'new ceremony': writing the word 'feminist' on a piece of paper and setting it on fire (*TGs*, p. 101). Gilbert and Gubar interpret this as a 'parodic enactment of Nazi book burning . . . the most ironic sign of [Woolf's] frustration at the alternatives available to women, for she cannot burn the words tyrant & dictator, which "are not yet obsolete" '.[30] One can read a heavy dose of irony in this scenario given the rest of her argument; one can also read a more genuine ambivalence toward feminism. Michele Barrett claims that 'the hostility expressed toward feminism in *Three Guineas* is . . . an indication of how difficult . . . were the issues that could not be resolved satisfactorily' in her argument.[31] The vision of a time when 'feminism' would no longer be necessary can alternately be interpreted as (foolishly) utopian – Jane Marcus says, 'This was rather premature and optimistic'[32] – or as part of Woolf's prescient advancement in feminist thinking that sees the need to move beyond gender-based identities to create real change.

Toril Moi states, 'The Woolf of *Three Guineas* shows an acute awareness of both liberal and radical feminism . . . and argues instead' for the rejection of the 'dichotomy between masculine and feminine as metaphysical'.[33] Moi persuasively demonstrates that the modernist rhetorical

devices of this text, Woolf's use of 'mobile, pluralist viewpoints' undermine the unitary point of view of 'Man', the 'seamlessly unified self' at
the heart of traditional, patriarchal humanism.[34] As part of this effort,
the end of *Three Guineas* superimposes a different picture on the photograph of the Spanish Civil War: 'It is the figure of a man; some say,
others deny, that he is Man himself, the quintessence of virility . . . He
is called in German and Italian Führer or Duce; in our own language
Tyrant or Dictator. And behind him lie ruined houses and dead bodies'
(*TGs*, p. 142). This passage illustrates not only that Woolf blames war
and violence on an extreme form of traditional masculinity; it also
demonstrates one of her techniques for employing multiple points of
view. By inserting 'some say, others deny', Woolf acknowledges multiple points of view – that of her addressee, her narrator, and among her
readers. She implicitly challenges the assertion she is making, preventing the narrator from becoming dictatorial. By adding, however,
'He is a man certainly', Woolf insists on her point of view even as she
has alerted her reader to be suspicious about certainties. *Three Guineas*
performs this operation on many levels through interruptions, juxta-
positions, letters within letters, qualifications, and irony, including on
the dystopian and utopian modes of the text. We can, however, read
the book as a whole as pessimistic[35] because it undermines the utopian
moments it presents with strong skepticism. Woolf explicitly rejects
utopian thought at the end of the book, refusing to tune out the 'bark
of the guns and the bray of the gramophones' because 'that would be to
dream' (*TGs*, p. 143). She leaves this dreaming to 'the poets' and focuses
instead on the 'fact' of the dystopian war photographs. The possibility
for change is slight.

Like Burdekin, Woolf gestures towards resistance in new uses of the
Christian tradition, particularly a feminist version of monk's vows. In
her imagining of the 'Outsiders' Society', women would embrace
'poverty', 'chastity' of mind, 'derision', and 'freedom from unreal loyalties' to maintain their difference from men, even as they joined the
professions and public life (*TGs*, p. 78). While this seems a powerful
potential way to resist assimilation into the masculine world associated
with capitalism and fascism, ultimately it seems not to change much:
as *Three Guineas* states, the Outsiders' Society 'squares with facts' –
those of women's exclusion and subjugation (*TGs*, p. 106). It attempts
to turn the difference between the sexes that the history of separate
spheres has inculcated – Woolf is very careful not to essentialize these
differences – into an asset in creating a better world. The very circumscribed utopian vision at the end of the book remains in the possibility

of women 'finding new words and creating new methods' based on their differences from men that should result in a better if not a perfect or utopian world. The utopian moments of *Three Guineas* make us as readers imagine another way to arrange our social relations, even if Woolf's vision was limited by the 'actual facts in the actual world' for which she had to account.

'Actual facts' are what Rebecca West ostensibly writes of in her travelogue about Yugoslavia, *Black Lamb and Grey Falcon*; she produces, however, an extraordinarily rich and imaginative work that weaves together in modernist fashion historical narratives, personal reflections, dialogue, philosophy, a fascination with the 'primitive', analyses of gender relations, and much more. West visited Yugoslavia three times, in the spring of 1936, spring of 1937, and early summer of 1938, the years during which Burdekin and Woolf were writing *Swastika Night* and *Three Guineas*.[36] West wrote this massive work (1100+ pages) through those years, but did not complete it until the Second World War was raging. Although West's ideological position was always quite different from Burdekin's or Woolf's, the difference in her perspective on fascism and gender relations was heavily influenced by the moment in which she completed the manuscript. She wrote the anti-fascist epilogue during the 'Blitz' on London, and some consider it 'one of the most stirring and intelligent pieces of straight-ahead war propaganda ever written'.[37] Because she was working out her ideas after the Second World War had begun, it seemed that West could not imagine a way for Europe to fight both misogyny and fascist-imperialist invaders. As I have demonstrated at greater length elsewhere,[38] West argues for a defiant military response to fascism that she believes will unfortunately but necessarily keep women in a subordinate position.

West's travelogue idealizes the land and one of the peoples, the Serbs, whom she visits in Yugoslavia and paints many aspects of their society in glowing colors. This is a work of fiction as much as a documentary work, and often comes close to utopian fiction in its depiction of this other land. Travel narratives and utopian literature share a number of features, including the creation of an alternative world against which one's own is measured, and the use of a traveler or guide to explain the other world. West takes her reader on a journey to another land geographically removed from England, rather than temporally removed as in Burdekin's novel and other utopian/dystopian works. In the prologue to *Black Lamb*, West uses utopian language to describe the land she will explore in this volume: 'It is more wonderful than I can tell you . . . there is everything there. Except what we have. But that seems very little' (*BL*, p. 23). Much of the volume describes the riches of the South Slav cultures as a counterpoint to the cultures of Western European nations degraded by fascism, capitalism, and other aspects of modernity.

West glimpsed connections between masculine militarism and the subordination of women and Jews but did not provide a critique of them in the manner of Burdekin and Woolf. For example, West says:

> Because it is a vigorous act to throw the Jews out of Germany and because it causes pain and disorder, it is taken as a measure of virile statecraft, although its relevance to the troubles of the country could be imagined only by an imbecile.
>
> (*BL*, p. 321)

I see the use of the adjective 'virile' as acknowledging the links between traditional conceptions of masculinity and fascist ideology. But West complicates the equation of masculinism with fascism by making her primary representative of fascism in *Black Lamb* a female character, Gerda, the German wife of her Yugoslav guide Constantine. This characterization admits that although fascist ideology may be linked with traditional masculinity, women can and did participate in it, as we now know well from studies such as Koonz's *Mothers in the Fatherland*.

West was very sensitive to the doctrine of separate spheres that both Burdekin and Woolf understood as central to fascist social organiza- tion. West provides the following key to traditional gender roles early in *Black Lamb*:

> Idiocy is the female defect: intent on their private lives, women follow their fate through a darkness deep as that cast by malformed cells in the brain. It is no worse than the male defect, which is lunacy: they are so obsessed by public affairs that they see the world as by moonlight, which shows the outlines of every object but not the details indicative of their nature.
>
> (*BL*, p. 3)

Despite the biological simile of 'malformed cells', West does not con- sistently analyze these gender differences as natural or biological; indeed in writing this book of history, politics, and philosophy, West transgresses the feminine sphere of 'private life'. At points she praises women for their refusal to participate in masculine violence. For example, after some killings in a village square, West spied several Croat women continuing their job of pulling up weeds in the square rather than joining the protests and violent altercations around them. West comments: 'I thanked God for the idiocy of women, which must in many parts of the world have been the sole defender of life against the lunacy of men' (*BL*, p. 1079). In West's text, women's 'idiocy' keeps them from participating in the bloody ethnic confrontations of Yugoslavia, as they withhold themselves from that 'masculine' realm of 'lunacy' like the members of Woolf's Outsiders' Society.

West detests these ethnic skirmishes not merely for the unnecessary loss of life they inflict, but because the Croats and Serbs were fighting each other rather than the German and Italian fascists (*BL*, p. 1077). West was not a pacifist as were Burdekin and Woolf; she saw the world as full of inevitable and violent conflicts, and in this case saw the fight against fascism taking precedence over more local ones. The 1930s led West to rely more heavily on an Augustinian 'fantasy of dualism'[39] which she reinterprets as the war in the human psyche between what Freud named Eros and Thanatos, the life instinct and the death instinct.[40] West claims the war between these forces, and the human preference for death over life 'causes the pain of history, the wars, the persecutions . . . the torture of poverty'.[41] This interpretation of the human psyche leaves no room for a utopian vision of perfectibility; the vision West summons that comes closest to utopian is of a people – the Serbs – who can defend their culture and customs, who can fight on the side of life, when the inevitable assault comes from fascists or other foes who serve death.[42]

West outlines this position most fully in a chapter of *BLack Lamb* that describes one of the Serb villages she visits on the Black Mountain of Macedonia. West describes the village as both a model of a close-knit and well-defended community, and as a dystopia for women. West paints the village as full of 'magnificent people. They had form, they had style', and they had been able to keep the imperialist Turks at bay for 500 years (*BL* p. 677). West's resistance to the modernity that produced fascism leads her to praise these people and their pre-modern social arrangements. At the same time, their defensiveness, and the artistic integrity of the village as seen in embroidery, dance and other cultural forms, demanded a high price from women: they were subject to 'masculine tyranny' and all manner of 'social persecution' (*BL*, p. 674). Surprisingly for this feminist, she counsels women: 'If the community is threatened by any real danger, and only a few fortunate communities are not, women will be fools if they do not accept' men's declaration of their own superiority, for that is what shores them up to fight invaders (*BL*, pp. 678–9). West here directly contradicts Burdekin's criticism of women contributing to their own subordination; she falls into the trap of the gendered superiority/ inferiority hierarchy that Woolf analyzes in *A Room of One's Own* and elsewhere.[43] West suggests women must pretend to be inferior to men in order to survive even if that means they are 'used as beasts of burden' (*BL*, p. 677). *Black Lamb and Grey Falcon* presents a dystopian vision for women on this score, and leaves feminist arguments behind to urge strong, military resistance to fascism. This Serb village becomes a model for England to emulate, an England that was too 'feminine' in its 'idiocy' of appeasement and pacifism and passivity for West's taste.

Ultimately, despite West's insights about how 'tyrannical' the Serb men are towards women, and we can extrapolate, how close they are to fascists, her own text presents a vision of gender relations that eerily corresponds to the fascist doctrine of separate spheres that Burdekin and Woolf, and West's own writing of this book, challenge.[44] West's 'solution' for Western Europe to avoid being invaded by fascists included a vision of the subordination of women to soldiers, just what Hitler and Mussolini had dictated in their nations. This work is finally more radically anti-utopian than Burdekin's. West's vision of an unchanging 'human nature' that prefers the death instinct to the life instinct will keep gender relations intact. As she concludes about women's subordination, with feminist despair rather than feminist hope: 'There is no known remedy for this disharmony . . . it will perhaps be reasonable till the end of all time within imaginable scope, to follow the ancient custom and rejoice when a boy is born and to weep for a girl' (*BL*, p. 680).

Each of these three writers, then, uses utopian and dystopian techniques and moments to probe the relations between fascist, militarist, and patriarchal oppression. None of these works maintains or ends with utopian visions; rather, these works end in rather pessimistic places regarding women's possibilities for fighting fascism at home or abroad. However, all three writers work satirically to call attention to the domination they see throughout Europe. Ironically, Burdekin's dystopian vision presents the widest latitude for change in the future while yet demonstrating that alternative ideologies are implicated in fascist thought. Woolf's modernist technique and Outsiders' Society suggest a continuing process of struggle without any definitively better future, but with the hope for one, an oscillation between dystopian and utopian visions that destablizes both. West analyzes women's oppression with no possibility in sight for a radical change in gender relations, primarily because of war, and in her work the collapsing of the dystopian and utopian modes is most clear and most extreme. In the context of the late 1930s, the works of these three writers demonstrate how dystopian understandings of modernity and utopian feminist visions were often at odds, and provide three different formulations of the conflict. This struggle continues in feminist theory today as Benhabib's work demonstrates. Modernity has bequeathed us a state of deep skepticism as well as a desperate need to believe, nonetheless, in a utopian future.

Afterword

Jane Marcus

Fascism lives. It lives in your country and my country. It lives in all our badly numbered worlds, first, second, and third. It flourishes in under-worlds and overworlds. It is at home in globalism as it was in national-ism. Fascism in one of its most virulent forms, the mimetic, as Roger Griffin defines it in the *Blackwell Dictionary of 20th Century Social Thought*, has run rampant in hate crimes and local forms of terrorism, calling for social rebirth to defeat what is perceived as the decadence of progress toward racial and sexual freedom. The fascisms of 2000 are nationalistic and elitist in cross-class alliances around race and sex hate. They breed in Iran, but also in Indiana.

Virginia Woolf's most important work as a public intellectual was in the struggle against the fascism of the 1930s in Europe, and expressed in that difficult, contorted, and problematic text, *Three Guineas*. Here she tried to combine a theory of feminism, socialism, and pacifism as an answer to the fascism of Hitler and Mussolini, and, most impor-tantly, the fascism she perceived at home in Britain. Virginia Woolf argued there that the origin of fascism was in the patriarchal family. This is her most important contribution to twentieth-century social thought. And yet her argument is still not taken seriously. The recent mimetic fascist attacks on homosexuals are explained by Woolf's theory. The mimetic fascist attacks on Muslim women who demand an education are explained by Woolf's theory. Immigrants, Asians, Jews, and Turkish workers have come under attack in ways that mimic the fascism of the 1930s.

If our students learn to read *Three Guineas* the way Merry Pawlowski and her colleagues in this volume do, they will find a usable critique of the world around them. Students will find in this book and the book it celebrates an analysis of state violence predicated on family violence.

Virginia Woolf developed her theory from her own experience and she wrote that experience in fiction and in one of the finest and most provocative pieces of political philosophy of our time. We are grateful to Merry Pawlowski for her continued efforts to place Virginia Woolf with the revolutionary thinkers as well as with the writers of genius.

Notes

1 Introduction: Virginia Woolf at the Crossroads of Feminism, Fascism, and Art

1 These clippings and notes scrapbooks, *Monks House Papers* B.16f., Vols 1, 2, and 3, are housed in the University of Sussex manuscript collection and catalogued in Brenda Silver's valuable resource *Virginia Woolf's Reading Notebooks* (Princeton, NJ: Princeton University Press, 1983). The speech by Hitler is from an article in *The Sunday Times*, September 13, 1936, entitled 'Praise for Women: Their Part in "Nazi Triumph" ', which Woolf clipped and pasted on page 22, Volume 2, *Monks House Papers* B.16f. These same three volumes are the core of a forthcoming archival edition which I am co-editing with Vara Neverow.

2 Sybil Oldfield's chapter on Woolf in her *Women Against the Iron Fist: Alternatives to Militarism, 1900–1989* (Basil Blackwell, 1989) pp. 96–130, offers valuable insight into the importance of Woolf's 3-volume scrapbooks, *Monks House Papers* B.16f., as research for *Three Guineas*.

3 The use of the term 'ideology' in this context suggests an Althusserian perspective, rather than a Marxian view of ideology as a set of illusions. That is, the view of ideology as 'a system of representations (discourses, images, myths) concerning the real relations in which people live', or, in Althusser's own words, ' "the imaginary relation of those individuals to the real relations in which they live" '. Catherine Belsey, quoted here along with her quotation from Althusser, provides a useful interpretation of Althusser's notion of ideology for feminist theory in 'Constructing the Subject, Deconstructing the Text', *Feminist Criticism and Social Change: Sex, Class and Race in Literature and Culture*, eds, Judith Newton and Deborah Rosenfelt (New York: Methuen, 1985) p. 46.

4 Zeev Sternhell, Mario Sznajder, and Maia Asheri, *The Birth of Fascist Ideology: From Cultural Rebellion to Political Revolution*, trans. David Maisel (Princeton: Princeton University Press, 1994) p. 3.

5 Sternhell, pp. 7–8.

6 George Mosse, *The Fascist Revolution: Toward a General Theory of Fascism* (New York: Howard Fertig, 1999) p. xvi.

7 Richard Golsan, ed., *Fascism, Aesthetics, and Culture*, ed. Richard Golsan (Hanover: University Press of New England, 1992) p. xi.

8 As examples, see Hannah Arendt, *The Origins of Totalitarianism* (New York: Harcourt, Brace & World, 1966); George L. Mosse, *Masses and Man: Nationalist and Fascist Perceptions of Reality* (New York: Howard Fertig, 1980) and *Nationalism and Sexuality: Respectability and Abnormal Sexuality in Modern Europe* (New York: Howard Fertig, 1985); H. R. Kedward, *Fascism in Western Europe 1900–1945* (New York: New York University Press, 1971); *Fascism, Aesthetics, and Culture*, ed., Richard Golsan (Hanover: University Press of New England, 1992); Zeev Sternhell, *The Birth of Fascist Ideology*;

and Alastair Hamilton, *The Appeal of Fascism: a Study of Intellectuals and Fascism, 1919–1945* (New York: Macmillan, 1971).

9 Two excellent studies on these topics include Renate Bridenthal, Altina Grossmann, and Marian Kaplan, eds, *When Biology Became Destiny: Women in Weimar and Nazi Germany* (New York: Monthly Review Press, 1984), and Victoria de Grazia, *How Fascism Ruled Women: Italy, 1922–1945* (Berkeley: University of California Press, 1992).

10 Barbara Ehrenreich, 'Foreword', in Klaus Theweleit, *Male Fantasies, Volume 1: Women, Floods, Bodies, History* 1977, trans. Stephen Conway (Minneapolis: University of Minnesota Press, 1987) p. xv.

11 Ehrenreich, in Theweleit, *Male Fantasies*, p. xiii.

12 Maria-Antonietta Macciocchi, 'Female Sexuality in Fascist Ideology', *Feminist Review* 1 (1979) 67.

13 Quentin Bell, *Virginia Woolf: a Biography* (New York: Harcourt Brace Jovanovich, 1972) vol. II, pp. 420–1.

14 See especially Jane Marcus's ' "No More Horses": Virginia Woolf on Art and Propaganda', in *Art and Anger: Reading Like a Woman* (Columbus: Ohio State University Press, 1988) pp. 101–21 and Brenda Silver's 'The Authority of Anger: *Three Guineas* as Case Study', *Signs* 6 (Winter 1991) 340–70.

15 A fine volume of essays which has been formative to the work of several of the authors included here is *Virginia Woolf and War: Fiction, Reality, and Myth*, ed. Mark Hussey (Syracuse University Press, 1991).

16 Marianne DeKoven, in *Rich and Strange: Gender, History, Modernism* (Princeton, NJ: Princeton University Press, 1991), provides a valuable discussion of the complex history of the debate over the politics of modernist form in her introductory chapter.

17 Pamela Caughie, *Virginia Woolf and Postmodernism: Literature in Quest and Question of Itself* (Urbana: University of Illinois Press, 1991) p. 116.

18 Other work on this topic which should be mentioned here includes David Bradshaw's two-part essay, 'British Writers and Anti-Fascism in the 1930s', *Woolf Studies Annual* 3 and 4 (1997, 1998) and Erin G. Carlston's *Thinking Fascism: Sapphic Modernism and Fascist Modernity* (Stanford: Stanford University Press, 1998). The *Woolf Studies Annual* serves as an excellent resource for scholarly work on numerous topics concerning Woolf; specifically, for work on Woolf and fascism, see my 'Reassessing Modernism: Virginia Woolf, *Three Guineas*, and Fascist Ideology', *Woolf Studies Annual* 1 (Spring, 1995) 53–74, among others. A second excellent resource for Woolf studies are the 8 volumes of selected papers from the International Virginia Woolf Conference. As examples of specific references to Woolf and fascism, see my ' "all the gents. against me": Virginia Woolf, *Three Guineas*, and the Sons of Educated Men', *Virginia Woolf: Emerging Perspectives, Selected Papers from the Third Annual Conference on Virginia Woolf*, eds., Mark Hussey and Vara Neverow-Turk (New York: Pace University Press, 1994) pp. 44–51 and 'On Feminine Subjectivity and Fascist Ideology: the "Sex-War" Between Virginia Woolf and Wyndham Lewis', *Virginia Woolf and the Arts: Selected Papers from the 6th Annual Virginia Woolf Conference*, eds Diane F. Gillespie and Leslie K. Hankins (Pace University Press, 1997) pp. 243–51.

19   Short excerpts of Hitler's speech were quoted under the headline 'Praise for Women, Their Part in the "Nazi Triumph" ' in the September 13, 1936, *London Times.*

20   H. G. Wells, *The Shape of Things to Come* (Hutchinson & Co., 1933) p. 138.

21   'Quentin's Bogey', *Art and Anger*, p. 204. Marcus was one among several American feminists who took Bell to task for his 1972 biography of his aunt. A debate in print ensued between Bell and Marcus in *Critical Inquiry* (1984) 10:4 and (1985) 11:3 and *The Virginia Woolf Miscellany*, Fall and Winter, 1983. Marcus, in her response to Bell's attacks in ' "No More Horses" ', 1988, p. 107, points out how deeply incapable she felt he was of understanding his aunt's pacifism, quoting him: ' "But were we then to scuttle like frightened spinsters before the Fascist thugs?" '. Marcus further quotes Bell's biography: ' "She [Woolf] belonged, inescapably, to the Victorian world of Empire, Class and Privilege. Her gift was for the pursuit of shadows, for the ghostly whispers of the mind and for Pythian incomprehensibility, when what was needed was the swift and lucid phrase that could reach the ears of unemployed working men or Trades Union Officials" ', quoted from Bell, *Virginia Woolf*, vol. II, p. 186.

22   Jeffrey Schnapp references this quote from a speech, 'Arte e civiltà', delivered by Mussolini on October 5, 1926. See 'Epic Demonstrations: Fascist Modernity and the 1932 Exhibition of the Fascist Revolution', in Golsan, pp. 1–32.

23   Golsan, p. 3.

24   Bridenthal, p. 7.

25   All of this factual information is taken from Hilary Newitt's eyewitness account of her travels through Nazi Germany in 1936, *Women Must Choose: the Position of Women in Europe Today* (London: Victor Gollancz, 1937), a work which Woolf read and took notes from in her *Reading Notes* manuscripts.

26   De Grazia, p. 7.

2   *A Room of One's Own* and *Three Guineas*

1   It should be noticed that the defence budget of 1935 which had been £122 million was increased in 1936 to £158 million – about half Virginia Woolf's figure. See Neville Williams' *Chronology of the Modern World: 1763 to the Present Time* (London: Barrie and Rockliff, 1966) p. 552.

3   *Three Guineas*, Fascism, and the Construction of Gender

1   Ernst Jünger, *Storm of Steel. From the Diary of a German Storm-Troop Officer on the Western Front*, introd. R. H. Mottram (New York: Howard Fertig, Inc., 1975) p. 316.

2   See Marie-Luise Gättens, *Women Writers and Fascism. Reconstructing History* (Gainesville: University Press of Florida, 1995), particularly the chapter on *Three Guineas*, 'Fascism as Gendered History'.

3   *Three Guineas* does not regard women as one unified group, but instead argues that important differences exist between middle-class and working-

class women. The speaker of *Three Guineas* refuses to assume authority to speak for working-class women, as this would be an arrogant imposition. Indeed, it would treat working-class women in the same way as middle-class men treat women.

4 See Gättens, p. 9.

5 Gertrud Scholtz-Klink in an interview with Claudia Koonz in Claudia Koonz, *Mothers in the Fatherland. Women, the Family and Nazi Politics* (New York: St. Martin's Press, 1987) p. xxiii.

6 See Koonz, p. 6.

7 See Koonz, p. 5.

8 Koonz, p. 3.

9 The Nuremberg party congress from September 5 to 10, 1934. Official report with all the speeches (Munich, 1935), pp. 169–72. Cited from Ute Benz, ed., *Frauen im Nationalsozialismus. Dokumente und Zeugnisse* (Munich: Beck, 1993) p. 43; my translation.

10 The Nazis strictly enforced the antiabortion law and shut down the birth control and sex counseling clinics. See Gisela Bock, 'Motherhood, Compulsory Sterilization, and the State', in Renate Bridenthal, Atina Grossmann, and Marion Kaplan, eds, *When Biology Became Destiny. Women in Weimar and Nazi Germany* (New York: Monthly Review Press, 1984) p. 276.

11 See Benz, pp. 16–17. Gertrud Scholtz-Klink claims that 6 million women, that means every fifth adult woman, was organized in one of the National Socialist women's organizations by 1941. See Benz, p. 14.

12 See Benz, p. 31.

13 Benz, p. 11, my translation. For a discussion of the categorization in 'valuable' and 'valueless' life see also Gisela Bock's article.

14 See Benz, p. 20.

15 See Koonz, p. 167.

16 See Koonz, pp. 172–3 and Renate Wiggershaus, *Frauen unterm Nationalsozialismus* (Wuppertal: Peter Hammer Verlag) 1984 p. 59.

17 See Koonz, p. xxxiv.

18 Koonz, p. 173.

19 Koonz, p. xxvii.

20 See Koonz, p. xxxiii.

21 Gisela Von Wysocki, *Weiblichkeit und Modernität: Über Virginia Woolf* (Frankfurt/Main: Quumran, 1982) p. 97. All translations from Wysocki are mine.

22 Woolf's description of the procession as it produces subjects, brings to mind Michel Foucault's description of the disciplines and the way they produce individuals: 'Discipline is an art of rank, a technique for the transformation of arrangements. It individualizes bodies by a location that does not give them a fixed position, but distributes them and circulates them in a network of relations.' *Discipline and Punish. The Birth of the Prison.* Trans. Alan Sheridan (New York: Vintage Books, 1979) p. 146.

23 Wysocki, *Weiblichkeit*, my translation, p. 99.

24 Foucault, p. 138.

25 See Kurt Sontheimer, *Antidemokratisches Denken in der Weimarer Republik: Die politischen Ideen des deutschen Nationalsozialismus zwischen 1918 und*

1933, 4th edn (Munich: Nymphenburger Verlagsbuchhandlung, 1962) p. 13.

26 Barbara Ehrenreich, 'Introduction' to Klaus Theweleit, *Male Fantasies*, Vol. I, trans. Erica Carter and Chris Turner in collaboration with Stephen Conway (Minneapolis: University of Minnesota Press, 1989) p. xvi.

27 Nina Schwartz explains Woolf's reinterpretation of the historical experience of nineteenth-century women that is at work in the 'four great teachers of educated men's daughters' in the following way: 'This redefinition of terms . . . does not presuppose that the new meanings of the old words actually arrive at some natural truth that had previously been obscured. Rather, in preserving but revising these old terms, Woolf (like Kristeva and others) does two things: she admits her determination by cultural forces she does not control, but she also recognizes and exploits the instability of language and history for transformative purposes.' *Dead Fathers: the Logic of Transference in Modern Narrative* (Ann Arbor: The University of Michigan Press, 1994) p. 126.

28 Wysocki, *Weiblichkeit*, p. 12.

29 Schwartz, p. 131.

30 Klaus Theweleit, *Male Fantasies*, Vol. I, p. 33.

31 See Ehrenreich, p. xiii.

32 Ehrenreich succinctly summarizes the fascist's experience of violence: 'As a theory of fascism, *Male Fantasies* sets forth the jarring – and ultimately horrifying – proposition that the fascist is not doing "something else", but doing what he wants to do . . . What he wants is what he gets, and that is what the Freikorpsmen describe over and over as a "bloody mass": heads with their faces blown off, bodies soaked red in their own blood, rivers clogged with bodies . . . these acts of fascist terror spring from irreducible human desire' (pp. xi–xii).

33 Theweleit writes in his conclusion: 'To the generation of young male Germans born around 1870 and 1920, it seemed easier to blow half the world to pieces, kill numerous millions of human beings, than to counter the demands of their various "educators" with anything identifiable as true resistance. More than this, they considered their response the *correct* one . . . The group they represented was large, with no clear limits; had it not been, they would have necessarily remained ineffective.' *Male Fantasies*, Vol. II, pp. 418–20.

34 Susan Sontag, 'Fascinating Fascism', in *Under the Sign of Saturn*, 6th edn (New York: Farrar, Straus, Giroux, 1980) p. 87.

35 See Theweleit, II, p. 408.

36 See Renata Berg-Pan, *Leni Riefenstahl* (Boston: Twayne Publishers, 1980) p. 111.

37 I have used the translation in Theweleit, II, p. 408.

38 See Berg-Pan, pp. 107–8.

39 Theweleit, II, p. 412.

40 Gisela von Wysocki, *Die Fröste der Freiheit: Aufbruchsphantasien*, 2nd edn (Frankfurt/Main: Syndikat, 1981) p. 80; my translation.

41 See Anton Kaes, *From Hitler to Heimat: the Return of History as Film* (Cambridge, MA: Harvard University Press, 1989) p. 5.

42 See Wysocki, *Fröste*, p. 79.

43 See Sontag p. 79. In a footnote on the same page, Sontag quotes from Leni Riefenstahl's *Hinter den Kulissen des Reichsparteientag-Films* (Munich, 1935): 'The preparations for the Party Congress were made hand in hand with the preparations for the camera work' (p. 31). Sontag, furthermore, states that this line is the caption to a photograph that shows Hitler and Riefenstahl bending over some plans. Thomas Elsaesser in *New German Cinema* makes a similar point: 'Leni Riefenstahl's *Triumph of the Will* is not so much the record of the 1934 National Socialist Party Congress in Nuremberg as its visual-dramatic-aural or architectural *mise en scene*' (New Brunswick, New Jersey: 1989) p. 267.

44 See for example Berg-Pan who maintains, 'the film is above all an achievement of editing rather than photography' (p. 103).

45 See Wysocki, *Fröste*, p. 79.

46 Wysocki, *Fröste*, p. 81, my translation.

4 Toward a Feminist Theory of the State: Virginia Woolf and Wyndham Lewis on Art, Gender, and Politics

1 *The Art of Being Ruled* 1926 (rept New York: Haskell House Publishers, 1972), p. 51. In addition to the abbreviations for Woolf's titles used in this volume, I would like to add the following abbreviations for the most frequently cited Wyndham Lewis titles for the purposes of this essay:

> *ABR: The Art of Being Ruled* 1926 (rept. New York: Haskell House Publishers, 1972).
> *Code*: 'The Code of a Herdsman', *The Little Review* IV (July, 1917).
> *Hitler: Hitler* 1931 (rpt New York: Gordon Press, 1972).
> *VW*: 'Virginia Woolf ("Mind" and "Matter" on the Plane of a Literary Controversy)', *Men Without Art* 1934 (rpt New York: Russell and Russell, 1964) pp. 158–71.
> *WL*: 'Mr. Wyndham Lewis ("Personal-Appearance" Artist)', *Men Without Art*, pp. 115–28.

2 See Jean Guiguet, 'Jeu de Miroirs: Jew de Massacre, Virginia Woolf et Wyndham Lewis', *Blast* 3, ed. Seamus Cooney (Black Sparrow Press, 1984) pp. 135–40, for a different argument regarding Woolf's 'looking in the mirror' of Lewis's criticism.

3 'Mr. Bennett and Mrs. Brown', *The Captain's Death Bed and Other Essays* 1950 (New York: Harcourt Brace Jovanovich, 1978) p. 96. This is the second version of the essay, derived from a paper read to the Heretics at Cambridge on May 18, 1924, and published first as 'Character in Fiction', *Criterion* (July, 1924), and then as 'Mr. Bennett and Mrs. Brown' in the Hogarth essay series in December, 1924. This version contains the quoted passage and is the one from which Lewis quotes. For the earlier 1923 version, see Andrew McNeillie's edition, *The Essays of Virginia Woolf: Volume Three, 1919–1924* (San Diego: Harcourt Brace Jovanovich, 1988) pp. 384–9; and for 'Character in Fiction', see the same volume of McNeillie, pp. 420–37.

4 Virginia Woolf, 'Mr. Bennett and Mrs. Brown', p. 96.

5　Jane Marcus argues that *Three Guineas* was, in fact, conceived as a response to male colleagues like Yeats, Forster, Eliot, and Huxley, who, Woolf felt, devalued her literary importance because she was female. ' "No More Horses": Virginia Woolf on Art and Propaganda', *Art and Anger: Reading Like a Woman* (Columbus: Ohio State University Press, 1988) p. 112.

6　*Toward a Feminist Theory of the State* (Cambridge, MA: Harvard University Press, 1989) p. 162.

7　Mackinnon, p. 160.

8　*Male Fantasies Vol. I: Women, Floods, Bodies, History*, trans. Stephen Conway (Minneapolis: University of Minnesota Press, 1987).

9　Barbara Ehrenreich, 'Foreword', in Klaus Theweleit, *Male Fantasies Vol. I*, p. xiii.

10　Anson Rabinback and Jessica Benjamin, 'Foreword', in Klaus Theweleit, *Male Fantasies Vol. II, Male Bodies: Psychoanalyzing the White Terror*, trans. Erica Carter and Chris Turner (Minneapolis: University of Minnesota Press, 1989) p. xii.

11　Rabinback and Benjamin, p. xiv.

12　See for support of this claim Lewis's biographer, Jeffrey Meyers, *The Enemy: a Biography of Wyndham Lewis* (London: Routledge & Kegan Paul, 1980) p. 16.

13　Trotter's work also formed the basis of an article by Leonard Woolf published in the *New Statesman* on July 8, 1916.

14　SueEllen Campbell, in *The Enemy Opposite: the Outlaw Criticism of Wyndham Lewis* (Athens: Ohio University Press, 1988) p. 174, substantiates this view and develops a later revision of this model by Lewis, which she claims is more ambiguous and vague.

15　*Wyndham Lewis and Western Man* (New York: St. Martin's Press, 1992) p. 49.

16　Quoted in Sandra Gilbert and Susan Gubar, *No Man's Land: the Place of the Woman Writer in the Twentieth Century, Vol. I: The War of the Words* (New Haven: Yale University Press, 1988) p. 22.

17　See for this argument George L. Mosse, *Nationalism and Sexuality: Respectability and Abnormal Sexuality in Modern Europe* (New York: Howard Fertig, 1985) p. 145.

18　*Group Psychology and the Analysis of the Ego* (New York: W. W. Norton, 1959) p. 51.

19　There are so many fine studies of Woolf's *Between the Acts* that I can only acknowledge a few of them here: Eileen Barrett's 'Matriarchal Myth on a Patriarchal Stage: Virginia Woolf's *Between the Acts*', *Twentieth Century Literature* 33 (1987) 18–37; Gillian Beer's 'Virginia Woolf and Pre-History', *Virginia Woolf: the Common Ground* (Ann Arbor: University of Michigan Press, 1996) pp. 6–28; Melba Cuddy Keane's 'The Politics of Comic Modes in Virginia Woolf's *Between the Acts*', *PMLA* 105, 2 (March 1990) 273–85; Mark Hussey's ' "I" Rejected; "We" Substituted': Self and Society in *Between the Acts*', in Bege K. Bowers and Barbara Brothers, eds, *Reading and Writing Women's Lives: a Study of the Novel of Manners* (Ann Arbor: UMI Research Press, 1990) pp. 141–52. I would recommend the reader to Mark Hussey's *Virginia Woolf A to Z* (Oxford: Oxford University Press, 1995) for a fuller bibliography through 1995 on this and all other works by Woolf.

20 John Constable, 'Wyndham Lewis's *Hitler:* Content and Public Reception, the Truth' (http://tori.ic.h.kyoto-u.ac.jp/pub/lewis/lewis.html) paragraph 2. I've indicated citations taken from this unpublished paper posted on Constable's website by paragraph number rather than page number as pagination is not indicated in the article and page numbers on printouts would be hard to standardize since individual computer printers may paginate differently.

21 See for the quote and support of this argument, William M. Chase, 'On Lewis's Politics: the Polemics Polemically Answered', in *Wyndham Lewis: a Revaluation*, ed. Jeffrey Meyers (London: Athlone Press, 1980) p. 156.

22 Constable, paragraphs 56–61, carefully details the array of reviews, one particularly cogent example of which comes from the *Daily Worker*: 'Mr. Lewis may worship his hero, but he seems to know singularly little about him. If he does know anything about him, this nauseating adulation of the Nazi leader, and the painting of his gang of bloodthirsty hooligan followers as angels of peace, can only be characterized as calculated, deliberate and frigid lying.' Anon., 'A Futurist Has Visions', *Daily Worker* (27 July, 1931) p. 2.

23 Constable, paragraph 5.

24 Jeffrey Meyers, pp. 186, 189.

25 Hitler, *Mein Kampf* (Boston: Houghton Mifflin, 1971) p. 456.

26 Hitler, p. 42.

27 David Ayers in *Wyndham Lewis and Western Man*, p. 12, repeats and expands this argument from Fredric Jameson's *Fables of Aggression: Wyndham Lewis, the Modernist as Fascist* (Berkeley: University of California Press, 1979).

28 David Ayers, p. 12.

29 Constable, paragraph 14.

30 Jameson, p. 183.

31 Jameson, p. 123.

32 See for another discussion of Woolf's conception of the Society of Outsiders, Sybil Oldfield's *Women Against the Iron Fist: Alternatives to Militarism, 1900–1989* (Oxford: Basil Blackwell, 1989) Chapter 5.

5 Freudian Seduction and the Fallacies of Dictatorship

I would like to thank my colleagues Patricia Cramer, Steve Larocco, and Jane Lilienfeld for taking the time to read earlier versions of this chapter and for offering excellent suggestions for revision.

1 'Name That Face', *Virginia Woolf Miscellany* 51 (Spring 1998) 4.

2 Elizabeth Abel, *Virginia Woolf and the Fictions of Psychoanalysis* (Chicago: University of Chicago Press, 1989) p. 14.

3 Abel, p. 6; pp. 103ff.

4 Shari Benstock, 'Ellipses: Figuring Feminism in *Three Guineas*', *Textualizing the Feminine* (Norman: University of Oklahoma Press, 1991) p. 221 n5.

5 Quoted in Abel, p. 13 from *Letters* 5, pp. 36, 91.

6 See Abel, pp. 16–17.

7 P. Meisel and W. Kendrick, *Bloomsbury/Freud* (New York: Basic Books, 1986) p. 22; see also Abel, p. 14.

8 Meisel and Kendrick, p. 308.

9 Quoted in Abel, p. 14 from Meisel and Kendrick, p. 264.

10 Abel, p. 14.

11 J. R. Noble quoted in Meisel and Kendrick, p. 309.

12 See also Louise DeSalvo, *Virginia Woolf* (New York: Ballantine Books, 1989).

13 For example, 'Three Contributions to the Sexual Theory', trans. A. A. Brill, *Journal of Nerv. Ment. Dis. Publ. Co.* (1910) Monograph Series 7; 'Three Essays on the Theory of Sexuality', *Standard Edition* (hereafter cited as *SE*), trans. J. Strachey, 24 vols (London: Hogarth Press, 1953–66) 7: 125–245. Most citations of Freud's works in this essay reference the publications that would have been available to Virginia Woolf. All citations include in square brackets the original date of publication in German and the translator and date of first translation into English. All citations are cross-referenced in square brackets to the *Standard Edition*, including variant essay titles, volume number, and full pagination.

14 'The Passing of the Oedipus Complex' [1924; trans. J. Riviere 1924], *Collected Papers* (hereafter cited as *CP*) vol. 2 , trans. under supervision of J. Riviere (London: Hogarth Press, 1924) p. 274 ['Dissolution of the Oedipus Complex', *SE* 19: 173–82].

15 'On the Sexual Theories of Children' [1908; trans. D. Bryan 1924], *CP* 2: 67 [*SE* 9: 207–26].

16 'Some Psychical Consequences of the Anatomical Distinctions Between the Sexes' [1925; trans. J. Strachey 1924], *CP*, vol. 5, ed. J. Strachey (London: Hogarth Press, 1959) pp. 186–204 [*SE* 19: 243–58, rpt. from *Int. J. Psycho-Anal.* 8 (1927)]. Freud's theory of penis envy has been challenged repeatedly. For responses of his contemporaries, see Helene Deutsch, *The Psychology of Women* (New York: Grune and Stratton, 1944); Karen Horney, *Feminine Psychology* (London: Routledge & Kegan Paul, 1967); Ernest Jones, 'Early Female Sexuality', *Papers on Psychoanalysis* (London: Ballière, Tindall and Cox, 1948) pp. 485–95.

17 *CP* 5: 190 [*SE* 19: 243–58].

18 'Psychical Consequences' *CP* 5: 191 [*SE* 19: 243–58].

19 'Psychical Consequences' *CP* 5: 196–7 [*SE* 19: 243–58].

20 In a later and even more scandalous essay, 'Female Sexuality', published in translation in 1932, Freud reiterates in a footnote these same points ('Female Sexuality' [1931; trans. J. Riviere 1932], *CP* 5: 189 n3 [*SE* 21: 225–43 rpt. from *International Journal of Psycho-Analysis* 13 (1932)]). See also 'Femininity' [1933; trans. W. J. H. Sprott, 1933], *New Introductory Lectures on Psychoanalysis* (London: Hogarth Press, 1933) [*SE* 22: 112–35].

21 See *Monks House Papers* B.16f (University of Sussex, England) vol. 3: 85–6.

22 *The Interpretation of Dreams* [1900; trans. A. A. Brill, 1913], trans. and ed. J. Strachey (London: Hogarth Press, 1953; New York: Avon, 1953) [*SE* 4–5].

23 See Abel, pp. 18–19. According to Freud, an *'obsessional neurosis . . .* rests on the premise of a repression by means of which a sadistic trend has been substituted for a tender one' ('Repression' [1915]. *CP* 4: 95 [*SE* 14: 143–58]).

24 See Abel, p. 86.

25 *Women and Fiction*, ed. S. P. Rosenbaum (Cambridge: Blackwell, 1992) p. 14.

26 See Abel, p. 19.

27 See also Woolf's 'Freudian Fiction', *Essays 3*, pp. 195–8.

28 James Strachey was translating the fourth essay of *Totem and Taboo* for Lytton Strachey in January 1925 (see Meisel and Kendrick, p. 171). Woolf may have discussed the essay with Lytton and would also have had access to A. A. Brill's English translation of the entire work (New York: Moffet and Yard, 1918; London: Routledge, 1919).

29 *Totem and Taboo* [1912–13; 1919] *SE* 13: 1–162; pp. 141–2.

30 *Totem and Taboo, SE* 13: 146.

31 *Totem and Taboo, SE* 13: 144.

32 *Totem and Taboo, SE* 13: 145–6.

33 *SE* 24: 286; 304.

34 'Types of Neurotic Nosogenesis' [1912; trans. E. C. Mayne 1924], *CP* 2: 113–21 ['Types of Onset of Neurosis', *SE* 229–44] p. 118; emphasis in text.

35 'Psychical Consequences', *CP* 5: 195 [*SE* 19: 243–358]; emphasis in text.

36 J. M. Masson, *The Assault on Truth* (New York: Farrar, Straus and Giroux, 1984) pp. xviii, 189.

37 See Benstock, pp. 123–37.

38 See also some of the observations of Woolf's contemporaries: Winifred Holtby, *Women and a Changing Civilization* (1935; Chicago: Academy Press, 1978) p. 161 and Hilary Newitt, *Women Must Choose* (London: Victor Gollancz, 1937) pp. 38–9.

39 Christine Froula, 'St. Virginia's Epistle to an English Gentleman', *Tulsa Studies in Women and Literature* 13 (Summer 1994) 52, n19.

40 See *Monks House Papers* B.16f.

41 Woolf's slang vocabulary was sufficiently sophisticated to accommodate this sexual play on such words (see for example, Woolf's memoir 'Old Bloomsbury', *MB*, pp. 195–6. See also Q. Bell, *Virginia Woolf* (New York: Harcourt Brace Jovanovich, 1972) 1:90 and 1:124; J. Malcolm, 'A House of One's Own', *New Yorker*, June 5, 1995: 58–82; Vanessa Bell, *Selected Letters of Vanessa Bell*, ed. Regina Marler, introduction by Q. Bell (London: Bloomsbury, 1993) p. 163).

42 See E. Partridge, *A Dictionary of Slang and Unconventional English*, 8th edn (New York: Macmillan, 1984); A. Richter, *Sexual Slang* (New York: HarperPerennial, 1993); M. E. Moore, *Understanding British English* (New York: Citadel Press, 1992).

43 L. Paros, *The Erotic Tongue* (New York: Henry Holt, 1984) p. 40.

44 Richter notes additional synonyms 'that relate to weaponry, including bayonet, club, poker, and sword'. 'Worm', another term Woolf uses (*TGs*, p. 53), is, as Richter points out, 'one of the few derogatory terms for penis, implying limpness, lowliness, and smallness' (p. 242). Freud himself indicates that all 'long, stiff objects' and 'weapons' are conventionally symbolic of the male genitals (e.g. *The Interpretation of Dreams*, p. 389).

45 I want to thank my colleague Steve Larocco for noting Woolf's curious disruption of the linear process of arousal, erection and ejaculation.

46 See also Abel, pp. 93–4.

47 See Abel, p. 160 n25.

6 Acts of Vision, Acts of Aggression: Art and Abyssinia in Virginia Woolf's Fascist Italy

1 Jan Morris, ed., *Travels with Virginia Woolf* (London: Hogarth Press, 1993) p. 174.

2 While Italy was crucial to the development of Woolf's feminism, Woolf was in turn vital to the growth of the Italian feminism: for example, the feminist center in Rome is called *Centro Culturale Virginia Woolf.*

3 Paul Fussell defines travel writing as 'a sub-species of memoir in which the autobiographical narrative arises from the speaker's encounter with distant or unfamiliar data, and in which the narrative – unlike that in a novel or a romance – claims literal validity by constant reference to actuality', Paul Fussell, *Abroad: British Literary Traveling between the Wars* (New York: Oxford University Press, 1980) p. 202. Even though Woolf's work may not be travel writing in the traditional sense, I consider the letters and diary entries Woolf generated during her stays in Italy as travel literature because they express and negotiate her expectations and experience of Italy as an actual place.

4 Virginia Woolf, introduction, *A Sentimental Journey Through France and Italy,* by Laurence Sterne (1768; London: Oxford University Press, 1928) p. xvi.

5 Virginia Woolf, *Flush: a Biography* (1933; rpt., New York: Harcourt Brace and Co., 1983) pp. 131–2.

6 Virginia Woolf, 'Memories of a Working Women's Guild', *Collected Essays,* vol. 4 (London: Hogarth Press, 1967) p. 137.

7 Although Kathy J. Phillips's recent study on Woolf and empire argues that Leonard Woolf's book highlights aspects of Woolf's novels, the issue of how Leonard's work connects with Woolf's touristic experience of Italy goes unexplored. See Kathy J. Phillips, *Virginia Woolf Against Empire* (Knoxville: University of Tennessee Press, 1994).

8 Leonard Woolf, *Empire and Commerce in Africa: a Study in Economic Imperialism* (1920; New York: Howard Fertig, 1968) p. 315.

9 Leonard Woolf, 1968, p. 173.

10 Virginia Woolf, notes, 'Anon', ' "Anon" and "The Reader": Virginia Woolf's Last Essays', ed. Brenda R. Silver, *Twentieth-Century Literature* 25 (1979) 403.

11 Adrian Lyttleton, *The Seizure of Power: Fascism in Italy 1919–1929* (London: Weidenfeld and Nicolson, 1973) p. 387.

12 Jeffrey Schnapp and Barbara Spackman, eds, 'Selections from the Great Debate on Fascism and Culture: *Critica Fascista* 1926–1927', *Stanford Italian Review* 8. 1–2 (1990) 236.

13 Alessandro Pavolini, 'Dell'arte fascista', *Critica Fascista* 4. 20 (1926) 393.

14 Quoted in Emilio Gentile, 'From the Cultural Revolt of the Giolittian Era to the Ideology of Fascism', *Studies in Modern Italian History: From the Risorgimento to the Republic,* ed. Frank C. Coppa (New York: Peter Lang, 1986) p. 116.

15 While women were not party members, the *Fasci femminili* organization established a separate network of women's *fasci* units that were distinct from the male *fasci* units. Paul Brooker notes an interesting difference between the way in which Italian fascists and Nazis treated their women: under fascism in Italy '[t]his very separation from the male members

suggests an inferior status to that enjoyed by the female members of the Nazi Party, who were at least members of the same units as the men even if, as women, they were never allowed to become unit leaders', Paul Brooker, *The Faces of Fraternalism: Nazi Germany, Fascist Italy, and Imperial Japan* (Oxford: Clarendon Press, 1991) p. 154.

16 Mario Puccini, 'Un'arte Fascista', *Critica Fascista* 4. 23 (1926) 436.

17 The image of the fish that in 1927 represented Woolf's wondrously uncon-strained passage through Rome serves as a symbol of impoverished stasis in its literalness in 1933; during that year's trip to Italy she encounters a 'melancholy' Tuscan peasant without the resources to escape his oppressive village who offers her 'his 6 or 7 little fish' (*Diary 4*, p. 156). The fish at the opening of *A Room of One's Own* is situated chronologically between these two touristic moments in 1927 and 1933, and it suggests the contrasting ideas of freedom and confinement. Although Woolf chooses the emblem of a fish in *A Room of One's Own* to symbolize intellectual freedom, the fish also demonstrates patriarchy's power to constrain and even to extinguish freedom of thought, expression, and movement in those groups marginal-ized by class (Italian peasants) or gender (British women). For the Oxbridge Beadle who chases the trespassing Woolf, lost in thought, back onto the path from a plot of grass because she is a woman sends her 'little fish into hiding' (*AROO*, p. 4).

18 After her 1927 journey, Woolf traveled to Italy next in the spring of 1933, this time on a motoring tour with Leonard. Woolf's diary entries from 1933 reflect little preoccupation with fascism. For instance, she closes a letter to Ethel Smyth by remarking, 'I dont [*sic*] like Fascist Italy at all – but hist! – there's the black shirt under the window – so no more' (*Letters 5*, p. 187). (A 'black shirt' refers to a fascist party member.) Woolf's sarcasm suggests that although the fascist state had consolidated its power in the six years since her last visit to Italy in 1927, her aesthetic concern with Italy in 1933 pre-vails over a serious political interest in fascism's menacing potential. This threat, however, overwhelms her just two years later in 1935.

19 Brenda R. Silver, 'Virginia Woolf: Cultural Critique', *The Gender of Modernism: a Critical Anthology*, ed. Bonnie Kime Scott (Bloomington: Indiana University Press, 1990) p. 648.

20 Leonard Woolf, 'Up and Up or Down and Down', *New Statesman and Nation* 227 (June 29, 1935) 958.

21 These maps represent what Schnapp and Spackman describe on page 236 as the regime's cultural-political move towards 'an explicitly Roman new-imperial iconography' in the mid to late 1930s.

22 Stephen Potter, 'The Ministry of Emotion', *New Statesman and Nation* 217 (April 20, 1935) 553.

23 For a discussion of the disturbing implications of the 'banal' aspects of fascism, see Alice Yaeger Kaplan, *Reproductions of Banality: Fascism, Literature, and French Intellectual Life* (Minneapolis: University of Minnesota Press, 1986).

24 One of Woolf's modernist contemporaries, Wyndham Lewis, offers a contrasting view of Italy's invasion of Abyssinia. In 1936 he asserts: 'that the industrious and ingenious Italian, rather than the lazy, stupid and predatory Ethiopian, should eventually control Abyssinia is surely not such

a tragedy', Wyndham Lewis, *Left Wings over Europe: or, How to Make a War About Nothing* (London: J. Cape, 1936) p. 164. Although Lewis is not the only writer in the 1930s to be wrong about Italian fascism and Nazism, his racist comments that justify Italy's invasion of Abyssinia highlight the power – and difference – of Woolf's critique.

25   Virginia Woolf, 'Virginia Woolf and Julian Bell', Appendix C, *Virginia Woolf: a Biography*, by Quentin Bell (New York: Harcourt Brace Jovanovich, 1972) p. 497.

26   Quoted in Bell, p. 497.

27   *Three Guineas* features the connected themes of outsider, anonymity, and androgyny that Woolf develops more fully in her final essay that is appropriately titled 'Anon': the triumphant figure of Anon is sequentially (rather than simultaneously) androgynous, 'sometimes man; sometimes woman' (Silver, 'Anon', p. 382), and is an outsider whose social isolation accords him or her freedom and 'outsiders [*sic*] privilege' (Silver, p. 383).

28   Michel Foucault, preface, *Anti-Oedipus: Capitalism and Schizophrenia*, by Gilles Deleuze and Félix Guattari, trans. Robert Hurley, Mark Seem, and Helen R. Lane (New York: Viking Press, 1977) p. xiii.

29   Virginia Woolf, 'Thoughts on Peace in an Air Raid', *Collected Essays*, vol. 4 (London: Hogarth Press, 1967) p. 174, p. 176.

7 'Thou Canst Not Touch the Freedom of My Mind': Fascism and Disruptive Female Consciousness in *Mrs. Dalloway*

I would like to thank Michael Chappell, Pat Cramer, Mark Hussey, Chella Courington, Merry Pawlowski, and members of the Feminist Research Group at Pace University – especially Walter Srebnick and Esther Labovitz – for helpful comments on this chapter.

1   See Alex Zwerdling, *Virginia Woolf and the Real World* (Berkeley: University of California Press, 1986); Susan Squier, *Virginia Woolf and London: the Sexual Politics of the City* (Chapel Hill: University of North Carolina Press, 1985); and Roger Poole, ' "We All Put Up With You Virginia": Irreceivable Wisdom about War,' pp. 79–100 in *Virginia Woolf and War: Fiction, Reality, and Myth*, ed. Mark Hussey (Syracuse: Syracuse University Press, 1991). Zwerdling, Squier, and Poole have all compared *Mrs. Dalloway* and *Three Guineas*, but none discuss Italian fascism as material history in the context of *Mrs. Dalloway*.

2   On the day after Mussolini's takeover of the Facta Government in October of 1922, Woolf writes in her diary that she must begin to think out her fourth novel. The entry reads: 'I dont want to be totting up compliments, & comparing reviews. I want to think out Mrs. Dalloway.' *Diary 2*, p. 209.

3   In his introductory remarks in *State Control in Fascist Italy: Culture and Conformity, 1925–42* (Manchester: Manchester University Press, 1991) p. 2, Doug Thompson argues that Mussolini's populism harnessed 'technological advances in the field of communications to seek to establish itself in the

hearts, minds and homes of all Italians' and that he created 'the illusion of a personal relationship with each one'.

4 Thompson details these methods of suppression, among others, in the second chapter of his book.

5 Thompson, p. 24.

6 *Downhill All the Way: an Autobiography of the Years 1919 to 1939* (New York: Harcourt Brace, 1967) p. 9.

7 L. Woolf, p. 48.

8 L. Woolf, p. 28.

9 L. Woolf, p. 27.

10 Two days after Mussolini's invasion *The Times*, October 30, 1922, 14c, in terms which might have laid a foundation for both *Mrs. Dalloway* and *Three Guineas*, one *Times* correspondent writes an essay of considerable length describing the hostility of the professional classes to the Bolsheviks and the collusion of the bourgeoisie with the fascisti in the suppression of Bolshevik cooperative exchanges.

11 *The Times*, October 28, 1922, 10g.

12 'The Fascists are a new organization representing new and vigorous forces in Italian national life', the reporter writes. 'There are very wholesome and very evil elements in Fascism; it has still to be seen which will triumph', *The Times*, October 30, 1922, 13c and d.

13 *Diary* 2, p. 248. See also *Letters* 5, p. 273, where Woolf writes to Quentin Bell that Leonard and the Labour Party 'think Moseley is getting supporters. If so,' she writes, 'I shall emigrate.'

14 See *The Orwell Reader: Fiction, Essays, and Reportage* (New York: Harcourt Brace, 1956) pp. 241–70.

15 Though Elizabeth Wiskemann suggests that the passage is by Mussolini, she indicates that the attribution may be problematic; the passage was written, if not by Mussolini himself, then by one of his chief administrators and theoreticians. See *Fascism in Italy: its Development and Influence* (London: Macmillan, 1969) p. 34.

16 See Zwerdling, p.130.

17 Wiskemann, p. 2.

18 Thompson, p. 64.

19 Thompson, pp. 63–4.

20 The *Duce* also portrayed himself as kind and fatherly, appearing in school textbooks, for example, like Jesus, surrounded by children.

21 Woolf's satire on Bradshaw's love for Conversion and Proportion is likely a response to her own experience with psychiatry. In *Downhill All the Way*, p. 51, Leonard Woolf describes a visit to Harley Street with Virginia in 1922: 'at our last interview with the last famous Harley Street specialist to whom we paid our three guineas, the great Dr. Saintsbury, as he shook Virginia's hand, said to her: "Equanimity – equanimity – practise equanimity, Mrs. Woolf." As the door closed behind us, I felt that he might as usefully have said, "A normal temperature – ninety-eight point four – practise a normal temperature, Mrs. Woolf." '

22 In *Gyn/Ecology: The Metaethics of Radical Feminism* (Boston: Beacon Press, 1990) pp. 293–312, Mary Daly compares modern American gynecology with Nazi experiments. See also Barbara Ehrenreich and Deirdre English,

For Her Own Good: 150 Years of the Experts' Advice to Women (New York: Anchor Books, 1989) and *Witches, Midwives, and Nurses: a History of Women Healers* (New York: Feminist Press, 1973).

23 In *Downhill All the Way*, Leonard records that Virginia spent the first seven months of 1922 visiting doctors on Harley Street for severe depression. In what is perhaps not only a coincidence, Woolf writes in her diary that she must begin to 'think out' *Mrs. Dalloway* one day after Mussolini's October 28 takeover. Surely it is tempting to think that, as she emerged from 'severe depression' to write *Mrs. Dalloway*, Woolf associated the Bradshavian, psychiatric menace at home with the victory of the *fascisti* abroad.

24 *The Times*, October 28, 1922, 11c.

25 Thompson, p. 24.

26 *The Death of the Moth and Other Essays* (New York: Harcourt Brace, 1970) p. 244.

27 Zwerdling suggests this in *Virginia Woolf and the Real World*, p. 138.

28 Thompson, pp. 109–10.

29 Thompson, p. 108.

30 De Felice in Thompson, p. 109.

31 Thompson, p. 108.

32 Wiskemann, pp. 9, 18.

33 *Virginia Woolf: a Study of Her Novels* (New York: New York University Press, 1979), p. 57.

34 *Virginia Woolf: a Critical Reading* (Baltimore: Johns Hopkins, 1977) p. 79.

35 'Mrs. Dalloway: the Communion of Saints', in *New Feminist Essays on Virginia Woolf*, ed. Jane Marcus (Lincoln, Nebraska: University of Nebraska Press, 1981) p. 126.

36 *Virginia Woolf and the Languages of Patriarchy* (Bloomington, Indiana: Indiana University Press, 1987) p. 117.

37 Clarissa is by no means purely heroic. Although transformed from Woolf's early representation of her as a supercilious socialite in *The Voyage Out*, Clarissa retains traces of her former self in *Mrs. Dalloway*. In fact, through various critical prisms – Peter Walsh, Doris Kilman, Richard Dalloway, and Sally Seton – we see Clarissa in a series of unflattering lights. We see that she 'cared too much for rank and society and getting on in the world' (p. 115); that she could be 'insincere' (p. 254); that she has 'great charm but lacks something'; that on the question of sexual harassment she took Hugh's side against Sally's; that she is 'at heart a snob' (p. 289); that she is 'hard on people' (p. 291). She prefers contemplating roses to the plight of the Armenians, and in fact, cannot remember whether it is the Armenians or the Albanians that are to be pitied. She is harsh and sometimes plays the prude. She marries for money, position, and security, and can turn suddenly cold, frightening others.

At the same time, Clarissa has her depths. Indeed, without them she could not be mentally chaste: she watches her sister die – from her father's carelessness – under a falling tree; she is upset by and identifies with, Septimus's suicide; she is a skeptic, saying 'we are a doomed race, chained to a sinking ship' (p. 117); and has more ability to judge character than Sally Seton. She is generous to her friends: But 'how generous to her friends Clarissa was!' (p. 291) Sally Seton thinks; and in this, Clarissa is 'pure-hearted' (p. 292). In the end, as Alex Zwerdling describes her, Clarissa is neither wholly good nor wholly bad, but rather stands between two worlds – between the governing class that in some ways saves her and the governed class in midst of which she might have drowned. For Zwerdling, pp. 139–40, Clarissa is – in however modified terms – ultimately redeemed for, 'though the decision to give up Peter and Sally and identify herself with the governing-class spirit is never reversed, it is also never final'; rather, 'Clarissa continually goes over the reasons for her choice thirty years later.'

38 Julia Kristeva, cited in Linda Alcoff, 'Cultural Feminism versus Post-Structuralism: the Identity Crisis in Feminist Theory', *Feminist Theory in Practice and Process*, eds, Micheline R. Malson *et al.* (Chicago: University of Chicago Press, 1989) p. 308.
39 *This Sex Which Is Not One*, trans. Catherine Porter (Ithaca, NY: Cornell University Press, 1985) p. 117.
40 Irigaray, p. 112.
41 Zwerdling, p. 138.
42 Irigaray, p. 113.
43 Makiko Minow-Pinkney, *Virginia Woolf & the Problem of the Subject* (New Brunswick, NJ: Rutgers University Press, 1987) p. 72.
44 Minow-Pinkney, p. 81.
45 Minow-Pinkney, p. 57.
46 Mark Hussey, ' "Hiding Behind the Curtain": Reading (Woolf) Like a Man.' Typescript for Keynote Speech for the Fifth Annual Virginia Woolf Conference, Otterbein College, June 15, 1995, p. 19.
47 Minow-Pinkney details these and other grammatical unravellings in Chapter 3 of *Virginia Woolf & the Problem of the Subject*.

8 Of Oceans and Opposition: *The Waves*, Oswald Mosley, and the New Party

1 Alice Kaplan, *Reproductions of Banality* (Minneapolis: University of Minnesota Press, 1986) p. 13.
2 Walter Benjamin, 'The Work of Art in the Age of Mechanical Reproduction', *Illuminations*, trans. Harry Zorn (New York: Schocken, 1969) pp. 217–52.
3 Kaplan, p. 32.
4 Russell Berman, 'Modernism, Fascism, and the Institution of Literature', in Monique Chefdor *et al.*, eds, *Modernism: Challenges and Perspectives* (Urbana: University of Illinois Press, 1986) p. 95.
5 Kaplan, p. 32.
6 Among them were several members of the Labour Party and of Woolf's intimate circle, including Harold Nicolson, Vita Sackville-West's husband, who was one of Oswald Mosley's strongest early supporters.
7 See Russell Berman, 'The Aestheticization of Politics: Walter Benjamin on Fascism and the Avant-Garde', *Stanford Italian Review* 8 (1990) 35–52.
8 This has prompted Jane Marcus to characterize them as signs of the British imperialist effort in 'Britannia Rules *The Waves*', in Karen Lawrence, ed.,

Decolonizing Tradition (Urbana: University of Illinois Press, 1992) p. 145. While Marcus's essay has been instrumental in helping us re-think *The Waves*, I do not agree that the novel condemns all its characters, as she seems to believe.

9 Klaus Theweleit, *Male Fantasies*, vol. 1, trans. Stephen Conway (Minneapolis: University of Minnesota Press, 1987) p. 230.

10 On the German fascist conceptions of sexuality see also George Mosse, *Nationalism and Sexuality: Middle-class Morality and Sexual Norms in Modern Europe* (Madison: University of Wisconsin Press, 1985), especially Chapters 5 and 8.

11 See for example, Richard Thurlow, *Fascism in Britain* (London: Basil Blackwell, 1987) pp. 92–118.

12 Zeev Sternhell, 'Fascist Ideology', in Walter Laqueur, ed., *Fascism: a Reader's Guide* (Berkeley: University of California Press, 1976) p. 320.

13 This is of course an argument Sternhell makes about France, and only by passing allusion, about England. See *Neither Right Nor Left: Fascist Ideology in France*, trans. David Meisel (Princeton: Princeton University Press, 1986).

14 By December 1930 there were over two-and-a-half million unemployed. Robert Benewick, *The Fascist Movement in Britain* (London: Allen Lane, Penguin, rev. 1st edn, 1972) p. 60.

15 See D. S. Lewis, *Illusions of Grandeur: Mosley, Fascism and British Society, 1931–81* (Manchester: Manchester University Press, 1987) p. 13.

16 The journal of the New Party, *Action*, sold 160 000 copies of its initial issue, according to Benewick, p. 76. Mosley counted among his followers in the early period of the New Party both John Strachey and Allan Young.

17 Oswald Mosley, *The Greater Britain* (London: British Union of Fascists, 1932, 1934) p. 20.

18 Mosley, *Greater Britain*, p. 34.

19 'Our Shabby Grandfathers', *Action 1.2* (October 15, 1931) 3.

20 'Crisis: by Oswald Mosley', *Action 1.1* (October 8, 1931) 1.

21 Leonard Woolf, *Downhill All the Way: an Autobiography of the Years 1919–1939* (New York: Harcourt Brace Jovanovich, 1967) p. 27.

22 She declared herself a Fabian in January 1915 (*Diary 1*, p. 26).

23 For a more complete discussion see Jessica Berman, 'Reading Beyond the Subject', in Helen Wussow, ed., *New Essays on Virginia Woolf* (Dallas: Contemporary Research Press, 1995) pp. 42–4.

24 For example, Labour leader C. R. Atlee states that the 'Trade Union movement is predominantly representative of men's interests . . . while the Co-operative movement is an expression of the interests of the woman in the home'. *The Labour Party in Perspective – and Twelve Years Later* (London: Gollancz, 1949) p. 70.

25 Labour Party, *The Rise of the Labour Party* (n.p., 1946) p. 8.

26 Naomi Black, 'Virginia Woolf and the Woman's Movement', in Jane Marcus, ed., *Virginia Woolf: a Feminist Slant* (Lincoln: University of Nebraska Press, 1983) p. 187.

27 See J. Berman.

28 'Other Books: Virginia Woolf,' *Action 1.1* (October 8, 1931) 6.

29 Kaplan, p. 23.

30 'Our Shabby Grandfathers', p. 3.
31 'The New Party Notes and News', *Action 1.1* (October 8, 1931) 29.
32 See most recently Kathy J. Phillips, *Virginia Woolf Against Empire* (Knoxville: University of Tennessee Press, 1994). While I agree with many of Phllips's claims about Woolf's politics, her book often falls into the trap of reducing all British politics to the politics of empire, and all the many nuances of political opposition to anti-imperialism, broadly defined.
33 Marcus, 'Britannia', pp. 136–7.
34 Gillian Beer, 'The Body of the People in Virginia Woolf', in Sue Roe, ed., *Women Reading Women's Writing* (New York: St. Martin's Press, 1987) p. 110.
35 Beer, p. 110.
36 Beer, p. 111.
37 See, for example, Labour Party, *Labour and the Nation* (Transport House, 1928).
38 'Our Shabby Grandfathers', p. 3.
39 Oswald Mosley, 'What is Personal Liberty?', *Action 1.9* (December 3, 1931) 1.
40 This tension also plays itself out in the hypocrisy of Mussolini's insistence on the traditional family model, and his notorious adultery. As George Mosse, p. 157, points out, this hypocrisy would not have been tolerated in Nazi Germany, where liberatory sexuality was not a part of the fascist sensibility.
41 Andrew Hewitt, 'Fascist Modernism, Futurism, and Post-Modernity', in Richard J. Golsan, ed., *Fascism, Aesthetics and Culture* (Hanover: University Press of New England, 1992) p. 49.
42 Theweleit, pp. 195–6.
43 On these images see also Mosse, p. 160.
44 Melba Cuddy-Keane, 'The Politics of Comic Modes in Virginia Woolf's *Between the Acts*', *PMLA 105.2* (March, 1990) 273. I am greatly indebted to this article.
45 Jean-Luc Nancy, *The Inoperative Community*, trans. Peter Connor *et al.* (Minneapolis: University of Minnesota Press, 1991).
46 Madeleine Moore has written persuasively on this subject. See 'Nature and Community: a Study of Cyclical Reality in *The Waves*', in Ralph Freedman, ed., *Virginia Woolf: Revaluation and Continuity* (Berkeley: University of California Press, 1980) pp. 219–40.
47 Garrett Stewart, 'Catching the Stylistic D/Rift: Sound Defects in Woolf's *The Waves*', *ELH* 54.2 (Summer, 1987) 424.
48 Stewart, p. 428.
49 'Our Shabby Grandfathers', p. 3.
50 Mosley, 'What is Personal Liberty?' 1.
51 Mosley, 'What is Personal Liberty?' 1.
52 Mosley, 'What is Personal Liberty?' 1.
53 Harold Nicolson, *Diaries and Letters, vol. 1, 1930–39*, ed. Nigel Nicolson (New York: Athenaeum, 1966) p. 107.
54 Nicolson, p. 97.
55 Nicolson, p. 91.
56 *Action 1.1*, 10.

57 James Lees-Milne, *Harold Nicolson: a Biography, 1930–1968* (London: Chatto, 1981) p. 17. According to Nigel Nicolson, she thought the venture 'insane', p. 67.

58 Nicholas Mosley, *The Rules of the Game: Sir Oswald and Lady Cynthia Mosley, 1896–1933* (London: Secker and Warburg, 1982) p. 160.

59 N. Mosley, p. 185.

60 Nicolson, *Diaries and Letters*, p. 68.

61 N. Mosley, p. 205. See also Nicolson, *Diaries and Letters, 1930–1939.*

9 Monstrous Conjugations: Images of Dictatorship in the Anti-Fascist Writings of Virginia and Leonard Woolf

1 According to Alex Zwerdling, 'Woolf's name does not appear among the sponsors of the many organizations engaged in war resistance between 1914 and 1941. . . . One does not find her mentioned in the histories of the Peace Pledge Union or the No-Conscription Fellowship or the League of Nations Society or the Women's International League for Peace and Freedom. . . . But she was intimate with many people whose primary activities were given to such work, most especially Leonard, and she was in deep sympathy with their aims.' Zwerdling, *Virginia Woolf and the Real World* (Berkeley: University of California Press, 1986) p. 274.

2 'Thoughts on Peace in an Air Raid', in *The Death of the Moth and Other Essays* (New York: Harcourt Brace Jovanovich, 1942) p. 244.

3 'Thoughts on Peace', p. 243.

4 Leonard Woolf, *The War for Peace* (London: George Routledge & Sons, Ltd, 1940) p. 180.

5 Leonard Woolf, *Quack, Quack!* (New York: Harcourt, Brace and Company, Inc., 1935) p. 20.

6 'Craftsmanship', in *The Death of the Moth*, p. 193.

7 'The Leaning Tower', in *The Moment and Other Essays* (New York: Harcourt Brace Jovanovich, 1948) p. 146.

8 Elizabeth Abel writes about Woolf's descriptions in *Three Guineas* of the fascist as a male mother. See *Virginia Woolf and the Fictions of Psychoanalysis* (Chicago: The University of Chicago Press, 1989) p. 92.

9 Rape is never far from Woolf's mind when she considers forms of authoritarianism. In *Between the Acts*, Isa Oliver keeps remembering a rape she reads about in the morning paper.

10 See '*Between the Acts*: the Play of Will' in *Virginia Woolf: Modern Critical Views*, Harold Bloom, ed. (New York: Chelsea House Publishers, 1986) p. 143.

11 Virginia Woolf, 'A Letter to a Young Poet', in Hermione Lee, ed., *The Hogarth Letters* (Athens: The University of Georgia Press, 1986) p. 230.

12 Leonard Woolf, 1940, pp. 200–1.

13 The sense of despair is heightened by a disparity: by 'nibbling', Woolf means her daily efforts to write – but the image of a mouse nibbling at a page actually suggests the *destruction* of the written word.

14 Leonard Woolf, 1940, p. 216.

15 Leonard Woolf, 1940, pp. 217–18.

16 Leonard Woolf, 1940, p. 219.

17 Leonard and Virginia's names were on a hit list compiled by the Nazis in case they did invade England. See Hermione Lee, *Virginia Woolf* (New York: Alfred A. Knopf, 1997), p. 718.

18 Leonard Woolf, 1940, p. 204.

19 'Thoughts on Peace', p. 247.

20 '[La Trobe] set down her glass. She heard the first words' (*BA*, p. 212).

10 'Finding New Words and Creating New Methods': *Three Guineas* and *The Handmaid's Tale*

For the purposes of this chapter, the following abbreviation will be used in addition to those which refer to Woolf's texts:

HT: Margaret Atwood's *The Handmaid's Tale* (London: Jonathan Cape, 1986).

1   Naomi Mitchison, 'The Reluctant Feminists', *Left Review*, 1.3 (December, 1934) 93.

2   Johanna Alberti, 'British Feminists and Anti-Fascism in the 1930s', in Sybil Oldfield, ed., *This Working-Day World: Women's Lives and Cultures in Britain 1914–1945* (London: Taylor and Francis, 1994) p. 118.

3   Brenda Silver, *Virginia Woolf's Reading Notebooks* (Princeton: Princeton University, Press, 1983) p. 292, quotes this segment from Elizabeth, Countess Bibesco's letter to Virginia Woolf dated January 1, 1935. The original is found in Virginia Woolf's *Reading Notebooks, The Monks House Papers* B. 16f, The University of Sussex, 3 vols related to *Three Guineas*, vol. 2, p. 51.

4   Virginia Woolf, *Three Guineas* (London: The Hogarth Press, 1938). Please note that in this chapter alone, all page references given in parenthetical citation are to the first British edition and not from the standard for the volume, the Harcourt Brace Jovanovich edition.

5   Jean Bethke Elshtain, *Women and War* (Brighton: The Harvester Press, 1987) pp. 3–4.

6   Elshtain, p. 4.

7   Elshtain, p. 4.

8   Letter from Margaret, Lady Rhondda to Virginia Woolf dated June 2, 1938. *The Letters of Virginia Woolf*, Vol. 6, Nigel Nicolson and Joanne Trautmann, eds (London: The Hogarth Press, 1976–1980) p. 236. Please note this is a different edition than the standard edition of Woolf's letters quoted from in the rest of this volume.

9   Letter from Virginia Woolf to Shena, Lady Simon, dated January 25, 1941, *Letters*, vol. 6 (Hogarth Press) p. 464.

10 Virginia Woolf, 'Thoughts on Peace in an Air Raid', in *The Death of the Moth* (London: Hogarth Press, 1942) p. 175.

11 Carol Gilligan, *In a Different Voice: Psychological Theory and Women's Development* (Cambridge: The Harvard University Press, 1982) p. 8.

12 Gilligan, p. 17

13 Gilligan, p. 22.

14 Toril Moi, *Sexual/Textual Politics* (London: Methuen, 1985) pp. 11–18.

15 Gill Plain, *Women's Fiction of the Second World War: Gender, Power, Resistance* (Edinburgh: Edinburgh University Press, 1996) p. 115.

16   Plain, p. 116.

17   Plain, p. 115.

18   Margaret Atwood, 'The Curse of Eve – Or, What I Learned in School (1978)', in Margaret Atwood, *Second Words: Selected Critical Prose* (Toronto: The House of Anansi Press, 1982) p. 227.

19   Atwood, 1982, p. 227.

20   Susan Faludi, *Backlash: the Undeclared War Against Women* (London: Chatto and Windus, 1992).

21   Winifred Holtby, *Women and a Changing Civilization* (London: John Lane, 1934) p. 152.

22   Edward Said, *Culture and Imperialism* (London: Chatto and Windus, 1993) p. 397.

23   Geoff Hancock, 'Tightrope-Walking Over Niagara Falls', in Earl G. Ingersoll, ed., *Margaret Atwood: Conversations* (London: Virago, 1992) p. 216.

24   Margaret Atwood, 'Amnesty International: An Address (1981)', 1982, p. 394.

25   Barbara Norden, 'American Nightmare', *Everywoman* (November, 1990) 14.

26   Bonnie Lyons, 'Using Other People's Dreadful Childhoods', in Ingersoll, p. 223.

27   Virginia Woolf, 'Thoughts on Peace in an Air Raid', *The Death of the Moth and Other Essays* 1942 (San Diego: Harcourt Brace Jovanovich, 1970) p. 247.

28   Margaret Atwood, *Surfacing* (London: Deutsch, 1985) p. 222.

29   Dale M. Bauer, *Feminist Dialogics: a Theory of Failed Community* (Albany: The State University of New York Press, 1988) p. 4.

30   Margaret Atwood, 'The Curse of Eve', 1982, pp. 222–3.

31   Barbara Rigney, *Margaret Atwood* (Basingstoke: Macmillan, 1987) p. 10.

32   Margaret Kaminski, 'Preserving Mythologies', in Ingersoll, p. 31.

33   Naomi Black, 'Virginia Woolf: the Life of Natural Happiness (1882–1941)', in Dale Spender, ed., *Feminist Theorists: Three Centuries of Women's Intellectual Traditions* (London: The Women's Press, 1983) p. 304.

34   Maria diBattista, *Virginia Woolf's Major Novels: the Fables of Anon* (New Haven: The Yale University Press, 1980) p. 193.

35   Patricia Jagentowicz Mills, *Woman, Nature, and Psyche* (New Haven and London: The Yale University Press) pp. 17–36.

36   Susan Stanford Friedman, 'Beyond White and Other: Relationality and Narratives of Race in Feminist Discourse', *Signs: Journal of Women in Culture and Society*, 2.1 (1995) 16.

37   Friedman, p. 19.

38   Quoted in Jim Davidson, 'Where Were You When I Really Needed You?', Ingersoll, p. 94.

39   Gregory Fitz Gerald and Kathryn Crabbe, 'Evading the Pigeonholers', in Ingersoll, p. 139.

40   Patricia Duncker, 'Heterosexuality: Fictional Agandas', in Sue Wilkinson and Celia Kitzinger, eds, *Heterosexuality: a Feminism and Psychology Reader* (London: Sage Publications, 1993) p. 138.

41   Jeanne Schulkind, ed., *Virginia Woolf, Moments of Being: Unpublished Autobiographical Writings* (London: The Sussex University Press, 1976) pp. 126–7.

42   Sudhakar Jamkhandi, 'An Interview with Margaret Atwood', *Commonwealth Novel in English*, 2.1 (January, 1983) 5.

43   Davidson, p. 96.

44 Jill Bihan, '*The Handmaid's Tale, Cat's Eye* and *Interlunar*: Margaret Atwood's Feminist (?) Futures (?)', in Coral Ann Howells and Lynette Hunter, eds, *Narrative Strategies in Canadian Literature* (Milton Keynes: The Open University Press, 1991) p. 94.
45 Fitz Gerald and Crabbe, p. 139.
46 Sybil Oldfield, *Women Against the Iron Fist: Alternatives to Militarism 1900–1989* (Oxford: Basil Blackwell, 1989) p. 112.
47 Alexander Zwerdling, *Virginia Woolf and the Real World* (Berkeley: The University of California Press, 1986) p. 217.
48 Gill Plain, p. 115.

11 Seduced by Fascism: Benedetta Cappa Marinetti, the Woman Who Did Not Write *Three Guineas*

I want to thank my friend Janet Dunolly who tried, I hope not in vain, to make my written English comprehensible and Merry Pawlowski for the chance she gave me. This chapter is dedicated to the memory of my friend Federica Manfredini, painter, teacher, and art-historian.

1 See Victoria De Grazia, *How Fascism Ruled Women. Italy 1922–1945* (University of California Press, 1992).
2 Grazia Deledda, who in 1926 won the Nobel Prize for Literature, devoted herself only to her novels.
3 'If the past (and present?) relationship between women and fascist ideology is not analysed, if we do not analyse how and why fascism has fooled women . . . then feminism is mutilated', Maria Antonietta Macciocchi, 'Female Sexuality in Fascist Ideology', quoted in Merry Pawlowski, 'An Editorial Comment on Woolf and Fascism', *Virginia Woolf Miscellany*, 44 (Fall, 1994) 1.
4 Ms Cappa Marinetti adopted her christian name as a pseudonym.
5 Vanessa Bell, *Notes on Virginia's Childhood*, in *Sketches in Pen and Ink*, ed., Lia Giachero (London: Chatto and Windus, 1997) pp. 57–8.
6 Woolf was born in 1882 and Benedetta in 1897.
7 Unfortunately the paintings by her that we know are fewer than 30 and it is hard to know, even roughly, how many she actually painted.
8 *Le forze umane. Romanzo astratto con sintesi grafiche* (Foligno: Campitelli, 1924); *Viaggio di Gararà. Romanzo cosmico per il teatro* (Milan: Morreale, 1931); *Astra e il sottomarino. Vita trasognata* (Naples: Casella, 1935). The third one is considered the most readable and in fact was republished by the Editori del Grifo in 1991 and in an anthology of futurist novels, by il Saggiatore in 1995. All three of them can be read in the most recent (although not very accurate) edition (Rome: Edizioni dell 'Altana, 1998), edited by Simona Cigliana. Many futurist scholars have written essays on Benedetta, the most recent ones can be found in Mirella Bentivoglio and Franca Zoccoli, *Women Artists of Italian Futurism – Almost Lost to History* (New York: Midmarch Art Press, 1997) and in Anna Maria Ruta, ed., *Fughe e ritorni. Presenze Futuriste in Sicilia. Benedetta* (Naples: Electa, 1998).

9   'Futurist project for recruitment for the next war', *Futurismo*, 4 (October, 1932).
10   *Motherland women in war* (Capania and Siracusa: INCF, 1942).
11

The whole system of military call-up should be reversed so that the first contingent would be made up of sixty and fifty-year-olds. Then the forty and the thirty-year-olds. This futurist solution would have the following principal advantages:

1. It would preserve the maximum number of young men of the victorious Motherland for the years following the war, thus eliminating the crisis of disturbed young soldiers. In the case that . . . the future war destroyed all the combatants in the first contingents the Motherland would still have all its young.

2. Upgrade the old men from the patriotic point of view by offering them a useful and glorious death on the battlefield . . . Not least because a future war . . . will not require . . . much physical strength . . ., but will require the conscious courage of the mature man.

3. Keep the young soldiers for the last effort . . . when the armies are exhausted . . .

4. Eliminate the problem of jealousy of the young at the front and that of their women besieged by the forty and fifty-year-olds left in the city. Many more sons will be born to the Motherland and only 'mature' women will be left alone.

12   Benedetta Marinetti, 'La leva rovesciata', *Futurismo*, 14 (December 11, 1932) 1.
13   'regarding the military and moral aspects'
14   'I am happy to believe that all women will be proud to contribute in time of war as they contribute in time of peace (both in the family and in society) to the glory of the Motherland.'
15   That is the years 1918–20. In 1918 the Partito Politico Futurista (Futurist Political Party) was founded; in 1919 Marinetti was candidate at elections, in Milan, together with fascists (there was with him – and perhaps few people are aware of it – also Arturo Toscanini); in 1920 Marinetti left the Fascist Party (Fasci di Combattimento) because of his disagreements with Mussolini. From this time on Marinetti and his movement would never meddle in active politics even when he and Mussolini forgot their disagreements.
16   Virginia Woolf, *Three Guineas*, from *A Room of One's Own and Three Guineas* (London: Chatto and Windus – The Hogarth Press, 1984) p. 113. Please note that this is a different edition from the standard edition abbreviated throughout the volume and that all future references to both *A Room of One's Own* and *Three Guineas* in this chapter will be from this edition.
17   'the next war'
18   Although in her case she married Marinetti (not in a church) after having lived together for some years.
19   Benedetta's three daughters, Vittoria, Ala, and Luce, during various interviews, said that they had received quite a conventional education.
20   Woolf, *Three Guineas*, p. 229.

21 'War is to man as maternity is to woman.'

22 See the quotation from 'La leva rovesciata'.

23 'The Italian woman is not and will never be in competition with men. She is too profoundly mother. When I say mother you have to understand the word in its broadest meaning of parent; of generator of men, of feelings, of passion, of ideas.' *Spirituality of the Italian Woman*, published in the *Giornale d'Italia*, is the text of a lecture Benedetta toured Italy with during the Ethiopian War.

24 'Since through fascism we have had the gift of being placed spiritually at the peak of life, since the united and inseparable family has been given more importance, since by encouraging our natural instinct we became blessed mothers and motherhood is a favourite and protected state . . .' This article was published in issues 3–4 of *Origini*.

25 'When the new life of our child blossomed in our mothers' hearts and he became for us the spring time of the world, we passed on to him our thoughts, our dreams, our will, so that he would become rich in human goodness . . . so that his creative intelligence would shed light on his daily toil; so that he would possess the strength which defends and creates . . . we gladly accepted that our flesh be torn, on condition that our son be spared our wounds on his flesh, but also, and perhaps most of all, so that his body would learn to accept the offer of sacrifice through obeying the law of the love of life.' *Italian Will* is a small book published by Edizioni Erre in 1944.

26 Useless to say that women belonging to the wealthy upper classes were seldom *prolific mothers* (although there were exceptions such as Virginia Agnelli). On the other hand it is important to note that Italy was the only industrialized country in which salaries diminished from the beginning of the 1920s to the Second World War.

27 Women's salaries had been cut down by half in 1927 by law.

28 See De Grazia.

29 See Lucia Aducci, 'Crisi del romanzo femminile', *anno XIII*, 22 (May 30, 1935). Benedetta's reply, in the succeeding issue, is synthetic, brilliant, telling.

30 'knows how to betray but not how to wait'

31

> I seek the voice which awakes echoes in the valleys
> laden with pleasure
> with warmth to disperse the cold of space,
> with blood to color the horizons
> with passion to populate life itself.
> (Benedetta, 1991, pp. 64–5)

32 'when events require it'

33 'from the fragile person a force of passion and of heroism which multiplies a hundred times physical strength, spreads a positive influence, transforms intelligence into vision and renders prodigious the acts of love'

34 'Life exists so that we can offer it to our country'

35 'mount through the solitude of implacable grief to rest among the highest peaks of pride'

36 Woolf, *A Room of One's Own*, 1984, p. 96.

37 *Mount Tabor*, 1939 ca., oil on canvas, 94 × 128.5 cm, private collection.
38 *Rhythms of rocks and sea*, oil on canvas, 80 × 130 cm, private collection.
39 *The big X*, 1930, oil on canvas, 129 × 90 cm, Paris, Musée d'Art Moderne de la Ville de Paris.
40 Marinetti accepted a position as member of the Accademia Italiana in 1929. Many futurists considered this fact a betrayal of the spirit of the movement.

12 Eternal Fascism and its 'Home Haunts' in the Leavises' Attacks on Bloomsbury and Woolf

1 Quentin Bell, *Virginia Woolf: a Biography* (New York: Harcourt Brace Jovanovich, 1972) vol. II, p. 205.
2 Alex Zwerdling, *Virginia Woolf and the Real World* (Berkeley: University of California Press, 1986) p. 293.
3 Maynard Keynes, *Two Memoirs* (London: Rupert Hart-Davis, 1949) pp. 98–100.
4 Zwerdling, p. 294.
5 Woolf's critique of the worship of reason conveys many of the concerns expressed by the Frankfurt School theorists in their critical analyses of the destructive effects of instrumental reason, in particular the technological domination of nature and atomization and annihilation of the individual.
6 Umberto Eco, 'Ur-Fascism', *The New York Review of Books*, XLII, no. 11 (June 22, 1995) 14.
7 Andreas Huyssen, *After the Great Divide: Modernism, Mass Culture, Postmodernism* (Bloomington: Indiana University Press, 1986) pp. 49–54.
8 Wyndham Lewis, *Men Without Art* (London: Cassell, 1934) pp. 170–8.
9 John Carey, *The Intellectuals and the Masses: Pride and Prejudice among the Literary Intelligentsia, 1880–1939* (New York: St. Martin's Press, 1992) p. 186.
10 Eco, p. 15.
11 Eco, p. 14.
12 Max Horkheimer, 'The End of Reason', *The Essential Frankfurt School Reader*, eds, Andrew Arato and Eike Gebhart (New York: Continuum, 1994) pp. 26–48.
13 Paul Berry and Alan Bishop, *Testament of a Generation: the Journalism of Vera Brittain and Winifred Holtby* (London: Virago, 1985) p. 172.
14 Eco, pp. 14–15.
15 See Queenie Leavis, 'Fresh Approach to *Wuthering Heights*', F. R. and Q. D. Leavis, *Lectures in America* (New York: Pantheon Books, 1969) p. 310. Queenie applies these characteristics to Emily Brontë and to the characters in the novel. She focuses on Nelly Dean as the normative center of the novel – mature, commonsensical, selfless, motherly, robust, and possessed of a 'wholesome classlessness'. By contrast, most of the other characters (the younger Cathy being the notable exception) are criticized as being immature, perverse, selfish, and/or sickly. Queenie is especially intolerant of immaturity and physical frailty.
16 See David Stephen Lewis, *Illusions of Grandeur: Mosley, Fascism and British Society, 1931–81* (Manchester: Manchester University Press, 1987) pp. 38–9.

Lewis points out that although the Nazis made ready use of racial theories produced by British philosophers and scientists who endorsed social Darwinism, the British Union of Fascists showed a reluctance to fully exploit these home-grown theories. The BUF avoided using stock racist terms such as 'Aryan', preferring instead 'Britishness' or 'Anglo-Saxon'. The BUF's particular brand of racism derived from its rabid nationalism rather than from the theories of pre-1914 geneticists.

17 Thus, for example, in Leavis's repeated criticism of Auden's 'failure to develop' and 'inverted development', I discern something more than poetical immaturity at issue.

18 Francis Mulhern, 'English Reading', *Nation and Narration*, ed., Homi Bhaba (New York: Routledge, 1993) p. 253.

19 Mulhern, p. 258.

20 David Carroll, *French Literary Fascism: Nationalism, Anti-semitism, and the Ideology of Culture* (Princeton: Princeton University Press, 1995) pp. 160–1.

21 Eco, p. 15.

22 Francis Mulhern, *The Moment of 'Scrutiny'* (London: NLB, 1979) pp. 38–9.

23 Queenie Dorothy Leavis, *Fiction and the Reading Public* (London: Bellew Publishing, 1990) p. 270.

24 Noel Annan, 'Bloomsbury and the Leavises', *Virginia Woolf and Bloomsbury*, ed., Jane Marcus (Bloomington: Indiana University Press, 1987) pp. 27–8.

25 Eco, p. 14.

26 Annan, pp. 31–2.

27 Mulhern, 1979, p. 56.

28 F. R. Leavis, *The Great Tradition: George Eliot, Henry James, Joseph Conrad*, 1948 (Harmondsworth: Penguin Books, 1966 repr.) p. 144.

29 F. R. Leavis, *A Selection from 'Scrutiny'* (Cambridge: Cambridge University Press, 1968) vol. II, p. 99.

30 F. R. Leavis, *D. H. Lawrence: Novelist*, 1955 (Harmondsworth: Penguin Books, 1968 repr.) p. 151.

31 F. R. Leavis, 1968, p. 235.

32 R. P. Bilan, *The Literary Criticism of F. R. Leavis* (New York: Cambridge University Press, 1979) pp. 267–8.

33 F. R. Leavis, *The Common Pursuit*, 1952 (Harmondsworth: Penguin Books, 1966 repr.) p. 256.

34 Bilan, pp. 212–13.

35 Jane Marcus, *Art and Anger: Reading Like a Woman* (Columbus: Ohio State University Press, 1988) p. 261.

36 Queenie Leavis, 'Caterpillars of the Commonwealth Unite!', *Scrutiny* 7.2 (September, 1938) 203.

37 Q. Leavis, 1938, p. 204.

38 Q. Leavis, 1938, p. 208.

39 Q. Leavis, 1938, p. 208.

40 Q. Leavis, 1938, p. 206.

41 In a letter dated December 2, 1939 to her niece Judith Stephen, Woolf focuses on the continuing discrimination against female students at Cambridge.

42 Q. Leavis, 1938, p. 206.

43 Q. Leavis, 1938, p. 209.

44 Q. Leavis, 1938, p. 212.
45 Mulhern, 1993, pp. 258–9.
46 Shari Benstock, *Women of the Left Bank: Paris, 1900–1940* (Austin: University of Texas Press, 1986) pp. 124–5.
47 Benstock, p. 125.
48 Neither Gramsci's nor Reich's perspective was feminist, however. Although Gramsci's concept of hegemony sought to explain the complexity of power relations in the spaces of everyday life, it stopped short of examining the ways power worked in sexual relationships. In his Freudian-Marxist synthesis, Reich preserved the phallocentricity of Freud's and Marx's theories. He focused on mass psychology and sexual repression, while overlooking sexual differences.
49 Maria-Antonietta Macciocchi, 'Female Sexuality in Fascist Ideology', *Feminist Review* 1 (1979) 67.
50 Macciocchi, p. 69.
51 Macciocchi, p. 76.
52 Virginia Woolf, 'Thoughts on Peace in an Air Raid', *The Death of the Moth and Other Essays* (New York: Harcourt Brace Jovanovich, 1942) p. 245.
53 Macciocchi, p. 73.
54 Jane Caplan, 'Introduction to Female Sexuality in Fascist Ideology', *Feminist Review* 1 (1979) 63.
55 Eco, p. 15.
56 In his excellent study of French 'literary fascism', David Carroll begins with the provocative observation that the long-lived explanation of fascism as an aberration within the dominant Western political tradition completely fails to account for why 'fascism could have appeared as an attractive alternative to democracy to political theorists, writers, and intellectuals who were not irrational nihilists but in fact were very committed to traditional values, art, and culture, and even to a form of classical humanism'. These writers and theorists saw fascism as a way of revitalizing a rational humanist tradition that had been nearly destroyed in modernity (p. 3).
57 The sources of the quotations are: (1) *The Letters of D. H. Lawrence*, ed., James T. Boulton (New York: Cambridge University Press, 1979) vol. I, p. 81; (2) H. G. Wells, *Anticipations of the Reaction of Mechanical and Scientific Progress upon Human Life and Thought* (London: Chapman and Hall, 1901) pp. 298–9; (3) Mosley's weekly column, *The Fascist Week* (December 22–28, 1933) 1; (4) T. S. Eliot, *Christianity and Culture* (New York: Harcourt Brace Jovanovich, 1968) p. 185; (5) Ezra Pound, *The Egoist* 1.2 (February 16, 1914) 67–8; (6) Carey, p. 186.

13 Dystopian Modernism vs Utopian Feminism: Burdekin, Woolf, and West Respond to the Rise of Fascism

For the purposes of this chapter the following abbreviations will be used in addition to those for Woolf's *Three Guineas*:

SN: Katharine Burdekin's *Swastika Night* (New York: Feminist Press, 1985).
BL: Rebecca West's *Black Lamb and Grey Falcon* (New York: Viking Press, 1941).

1   John Maynard Keynes, 'My Early Beliefs', *The Bloomsbury Group: a Collection of Memoirs, Commentary and Criticism*, ed., S. P. Rosenbaum (London: Croom Helm, 1975) p. 62.
2   See Nan Bowman Albinski, *Women's Utopias in British and American Fiction* (London and New York: Routledge, 1988); M. Keith Booker, *The Dystopian Impulse in Modern Literature: Fiction as Social Criticism* (Westport: Greenwood Press, 1994); Tom Moylan, *Demand the Impossible: Science Fiction and the Utopian Imagination* (New York and London: Methuen, 1986); Peter Ruppert, *Reader in a Strange Land: the Activity of Reading Literary Utopias* (Athens and London: University of Georgia Press, 1986); and Chad Walsh, *From Utopia to Nightmare* (Westport: Greenwood Press, 1962).
3   Seyla Benhabib, 'Feminism and Postmodernism: an Uneasy Alliance', *Feminist Contentions: a Philosophical Exchange* (New York and London: Routledge, 1995) pp. 29–30.
4   Benhabib, p. 30.
5   See Albinski pp. 87–94, for more dystopian women writers of this era.
6   The self-reflexive modernism of male contemporaries such as Eliot, Pound, Yeats, and Lawrence has long been associated with fascist ideology. Among many works suggesting this link are Frank Kermode's *Sense of an Ending* (New York: Oxford University Press, 1967), John R. Harrison's *The Reactionaries* (New York: Schocken Books, 1967), Elizabeth Cullingford's *Yeats, Ireland and Fascism* (New York: New York University Press, 1981), Tim Redman's *Ezra Pound and Italian Fascism* (Cambridge: Cambridge University Press, 1991), and Anne Fernihough's *D. H. Lawrence: Ideology and Aesthetics* (Oxford: Clarendon Press, 1993).
7   I am not interested in categorizing these works according to strict generic definitions, and many fine distinctions are made in the criticism of utopian, dystopian, and anti-utopian literature; for example, differences exist between a utopia, a representation of a 'good place' (eutopia) that is 'no place' (outopia); a dystopia, a representation of a 'bad place'; and an anti-utopia, a narrative that critiques the desire for utopia, a cynical text that suggests perfectibility is impossible. Rather, I find the concepts of 'utopia' and 'dystopia' richly suggestive and use them loosely.
8   See Max Horkheimer and Theodor W. Adorno, *Dialectic of Enlightenment*, trans. John Cumming (New York: Continuum, 1993).
9   See David Harvey, *The Condition of Postmodernity* (Oxford: Basil Blackwell, 1989) p. 13.
10 See George Mosse, *The Crisis of German Ideology* (New York: Grosset & Dunlap, 1964) and *Masses and Man: Nationalist and Fascist Perceptions of Reality* (New York: Howard Fertig, 1980), especially pp. 69–86. Mosse analyzes literary works such as fairy tales that proposed a utopian vision of a Volkish nation. One result of this utopian impulse was to 'stimulate the yearning for the actualization of the ideology . . . here and now', for example in agrarian communities, Mosse, 1964, p. 123. Alfred Rosenberg, Nazi theorist and ideologue, described his vision of the total state as 'the means by which National Socialism, the mightiest phenomenon originating in the twentieth century' embodies the *Weltanschauung* of the 'collective German Volk . . . its blood and character'. See Alfred Rosenberg, *Race and Race History and Other Essays*, ed., Robert Pois (New York: Harper and Row, 1970) p. 192.

11 Barbara Goodwin and Keith Taylor, *The Politics of Utopia* (New York: St. Martin's Press, 1982) p. 235. They further explain that 'a well-established school of thought . . . equate[s] utopianism and totalitarianism', p. 181. At the same time, a debate exists between this analysis and that which links utopianism with 'communitarianism' in which 'utopianism . . . becomes synonymous with hostility to the large, powerful nation-state', p. 181. Goodwin and Taylor conclude that 'it is by no means easy to classify Fascism in any straightforward fashion as utopian or non-utopian', p. 23.

12 Darrell Fasching, *The Ethical Challenge of Auschwitz and Hiroshima: Apocalypse or Utopia?* (Albany: State University of New York Press, 1993) p. 28.

13 Victoria de Grazia, *How Fascism Ruled Women: Italy, 1922–1945* (Berkeley: University of California Press, 1992) p. 1.

14 Adoph Hitler, *Mein Kampf*, trans. Ralph Mannheim (Boston: Houghton Mifflin, 1962) p. 441.

15 Daphne Patai, 'Imagining Reality: the Utopian Fiction of Katharine Burdekin', in *Rediscovering Forgotten Radicals*, eds., Angela Ingram and Daphne Patai (Chapel Hill and London: University of North Carolina Press, 1993) p. 243.

16 Brenda Silver, *Virginia Woolf's Reading Notebooks* (Princeton: Princeton University Press, 1983) p. 311.

17 De Grazia shows, however, that the implementation of this ideology did not always maintain such a strict division of labor.

18 At points, Burdekin makes explicit jabs at England, for example when a German character tells Alfred 'You ought to be ashamed of your race, Alfred, even though your Empire vanished seven hundred years ago. It isn't long enough to get rid of the taint' (*SN*, p. 78).

19 Daphne Patai, 'Introduction', Katharine Burdekin, *Swastika Night*, p. vi.

20 Susan Kingsley Kent explains in 'The Politics of Sexual Difference: World War I and the Demise of British Feminism', *Journal of British Studies* 27 (July, 1988) 249, that '[a]lthough postwar crimes did not rise dramatically' in England, newspapers were filled with reports about violent acts against women often by ex-soldiers.

21 Patai, 'Introduction', p. vii.

22 Klaus P. Fischer, *Nazi Germany: a New History* (New York: Continuum, 1995) p. 366.

23 Booker, p. 11.

24 Rachel Blau duPlessis describes 'feminist apologues – including utopian and science fiction – as "teaching stories contain[ing] embedded elements from 'assertive discourse' – genres like sermon, manifesto, tract, fable – . . . in which elements like character and plot function mainly as the bearers of philosophical propositions or moral arguments" '. Quoted in Jane L. Donawerth and Carol A. Kolmerton, eds, *Utopian and Science Fiction by Women* (Syracuse: Syracuse University Press, 1994) p. 3.

25 Jean Pfaelzer, *The Utopian Novel in America 1886–1896* (Pittsburgh: University of Pittsburgh Press, 1984) p. 78.

26 Booker, p. 15.

27 Cranny-Francis claims that 'One of the major conventions of utopian fiction, in common with other generic forms such as science fiction and

fantasy, is estrangement' in *Feminist Fiction: Feminist Uses of Generic Fiction* (Cambridge: Polity Press, 1990) p. 110. Patai emphasizes the term 'defamiliarization' as used by Victor Shklovsky and Bertolt Brecht in 'Beyond Defensiveness: Feminist Research Strategies', in *Women and Utopia*, eds, Marlene Barr and Nicholas D. Smith (Lanham and London: University Press of America, 1983) p. 152.

28 Alex Zwerdling, *Virginia Woolf and the Real World* (Berkeley: University of California Press, 1986) p. 293.

29 Marie-Luise Gättens, *Women Writers and Fascism* (Gainesville: University Press of Florida, 1995) p. 20.

30 Sandra M. Gilbert and Susan Gubar, *No Man's Land*, Vol. 3 (New Haven: Yale University Press, 1994) p. 223.

31 Michele Barrett, '*A Room of One's Own* and *Three Guineas*: Introduction', in *Virginia Woolf: Introductions to the Major Works*, ed., Julia Briggs (London: Virago, 1994) p. 385.

32 Jane Marcus, ' "No More Horses": Virginia Woolf on Art and Propaganda', in *Critical Essays on Virginia Woolf*, ed., Morris Beja (Boston: G. K. Hall, 1985) p. 154.

33 Toril Moi, *Sexual/Textual Politics* (London and New York: Methuen, 1985) p. 14.

34 Moi, p. 8.

35 Michele Barrett says '*Three Guineas* is often thought to be more pessimistic about women's solidarity than *A Room of One's Own* . . . but in [some] passage[s] we see a flash of Virginia Woolf's earlier optimism', pp. 375–6.

36 Victoria Glendinning, *Rebecca West: a Life* (New York: Alfred A. Knopf, 1987) pp. 163–4.

37 Brian Hall, 'Rebecca West's War', *The New Yorker* (April 15, 1996) 74.

38 See my 'Female Sacrifice: Gender and Nostalgic Nationalism in Rebecca West's *Black Lamb and Grey Falcon*', in *Nostalgia, Gender, and Nationalism*, eds., Suzanne Kehde and Jean Pickering (New York: New York University Press, 1996).

39 Rebecca West, *St. Augustine*, 1933, in *Rebecca West: a Celebration*, ed., Samuel Hynes (New York: Viking, 1977), p. 234.

40 Glendinning, p. 223.

41 West, *Augustine*, p. 234.

42 Completing this chapter during the military crisis in Kosovo raises multiple ironies about West's interpretations of the Balkans.

43 In *A Room of One's Own*, Woolf criticizes the 'obscure masculine complex which has had so much influence upon the women's movement; that deep-seated desire, not so much that *she* shall be inferior as that *he* shall be superior', p. 57.

44 Glendinning, p. 166.

Select Bibliography

In this bibliography I cannot offer an exhaustive guide but rather it is my intention to direct the reader to works that have been most helpful to the contributors of this volume. There are few works to date which explore Woolf in the context of fascism directly, so I have tried to be as complete as possible on that topic. My other criteria for selection to this list included choosing several good introductions to historical fascism; works which Woolf herself read on the topic; those which explore writers and fascism; those which focus on British fascism, works on women, gender, and fascism; and, finally, works which examine the insemination of culture with fascist ideology.

Abel, Elizabeth, *Virginia Woolf and the Fictions of Psychoanalysis.* Chicago: University of Chicago Press, 1989.

Affron, Matthew, and Mark Antliff, *Fascist Visions: Art and Ideology in France and Italy.* Princeton University Press, 1997.

Alberti, Johanna, 'British Feminists and Anti-Fascism in the 1930s', in Sybil Oldfield, ed., *This Working-Day World: Women's Lives and Cultures in Britain 1914–1945.* London: Taylor and Francis, 1994.

Berman, Russell, 'The Aestheticization of Politics: Walter Benjamin on Fascism and the Avant-Garde', *Stanford Italian Review* 8 (1990): 35–52.

——, 'Modernism, Fascism, and the Institution of Literature', in Monique Chefdor *et al.*, eds, *Modernism: Challenges and Perspectives.* Urbana: University of Illinois Press, 1986, pp. 94–110.

Bradshaw, David, 'British Writers and Anti-Fascism in the 1930s', *Woolf Studies Annual* 3 (1997): 3–27; and 4 (1998): 41–66.

Bridenthal, Renate, Altina Grossmann, and Marian Kaplan, eds, *When Biology Became Destiny: Women in Weimar and Nazi Germany.* New York: Monthly Review Press, 1984.

Caplan, Jane, 'Introduction to Female Sexuality in Fascist Ideology', *Feminist Review* 1 (1979): 59–66.

Carlston, Erin G., *Thinking Fascism: Sapphic Modernism and Fascist Modernity.* Stanford: Stanford University Press, 1998.

Carroll, David, *French Literary Fascism: Nationalism, Anti-semitism, and the Ideology of Culture.* Princeton: Princeton University Press, 1995.

Casillo, Robert, *The Genealogy of Demons: Anti-Semitism, Fascism, and the Myths of Ezra Pound.* Evanston, IL: Northwestern University Press, 1988.

Cullingford, Elizabeth, *Yeats, Ireland, and Fascism.* New York: New York University Press, 1981.

Drennan, James, *BUF: Oswald Mosley and British Fascism.* London: J. Murray, 1934.

Durham, Martin, *Women and Fascism.* New York: Routledge, 1998.

Elshtain, Jean Bethke, *Women and War.* Brighton: The Harvester Press, 1987.

Gättens, Marie-Luise, *Women Writers and Fascism: Reconstructing History.* Gainesville: University Press of Florida, 1995.

Gilbert, Sandra, and Susan Gubar, *No Man's Land: the Place of the Woman Writer in the Twentieth Century.* 3 vols. New Haven: Yale University Press, 1988–96.

Golsan, Richard, ed., *Fascism, Aesthetics, and Culture.* Hanover: University Press of New England, 1992.

de Grazia, Victoria, *How Fascism Ruled Women: Italy, 1922–1945.* Berkeley: University of California Press, 1992.

Griffin, Roger, ed., *International Fascism: Theories, Causes, and the New Consensus.* New York: Oxford University Press, 1998.

——, *The Nature of Fascism.* New York: Routledge, 1993.

——, *Women and Fascism.* New York: Oxford University Press, 1995.

Hamilton, Alastair, *The Appeal of Fascism: a Study of Intellectuals and Fascism, 1919–1945.* New York: Macmillan, 1971.

Harrison, John R., *The Reactionaries: Yeats, Lewis, Pound, Eliot, Lawrence.* New York: Schocken Books, 1967.

Hewitt, Andrew, *Fascist Modernism: Aesthetics, Politics, and the Avant-Garde.* Stanford University Press, 1993.

——, *Political Inversions: Homosexuality, Fascism, and the Modernist Imagination.* Stanford University Press, 1996.

Holtby, Winifred, *Women and a Changing Civilization.* 1935. Chicago: Academy Press, 1978.

Hussey, Mark, ed., *Virginia Woolf and War: Fiction, Reality, and Myth.* Syracuse University Press, 1991.

Jameson, Fredric, *Fables of Aggression: Wyndham Lewis, the Modernist as Fascist.* Berkeley: University of California Press, 1979.

Joannou, Maroula, *'Ladies, Please Don't Smash These Windows': Women's Writing, Feminist Consciousness, and Social Change 1918–38.* Oxford: Berg, 1995.

Kaplan, Alice Yaegar, *Reproductions of Banality: Fascism, Literature, and French Intellectual Life.* Minneapolis: University of Minnesota Press, 1986.

Kedward, H. R., *Fascism in Western Europe 1900–1945.* New York: New York University Press, 1971.

Koonz, Claudia, *Mothers in the Fatherland. Women, the Family and Nazi Politics.* New York: St. Martin's Press, 1987.

Laqueur, Walter, ed., *Fascism: a Reader's Guide, Analyses, Interpretations, Bibliography.* Berkeley: University of California Press, 1976.

Larsen, Stein, and Beatrice Sandberg, eds, *Fascism and European Literature.* New York: Peter Lang, 1991.

Lewis, D. S., *Illusions of Grandeur: Mosley, Fascism and British Society, 1931–81.* Manchester: Manchester University Press, 1987.

Lyttleton, Adrian, *The Seizure of Power: Fascism in Italy 1919–1929.* London: Weidenfeld and Nicolson, 1973.

Macciocchi, Maria-Antonietta, 'Female Sexuality in Fascist Ideology', *Feminist Review* 1 (1979): 67–79.

Marcus, Jane, *Art and Anger: Reading Like a Woman.* Columbus: Ohio State University Press, 1988.

——, *Virginia Woolf and the Languages of Patriarchy.* Bloomington, IN: Indiana University Press, 1987.

Martin, Elaine, ed., *Gender, Patriarchy, and Fascism in the Third Reich: the Response of Women Writers.* Detroit: Wayne State University Press, 1993.

Mosley, Oswald, Sir, *Fascism in Britain*. Westminster: British Union of Fascists, n.d.

Mosse, George, *The Crisis of German Ideology: Intellectual Origins of the Third Reich*. New York: Grosset and Dunlap, 1964.

——, *The Culture of Western Europe*, 2nd edn. Chicago: Rand McNally College Pub Co., 1974.

——, *The Fascist Revolution: Toward a General Theory of Fascism*. New York: Howard Fertig, 1999.

——, *The Image of Man: the Creation of Modern Masculinity*. New York: Oxford University Press, 1996.

——, and Walter Laqueur, eds, *Literature and Society: Literature and Politics in the Twentieth Century*. New York: Harper and Row, 1967.

——, *Masses and Man: Nationalist and Fascist Perceptions of Reality*. New York: Howard Fertig, 1980.

——, *Nationalism and Sexuality: Respectability and Abnormal Sexuality in Modern Europe*. New York: Howard Fertig, 1985.

——, ed., *Nazi Culture: Intellectual, Cultural, and Social Life in the Third Reich*. New York: Grosset and Dunlap, 1966.

Mussolini, Benito, *The Political and Social Doctrine of Fascism*, trans. Jane Soames. London: L. and V. Woolf at the Hogarth Press, 1933.

Newitt, Hilary, *Women Must Choose: the Position of Women in Europe Today*. London: Victor Gollancz Ltd, 1937.

Nolte, Ernst, *Three Faces of Fascism, Action Française, Italian Fascism, National Socialism*, trans. Leila Vennewitz. New York: Holt, Rinehart and Winston, 1966.

Oldfield, Sybil, *Women Against the Iron Fist Fist: Alternatives to Militarism, 1900–1989*. Oxford: Basil Blackwell, 1989.

Pawlowski, Merry M., ' "all the gents. against me": Virginia Woolf, *Three Guineas*, and the Sons of Educated Men', in *Virginia Woolf: Emerging Perspectives, Selected Papers from the Third Annual Conference on Virginia Woolf*, eds, Mark Hussey and Vara Neverow-Turk. New York: Pace University Press, 1994: 44–51.

——, 'An Editorial Comment on Woolf and Fascism', *Virginia Woolf Miscellany* 44 (Fall, 1994).

——, 'On Feminine Subjectivity and Fascist Ideology: the "Sex-War" Between Virginia Woolf and Wyndham Lewis', in *Virginia Woolf and the Arts: Selected Papers from the 6th Annual Virginia Woolf Conference*, eds, Diane F. Gillespie and Leslie K. Hankins. Pace University Press, 1997: 243–51.

——, 'Reassessing Modernism: Virginia Woolf, *Three Guineas*, and Fascist Ideology', *Woolf Studies Annual* 1 (Spring, 1995): 53–74.

Pickering-Iazzi, Robin, *Mothers of Invention: Women, Italian Fascism, and Culture*. Minneapolis: University of Minnesota Press, 1995.

——, *Politics of the Visible: Writing Women, Culture, and Fascism*. University of Minnesota Press, 1997.

Plain, Gill, *Women's Fiction of the Second World War: Gender, Power, Resistance*. Edinburgh: Edinburgh University Press, 1996.

Phillips, Kathy J., *Virginia Woolf Against Empire*. Knoxville: University of Tennessee Press, 1994.

Reich, Wilhelm, *The Mass Psychology of Fascism*, trans. Theodore P. Wolfe. 3rd edn. New York: Orgone Institute Press, 1946.

Schnapp, Jeffrey, and Barbara Spackman, eds, 'Selections from the Great Debate on Fascism and Culture: *Critica Fascista* 1926–1927', *Stanford Italian Review* 8. 1–2 (1990): 235–72.

Shaw, Bernard, *The Intelligent Woman's Guide to Socialism, Capitalism, Sovietism, and Fascism*. 1928. New York: Random House, 1971.

Silver, Brenda, 'The Authority of Anger: *Three Guineas* as Case Study', *Signs* 16 (Winter, 1991): 340–70.

——, *Virginia Woolf's Reading Notebooks*. Princeton, NJ: Princeton University Press, 1983.

Sternhell, Zeev, 'Fascist Ideology', in Walter Laqueur, ed., *Fascism: a Reader's Guide*. Berkeley: University of California Press, 1976.

Sternhell, Zeev, Mario Sznajder, and Maia Asheri, *The Birth of Fascist Ideology: From Cultural Rebellion to Political Revolution*, trans. David Maisel. Princeton: Princeton University Press, 1994.

Theweleit, Klaus, *Male Fantasies*. 2 vols, trans. Stephen Conway. Minneapolis: University of Minnesota Press, 1987.

Thompson, Doug, *State Control in Fascist Italy: Culture and Conformity, 1925–42*. Manchester: Manchester University Press, 1991.

Thurlow, Richard, *Fascism in Britain from Oswald Mosley's Blackshirts to the National Front*. London: Basil Blackwell, 1987.

Wiskemann, Elizabeth, *Fascism in Italy: its Development and Influence*. London: Macmillan, 1969.

Writers Declare Against Fascism. London (?): Association of Writers for Intellectual Liberty (?), 1938 (?).

Woolf, Virginia, *Monks House Papers* B.16f., Vols 1, 2 and 3.

——, *Three Guineas*. 1938 rpt. New York: Harcourt Brace Jovanovich, 1966.

Zwerdling, Alex, *Virginia Woolf and the Real World*. Berkeley: University of California Press, 1986.

Index

Abel, Elizabeth, 6, 58, 60, 66
abortion
    fascist art characterized as, 7, 67,
        81–3, 128, 164
    under Nazis, 199n. 10
Abyssinia, 75, 84, 85, 87, 131–2,
    207n. 24
Action (New Party journal), 108–10,
    119–21, 212n. 16
Adorno, Theodor, 180
aesthetics vs. politics
    in Atwood's *Handmaid's Tale*,
        147–54
    in Cappa Marinetti's works, 156–64
    under fascism, 6–8, 81–3, 105–21,
        156–64
    as issue between Woolf and Lewis,
        39–55
    in Leonard Woolf's works, 7–8, 123,
        125–7, 129–30, 132–4
    in Woolf's views of Italy, 75–91
    in Woolf's works, 4, 6, 10, 13–20,
        123–6, 155, 185–9
    see also objectivity vs. subjectivity
Alberti, Johanna, 139
Aldington, Richard, 16
Amnesty International, 144
androgyny, 75–6, 83–4, 208n. 27
anger, 4, 13–14, 64
    see also mockery
'Anon' (Woolf), 80–1, 208n. 27
anonymity, 75–6, 78–81, 83, 87–9
Antigone (Sophocles), 54, 69, 150, 152
Apter, T. E., 99
Armistice Day, 109
art. *see* aesthetics vs. politics
The Art of Being Ruled (Lewis), 42,
    44–8, 53
Astra il sottomarino (Cappa Marinetti),
    162, 164
Atlee, C. R., 212n. 24
Atwood, Margaret, 143–54
Auden, W. H., 128, 179, 221n. 17

Austen, Jane, 16
Ayers, David, 45

Backlash (Faludi), 143
Bakhtin, Mikhail, 147
Barrett, Michele, 187
Barrett Browning, Elizabeth, 77
Barry, F. R., 18
Bauer, Dale, 147
BBC, 75, 84, 127
Beckett, Samuel, 185
Beer, Gillian, 112
Bell, Angelica, 84–6
Bell, Clive, 43, 131, 133
Bell, Julian, 14, 19, 87–8
Bell, Quentin, 84
    on Woolf, 4, 5, 13–20, 166
Bell, Vanessa ('Nessa'), 78–9, 84–6,
    157
Belsey, Catherine, 196n. 3
Benhabib, Seyla, 178–9, 193
Benjamin, Walter, 105
Benstock, Shari, 58–60, 175
Benz, Ute, 26–7
Berman, Jessica, 7, 105–21
Berman, Russell, 105
Bernikow, Louise, 175
Between the Acts (Woolf), 4, 42, 47–8,
    53–4, 114–15, 122–36, 142
Bibesco, Countess (Elizabeth), 139
Bible, *see* Genesis
Bihan, Jill, 153
Bilan, R. P., 172
Birrell, Francis, 109
Black Lamb and Grey Falcon (West),
    179, 180, 189–92
*Blackwell Dictionary of 20th Century
    Social Thought*, 194
Blake, William, 98
Bloomsbury
    Freud's influence on, 59
    Leavises' antagonism to, 168–73
    Lewis's opposition to, 169

reception of *Three Guineas* by,
166–8, 175
values of, 186
Blunden, Edmund, 16
Bottai, Giuseppe, 81
Bournemouth Conference, 16
Boy Scouts, 109
British Union of Fascists (BUF), 107,
168
see also New Party
Brooker, Paul, 206n. 15
Browning, Elizabeth Barrett, 77
BUF, *see* British Union of Fascists
Burdekin, Katharine, 9, 179–86, 192
Butler, Josephine, 154
Butler, Judith, 174

Campagna (Italy), 78–81, 91
Campbell, SueEllen, 202n. 14
Caplan, Jane, 176
Cappa Marinetti, Benedetta, 9,
156–64
Carroll, David, 222n. 56
Casagrande, Marquess, 176
castration, *see* phallus
Caterina da Siena, 163
'Caterpillers of the Commonwealth
Unite!' (Q. Leavis), 173, 174
Caughie, Pamela, 4
Chamberlain, Neville, 5
chastity (mental), 99–104
Chiara d'Assisi, 163
Christianity, 181–5
see also Church of England
Churchill, Winston, 5
Church Lads' Brigades, 109
Church of England, 25, 61
Cian, Vittorio, 99
Clarke, E. R., 18
class
Nazi claims about, 36
Woolf on, 23, 24, 198n. 3
Woolf on gender differences
within, 23–4, 32–3, 98–121
clothing (uniforms)
of British fascists, 119, 120
in *Three Guineas'* photographs, 58
Woolf on link of, to war, 30, 31,
134–5, 186

'The Code of a Herdsman' (Lewis),
42–4, 51
Coleridge, Samuel Taylor, 83
communism, 44, 175
community
West's vision of, 179
Woolf's vision of, 53–4, 103, 115,
124–5
Companions of Honour, 85, 87, 89
Conrad, Joseph, 171
Conservative Party (Britain), 16
Constable, John, 48, 49, 51, 203n.
22
Constantine, Murray, 178
cows, *see* herd imagery
'Craftsmanship' (Woolf), 127, 130
Creon, *see Antigone*
Critica Fascista, 81, 82
Croats, 191
Cuddy-Keane, Melba, 114
Culture and Imperialism (Said), 144
Daily Worker, 203n. 22
Daly, Mary, 97
Day-Lewis, C., 128
De Grazia, Victoria, 8
DiBattista, Maria, 128, 150

'dick,' 71
Dickens, Charles, 171
Dickinson, Violet, 77
dictators, *see* leaders
'dirk,' 71
Discipline and Punish (Foucault), 30
Donati, Ines, 163
Donne della Patria in guerra (Cappa
Marinetti), 158, 162–3
Downhill All the Way (L. Woolf), 93,
209n. 21
Duckworth, George, 59
Duckworth, Gerald, 59
Duncker, Patricia, 151
duPlessis, Rachel Blau, 224n. 24
dystopias, 143–54, 178–93

Eco, Umberto, 168, 169, 177
economics (of women), *see*
professions
'Editorial Comment on Woolf and
Fascism' (Pawlowski), 157

education (of women), 22, 62–3,
  186–7
egg imagery, 40, 61, 67, 71, 173
Ehrenreich, Barbara, 3, 30, 97, 200n.
  32
Eliot, T. S., 17, 39, 172, 177, 185,
  202n. 5, 223n. 6
elitism
  of the Leavises, 168–70
  of Wyndham Lewis, 40, 43, 44–7,
    49, 52
Elizabeth (Countess Bibesco), 139
Elsaesser, Thomas, 201n. 43
Elshtain, Jean Bethke, 140
Emma (Austen), 16
Empire and Commerce in Africa (L.
  Woolf), 77
Enciclopedia Italiana, 94–5
England, *see* Great Britain
English, Deirdre, 97
eugenics, *see* racism
Exhibition of the Fascist Revolution, 7

Fabian Society, 108–9
Falklands War, 5, 20
Faludi, Susan, 143
Falwell, Jerry, 145
'Familiar Fascism' game, 165–6, 177
family
  as metaphor for nation, 24, 27, 134,
    136
  as metaphor for Nazi Women's
    Bureau, 23
  women's work within, as
    non-political, 26–7
  Woolf on role of, in patriarchal
    society, 22, 24–5, 31–3,
    149–51
  see also patriarchy; women:
    reproductive role of
fascism
  aesthetics vs. politics under, 6–8,
    81–3, 105–21, 156–64
  alternatives to discourse of, 7–8,
    106, 122–36
  art of, as abortion, 7, 67, 81–3, 128,
    164
  British views of, 5, 93–6, 105–21,
    167, 168, 177
  characteristics of, 168, 169–71, 173,
    176–7
  contemporary, 194
  ideology of, as contradictory, 2, 7
  in Italy, 3, 93, 156–64, 180–1, 218n.
    15
  Leavises' criticism of Woolf as kind
    of, 9, 168–77
  Lewis's favoring of, 39–55
  link between patriarchy and, in
    Woolf's works, 1, 4, 10, 21, 25,
    31, 38, 42, 52–3, 56–72, 89–90,
    94–6, 113, 140, 142–3, 149–51,
    153, 166, 177, 180, 186, 194
  as masculine ideology, 2, 3, 7, 30,
    34–7, 39–55, 69–72, 81–2, 84,
    93–5, 113–14, 119–21, 126, 188
  and modernism, 6, 7, 105, 168–9,
    223n. 6
  as rejection of individualism,
    liberalism, and democracy, 2,
    39–55, 134
  rise of, in Europe, 14, 30–1
  as seductive ideology, 1, 3, 34–8,
    93, 176–7, 222n. 56
  and sexuality, 169, 175–7, 199n. 10,
    213n. 40
  women's role under, 1, 2, 5, 8–9,
    23–4, 65, 174, 180–1, 206n. 15
  see also futurism; Nazism; New
    Right; patriarchy; racism;
    specific fascists
fathers, *see* leaders; patriarchy
Faulkner, William, 39
'Female Sexuality' (Freud), 204n. 20
'Female Sexuality in Fascist Ideology'
  (Macciocchi), 175–7
femininity
  associations with, 39–55, 99–109,
    168–9
  Nazi conception of, 24, 26, 34
  as socially constructed, 31, 33,
    141–3
  see also gender; objectivity vs
    subjectivity; women
feminism, 9
  Atwood on, 153–4
  backlashes against, 143–4, 154
  Bell on, 13–14

decline of, in anti-fascist
movement, 139, 166
and dystopianism, 178–93
Queenie Leavis's rejection of, 173–5
and theory of the state, 6, 41–2,
47–56
as threat to patriarchy, 39–41, 46–7,
52, 54, 61, 66, 98, 107, 118–19
Woolf as advocate of, 1–5, 9–10, 31,
33, 153–7, 167, 179, 185–9
Woolf's burning of word, 70, 153,
187
see also Three Guineas; utopianism;
women's suffrage movement
Feminist Dialogics (Bauer), 147
Fiction and the Reading Public (Q.
Leavis), 170, 173–4
fish imagery, 79, 83
Fitzgerald, F. Scott, 185
Fleishman, Avrom, 99
Flush (Woolf), 77
Ford, Ford Madox, 16
Forster, E. M., 167, 202n. 5
Foucault, Michel, 30, 89, 184, 199n.
22
France, 143
Frankfurt School, 177, 220n. 5
Freikorpsmen, 3, 31, 34, 42, 113–14,
168
Freud, Sigmund, 191
gender hierarchy in theories of, 56,
204nn. 16, 20
Hogarth Press as publisher of, 59,
60
as influence on Woolf, 6, 43, 47,
53, 58–9, 130, 167, 205n. 28
Woolf's meeting with, 123–4
Woolf's subversion of ideas of, 48,
56–72, 128
Friedman, Susan Stanford, 151
Froula, Christine, 70
Le Forze umane (Cappa Marinetti), 164
Fry, Roger, 43
Führer, *see* Hitler, Adolf; leaders
Fussell, Paul, 206n. 3
futurism, 9, 113, 157, 158–60, 162,
164, 218n. 15
see also fascism
Futurismo (journal), 158, 159

Galsworthy, John, 66
Garibaldi, Anita, 163
Gättens, Marie-Luise, 6, 21–38
gender
construction of, by fascism and
psychoanalysis, 6, 21–72, 169,
180–1
differences in outlook of, within
class and nation, 32–3, 98–121
fascist ideology of, 2–3, 6, 26, 30,
69–70, 82, 94–5, 141, 180–1,
192
hierarchy of, 56–72, 82, 98, 174,
192
as socially constructed, 31, 33, 103,
134–5, 141–3
tensions relating to, after First
World War, 8, 22–3
and war, 5, 15–17, 20, 30–6, 51–3,
121, 140–3, 149, 159, 160,
188
see also femininity; masculinity;
separate spheres
Genesis (Biblical story), 125, 129, 136,
146
genocide, *see* racism
Germany
anti-feminist backlash in, 143–4
Lewis's views of, 45, 48–50
as superior to other countries, 26,
27, 34
Woolf's visit to, 84, 140
see also fascism; Freikorpsmen;
Nazism
Giachero, Lia, 9, 156–64
Gilbert, Sandra, 187
Gilligan, Carol, 141
Girl Guides, 109
Golsan, Richard, 2
Gramsci, Antonio, 175
Il grande X (Cappa Marinetti), 164
grandmothers, *see* hag imagery
Graves, Robert, 16
Great Britain
anti-feminist backlash in, 143
Burdekin on, 181–2
colonialism and nationalism in, 25
discrimination against women in,
21–2, 25, 29, 63, 69–70

Great Britain (*continued*)
  post-First World War conditions in, 93
  support for fascism in, 5, 93–6, 105–21, 168, 177
  West's criticism of, 192
The Great Gatsby (Fitzgerald), 185
The Great Tradition (F. R. Leavis), 171
Grensted (professor), 61, 68
Griffin, Roger, 194
Group Psychology and the Analysis of the Ego (Freud), 47
Gubar, Susan, 187
'Guernica' (Picasso), 185
Gypsies, 27

hag (grandmother) imagery, 119, 120, 128
  see also misogyny
The Handmaid's Tale (Atwood), 9, 143–54
Harris, Leigh Coral, 7, 75–91
Hart, Philip, 19
Hegel, G. W. F., 150
Hemingway, Ernest, 16, 39
Henke, Suzette, 99
herd imagery, 42–8, 54
heteroglossia, 147
Hewitt, Andrew, 113
Himmler, Heinrich, 2, 35
Hindenburg, Paul von, 35
Hitler (Lewis), 42, 48–51, 53
Hitler, Adolf, 52, 89, 123, 134, 144, 168
  on gender roles, 26, 30, 69–70, 141, 180, 192
  influences on, 45–6
  Lewis's view of, 45, 48–51
  on Nazi Women's League, 1, 5
  speeches of, 53, 128
  in *Triumph of the Will*, 35–6
  see also fascism; Nazism
The Hitler Cult (Lewis), 51
Hitler Youth Movement, 28
Hogarth Press, 58–60, 93
Holtby, Winifred, 144
homophobia, 169–71
Horkheimer, Max, 149, 177, 180
Hulme, T. E., 168

Huxley, Aldous, 202n. 5
Huyssen, Andreas, 168

identitylessness, *see* anonymity
incest, 59, 67–9
  see also rape
income, *see* professions
indifference (as political strategy), 57–8
  see also 'Society of Outsiders'
Instincts of the Herd in Peace and War (Trotter), 43
Interpretation of Dreams (Freud), 64
Iran, 144
Irigaray, Luce, 101, 102
Isherwood, Christopher, 109
Islamic fundamentalism, 144
Italy
  Abyssinian invasion by, 75, 84, 85, 87, 207n. 24
  fascism in, 3, 93, 156–64, 180–1, 218n. 15
  and feminism, 143, 156–64, 206n. 2
  Lewis on, 44–5
  women's repression in, 8–9, 65, 98–9, 143
  Woolf's dual visions of, 6, 7, 75–91
  see also fascism; futurism; Mussolini, Benito

James, Henry, 17, 171
Jameson, Fredric, 51
Jews, 27, 45, 49, 190
Jex-Blake, Sophia, 69
Joannou, Maroula, 9, 139–55
jobs, *see* professions
Joyful Wisdom (Nietzsche), 43
Jünger, Ernst, 21

Kaplan, Alice, 105, 107, 110
Kendrick, Walter, 59
Kent, Susan Kingsley, 224n. 20
Keynes, John Maynard, 166, 167, 172–3, 178, 179, 185, 186
Kipling, Rudyard, 5, 66
Koonz, Claudia, 23, 24, 27, 28, 190

Labour Party (Britain), 16, 19, 107–9, 120

Lacan, Jacques, 57
language, *see* aesthetics vs politics
Lawrence, D. H., 4, 171, 172–3, 177,
    223n. 6
Lawrence, T. E., 16
leaders (dictators)
    Leonard Woolf on, 126
    Lewis on, 45–52
    psychiatrists compared to, 97–8
    Virginia Woolf on, 47–8, 51–3,
        56–72, 114–15
    see also names of specific leaders
League of Nations, 109, 134
'The Leaning Tower' (Woolf), 128
Leavis, F. R., 9, 168, 169–74
Leavis, Queenie, 9, 168–71, 173–5
Left Review, 139
Lehmann, John, 129
Lewis, David Stephen, 220n. 16
Lewis, Wyndham, 6, 39–55, 168, 169,
    177, 207n. 24
Life As We Have Known It, 77
Literary Supplement, 39
London *Daily Telegraph*, 70
London *Times*, 1, 5, 94, 180–1
Low, Lisa, 7, 92–104

Macciocchi, Maria-Antonietta, 2–3,
    157, 175–7
MacDonald, Ramsay, 109
Macedonia, 191
machismo, 169
Mackinnon, Catherine, 41
Male Fantasies (Theweleit), 3, 34–5,
    42, 168
Männerbund, 2
Männerstaat, 2, 50, 51, 54
Manx cat imagery, 66
Marcus, Jane
    on contemporary fascism, 194–5
    on Woolf as feminist writer, 4, 5,
        99, 187, 194–5, 202n. 5
    on Woolf's anti-imperialism, 111,
        114, 117, 211n. 8
Marcuse, Herbert, 149
Margaret (Lady Rhondda), 141
Marinetti, Filippo Tommaso, 9,
    113, 157, 158, 164, 218n. 15,
    220n. 40

see also Cappa Marinetti, Benedetta;
    futurism
marriage, *see* family; women:
    reproductive role of
masculinity
    fascism's association with, 2, 7, 30,
        34–7, 39–55, 69–72, 81–2, 84,
        93–5, 113–14, 119–21, 126, 188
    as generated by female
        subordination, 56–72
    Hitler's conception of, 26
    Lewis's conception of, 39–55
    modernism and crisis of, 50
    psychoanalytic theory and crisis of,
        56–72
    as socially constructed, 31, 33,
        134–5, 141–3
    see also gender; machismo; men;
        objectivity vs subjectivity;
        phallus
maternity, *see* women: reproductive
    role of
Maurras, Charles, 42
medicine *see* professions
Mein Kampf (Hitler), 49, 180
Meisel, Perry, 59
Memoirs (Keynes), 172
men
    bonds between, in fascism, 2, 34–6,
        42, 50
    bonds between, in Freud's theories,
        67–8
    in procession metaphor, 29
    relation of, to war, 5, 15–16, 20,
        30–1, 34–6, 51–3, 140–3, 149,
        188
men (*continued*)
    see also gender; masculinity;
        misogyny; patriarchy; phallus
mentally retarded persons, 27
Men Without Art (Lewis), 39, 41, 55,
    169
military *see* clothing; procession; war
Mills, Patricia Jagentowicz, 150
mirror imagery, 65–6
misogyny, 42
    of British fascist movement,
        119–21
    as component of patriarchy, 5

misogyny (*continued*)
  of fascists, 3, 34, 42, 45, 60–1,
    113–14, 119, 168–9
  of Freikorpsmen, 3, 34, 42, 113–14,
    168
  as natural in Freud's view, 60–1
  Weininger's, 45
  Woolf's exposure of, 64–5
  see also hag imagery
Mitchison, Naomi, 139
mockery (satire)
  Atwood's use of, 144
  Lewis's use of, 39–55
  Woolf's use of, 8, 57–8, 122–3, 186,
    187, 209n. 21
modernism
  and crisis of masculinity, 50
  dystopias associated with, 9–10,
    178–93
  and fascism, 6, 7, 105, 168–9, 223n.
    6
  women exemplars of, 175
Moi, Toril, 142, 187–8
Il monte Tabor (Cappa Marinetti), 164
Moore, Madeleine, 213n. 46
Moral Majority, 145
Morrell, Ottoline, 75
Morris, Jan, 76
Mosley, Cynthia, 113, 120–1
Mosley, Oswald, 7, 107–9, 119–21,
    168, 169, 177, 211n. 6
'The Mosley Memorandum', 107
Mosse, George, 2, 213n. 40, 223n. 10
motherhood, *see* women:
  reproductive role of
Mothers in the Fatherland (Koonz),
    190
'Mr. Bennett and Mrs. Brown'
  (Woolf), 39, 40, 128
Mrs. Dalloway (Woolf), 6, 7, 76,
    92–104, 142
Mulhern, Francis, 174
Mussolini, Benito, 44, 218n. 15
  Abyssian invasion by, 75, 84, 85,
    87, 131–2, 207n. 24
  British support for, 5, 94, 119
  on fascist art, 6, 7, 81–3
  as fascist leader, 47, 65, 75, 84, 87,
    89, 92–4, 164, 176, 210n. 23

  on gender differences, 82, 94–5,
    180–1, 192
  hypocrisy of, on sexual matters,
    213n. 40
  reproductive policies of, 160, 161,
    180–1
  see also fascism; Italy
Mütterschulung, 26–7

Nancy, Jean-Luc, 115
Napoleon, 16, 65
nationalism (state)
  and fascism, 2, 24, 108, 110,
    119–21, 169, 171
  and gender arrangements, 25
  and gendered images of the body,
    112–14, 169–70
  as indicating superiority over other
    nations, 26, 27
  and the suppression of the
    individual, 94–6
  Woolf's rejection of, 17, 27, 33–5,
    52, 86–9, 111, 115, 124, 152
National Socialism, *see* Nazism
Nazi Party Congress (Nuremberg
    1934), 35, 37, 201n. 43
Nazism (National Socialism), 3
  Clive Bell on, 131, 133
  dystopian view of, 181–5
  First World War roots of, 30–1, 124
  ideology of, linked to myth, 180
  portrayal of, as historic mission,
    35–7
  racism of, 45–6, 49–52, 180, 221n.
    16
  repression of women under, 8,
    23–4, 26–7, 36–7, 69–70, 139,
    143–4, 199n. 10
  and sexuality, 169, 199n. 10, 213n.
    40
  women's contributions to, 1, 5,
    23–4, 26–8, 35–7, 146, 180–1
  women's role in, 1, 5, 23–4, 146–7,
    180–1
  Woolf likened to, 173
  see also fascism; Freikorpsmen;
    Germany; Hitler, Adolf; Nazi
    Party Congress; Nazi Women's
    Bureau

Nazi Women's Bureau, 1, 5, 23–4, 26–8, 37
Neverow, Vara S., 6, 56–72
Newitt, Hilary, 198n. 25
New Party (Mosley's), 7, 107–10, 119–21
see also British Union of Fascists
New Right (US), 144–5
New Statesman, 84, 85
Nicolson, Harold, 108–10, 113, 119–21, 211n. 6
Nietzsche, Friedrich, 42

objectivity vs subjectivity, 41, 42, 45, 54, 99–104, 167–9, 178–80, 186
see also aesthetics vs politics
oceanic feelings, 105–21
Oedipus (Sophocles), 69
Oedipus complex, 60, 61–2
Oldfield, Sybil, 154
'On the Sexual Theories of Children' (Freud), 60
Orwell, George, 94
Outsiders' Society, *see* 'Society of Outsiders'
Owen, Wilfred, 15, 16

pacifism
Burdekin's, 184
Hitler on, 141
Leonard Woolf on, 132–3
as natural to women, 15, 33–5, 121, 140–3
Woolf on, among men, 15, 16, 142
Woolf's, 18–20, 109, 156–7, 179
parades, *see* procession metaphor
The Pargiters (Woolf), 40
see also Three Guineas; Years
Partridge, Eric, 65, 71
'The Passing of the Oedipal Complex' (Freud), 60
Patai, Daphne, 181
patriarchy
feminism as threat to, 39–41, 46–7, 52, 54–5, 61, 66, 98, 107, 118–19
and incest, 67–9

link between fascism and, in Woolf's works, 1, 4, 10, 21, 25, 31, 38, 52–3, 56–72, 89–90, 94–9, 111–13, 140, 142–3, 149–51, 153, 166, 177, 180, 186, 194
within Nazi institutions, 23–4, 26–8
as producing war, 22, 25
as underpinning fascism and communism, 175
see also fascism; leaders; masculinity; misogyny; separate spheres; violence
Paul (saint), 184
Pavolini, Alessandro, 81
Pawlowski, Merry M., 1–10, 39–55, 157, 194, 195
penis envy, *see* phallus
Pfaelzer, Jean, 184
phallus
Lewis's use of symbolism of, 40
Woolf's mockery of privileging of, 6, 56–72
Phillips, Kathy J., 206n. 7, 213n. 32
Picasso, Pablo, 185
Plain, Gill, 142–3, 155
Pointz Hall (Woolf), 53
see also Between the Acts (Woolf)
Pommer, Frau, 152
Pound, Ezra, 168, 177, 223n. 6
'Praise for Women' (London *Times* article), 1, 5
procession metaphor
and fascism, 105
in *Mrs. Dalloway*, 94, 95–6, 102, 104
in *Three Guineas*, 29–31, 34, 186
in *Triumph of the Will*, 35–7
see also clothing
professions
Cappa Marinetti's lack of interest in, 162
fascism's removal of women from, 8–9, 98–9, 143–4
as involved with war and oppression, 93, 96–8, 102–3, 186
Woolf on women in, 6, 22, 25, 32, 52, 68–70, 153

professions (*continued*))
  Woolf on women's exclusion from, 21–2, 25, 29, 63, 69–70
  see also procession metaphor; psychoanalysis
'Progetto futurista di reclutamento per la prossima guerra' (Cappa Marinetti), 158–61
propaganda, *see* aesthetics vs. politics
Proust, Marcel, 83
psychiatry, *see* professions
psychoanalysis
  relation of, to fascism, 6, 56–72
  Woolf's aversion to, 58–9
  see also Freud, Sigmund; professions
Puccini, Mario, 82

Quack, Quack! (L. Woolf), 8, 123, 126, 127

racism (eugenics; genocide)
  of British Union of Fascists, 221n. 16
  Hitler's, 45–6, 49–52, 180, 221n. 16
  Leavises', 169
  Lewis's, 44, 50, 51, 207n. 24
  women's role in carrying out Hitler's, 8, 26, 27
The Rainbow (Lawrence), 172
rape
  in *Handmaid's Tale*, 146
  psychiatry as kind of, 97–8
  by soldiers, 169, 224n. 20
  in *Swastika Night*, 182
rationality, *see* objectivity vs subjectivity
Reading Notebooks (Woolf's), 1, 145
Reagan, Ronald, 144
Reich, Wilhelm, 175
Remarque, Erich Maria, 16
Rhondda, Lady (Margaret), 141
Richter, Alan, 71
Riefenstahl, Leni, 35–7
Rigney, Barbara, 149
Ritmi di rocce e mare (Cappa Marinetti), 164
Rome (Italy), 77, 78–81, 84–6, 90, 91
A Room of One's Own (Woolf)
  androgyny in, 75, 83–4

Bell's analysis of, 13–14, 20
  on fascist poetry, 7, 67, 81–3, 127–8, 164
  impact of Woolf's travels to Italy on, 76, 81–4
  Leavises' attacks on, 173–4
  as political work, 4, 13
  Woolf's analysis of patriarchy in, 56–7, 60–72
Rosenberg, Alfred, 180, 223n. 10
Rosenfeld, Natania, 7–8, 122–36
Russell, Bertrand, 97
Russia, 44

Sackville-West, Vita, 108, 109, 120, 152, 211n. 6
Said, Edward, 144
St. Mawr (Lawrence), 172–3
'St. Virginia's Epistle to an English Gentleman' (Froula), 70
Saintsbury (doctor), 209n. 21
satire *see* mockery
Scarborough Conference, 16
Schnapp, Jeffrey, 7
Scholtz-Klink, Gertrud, 23–4, 26–8, 34, 37, 146–7, 199n. 11
Schwartz, Nina, 33, 200n. 27
Scrutiny, 168, 171–3
A Sentimental Journey through France and Italy (Sterne), 76
separate spheres
  fascism's domination of private, by public, 93, 123, 128
  fascism's emphasis on, 2, 5, 8–9, 23–4, 28, 45, 69–70, 72, 98–9, 180–1
  West on, 190–2
  Woolf's view of fascism and patriarchy as link between, 1, 4, 10, 21, 22, 24, 25, 29–34, 38, 52–3, 56–72, 89–90, 94–9, 111–12, 140, 142–3, 149–51, 153, 166, 177, 180, 186
  see also gender
Serbs, 189–92
Sex and Character (Weininger), 45
Shakespeare, William, 67, 83
Sherman, William Tecumseh, 16
Silver, Brenda, 84

Sitwell, Osbert, 109
'A Sketch of the Past' (Woolf), 59
Smyth, Ethel, 86, 207n. 18
'The Society' (Woolf), 113
'Society of Outsiders' (Woolf's concept)
   Atwood's use of, 151–2
   Bell on, 5, 17–19
   as Woolf's strategy for preventing war, 22, 32–3, 53, 54–5, 88–90, 99–104, 124–5, 152, 188–9, 192, 208n. 27
soldiers, *see* war
'Some Psychical Consequences of the Anatomical Distinction Between the Sexes' (Freud), 60, 63
Sontag, Susan, 35, 37
Sophocles, 58, 69, 150
Spain, 143
   civil war in, 14, 18–19, 69, 185, 186, 188
spectacles, *see* procession metaphor
Spender, Stephen, 84, 128
'Spiritualità della donna italiana' (Cappa Marinetti), 160, 161
state, *see* nationalism
Stavely, Alice, 58
Stec, Loretta, 9–10, 178–93
Stephen, Adrian, 59
Stephen, Karin Costelloe, 59
Stephen, Leslie, 53, 59, 170, 173
Sterne, Laurence, 76
Sternhell, Zeev, 2, 107
Stewart, Garrett, 118
Strachey, Alix, 59
Strachey, James, 59, 60
Strachey, John, 108, 119, 212n. 16
Strachey, Lytton, 170, 171
Suffer and Be Still (Vicinus), 26
suffrage, *see* women's suffrage movement
Surfacing (Atwood), 147
Swastika Night (Burdekin), 178, 180–6

Talleyrand, Charles Maurice de, 13
Thatcher, Margaret, 5, 16, 20, 144
Theweleit, Klaus, 2–3, 34–6, 45, 52, 106, 113–14, 168

Thompson, Denys, 174
Thompson, Doug, 93, 96, 98–9
'Thoughts on Peace in an Air Raid' (Woolf), 90, 98, 132, 134–5, 141, 146, 176
Three Guineas (Woolf)
   Bell on, 14–15, 17–20
   construction of gender in, 21–2, 103, 140–1
   contrast of, with Leonard Woolf's works, 8, 122–7
   as dystopian work, 179, 180, 185–9
   impact of Woolf's travels to Italy on, 76, 88–91, 140
   link between patriarchy and fascism in, 22, 24, 29–34, 38, 52–3, 56–72, 89–90, 94–9, 113, 140, 142–3, 149–51, 153, 166, 177, 180, 186, 194
   Mrs. Dalloway's anticipation of ideas in, 93–104
   photographs in, 58
   as political work, 4, 54–5, 96, 144–6, 175
   reception of, 92, 166–8, 173, 174
   research materials for, 1, 9, 145, 180–1, 186
   Woolf's strategies for preventing war in, 22, 32–3, 53, 54–5, 57–8, 88–90, 99–104, 124–5, 152, 188–9, 192, 208n. 27
   Woolf's writing of, 132, 202n. 5
   working titles for, 41
   see also fascism; feminism; patriarchy; 'Society of Outsiders'; war
Time and Tide, 48, 49
Toscanini, Arturo, 218n. 15
Totem and Taboo (Freud), 67–9
To the Lighthouse (Woolf), 76, 80, 171
Trade Union Congress, 109
Travis, Molly Abel, 9, 165–77
Triumph of the Will (film), 35–8
Trotsky, Leon, 120
Trotter, Wilfred, 43, 47
Trouton, Rupert, 109
Tuscany (Italy), 77
'22 Hyde Park Gate' (Woolf), 59

'Types of Neurotic Nosogenesis' (Freud), 68

Umbria (Italy), 77
uniforms *see* clothing
'Ur-Fascism' (Eco), 168, 169
utopianism, 9–10, 92, 105, 151, 178–93
 see also dystopias

Vansittart, Robert Gilbert, Baron, 19
Viaggio de Gararà (Cappa Marinetti), 164
violence
 masculine enjoyment of, 34–5, 42, 43
 and survival, 80–1
 West's analysis of, 179, 191
 Woolf's analysis of, 56–72
 Woolf's defamiliarization of, 185–6
 see also war
Virginia Woolf and the Real World (Zwerdling), 13
Virginia Woolf Miscellany, 157
virility, *see* masculinity; phallus
Volontà italiana (Cappa Marinetti), 161
'VOLT' (New Party's motto), 110, 121
The Voyage Out (Woolf), 76

war
 as dramatic national project, 35
 Italian displays relating to, 84
 men's relation to, 5, 15–16, 20, 30–1, 34–6, 51–3, 140–3, 149, 188
 patriarchy's role in producing, 22, 25
 professions' role in, 93, 96–8, 102–3, 186
 societies built on values of, 182
 and subordination of women, 189–92
 women's relation to, 15, 16–17, 33–5, 121, 140–3, 159, 160
 Woolf's strategies for preventing, 22, 32–3, 53, 54–5, 88–90, 99–104, 124–5, 152, 188–9, 192, 208n. 27

 see also clothing; pacifism; patriarchy; procession metaphor; violence
The War for Peace (L. Woolf), 8, 123, 125, 129–30, 132–3
Warmongers (C. Bell), 131
The Waste Land (Eliot), 172, 185
The Waves (Woolf), 6, 7, 77, 78, 80, 105–21, 171
Weininger, Otto, 45–6, 52
Wells, H. G., 5, 177
West, Rebecca, 9, 66, 179–82, 189–92
Wiggershaus, Renate, 28
Wiskemann, Elizabeth, 96, 209n. 15
Woermann, E., 180–1
women
 as compliant with fascism, 9, 23, 26–9, 34, 156–64, 174–7, 181, 182, 190, 199n. 11
 discrimination against, in England, 21–2, 25, 29, 63, 69–70
 discrimination against, in Nazi Germany, 23–4, 26–7, 36–7, 69–70, 143–4, 199n. 10
 education of, 22, 62–3, 186–7
 fascism's divisions among, 27
 fascists' views of bodies of, 3, 34, 42, 45, 60–1, 113–14, 119, 168–9
 relation of, to war, 15–17, 33–5, 121, 140–3, 159, 160
 repression of, under Christianity, 183–4
 repression of, by fascism, 5, 8–9, 23–4, 26–7, 36–7, 54, 65, 69–70, 98, 139, 143–4, 199n. 10
 repression of, in *Handmaid's Tale*, 143–54
 repression of, by psychoanalysts, 56–7, 60–70
 reproductive role of, 8, 22, 25, 26, 32, 160–1, 169, 174, 175–7
 reproductive role of, in *Handmaid's Tale*, 145–6
 reproductive role of, in *Swastika Night*, 181–2
 as responsible for racial purity, 8, 26, 27

role of, under fascism, 1, 2, 5, 8–9,
    23–4, 65, 146–7, 174, 180–1,
    206n. 15
  as threat to male power and
    fascism, 39–41, 46–7, 52, 54,
    61, 66, 92–104, 107, 118–19,
    177
  see also feminism; misogyny;
    patriarchy; professions;
    separate spheres; women's
    suffrage movement
Women and Fiction (Woolf), 66
Women Must Choose (Newitt), 198n.
  25
Women's Co-operative Guild, 109
Women's Peace Conference, 120
women's suffrage movement
  Bell on, 13, 14
  men's reaction to, 67, 68, 166
  post-First World War success of, 14,
    22, 139
  see also feminism
Woolf, Leonard, 75, 167, 202n. 13,
    207n. 18
  fascist context of writings of, 6, 84
  political writings of, 77, 123–36
  politics of, 19, 108
  on post-First World War
    conditions, 93
  on Virginia Woolf's politics, 4, 13
  see also Hogarth Press

Woolf, Virginia
  as apolitical aesthete, 3–5, 9, 13–20,
    92, 166–7, 171, 173
  attacks on, 9, 39–55, 166–7, 171–5
  as political writer, 1–4, 92, 108–9,
    111, 114, 117, 121, 177, 180,
    181, 192, 211n. 8
Woolwich, Mayoress of, 17–18
words, *see* aesthetics vs politics
World War I
  blaming of German and Italian
    women for losing, 8
  images of suffering in, 37–8
  and *Mrs. Dalloway*, 7, 92
  Nazism's roots in, 30–1, 124
  suffrage granted to British women
    after, 14, 22
  women's support for, 34
World War II, 163, 189
'worm,' 71, 205n. 44
Wysocki, Gisela, 29, 30, 33, 37
The Years (Woolf), 14, 142, 171
  see also Pargiters (Woolf)

Yeats, W. B., 202n. 5, 223n. 6
Young, Allan, 212n. 16
Yugoslavia, 189–92

Zwerdling, Alex, 13, 154, 167,
    214n. 1
  on *Mrs. Dalloway*, 101, 211n. 37